THE WAY

VOLUMES OF THE VEMREAUX
BOOK ONE

MARY E. TWOMEY

MARY E. TWOMEY, LLC

THE WAY

VOLUME ONE
OF
The Vemreaux

By
Mary E. Twomey

COPYRIGHT

DEDICATION

For Maybee

May you be only as beautiful as you are kind,
And only as strong as you are gentle.

ACKNOWLEDGMENTS

Special thanks to Sara-Beth,
For your editing and constant cheerleading.

And to the Write Club,
For slaughtering my excess adjectives, tearing apart the weaker characters, and amputating whole sections that did not work, despite my best efforts.
For all the times I wanted to shake my fist in the air at you, here in print,
I admit...you were right.

PROLOGUE

"Can't you move any more than that?" Baird complained, his tone exhibiting its usual unforgiving tenor.

"I'm doing the best I can!" Blue responded in like frustration as she hurled a pitchfork full of scratch onto the conveyor belt. The squishy "slurp" the slop made as it spread out sickened her.

"The best you can," Baird scoffed. "Is there a reason you're lying?"

"Fine. The best I can for how much I'm supposed to be able to do." Flies buzzed around them and even had the audacity to land on their arms when they were still for too long. She'd only been in Building Three of The Way for a month, but she caught on quickly. The one thing she'd not grown immune to was the smell. The sting of the warm scratch pies in her nose left a lingering pungency all day long. She'd been prepared in the same manner as every other Wayward before they graduated from Building Two, but nothing could match first-hand experience. Cows were the bread and butter of Vemreaux society, and their reeking excrement piles were the stuff that currency in the real world was based on. They'd made it sound like such an honor in Building Two. A month spent knee-deep in poop told another tale.

Baird urged her on. "No one can see us, Blue. It's one of the few times you can actually challenge yourself. Why are you holding back?"

"For you. So you don't feel bad you're not as strong as me," she grinned.

Baird rolled his eyes, but refused to be baited. He was the largest and strongest Wayward in his year, and Blue made sure to remind him as often as she could that even he was no match for her. "Ha," he commented, offering a rare half-smile. "Real reason?"

"Baird, what if somebody sees? They'll know I'm the..." Blue looked over her shoulder to make sure again that no one was near, and mouthed *"Light."* She'd waited years to be old enough to graduate to the next building so she could be with her big brother, but since she'd arrived, the training Baird insisted upon was relentless.

Her brother shook his head in disappointment. "I'm watching your back. You're supposed to be watching mine, remember? The system doesn't work if you don't trust me. Now I want to see how much your puny girl arms can lift."

That did it. Being gently nudged had little effect on the eight-year-old girl. It was the criticism and direct challenge that painted defiance onto her muscles and narrowed her eyes. She shoved her pitchfork at her brother and moved to the wheelbarrow. Without hesitation, she hefted the barrow over her head, and then dumped the contents onto the conveyor belt. She looked to him with a shining smile that revealed her need for his approval. Baird kept his praise confined to a single nod of his head.

Making do with less was a survival skill of the Waywards, so her brother's unspoken affirmation was translated in her mind to, *"Wow! I can't believe how strong you are. I bet you're stronger than I am, and I'm one of the best workers in the whole facility."* A thick bead of sweat forced Baird to blink. Blue imagined the squint giving way to a paternal smile. *"I'm so glad you're my sister. Don't worry. We're in this together. No one will find out who you are. No one will take you away from me."*

Of course, he said nothing, so Blue pushed the dreams of how she wished she was loved deeper down into the scraps that were left of her youthful softness. She surrounded the naïveté with tall bricks, guards and barbed wire to match the barriers that separated A-blood types from the Bs. The Waywards from the Vemreaux. The Way from the real world.

"You can do more than that," he chided.

Blue nodded. "Sure. But where do you expect me to find something heavier to lift?" She held out her small hand expectantly, the tattooed barcode standing out on her tanned skin. She'd already memorized her own serial number, Baird's, and now every time a Wayward's wrist exposed itself to her, the digits imprinted themselves on her brain as permanently as the ink that marked them. It annoyed her that she couldn't turn it off, but Baird assured her it was useful.

Baird shoved his own pitchfork into the pile with a steady understanding of how much force was necessary for the job. "Back to work."

"Let me try again," she whined, shaking off a fly from her sleeve. "I'll go fill up the wheelbarrow with a lot more scratch this time, so it'll be heavier."

He shook his head in all of his ten-year-old wisdom. "That's enough for now. The others'll be coming this way soon."

"I hate that stupid prophecy."

"It doesn't much matter how you feel, Blue. Love it or hate it, you're the Light who's supposed to *free the Vemreaux from the tyranny.*"

Blue shrugged her shoulders and looked around. "What tyranny? They're the only blood type in the free world. Everyone else is in work camps that *they* control. What could they possibly need protection from?"

Baird swallowed his real answer and replied, "Be glad the Vemreaux all feel that way, or you'd be the object of a witch hunt. I can't stand those stupid blood guzzlers."

Blue nodded with conviction. "Yeah. Stupid blood guzzlers."

Baird swallowed a smile at how readily his sister followed his every move. "Right now, all we have to do is hide you from other

Waywards." He cleared his throat and did his best not to look at the innocent face that was genetically similar to his. Though she was two years younger than he, they shared thick auburn hair, a peak in their left ear, and the same barely controlled temper. Yet it was the piercing, unnaturally blue eyes that gave them away as siblings most of all. He tried to turn off his heart as her vivid orbs looked up at him for guidance, understanding and love.

Guidance. That one, he could give.

He reached his hand down into the balmy muck with the iron stomach of experience and fished out an errant piece of hay while Blue tried not to blanch. "Challenge yourself when no one's watching. The rest of the time, be the weak newbie you look like. Be who they expect you to be, and you'll stay hidden just fine."

"I would've been able to lift more if the wheelbarrow'd been fuller," she muttered.

"That sounds like an excuse. Who makes excuses?"

Blue's shoulders dropped from their previous position of elevated pride. "Lazy people."

"And who whines?"

"Children whine. Whiners whine." She repeated the Baird-ism perfectly.

"Are you lazy?"

"No, Baird."

"Are you a child?" he asked, tone sharp as he heaved his shovel into the pile of scratch.

"No, Baird."

"Are you a whiner?"

"No, Baird." Blue looked down at her tool forlornly. She hated disappointing her brother.

"Good. Then get back to work. We've got to empty this pile before noon if we want to eat."

Blue worked in silence next to her brother for a full three minutes before daring to annoy him with her thoughts. "Baird, do you ever wish you were *B*-blood?"

"I don't waste my time on wishing, and neither should you."

"Okay." Blue scooped up a puny amount of cow poop and moved it onto the conveyor belt. "It would be kinda cool if we were the ones who reacted to the Fountain of Youth, like the *B*-bloods. Stop aging, live an extra hundred twenty years." Distracted by her daydream, Blue hefted too large a pile for her slight size. Baird cleared his throat, and Blue remembered the façade. She dropped half the excrement back to the grass and sighed. "Beats shoveling scratch in a work camp."

"Yeah. Except for that little tradeoff of the hankering for *O*-type human blood."

"Right. Except for that."

Four boys came out to the yard with pitchforks in hand to attend to the pile of scratch several meters from them. Two were older and two were Blue's age. It would be a while before the eight-year-olds could be expected to be left on their own to work in the field, so all those in Blue's year had a guide. Blue clicked her tongue against the roof of her mouth twice to signal to her brother that they were no longer alone. Baird returned the signal to indicate that he'd heard and watched out of the corner of his eye to make sure that his sister went back to pretending to struggle with meager scoops of scratch.

"Hey, Baird. How's the fledgling working out?" Androo asked.

"Fine," Baird made it a point not to invite conversation.

This did not deter Androo. He elbowed the boy next to him and grinned. "Barnafer here's doing okay. Just needs to stop staring at the pretty girls and concentrate on his work, you know?"

Barnafer blushed and kept his head down.

Baird's knuckles tightened around his shovel, but he kept working as if no one had spoken.

Once the boys were out of hearing range, Blue mumbled, "Clear."

"Come here," Baird ordered. He bent down and picked up a clump of acrid scratch that squished in his fingers.

Blue stood before him obediently, and did not pull away when her brother smeared the filth on her forehead and cheeks. She did not blink when the stench threatened to make her eyes water, nor did her lip quiver as she fought down the urge to vomit. Disgust and mortification lacerated where the scratch marked her, but she did not dare question Baird.

He had a plan. He *always* had a plan.

When she'd been marked up to his satisfaction, he nodded for her to get back to work. "That's better," he commented. "Can't afford to have guys looking at you. Best put a stop to that early on. Don't worry. No one'll pay attention to you now. You're disgusting."

Blue could tell by his tone that his words were meant to be comforting, or at the very least, reassuring. Secrecy was paramount, given her extraordinary abilities. However, his last sentence punched her chest and sunk down into her gut, making her stomach turn. She was utterly grotesque, and now she would be reminded of that fact all day by the inescapable stink of scratch right next to her nose. The flies that plagued her legs and arms would now venture to her face and make their presence constantly known. Blue swallowed the inexcusable lump in her throat and wished for invisibility, so she could disappear from the world completely.

1

GRETTEL'S HEALING TOUCH

Six Years Later

"Can I go now?" Baird asked impatiently. He loathed the stench of antiseptic, and it permeated every breath. He'd been sitting on the paper-covered patient's table for twenty-five minutes. He glanced out the window and watched his sister muck scratch. If he had not been so predisposed to focus on her training, he might not have noticed her at all. She kept her head down and made sure she had scratch marking her arms, legs and face. Six years passed since she'd joined him in Building Three, and he couldn't have been prouder of her progress. Of course, he would never tell her that. No sense in spoiling her.

"Not yet. I still have to bandage you up," Nurse Kalista reminded him in her clipped tone. She had yet to take a good look at his injuries. "You're not my only patient, you know."

Supervisor Tum had been in a temper that morning, handing out beatings at the slightest hint of rebellion or ineptitude. Baird and Blue's younger brother, Griffin, only ten, had messed up twice in the sewing room. One mistake was tolerable, but two was usually cause for a point taken away. When Tum was in a mood, though, one misstep could land you at the whipping post. Baird had volunteered to take his brother's beating. Griffin was too young, too emotional. Plus, Blue was about to take his place, and Baird wouldn't have that.

"I can do that myself. I did last time." Baird grabbed a roll of gauze from the tray next to the window. His lashings were starting to annoy him. He hated when his jumpsuit stuck to the clotting blood.

"You'll do no such thing. Bad enough you kids all decide to cause problems on the same day. Plus, my assistant's useless. A little patience, Baird." She shook her head at the Wayward. Most were not on a first-name basis with the nurse, but Baird was no stranger to the whipping post. "Stop wasting my time. Remove your jumpsuit to the waist and lay on your stomach. You know the drill." She glared at Baird until he complied. Her perpetually bugged eyes were staring at him, blaming him for wasting her time. Just then, the door opened and yet another Wayward was brought in, blood seeping through the back of the orange jumpsuit in stripes. "Ugh, my lucky day. I'll be back." She tore open the curtain and moved out to scold the barely upright new arrival for adding to her workload. "Grettel! Get in here and fix this one up. Do you think we have all day, here?"

Real inconvenient for you, Baird wanted to say. He sat up on the table and glanced over his shoulder, grimacing at the damage on his back. There was one mirror in the entirety of The Way, and it was in the entryway of the Nurse' station. It was supposed to look decorative, but Baird reasoned it was there so the Waywards could see the damage they'd caused themselves.

Supervisor Tum had broken off one of the whip's shards in his back. Baird had wondered why the sting was lasting longer than usual. His eyes flickered to the window, where he checked on his sister again. *Good. She's fine. Still keeping her head down, like she should. Stop worrying.*

An intake of breath from behind him ceased his hand from reaching around and yanking the embedded pottery piece out of his wound. He turned and saw Nurse Kalista's assistant. The girl's short, slight frame was made even more petite by her hunched shoulders that looked predisposed to cowering. Her orange jumpsuit hung on her like a bag, and Baird wondered if her meals were being bullied away from her by the bigger Waywards. Baird guessed that she was even shorter than Blue. Something about the skittish dart of her eyes to the partition and back to the floor made him want to speak softer, so as not to further frighten her.

The rotation of nursing assistants changed every month, and this one was new to Baird. He tried to memorize every barcode in the building, but there were thousands of Waywards. This girl kept her head bowed as much as she could, while still observing the bloody scores.

Assisting the nurse was a privilege not many were granted. You needed a spotless record and to pass several tests, both textbook and psychological. There were scissors, needles, and chemicals in the nurse's station. Only the most trusted were permitted the demanding rotation. The girl, not much older than Blue, opened her mouth to speak, but no sound came out.

Baird was used to girls growing shy around him; he was very handsome. He'd overheard one hormone-laden girl saying to her friend that Baird had "a face to die for, and a butt to kill for."

Grettel's was a different kind of timidity. The girl looked positively afraid of her own shadow, not to mention Baird's. Grettel's fingers twisted, and she swallowed three times as she worked her way up to speaking. "It's okay. I got it." Baird reached behind him to grab for the foreign object in his back, but the girl shook her head, finally daring to move toward him.

Wordlessly, she pointed to the table. She was so unimposing with her short brown hair and cocoa-colored eyes; he found his usually obstinate demeanor complying without question. Dainty fingers ghosted over his naked flesh, causing goosebumps to erupt. Every now and then, Blue's best friend Elle would flirtatiously stroke his arm or back. That was a different reaction from this. The assistant was tender as she touched the wounds, and he found that her sweetness softened him without his consent.

"Grettel, I swear!" Nurse Kalista steamed, barging through the curtain that separated Baird from the numerous other patients. "I told you, I needed the antiseptic at station three refilled! I have patients piling up, here, and I can't keep repeating myself." Nurse Kalista grabbed at Grettel's collar and shoved the petite girl toward the curtain.

Grettel nodded meekly and darted out of the area, reappearing a moment later with a large bottle of clear liquid. She handed it to the nurse with shaking hands, and then returned to Baird's bedside.

"Where was this?" Nurse Kalista asked, flipping her shiny black hair over her shoulder.

"S-station three, ma'am."

Without warning, the nurse pulled back her hand and slapped Grettel across the face. The girl staggered back, tears springing to her eyes. "It was not! I looked, and it wasn't there. Now, get on the ball!" She slapped Grettel again. Baird's jaw tightened at the nurse's abuse of Grettel. It was clear she often used the Wayward girl as a means of relieving the stress of her job. "Clean him up," Nurse Kalista ordered before leaving for another patient in a huff.

Every bit the model Wayward, Grettel obeyed, keeping her tears silent as she turned to face the intimidating older boy nearly every Wayward revered or feared. She motioned for him to lay back down with a trembling finger, and Baird obeyed. She cried through the entire ordeal of pulling out the broken piece of pottery and three other fragments that splintered off and had to be removed with tweezers.

Baird scarcely noticed the pain of the metal gouging into his torn flesh.

Nurse Kalista barged back in, her unwrinkled thirty-something face pinched with frustration. "Where are the – oh, you have them. Of course. Of course you would use the tweezers and not put them back. You know how tightly we have to keep an eye on our supplies with all these delinquents in and out today. What are you thinking?" She yanked the tweezers from Grettel's shaking hand and slapped the girl across the face for the third time in less than ten minutes.

"Idiot!" She wound up for another strike, but Baird would have no more.

His plan to distance himself from everyone, save for his family and Elle crumbled as he twisted off the table and planted himself between the nurse and Grettel. He was sixteen, and well-built for his age. Naked chested and strong arms bared, he stared the nurse down with a sneer he reserved only for his enemies. "Hit me," he dared her.

Nurse Kalista tried to return his glare, but her trepidation was palpable as she took a step back from him. "Baird, you lay down on that table right now!"

His eyes widened, and he knew he was bordering on psychotic as he kept his voice low and steady. "You mad about something? Hit me."

"Stop it!" Nurse Kalista scolded.

Grettel whimpered and clung to the wall. Baird moved in front of the girl, acting as her shield. Though he did not know her, he knew that he could not leave Grettel to fend for herself. The marks of abuse were evident, and Baird hoped Grettel had not been scarred for life by the nurse. It took thick skin to make it through the daily tasks of The Way, and he feared what any more toughening of this tender girl would do to her. Not many things softened him, but when they did, Baird clung to the lifeline with ferocity.

"Hit me, Vemreaux. You seem to like beating on little girls. Try me on." He cracked his knuckles ominously. "I think I might like it. Hit me."

"Young man, you'll sit down right now and..."

"Hit me!" he shouted in her face, towering over her.

Nurse Kalista stumbled back a few steps, tripping over her own foot and dropping her clipboard. She snatched her patient files back up off the ground, embarrassed at being intimidated by a mere Wayward. "Grettel, you clean him up and get him out!"

Once she'd left, Baird turned and lay back on the table, making sure not to look at Grettel or her overflowing tears.

It took an entire minute before Grettel approached him. This time when she touched his skin, it was with the air of blessing his wounds with her gratitude. "Why?" she whispered. "Why'd you do that?"

Baird shrugged. "She pissed me off. Besides, you didn't look like you were up for the task of putting her in her place."

"In her place? But she's Vemreaux. We're *beneath* her."

Baird reached out and gripped Grettel's wrist, reminding himself to be gentle. "No. No, we're not. You're not." He met her watery eyes, and for the first time, was not repelled by the show of tears. "She hit you often?"

Grettel nodded, sniffing back as much emotion as she could, so that she could further attend to Baird's back. "It's okay. She doesn't leave marks. Not like these." She pointed to Baird's bloody back. "Now, this is going to sting, so get ready." She squirted a healthy stream of antiseptic onto the wounds, making sure to cover every raw bit. Her dainty fingers rested on his bicep in a gesture of comfort.

Baird had never been babied. Everyone assumed that he did not need consoling, so they never bothered. He loathed the release of tension that came from Grettel's kindness, and tensed his fist to stave of any further softening on his part.

"Did that hurt too badly? Are you okay?"

"I'm fine. She shouldn't be hitting you, Grettel."

"It's okay." Grettel ducked her head toward his to ensure no one overheard. "Thank you, though. I'll probably get worse from her later for it, but thank you for doing that. You don't even know me."

"You don't know me, and you're helping me out." Baird refused to look at her, not wanting to own up to his kind words. "Only fair I return the favor."

At this, Grettel managed a small smile through her sniffling. "Everyone knows you."

"No one knows me," Baird countered, cursing his blatant melancholy.

Grettel placed her delicate hand on his shoulder and rubbed a light circle on the flesh. "That's a shame. You seem...worth knowing. Worthwhile."

Baird did not know what to say to this, so he settled for patting her hand. "Thanks."

Grettel kept her mousy voice low and bent in, so there would be no chance at being overheard. "Maybe I don't know you, but I've seen you."

Baird stiffened and stopped breathing simultaneously. "You've seen me do what?"

He could hear the gentle smile in Grettel's response. "You watch your sister. Protect her. No one bothers her because they're afraid of you. I've seen you finish your brother's workload, too. He's young, and they sometimes give the children more than they can handle. You always step in and make sure he's taken care of." She glanced down at his torn back. "How many of these beatings did you actually earn, and how many were Griffin's?"

"Do you know Griffin or something?" Baird was surprised anyone watched him that closely.

"No. But don't worry. I know it's supposed to be a secret that you're nice. I can keep my mouth shut." Grettel pointed to the gash she'd dug the pottery from. "I think you might need stitches here. I don't do those, though. Let me call the nurse back in."

Baird wasn't sure what to make of the observant girl. "No, thanks. I'll take my chances. It'll heal. It always does."

"At least let me bandage it up." Her petite fingers made quick work of concealing the abrasions. She gathered up the gauze and bloody scraps to throw them in the trash.

"Wait. I'll take those." Baird sat up.

"The garbage?" Grettel wrinkled her nose in confusion. "But it's unsanitary."

"It's my blood. I earned every bit of that whip, so I should get to keep my blood. It's mine. They don't need it for anything."

Grettel's fearful eyes darted to the curtain. "But that's against the rules. Nurse Kalista would be mad."

"Nurse Kalista won't find out. I'll burn it all in the furnace later."

It was a test, as everything was with the people he trusted most. Baird needed to know if he'd earned Grettel's allegiance.

Hesitantly, Grettel handed the sodden mess over to the large man, who tucked the contraband in his armpit. She surprised Baird by resting her petite hand on his arm to stay his exit. "Please don't get caught. And let me get you a fresh uniform. That one's ruined."

"Nah. I like it. Sends a message to the Supervisors."

"Oh. Um, well, just be careful with those bandages. Nurse Kalista...she's a lot worse when I've actually done something to make her mad."

Just like that, Grettel passed the test. Baird glanced out the window to his sister, who was still hard at work in the yard. He knew Blue wouldn't be opposed to adding the meek girl to their exclusive group. Baird mentally shifted his worldview to include Grettel, tucked securely under his wing of protection.

Baird stood, buttoning up his bloodied jumpsuit as he gave an evil grin to the girl. "I wouldn't worry about Nurse Kalista, Grettel. She won't be bothering you much longer."

2

THE BLACKOUT

Two Years Later

Blue's arms were not tired as she hauled the fifteenth load of housing bricks to the refinery, but she was bored. Tasks that had once been exciting with their newness had grown mundane through the years she spent with her brother in The Way. Baird let her switch up jobs occasionally. She'd worked in the yard mucking scratch, in the kitchen, pressing paper, sewing clothes, laundry, in-house maintenance and even S-brick production. Finally, she'd convinced him that she should work with the housing bricks. Well, it wasn't so much her as it was her best friend Elle who did the convincing. Elle was a year older than Blue, and even the stoic Baird was not immune to her blonde hair and beguiling emerald eyes. They'd used the angle of hauling housing bricks as inconspicuous weight training. It also helped that the furnace shed they were fired in was a kilometer away from the yard workers, so she would have more opportunities to train without fear of being seen. He reluctantly agreed. The preparation he'd had her doing of sewing clothes with her eyes shut had reached its maximum level of effectiveness.

When Baird finally conceded, Blue was so happy not to have to sit still for hours on end anymore that she almost jumped up and hugged him. Almost. Hugging was not something Baird suffered, so she settled for a grateful shove, which he returned with a smile. The condition was that either he or Elle had to work the shift with her. After much pretense of debate, Blue decided she'd like to spend her days with Elle, who knew her secret and promised Baird that she'd keep an eye on his sister.

After a month hauling housing bricks, it proved to be like every other job. The repetition of the task was taxing, not the work itself. When she and Elle were alone, stacking bricks in the sweltering furnace room, Elle got a much needed break while Blue moved both their loads from the trolleys. The Vemreaux Supervisors never bothered them much; the room was too hot for their liking.

"So, you think Baird noticed?" Elle asked, looking down approvingly at her chest.

"Normally, I'd say that Baird notices everything, so of course he'd see that you went up a bra size. But since you happen to be the one area he's clueless about..." Blue nodded as Elle placed the fortieth brick in Blue's outstretched arms. Each brick weighed two kilograms. This was not a challenging amount for Blue to carry, but she had to do it while having a conversation and being careful not to drop any. Baird instructed them that if her voice wavered at all while lifting, that would count as showing weakness, and she would fail his lesson for the day.

"I know, right? He can obsess about the correct form for your inverted one-handed pushups, but can't see what's right in front of his face."

"That's the brilliance of Baird for you. I saw Larry giving you the glad eye at breakfast."

Elle grinned and winked. "I coulda sworn he was looking at you, girlfriend."

Blue rolled her eyes. Although it was true that at sixteen, her body was changing, and no amount of strategically smeared scratch could hide that, it was laughable to think that any guy would give her a second look when they had Elle to ogle. "You're sweet, but wrong. And if you want to be with Baird, then you've got to make the first move. And the second. And probably the third. And you've got to be more obvious."

Elle flipped her hair over her shoulder and huffed. "How many more times can I do the lean and laugh?" She demonstrated by unbuttoning the top snap of her orange jumpsuit, leaning forward so her ample bosom pressed into her folded arms and let loose her best tinkling giggle.

Blue quirked her eyebrow at her best friend. "You may have to revise your takedown."

"Ugh. Everything is a fighting term with you two. Not sexy."

Blue shrugged at the nature of the beast. Sweat was sliding down her forehead, not from the work, but from the furnace. Their job was to move the dried and pressed housing bricks from the workshop to the refinery, and then another Wayward, usually Marxus or Grent, fired the bricks to ensure their purity and durability. Then the girls moved them to the storage shed on the east end of The Way's vast property.

Today, however, Marxus was in the infirmary with a bloody fist and sprained wrist. Marxus was Baird's right hand, and the two worked the yard together. When Baird permitted Blue to sign up for a position moving housing bricks, it was no surprise that it came with strings. Elle knew her secret, but it was apparently not enough for her to watch Blue and help her train. Marxus had to be there, as well. Marxus and Baird unofficially ran the yard, which, until they'd established themselves as Alpha dogs, was where most of the fights broke out. Both men would turn nineteen at the end of the month, and even though there were plenty of older Waywards out there, Baird's rule was absolute. Any fights would have to go through him, and he liked a quiet work atmosphere.

When Blue switched jobs, she should not have been surprised that Marxus was asked to put in for a similar job trade. Though he was no Baird, and he did not know their secret, Marxus looked so forbidding and had the reputation of being Baird's dirty work enforcer, that there was no chance the girls would have a hard time in the mostly-male housing bricks job site.

The fight Marxus had been in that morning churned in the rumor mill like a hurricane. He'd apparently taken down three older boys single-handedly for trying to get him kicked off his lead position in the furnace room. The gossip was that they hadn't been able to land a single blow, and that Marxus' injuries had come from punching a wall. That was how it went with rumors in The Way, though. In another day, the sprained wrist would be omitted, and there would be twelve guys he obliterated.

Blue heard Grent approaching with Marxus' replacement, and immediately set down the forty bricks she'd been moving. She rolled her eyes and pretended to struggle as she lifted two bricks, ignoring Elle's quiet laughter at the theatrics. There were additional sets of footsteps now, and Blue warned Elle with a look to keep alert.

The mask was effortless. Blue's perfect posture slumped, shoulders inverted, and feet shuffled at the first hint of eavesdroppers. She lowered her chin so that her auburn hair tilted forward to obscure most of her face.

"Hey, Elle," Grent called as he strolled into the hot room. He had four older guys with him, each of whom looked like they were approaching the age limit for Building Three. Grent looked her up and down more overtly than his usual stolen glances. "You're looking good today."

Elle gave him an appreciative half-smile. "You think I look good now? Wait till I'm not stuck in this hot box." She nodded to acknowledge the four guys brought in to replace one Marxus. "Why all the extra help? Hey, Evan. Perry." She could not recall the other two men's names.

"This one looks like she could use a break," suggested Evan as he motioned to Blue. He held the door open for her to exit. "Go on, kid. Supervisor's tied up on the yard right now, but you could probably use a water stop."

Haulers and refiners went through a lot of water, true, but the menace in Evan's tone made the hairs on the back of Blue's neck stand on end. Grent was usually quiet with the occasional covert flirt for Elle, but his confidence had not been as obvious with Marxus around to keep watch. She did not like the bravado, or the fact that there were five guys when a Vemreaux Supervisor would only have sent two for the task.

Elle had the same thought. "Now that you mention it, I could use some water, too. Come on, Blue."

Grent moved to block her way out. "I already told you that you look good. It's not water you need, and you know it."

The two men Elle did not know closed in behind her. She held her ground and acted as if she was not in the middle of an impending attack. "What's this about, guys?" Elle tried to keep her voice steady. Bored, even.

"It's about you."

Perry's brown eyes glinted with mischief and malice as he stepped in front of Elle. "You're Baird's girl, right?"

"Why? You hoping to be Baird's girl?" she joked boldly, unwilling to cower beneath the threat of their combined height, weight and strength. In truth, she and Baird never made anything official. It was simply understood that the two were together. For years, stories circulated about their various wild sex adventures, when in reality, Baird had never even kissed her. Elle squared her shoulders to Perry's, ignoring the two men behind her whose breath she could feel through her hair.

Perry cracked his knuckles as he looked her up and down. "Baird needs to know that he's not in charge around here anymore. Marxus got our message this morning, but there're too many supervisors in the yard to get close to Baird. You, on the other hand. Well, he left you wide open."

One of the men behind Elle surprised her by gripping her arm hard with his calloused and dirty fingers. She looked up, scowling, but her bravery did not deter his strength. Her eyes met Blue's across the room, and she shook her head almost imperceptibly.

Blue caught Elle's silent warning to let her handle this, but did not even consider obeying. Evan's heavy hand pressed down on Blue's shoulder, causing her to stiffen. "Out you go, now," he ordered.

Blue froze as black wisps crept in at the edges of her vision. "Don't touch me," she warned in a quiet voice.

Perry turned to acknowledge the open door. "That's Baird's sister, right?"

Grent looked uneasy, but nodded. "She's young, though. She's a Jane." He indicated her middle name. Every Wayward girl born in Blue's year was given the middle name Jane. Elle was a year older, so she was a Louise. The guys surrounding them were older than Baird. Franklins, at least.

"Yeah, yeah. The quiet one. I don't know, Grent. A two-fer sounds good. What do you say, Perry?" Dureck suggested.

"She's just a kid, Dureck. Let her go. You want to take down Baird, go for his girlfriend," said Grent. Elle walked around like a beacon all other women should aspire to, and every man should fantasize about. She practically screamed sex. But Blue? Grent could not justify manhandling the quiet girl who'd barely ever opened her mouth in his presence.

Evan's hand shoved Blue forward. "You want the sister, Dureck? Take her. I had dibs on Elle."

Dureck released his grip on Elle's arm and moved toward the timid-looking girl with purpose. "Don't be afraid. I'm doing you a favor. Word gets around that you gave it up to me, you'll be set. Envy of all the Janes."

Blue shook her head, afraid not of what he'd do to her, but of what she might do to him. She couldn't let that happen again. Baird had warned her about staying in control, dealing with problems without losing her head. She fought to stay in the moment, to handle Dureck without blacking out. The wisps were mutating into a fog that clouded her clarity. "You should leave," she whispered to him. "Please. I'm begging you. Just go."

Desperation gripped Elle as she watched Blue struggle to remain timorous. Panic pinched Elle's voice as she pleaded frantically. "No,

Dureck! Take me instead! Leave her alone! Do what you want with me. You know you want to. I'm the one you came for. All of you. Just let her go." Perry grabbed her roughly, mashed his face to hers and kissed her without mercy. Elle jerked away. "Run, Blue! Get out of here!"

Dureck stood in front of her, but Blue saw only Elle. The edges of her vision were completely dark, cutting off her periphery. Elle's fearful scream narrowed the focus until the alarm on her best friend's face was all Blue could see. Blue could not run. She could not call out for help. In the fog of the fray, she vaguely heard Dureck unsnapping his jumpsuit.

She felt the air move when his hands approached her, as if in slow motion. The black narrowed so she could see only a tunnel in front of her, gray bleeding in like vapors of smoke at the edges. Her breath caught as Dureck made contact with her orange jumpsuit.

Without pause, she clamped her small hands around Dureck's fingers and squeezed, not stopping until she felt several bones snap beneath his howls of pain and surprise.

Her vision tapered yet further, and she did not hesitate as she grabbed a handful of his black hair and bashed his head down against a pile of bricks. Over and over she thrust him down, not stopping even when the fight and life went out of him.

Shouts of surprise echoed around her, but she registered none of it. Turning on the remaining men, her sight faded to darkness as she stepped forward to pay them the justice they deserved.

She was no longer a girl, but death incarnate.

Bones shattered beneath her capable hands, but she registered no victory. The men cried for help while Elle shrieked, but she did not slow. Blood spread out over her, dripping from her hands and pooling at her feet, but she felt none of it. An abyss of nothing flooded her, blinding her brilliant blue eyes from the torment she inflicted. Her body continued while her mind retreated to a place in her subconscious where the violence couldn't reach her.

Seconds. Minutes. Hours? She could not remember her own name as she repeatedly slammed Grent's head into the concrete floor while humming a dismal melody. His skull had long since caved in, face unrecognizable, but Blue was stuck on autopilot. Having wreaked all the carnage she could, her muscles would not stop, even at absolute death. She was encased in the black that would not lift, despite the glow of the furnace and fluorescent bulb dangling overhead.

It was not Elle's sobs and vomiting that roused her, but her brother's voice that finally found her in the fog. "Blue!" he cried, his shock only just breaking through her daze as she continued to bash Grent's head on the floor while humming the Wayward Anthem eerily. "Blue, stop! You're done now."

When this did not produce the lucid results he'd been hoping for, Baird pulled back his arm and let it fly, slapping her so hard that her head bobbed to the side.

The room came back to her in trickles and small details, the black giving way to the light. The bulb. The furnace. A pile of housing bricks. Elle biting her fist as she screamed into it in the corner. Pile of dismembered bodies scattered around her. Blood coating the floor, dripping from her fingers.

Baird's face. Control trumped the worry on his features as he moved in front of her and locked in on her unfocused gaze. "Blue," he whispered. "That's enough."

When Blue found that her hands would not relent in their punishment of Grent's shattered skull, she whimpered. Her brother's firm palms gripped her face, forcing her to see only him. "Br-aird?" Her voice sounded far away and foreign. Surely that scared girl couldn't possibly be her.

"I'm here now. I'll take care of it." He nodded until she mirrored the motion. "Now, let him go."

When her fingers finally granted Grent's head permission to slump on the floor, Blue let out a single scream that Baird's hand muffled. He shook his head. "You don't get to freak out here. Do that on your own time. It's done. I need you back in the room with me, not wherever you just went to in your head."

She tried to move her mouth, but only mushy ramblings spilled out.

"Get it together, Elle," he said of Elle's quiet sobs. She was huddled in the corner, tears streaming down her face as she hugged herself. Baird shook his head at the mess. "This was sloppy," he criticized. "These breaks...why here?" Baird lifted a leg to indicate the broken shin. "That's not the place to incapacitate. All you'll do is slow him down a little, which you don't need, given how fast you are. That was wasted effort." He scoffed at another odd fracture. "Well, at least you kept it quiet this time."

Blue watched in confusion as her brother continued his lecture on the importance of a clean, swift takedown. She tried to make sense of his words, to pick out the important ones and force them to mean something, but she couldn't. The room tilted as Elle's red face came into view. Her eyes were swollen from crying and her face splotchy with emotion. Elle clutched her knees to her chest as she wept.

"Go ahead," Baird urged, and it occurred to Blue that he had been instructing her to no avail.

"*What*?" she mouthed, her voice adding no volume.

"Snap out of it!" Baird clicked his fingers in front of her face. To test her awareness, he slapped her cheek, dismayed when she did not punch him back. "Blue." He laid a dismembered leg across her lap. "The femur. Practice snapping the femur. It's the strongest bone in the body, so it might compare to a Vemreaux's arm or something."

Blue did not respond as the room tilted once more, shifting the order of everything like sand to one side and then back again. She felt him move her hands to either end of the thigh and heard one command: "Break it!"

Blue finally obeyed. Without much hesitation, the strong bone splintered and cracked in half. She did not register Baird's satisfaction, or the second leg he placed in her lap. Over and over he had her break femurs until each one was properly assaulted.

Baird pulled her up, unsettled when her legs gave out beneath her. "Get yourself together, Blue. This isn't finished. We've got to clean this mess up." When he judged that she could stand without assistance, he opened the door to the furnace and thrust in what was left of Grent's head, careful not to get blood on his jumpsuit.

Blue followed his example, shoving pieces of her soul into the chute along with each body part she burned. The heat was unforgiving, but the fire inside proved a welcome distraction from the agony that threatened to show itself at any moment. The thought to climb into the conflagration and burn away her many sins seemed a viable option, but the saner part of her reasoned that Baird would probably not approve.

Arm. Leg. Head. Torso. Arm. Leg. Head. Torso. Penis. Blue screamed at the foreign appendage and jumped back, earning a glare from her brother. "Finish it!" he commanded.

Arm. Leg. Head. Torso. Blue could scarcely believe the destruction she'd caused, the utter obliteration of these men at her hands. There could be no absolution from this. Despite their intentions, she knew she would carry the weight of their deaths for years to come, as she did the others she'd destroyed in the black.

So entranced was she that she did not hear the door open. She did not see the intruder enter the furnace room. Only when the beginnings of a shrill screech reached her ears did Blue turn around.

Ariel. Number 0-6396829527-8. Blue remembered the girl with frizzy red hair. She was three years younger than Blue, a Linda. There she stood in the doorway, eyes wide with Baird's hand over her mouth. He checked the surrounding area to see if anyone had heard her noise, and then shut the door again, dragging her into the mess. "This," he spat with anger at his sister, "this is what happens when you lose your mind. This is what happens when you lose your temper." He shook the girl, his hand still stifling her screams. "This is what happens when you aren't careful." He looked into Ariel's young eyes that were filled with terror. Bad enough to be this close to the infamous Baird. Even worse to walk in on mangled corpses and Blue covered in blood. Baird jostled her to evoke another cry for help that would go nowhere. "She won't be able to keep your secret like Elle or Grettel. So now, because you lost your temper, she has to die." He thrust the rag doll at his sister with disgust. "Finish her."

Blue was sure she'd misunderstood. She was positive he couldn't mean she must kill this thirteen-year-old girl who recoiled from her in horror. "B-Baird! No! I can't do that! She h-hasn't d-done anything wrong."

"No, but you did." Baird's was tone icy. "Your mistakes have consequences, and she has to pay for it. Do it," he commanded.

"N-No!" Blue bent down to Ariel, who'd dropped to the floor, nose running as she bawled. "Shh. Quiet, Ariel! You can keep quiet, right?" When her words did not penetrate, she pleaded with the girl. "Please! Be q-quiet, Ariel! I don't want to hurt you!"

Elle crawled toward the girls to lend her support, but she had no words that could help. She simply offered her tears to the growing pile as she touched Ariel's bony back.

Baird knew his sister like the back of his hand, the hand that was dripping with the blood of her mistake. He looked down at Blue and knew she was not capable of killing on her own without blacking out. He shook his head, hoping to convey his utter disappointment in her. "You're not ready," he ruled.

In one swift motion, Baird picked up the gangly girl. "Shh," he cooed, almost tenderly. He smoothed her fiery tangles from her tear-stained face as she begged for help Baird could not give. Then, just as quick as her scream built up, it ended with a sharp twist of her head. Ariel slumped to the floor, every bit as dead as Grent and the others.

Elle shoved her fist into her mouth and howled, muffling the sound and the horror as much as she could. She backed away from Baird, now only pretty sure he wouldn't do the same to her. She'd kept quiet. She'd been helpful, even. Still, Baird possessed little mercy, and she didn't want to use up the last of it. She tried to breathe as he pushed Ariel into the furnace, but the air was too thick to pull in a proper gasp.

After Baird tossed the last torn body part into the heat and shut the heavy door, he set about dealing with the rest of the mess. He ventured outside the building and turned on the hose. Without addressing either woman, he sprayed down the floor, chasing the blood and bile down the drain in the center of the room.

Logistics he could deal with. Elle needing comfort as she sobbed? There never seemed a right way to handle that, so he settled on ignoring her for the time being. "Blue, I'll run back to Laundry and get you a new jumpsuit, but you'll have to hose off while I'm gone. Burn the uniform you're wearing. Nothing can tie you to this, understand?"

Blue's mouth opened to scream, but Baird closed the distance between them in two of his long strides. He palmed her forehead and pushed her down on her knees roughly. "Ariel's gone, and you don't need to think about that right now." He stiffened against her violent shaking. Baird was grateful his sister did not seem capable of crying. "I want you to picture her body and put it in a box. Can you do that?" His voice was unnaturally calm as he spoke to her. "Put Ariel in a box and shut the lid tight. Now dig a hole and stuff the box in." When Blue did not confirm his words, his tone hardened. "I can't hear you."

"Yes, Baird," she whispered.

"Good. Now shove the box in the ground and cover it up. Nice and deep, shove it down. Shove it down." He pushed her forehead and squeezed his fingers tighter around her cranium. "Stuff it all down, Blue." Baird watched her eyes slide out of focus. "Did you bury the bad things?"

"Yes, Baird," she answered soullessly.

"Good girl. Hold it back. Hold it all back. Push it down. Way down." His voice was hypnotic as he watched her obey. The angst slid from her, as did her fight. "There you go. Never touch that box again. If you see any sign of it, beat it back down. Push it down."

Blue nodded, her eyes empty as her brother released her, finally giving her the space to breathe. "Now, wash up," she heard him order.

Blue moved without thinking. Her mind was numb to the terror. She heard only the blood rushing in her ears as she turned on the water. Blue held the hose over her head and let the cold water hit her, though she doubted she would ever feel clean again. Life began to return to her as the chill awakened her senses one by one. When she found Elle standing at her side, Blue scolded herself for allowing someone to surprise her. Elle's trembling hand motioned for the hose, and Blue handed it over without a word.

"Why didn't you run?" Elle asked, her voice barely audible above the trickle of water.

Blue shrugged. "Would you have left me alone with those guys?"

Elle did not respond, but hardness glinted in her emerald eyes. "Still, you stayed. For what it's worth, you were pretty amazing." She bunched Blue's hair in her fist and ran the water over her friend's neck. Elle swiped at her tears, still trying to steady herself. "You've got to take this suit off, sweetie. Baird's right. It's gotta be destroyed."

Blue unsnapped her jumpsuit and peeled the uniform off. After casting the last bit of evidence into the furnace, she sat on the floor under the stream of water, clad only in her underwear and bra. She shivered from a cruel combination of cold and nerves. Even though the water from the hose would have covered her indiscretion, Blue did not cry. Baird would not have tolerated such a disgusting act. Blue stared vacantly ahead and permitted Elle to weep for the both of them.

3

TEMPER

Three Years Later

"**H**urry, George!"

"Oh, this is not good. This is really not good," George worried aloud to himself as he struggled with the bag of feed. The sturdy burlap sack weighed half as much as he did and did not lighten with his valiant attempts at speeding up.

"We have to finish our chores soon," Griffin insisted. "This is the last day I can see my sister, you know."

George stopped once again to give his pubescent muscles a rest. "Griff, I can't go any faster than this. These bags are heavy!" He stretched his back up straight and groaned, already getting annoyed with the flies that grew thicker as they neared the scratch piles and cow pens. "Why did we get barn duty today of all days? Wouldn't mind scrubbing a toilet right now."

Griffin smirked, despite the growing urgency that plagued him all morning. "I'll remember you said that next time we get bathroom detail. C'mon, now. We're almost done. Just four more bags."

"After these two!" George corrected him.

Griffin could not be deterred. Heavy sack flung over his back, he walked steadily forward – George or no George.

George pushed the bent frame of his gold-rimmed glasses up onto his nose, but the profuse perspiration made his preference for their placement irrelevant. When he hefted the too-large bag over his unsteady shoulder, his glasses slid down even further than they were before. George huffed as his leaden feet followed his best friend faithfully.

"Hurry, George!" Griffin called out over his sturdy shoulder.

George pursed his lips and bit back the grunts he wanted to make. After all, this might be the last day Griffin would be allowed to see his sister on the inside. If their older brother Baird was successful in purchasing her for his owner that night, it would be the end of the threesome. Griffin, Blue and George would become just Griffin and George. Griffin would be without family in The Way. While this devastated Griffin to no end, it made George equally wary. Blue had an uncanny ability to calm her younger brother's oft-flaring temper. George did not know how well Griffin would fare without his sister's gentle hand on his arm to quiet his sometimes violent irritability.

With new determination, George fought against his strained muscles and the itch from the sweat that ran down his back, soaked up by his orange jumpsuit. He was glad for the calluses that already marked his fingers from the many hard years of work he'd lived through. His hands were shaking with the effort of keeping the sack in place. Griffin made it look so easy.

"You take that back!" George heard Griffin's voice yelling from up ahead.

"Look, kid. I'm not saying anything against your sister. I just think it's rough, is all." Clarense shrugged as he leaned on the fertilizer rake in front of him. He bore a large smear of scratch across his cheek, not to mention several smelly trails down his arms. His barcode was scarcely visible under the brown stains.

"She'll be fine!" Clarense had voiced Griffin's biggest concern, though the fiery teenager didn't want to admit it. "Baird's owner is buying her. My brother'll look after her, no problem. You remember Baird, right? The giant Wayward that broke your arm when you couldn't watch your mouth?"

"Hey, no need to bring that up. I'm sure you're right, Griff." Clarense held up his free hand in surrender. "I just hope Baird's owner isn't into renting out his A-bloods for prostitution. I've heard they don't screen as carefully for that anymore."

Griffin's right fist began to shake, and George knew his time was just about out. He huffed and puffed closer to the two who were garnering much unwelcome attention. Just a little further and he could drop his heavy load and coax his best friend away from the older Wayward who had yet to learn tact.

"My sister's not a prostitute! Baird would never let her get bought by someone like that."

Good, George thought. *Use logic instead of your fists this time.*

"C'mon, Clarense!" A second older boy by the name of Willyum chimed in as he refilled his bucket with wet scratch. "That's crazy. You know who his sister is. She's that scrawny one named Blue. No Vemreaux in his right mind would pay for her."

George closed his eyes and hissed out the air he was saving to talk Griffin into walking away. There was no hope for that now. Griffin had the same auburn hair as his siblings, the same peak in his left ear, unsettlingly blue eyes, and unfortunately, he also had his brother's temper – but without the silent intimidation or moderate level of self-control. When Griffin exploded, there was no containing the damage.

Griffin leapt over the puddle of muck and slammed into Willyum, knocking the older boy onto his back. Misdirected rage filled Griffin's fist as it collided with Willyum's jaw once, twice, and geared up for a third time.

Blue was blessed with unnatural strength, but a varying degree of that same power was shared between the siblings. Plus, Griffin trained with Baird and Blue every chance he got when Baird lived in The Way, so his fury packed some definite pain.

"Don't talk about my sister like that!" Griffin stormed. Even the flies knew to leave him alone in that moment, not one daring to land on him as he gave in to the volatile anger that had been bubbling beneath the surface for days.

"Griffin, leave it alone!" George pleaded, his breath squeezing through gritted teeth as he struggled to pry his friend off of his victim. "Do you want to get a punishment today of all days? What if you get solitary again? You won't be able to say goodbye to her or see Baird."

Griffin's fist slowed before it could deliver Willyum's final blow. "This isn't over," he warned.

"It is if I go to the infirmary and report you!" Willyum spat out a mouthful of blood as Clarense helped him up off the ground.

George sighed. If Griffin wasn't his best friend, he would have so many more points by now. "Will three points convince you to tell the nurse you fell onto your shovel?" He tapped his barcode reluctantly.

Griffin snorted, unwilling to give up even one point to make things right.

Willyum would never have admitted to being taken down by a fifteen-year-old, even if it was a relative of the ominous and infamous Baird. Though Baird had been bought by a Vemreaux years ago for indentured work in the real world, the Waywards still told stories about him in hushed, deferential tones. There were rumors that Marxus was still working on Baird's orders, though no one knew how they communicated.

Willyum tried to sound tough. "Make it five points. You know I could get him beaten if I told Supervisor Tum."

"Fine." George shook his head as Griffin stomped off. "Lay off him. He's losing all he's got today."

4

VIOLATED

Age of Peace Law 17, Subset 2b
All emergency personnel should respond to Vemreaux distress calls first.
Second, a freed Wayward, and third, an owned Wayward.

"I s there a problem? You look weird." Baird spoke with his signature note of annoyance that had not lessened over the years. He shifted the 4x4 to third gear as they exited the main street and traveled down a series of dark and winding side roads.

"No problem," Blue answered. "Just nervous. Excited."

"Don't be nervous," he commanded. "Your job isn't to feel; it's to listen. How do you think you're doing at your job so far?"

"Go ahead. I'll do better."

Baird grumbled under his breath before continuing with his debriefing, checking off the key points one at a time. "One thing to remember when you're waiting tables at your owner's diner is that there're two sides to the menu. There's one set of meals for changed Vems and one for unchanged. You've never spent time around unchanged Vemreaux before. Tell me how to spot an unchanged."

Blue fought with her sass at being asked such a rudimentary question. "Unchanged Vemreaux haven't bathed in the Fountain of Youth yet, so they age like us. Once they dip, they go through the change." *Obviously. I'm not an idiot.* "Their eyes turn black, their bones are harder to break, they stop aging and they have heightened senses, except for their sense of taste, which dulls."

"The unchanged can't smell us," Baird added. "Only the changed ones with their heightened sense of smell can tell we're *A*-blood."

Blue rattled off the facts every Wayward knew. "Changed ones have an iron deficiency, so most of them drink filtered *O*-type blood to keep from being anemic."

"I didn't ask you to tell me everything a five-year-old knows. I asked you how to spot an unchanged." He tapped his ear. "Listening, remember?"

"I already answered how to spot an unchanged Vem!"

"Then what's with all the extra chatter?"

Blue crossed her arms over her chest and frowned. "You're meaner than I remembered."

"Then you'll have to work on your listening and your memory."

Blue groaned. "So the moral of your boring story is?"

"When Elle and –" Baird began.

Blue interrupted by snoring loudly.

"You wanna survive out here, or not?"

"I don't know. How much more of this story's left?"

Baird scowled at his sister. "Shut up, Blue." He could not remember when he'd permitted her to mock him, but somewhere in her teens, she'd come into her moxie. It was annoying, but at times, he secretly found it amusing. Baird palmed the crown of his sister's head and shoved her to the side, earning a punch to his arm. "When Elle and Grettel lived in The Way, you would wear their dirty jumpsuit from the day before. That way you'd have the sulfuric *A*-blood scent on you so the Vemreaux monitoring us wouldn't catch on you were weird and didn't smell like a normal Wayward. You'll have to do the same thing in the real world."

"I figured."

"You wanna run this conversation?"

"No, Baird. Go ahead." *Tell me more things I already know,* Blue thought bitterly.

"Be yourself at home, but out of the hut, you have to stay under people's radar until you find your calling. Let Elle be the thing that draws their eyes, just like in The Way. She looks more like a Femreaux anyway, carries herself prouder than a Wayward. Fem is slang for a female Vemreaux, by the way."

"Then why'd you have Master Joe buy me as a waitress instead of a cook or something? Won't that make me more visible?"

Baird's teeth ground together. "The correct answer is: thank you, Baird. Thank you for getting me out of The Way before I turned sixty and got terminated at life expectancy."

"Thank you, Baird. Blah, blah, blah, life expectancy."

Baird's knuckles tightened on the steering wheel, but he did not address her back-talk. He'd been looking forward to having her out in the real world with him for a long time, and didn't want to ruin it with a fight right away. "Joe needed a waitress, and I have no idea how long it'll be before he asks me to find him another slave. I saw the opportunity and took it. I'm warning you that even though you'll be taking their orders, you'll have to do your best to stay out of their way. Hide your eyes, walk around like Grettel, and you know, be forgettable."

No trouble with that one, Blue sighed inwardly. "Okay."

The amazing assortment of cars, buildings, people and nature that blurred by them was so incredible, Blue scarcely had room in her brain to process it all. It was two in the morning as they drove to her new home, but her keen eyes picked out details in the black that no one else could. Each new object she saw was catalogued in her brain, with a name and purpose to be assigned later. The grin on her face would not move, no matter that it announced a blatant emotion to the world...the *real* world. The *free* world.

I'm never going back to The Way. I'm in the real world now! I'm not gonna die in The Way! Blue tried her best to keep the excited smile hidden, lest her brother find fault with it. *No more cleaning up the cows' scratch. No more beatings. The real world! I made it!*

As she took in the stark difference from the sameness of The Way, her grin settled into a contemplative expression. "Baird? Do you sometimes wish that *A*-bloods reacted to the Fountain of Youth, too? Kinda sucks that the real world is only for the *B*-blood Vems to enjoy. Everything's so pretty out here. These buildings? Amazing! Like, how'd they build them so high? Could you take me to see some of them up close once I get settled?"

Baird's response was quick and harsh. "You know I don't waste my time on wishes. You shouldn't, either." He looked out the window before making a turn. The 4x4 vehicle Master Joe provided for them had no side mirrors, or even a rearview mirror, for that matter. "You'd be surprised what a curse that Fountain is. After you meet a few of the changed Vems that aren't worth the scratch their world's built on, you'll understand what I mean." He glanced over at his sister. "Unclench your fists. You'll get used to riding in a car eventually."

"Eventually," Blue repeated, trying to stifle her happiness so as not to annoy Baird. The car ride was a brand new experience, and she didn't care that it nearly made her sick. She had been fighting down the bile since the first turn. Her brother's silent scrutiny for over an hour had not helped matters much.

Baird cleared his throat as the car turned left around the corner leading to their home. "I'm surprised they finally got all the paperwork together to sell you. I've been back to The Way three times this week, and each time, your Vemreaux Studies professor had another excuse why my master couldn't buy you."

"Jack's thorough."

"Jack's an idiot."

"He's nice to me and Griff. He was nice to you, too, if you recall."

"Not right for a professor to care that much about us. Unnaturally friendly only to the three of us? Something's wrong with him."

"Curse Jack for being friendly!" Blue shouted with her fist in the air, unable to contain her bliss any longer. She directed her grin at her brother, and for a moment, she forgot that she was trying not to anger him. "Welp, nothing you can do about it now. We're on the outside. No way you can make him 'disappear' from out here."

"Don't be so sure," Baird mumbled. "Don't be so cocky, either. I'm allowed to have suspicions."

"And I'm allowed to have friends," she challenged him, fighting the urge to stick her tongue out at her brother.

"You know, a smart mouth like that makes me wonder why I was so anxious to get you outta there." Elle had warned him about being too harsh with Blue on her first day out in the real world. It was the fifteenth item on her verbal list of things he needed to be sensitive to on Blue's inaugural day of indentured freedom.

"Were you anxious because you worry about my safety among all those mean ole' Waywards?" Blue feigned fear for his entertainment.

"Maybe about *their* safety, sure." Baird gave her a shove when she kept up the theatrics, resting the back of her dainty hand on her forehead.

"Aw! Someone pickin' on you, Baird? You need me to beat up a bully for you?" She reached over to place her hand on his arm, laughing when he batted it away.

"Shut up."

"Is it because you missed me something terrible?" she joked. When Baird swallowed instead of fighting with her, Blue took that as confirmation. Her delight beamed, and she did not care anymore if he saw it.

"I just feel better when I can keep my eye on you. Know you're staying out of trouble."

Blue met her brother's eye, and they shared a smile that communicated the things they were unwilling to say. "I missed you, too, Baird."

"The girls've been really..." He squinted, focusing on a point at the end of the road with sudden fury. A swelling of rage, anger and violence all fought for first place on his face as he roared a filthy curse.

A simple shack with four cement walls and a sunken-in roof stood with determination as the only house on the dark, dead-end road. A bright green vehicle with obnoxious fire decals on the side was parked on the grass in a way that conveyed disrespect for the humble property.

Baird sucked his lower lip to his teeth in thought.

Blue recognized this as Baird's planning face, and readied herself for action.

"How much muscle mass have you lost?"

"None!" Blue was affronted at the insult.

"You still as fast as when I left you?"

"Exactly how you left me." *Maybe better,* she thought to herself, though she dared not provoke him by mentioning this aloud. "Baird, what's going on?"

"That car belongs to Vemreaux who think we're easy prey. That pile of sticks is where we live, and they think we don't deserve even that. They're robbing us right now."

"What about the girls?" Blue leaned forward, ready to jump out of the car at first command. Elle and Grettel were a year older than her, and on Baird's recommendation, Blue's new master purchased the two girls as soon as they became of age a year ago. To think of her best friends in danger diminished the beauty of all the lush vegetation, the excitement of riding in a car, and the thousand other amazing new possibilities that just seconds ago enticed her.

Baird's hawk-like gaze fell upon the storm cellar. The large rock that usually sat on the doors had been moved from its position. "They're fine for now." He steadied himself and turned to his sister. "You can go in there with me and learn how we deal with problems like this, or you can wait out here."

Blue was insulted that he would insinuate she was anything less than ready to defend the girls to the death. "Let's go!" Blue palmed the car door's handle.

"Alright." Baird's face transformed to a calculating expression he wore when he was about to teach her something unpleasant. "They're in our home, so we can either phone Master Joe and ask him to call the cops, then wait for them to respond to a Wayward's distress call, which gets lowest priority..." Baird took a deep breath as he stared at the hut, unblinking.

"Or?" Blue queried, hoping he had a better option than that. She'd never seen her brother hesitate to do what needed to be done. Even in a foreign scene like the real world, Vemreaux logic didn't suit him.

"Or we deal with them ourselves."

"Meaning?" she questioned, though she suspected the answer.

"Remember when you'd get sloppy in The Way and someone would see you doing something...too powerful?" He watched his sister swallow with shame. "Used to be my job to protect your secret. Now it's *our* job to protect Elle and Grettel."

"So they can see my face?" Blue clenched her fist.

"They signed their death warrant the second they walked onto Master Joe's property."

"But Baird, I've never killed anyone on purpose," she admitted. "That's your job." Suddenly, the car was far too hot. The air thick with gravity and duty. Blue struggled to take in a full breath. Her chest caught with the fear she dared not give voice to.

"It's like anything else. Do it enough times and, well, you'll get the hang of it. Just do what I taught you. Stay in control." He forced out a small smile of encouragement. "Finally, you'll get some hands-on training. You won't have to hold back this time!" When he sensed the dread she would not speak, he fisted the handle and quietly shoved it open, all camaraderie disappearing into the black of the night sky. "Or wait in the car. It's only a handful of Vemreaux at most. I've killed that many before on my own. If you're not ready to protect the girls yet..."

Her initiation into the real world was much more than signed papers and a large check to The Way West from a wealthy Vemreaux. Blue swallowed the last of the moisture in her mouth as she willed herself not to be afraid. "I can do it. I've just never killed anyone without, you know, blacking out."

"I know, but this'll be good training for you. Just don't get angry. Focus on a clean takedown. Easier than you think."

Baird exited the car, and Blue allowed herself only the briefest of seconds before she followed in her brother's large, all-consuming footsteps. "Okay, let's give it a shot." Her voice was small, but she forced it not to waver. She wasn't eight anymore; she was nineteen. Fear wasn't appropriate when she was a child, so there was no excuse for it now.

As always, Baird had a plan.

"So how're we going to play this? Damsel? Giant? Tum's Rage? I've never done Blind Man against more than one person, though." She ticked off a few more code names they'd used in fights back in The Way.

"Damsel's fine. Got any tears in you?"

"Very funny," she snarled. Each step she took distanced her from the dread that would swallow her, were she to stop and examine it. On she marched, the anxiety chasing at her heels.

As they approached the hut, the two parted ways. Blue went for the front door, and Baird sneaked around the back. Without her brother's scrutiny, she permitted her heart to race and the fear to climb up to her chest before she could gulp it down. It clung to her with its vice grip until she shook it off and forced herself to focus on the task at hand.

"Nothin' in here's worth liftin'," the first man jeered.

"Don't know why we even bothered. *A*-bloods don't own shit!"

"Yeah, but this is Joe's *A*-blood, Aaron. That bar's crowded every night. You know Joe's got money."

"Don't mean he's sharing it with his slaves." A loud belch echoed through the thin walls of the shack.

Blue exhaled out the last of her fear as she listened to their infuriating chatter. She knew that to punch any of them before Baird was in place would be a mistake, but her fingers itched to do the job. Taking a steadying breath, Blue fumbled loudly with the door's round knob. She flung it open and let out the loudest feminine scream she could muster, hating how stupid she sounded. Taking a page from timid Grettel's book, she huddled against the wall, shrieking and pretending to sob as best she could. "Help! Help!" she cried, her hands cupping her cherubic cheeks. She could imagine her brother hiding his laughter at the show.

"Aw, look at the little Wayward, Mosely," the taller man laughed. "She's just an itty bitty thing." Aaron took two steps toward her and leaned down to make sure he dominated her view. "Who do you think's gonna hear you, A-word-Wayward?"

Blue almost forgot her feigned fright, pausing her fake crying at the idiotic insult. "Take anything you want! Just don't hurt me, please!"

Mosely bent toward her and sniffed, making a face. "Lucky you stink like a rotted egg and scratch, kid. Anything my eyes want, my nose can't handle."

In her periphery, Blue could see Baird through the thin screen of the back door. The familiar black snaked its way into her vision, but she fought to regain control. She waited for Baird to nod, and then reached down to her side. "Here," she whispered, her balled-up hand shaking. "It's all I have." Of course, Blue had no money, but Mosely reached for her fist all the same.

Once he was close enough, Blue snatched his outstretched hand and yanked him forward. The surprise in his eyes was nothing compared to the agony that swept across him when she pulled his arm out of its socket and delivered a swift kick to his groin. She'd always ruled that one as a cheap shot, but didn't resent its use this time so much since they were bent on robbing a slave girl who had yet to be given a single possession. The action thrilled her, exciting each of her nerves in a chorus of brutality. Rarely had she been able to fight so uninhibited without losing her mind to the blackouts.

If this was to be her first scrap with a Vemreaux, she would be sure to win it.

Baird moved like a shadow. He quickly and silently maneuvered the tall Aaron into a chokehold, taking him down without being seen by his victim.

Blue focused her strength on Mosely. He was bent over in pain and confusion, so Blue took her opportunity. She cuffed him on the nape of his neck and shoved the crown of his head hard into the concrete wall, grimacing at the sickening crack it made.

Blue stilled even as Baird brought the grand prize to his knees right next to her. Using her strength was exhilarating; her muscles thrilled at finally having their moment of action. In that same moment, her conscience ached, taking a worse beating than Mosely as she looked down at the destruction.

Restraint. Control. Cover.

Killing was something she'd grown to accept as her fate. The prophecy that foretold her fight to the death gave that much away. In The Way, the *A*-blood types were fragile. Their bones shattered under her capable hands, so she had to practice superior self-control at all times. Now she was in the real world. The Vemreaux – those with *B*-type blood – had bones that were far more difficult to break, though the punishment for assaulting one of the superior race was swift and harsh.

If you were caught.

Blue never dreamed she'd roughen her hands and toughen her soul so quickly upon her purchase. Yet, here lay Mosely, looking defeated and not-so-dearly departed at her feet. He was a stranger who made the mistake of robbing the wrong person, and would never live to repeat the folly.

The adrenaline ebbed, and her hands tingled with regret and terror. Fingers that wanted to do schoolwork and help her family mutated into violent weapons that could not be matched. Nineteen was young, but standing over Mosely, willing her legs not to shake, she felt ancient, doomed...and tired. Always tired.

Aaron lay without breath on the floor of the hut with Baird towering over him. His head was turned at an unnatural angle, and Blue guessed that Baird broke the Vemreaux's neck to assure ultimate victory.

Baird eyed Mosely, and then grabbed hold of his sister's arm. "See that, Blue? He's still breathing. Your job was to kill him, not give him brain damage." He smirked at her, but sobered once he took in Blue's petrified stare and quaking limbs. "You did the hard part already.

Now finish the job." When his sister did not move to obey, his grip on her softened. "This is what you were meant for."

Dread engulfed her when his words coupled with her deeds. The onyx vapor crept into her sight once more. She trembled as she fought to control it. Her lower lip shook, but her eyes remained dry. Mortified at her weakness, Blue choked out a whisper before she degraded herself further. "No, Baird. P-Please don't make me do this. I...I don't think I can stop the dark from taking over."

Victory vanished, and Baird assumed the cold and detached face he often used when giving her unpleasant tutorials. "You're not ready," he stated, daring her to stand under the weight of his disappointment. "I thought you were. Sit down until you're under control. I'll finish it."

Guilt fell hard on Blue's shoulders as she bore his displeasure in silence at his feet. Heavy was Baird's stony stare and weighted were his words as he showed his sister how to suffocate an incapacitated man. Of course she knew how. It was simple. She'd seen Baird snuff the life out of a few Waywards in the same manner. She just couldn't will her hands to so thoroughly destroy. Blue nodded hollowly as Baird explained that killing was not a joy, but a job. The girls were his responsibility, and he was the only one who would protect them and their humble way of life. Blue was supposed to add to that protection, not run from her duty.

The trick to killing was to end the foe as quick as possible. There was no room for a fair fight, chivalry, or mercy. If someone needed to die, there was no use beating around the bush. Just beat them about the head and be done with it.

He did not look at her as he rose, but instead pulled from his pocket a dated phone and punched in eight digits. "Lawrence, it's Baird. I've got two deliveries for you at the hut." He grunted twice more, and then hung up, still keeping his eyes from his sister. "No more black?"

"It's gone," she informed him, ashamed. "I'm sorry, Baird." When he did not answer, she gave herself a few more minutes before speaking. "Who's Lawrence?"

"Lawrence is a regular at the diner. He drinks for free and holds his business meetings at the restaurant. In return, he takes care of the bodies for us."

"How often does this happen, Baird?"

"Once every couple months. Not too often. But it has to be dealt with the same way every time. They come for us, we kill them. Quiet and quick." He pocketed his phone and crossed the hardened muscles of his arms over his stone of a heart. "Then Lawrence deals with the bodies. We get caught with them, we get arrested and then killed after the 'fair' trial. A Vemreaux like Lawrence is connected. He gets caught with a body, he can claim self-defense and it's overlooked."

"How does he do it? I mean, there's no scratch pit for the bodies to decompose in undetected."

"He owns concrete and construction companies, a few boats. Sometimes he throws the bodies in a giant freezer to throw off time of death to make sure nothing gets traced back to us. He's smart, rich and well-connected. His job to figure out how to get rid of them. My job to hand them over in a bag." He pulled out a roll of thick black plastic from under the sink. "These bags."

"He does all that for free drinks?"

Baird smirked as he pulled his sister to her feet. "You haven't tried my Green Abby shots. They're barter-worthy. Lawrence doesn't like the system and wants to clean up the streets. Thieves are bad for business. I help him out with that when I can."

"So, just like that?"

"Quiet and quick," he repeated. "Most Vemreaux turn a blind eye to how slaves are treated, but there are always sympathizers. Not everyone wants *A*-bloods in The Way. Find the right one, ply him with his vice, and you've got a two-man crew."

"It's that simple?"

"The more complicated a plan is, the more ways it can fall apart."

Blue's hand was still trembling, so she crossed her arms to give herself the hug she wished she didn't need.

Baird rummaged through Mosely's pants and dug out his keys.

"We don't get robbed too often, but there's the occasional bar fight at the diner. When that happens, find Lawrence and pretend to be useless. Gather the girls and stay with him. He doesn't know who you really are, so he'll try to protect you. Let him."

"Baird, I don't need anyone to protect me," Blue protested with a frown.

"Says the girl who couldn't finish the job." Baird motioned to the men on the floor. "You'll get used to it."

"I wouldn't be so sure," she murmured, glancing to the bodies at her feet.

5

HOME SWEET HUT

Age of Peace Law II, Subset 2c
Vemreaux owning Waywards must provide them with lodging according to
code 27a. Vemreaux are not required to fraternize or live with their slaves.

*L*awrence assured Baird that he would remove the bodies before daybreak, so the next job was to make sure the girls were okay. Blue followed her brother outside. She was careful to give the two dead Vemreaux in plastic bags a wide berth as she exited the hut.

Baird disappeared down into the cellar that lay several meters from the hut. He pulled up the steel door and vanished into the hideaway. No sooner had he left Blue's vision did a familiar face pop up out of the hole like a groundhog. "Blue!" shouted Elle.

"Elle!" Blue tried to exclaim the joy she felt, but her throat had gone dry. Blue ached at the sight of her best friend. Elle was ever herself – tall, gorgeous blonde hair, strong and lean, with a smile that lit up the night sky. Her stained, threadbare undershirt and plain shorts did not detract from her beauty, but somehow made it stand out even more.

The hug was without hesitation, like two puzzle pieces parted for far too long. It had been over a year since she'd held her friend. Most people that left The Way were never seen again. They gripped each other as Elle squealed over and over the extremes of her enthusiasm, her smile breaking up the intensity of the night.

"You're here! You're here!" she crooned, kissing Blue's cheeks and hair. "I missed you so much!" Elle squeezed her around the ribs. "Those stupid Vems! I can't believe they did something like this your first day here!"

A second figure came timidly out of the cellar, head darting every which way nervously. "Blue?" Grettel always spoke with a note of fear, her voice tiny. Baird nudged her out, and though she wanted to run toward her friend, she was too shaken to be more than a few meters from Baird's protection.

Grettel's russet eyes sparkled with moisture as she joined the entanglement of limbs. Blue and Elle welcomed her to the hug, and the three giggled and cooed over each other, noting the changes just one year played on each of them. "I missed you so much!" Grettel sobbed.

"I'm here now! Your hair! It's shorter! I can't believe you cut it!" Blue marveled at the short brown hair that was cropped unevenly around Grettel's face. "It's so cute!"

"You can cut your hair whenever you want in the real world, Blue," Grettel explained through her tears.

"So cool! And Elle, you look taller or something."

"Nope. Just more beautiful," Elle commented churlishly. "That's my curse. More gorgeous every year. Good thing we only missed out on a year. You might not recognize me if you waited much longer."

Blue laughed, ignoring her brother's rolled eyes. The girls laughed and chatted at such an accelerated pace that an onlooker may have needed a translation guide to cut through all the inside jokes and half-verbalized sentiments that held whole truths in their hearts.

It was only when Baird cleared his throat that the three were reminded of the pace held by the rest of the world. The embrace broke, but they still found a way to remain connected. Elle linked her arm possessively through Blue's, and Blue held onto Grettel's thin hand.

It had been a year Blue had lived without the shy pixie, and every day she felt the absence of the thing that kept her warm heart from freezing over. "Do you like your new house?" Grettel asked sheepishly.

"Are you kidding? Does it smell like scratch?" Blue wore a giddy grin, bouncing on the balls of her feet.

Grettel shook her head, smiling.

"This is the only house on the whole road! Does Master Joe own it all?" Blue was grateful the girls would not tire of her questions. Baird was never so generous with her rare moments of incompetence. "And the grass is different here. Do you have a garden? Like a real Vemreaux garden with flowers, or is it just a food garden like in The Way?"

"Inside," Baird commanded. He'd moved the bodies out the back door already, so as not to upset the sensitive Grettel.

Blue caught the hint of her brother's suppressed smile when Elle's index finger tickled his ribs discreetly. She noticed that he did not grumble or glare at her, as he'd done most of the time when she'd tried to cozy up to him in The Way. Blue grinned even more widely that her brother had finally gotten some sense concerning the blonde who never relented in her pursuit of him.

The familiar scent of scratch that Blue brought into the hut was replaced with urine-soaked air. Elle and Grettel both groaned at the damage the two intruders had done in such a short time. One of them peed all over the east wall. The other lost bowel control when he died. All of the cupboards had been rifled through. Their clothes were in disarray.

Baird's anger was in check, though still evident on his features in the form of a scowl as he moved past the girls to the kitchen. "Let's start with the walls." Wetting a few discolored rags with soapy water, he handed them out to each of them. "You can show her around when we're done. Grettel, start with washing the floor." Baird interrupted Blue and Elle's chatter with business. "In case I'm not here the next time this happens, Blue, here's how this works. After I call Lawrence, I put the lowlife bodies in a black trash bag, drag them out back and put them in the garden box marked 'compost'. Lawrence'll come by in an hour or two and pick them up."

Elle groaned. "Could we please put a hold on your lessons for one day? She just got here! A couple hours out of The Way and she's already cleaning piss off the walls and learning how to get rid of bodies. Grrr-oss!" She flipped her golden hair over her shoulder. Elle was always good at lightening a dismal mood. "Tell me you didn't make her kill those guys on her first day out."

Blue shook her head, speaking for her brother. "It's fine, Elle. I'm just glad you're both okay."

"Okay?" Elle scoffed, motioning to her curves. "I'd say I'm doing more than okay." Somehow she made disgusting housework look glamorous.

They all scrubbed as Baird filled them in on the details of Blue's purchase. Elle made the most of every nuance to the story, settling for nothing less than an absolutely Technicolor mental picture of the event. It was a welcome distraction to the less than amazing homecoming the vandals delivered.

"Buying her wasn't all that different from buying you," Baird assured Elle, exasperated from talking so much. "Except for that stupid, overbearing professor, Jack. He was a pain."

"He was fine, Baird. It's okay that he's thorough. It's kind of a big deal to purchase a slave."

"Incompetence pains me. So yes, Jack was a pain."

"Oh, brother." Blue huffed as she shook her head. She'd been taught by him to keep her hair forward to cover her vibrantly blue eyes, but in the privacy of the hut, it was not necessary. She could be a real person without hiding, even if it was only behind closed doors. Today, her true self felt like sassing her brother, so she used the isolation of the hut to her advantage. "You're a pain."

"Good one." Baird snorted as he threw his soiled rag in the sink.

"Um, Griffin was there at Blue's purchase. That's different," Elle argued. "How'd he take it?"

"Fine, Griffin was there. He'll survive. The whole thing took longer than it should have. Big deal. She's here now, cleaning piss off the wall, just like us, living our grand dream." Baird sighed when he caught a hurt look from Grettel.

"Man, Baird," Elle said as she glared at him. "Stop being such a grump. You didn't have to kill those Vemreaux. You coulda called the police."

"That's a great idea. We'll try that next time." Baird rolled his eyes. "How about you show her the house while I finish up. See if anything else was damaged."

"Excellent idea, slave," Elle kidded as she stood.

"Here, take these, slave," Baird handed her the rest of the filthy rags, suppressing his amusement.

Elle hugged Blue once she scrubbed her hands clean of the urine stench. Elle donned her most dazzling smile. She acted as spokesperson for the household since Baird was not prone to idle chatter, and Grettel was too introverted to take the attention on herself for a prolonged period of time.

The entire shack was comprised of two rooms: the bathroom and everything else. The living room, bedroom and kitchen were all open, separated only by a single post in the center of the structure running from ceiling to floor (which no doubt existed to keep the sagging roof from collapsing down on their heads at the first sign of a stiff breeze). In this instance, it was a good thing that there was not much surface area to clean.

"So, this is the couch." Elle's fingers rested on the silver tape that kept the pale green cushions from further splitting. "Can you believe we found it in some Vemreaux's trash? All it needed was a good cleaning and some tape. With it pushed up against the beam like this, it's easier to imagine that this is a whole separate room from the kitchen. Baird sleeps there, but during the day, we all can sit on it." She demonstrated the usefulness of the object by lazily flopping on it, undoing the top button of her jean shorts and miming a can of blood beer in her hand. Then she picked up an imaginary remote control and began flicking through channels on a television that was not there. "See? We can pretend to be Vemreaux. Oh, slave!" Elle called over her shoulder. "This remote is tiresome. Change the channel for me and fetch me a cocktail."

Blue snorted a laugh and handed her friend an invisible drink. "Ever at your service."

Elle motioned to the mattress at her feet as she refastened her pants. "The bed is where Grettel and I sleep." Her use of "bed" instead of mattress was purposeful. This was their home, and though money was not abundant, their imaginations were still theirs.

The simple full-sized mattress was covered in a yellowed sheet that had once upon a purchase been white, and now sported a violent slash clear down the middle, making the reason for its abandonment to the trash perfectly obvious. A green sleeping bag rested unzipped like a comforter across the sheet. Grettel bent down and smoothed out the boot prints the destructive Vemreaux made during their intrusion.

It was difficult to decide which was better – a controlled life in The Way working knee-deep in scratch, or this impoverished existence where you could earn a wage and rub elbows with the Vemreaux, but you made do on the lowest standard of living and highest rate of crime.

"It's amazing," Blue offered kindly.

Gesturing to each makeshift room as though it was not already self-explanatory, Elle gave long dissertations on how they acquired each belonging, down to the torn rug laid on the wood floor of the kitchen that she bragged gave the place a "homey feel."

Taking a brief inventory of the cupboards' contents, Elle called over her shoulder to Baird. "Everything's here! They didn't take a thing!"

"Glad to hear they didn't steal back Vemreaux trash," Baird grumbled as he inspected the wall. "Of course they didn't take anything. I killed them."

Blue grimaced that her brother had done the brunt of the dirty work, while she'd stood on the sidelines, chickening out.

Elle swayed her hips as she walked over toward Baird and pinched his cheeks. "Except your smile. I think they got away with that."

"Are you trying to piss me off?" Baird glowered at her grin. Blue could see that perhaps Elle had not made as much progress with her brother as she'd hoped.

Elle ignored his sour remark. "This gets to be your cup, Baby Blue." She opened a cabinet to pull out one of the few things resting on its shelf.

"Wait, what?"

Elle grinned. "This cup is for you. Your very first thing that's just yours."

Blue spluttered, "But I don't need something so nice. We should all share it."

"We each have our own, and this one's yours."

Blue examined every detail of the plastic vessel in awe. "Seriously? All mine? Whoa."

"We found it last week. Isn't it perfect? See that?" Elle pointed to the design of the New World King on the cheap vessel. Despite the cartoon-like depiction, the benevolent eyes of King Sinclair shown clear. "It's like owning a cup and a portrait all in one. Like a rich Vemreaux!" Elle spoke to the cup in an exaggerated feminine voice. "I think I'd like a drink, King Sinclair." Then she answered back in a low imitation of a man's cadence, "Why yes, mi'lady. Happy to serve you. You're an invaluable part of society. Your beauty alone could..." Elle stopped at Blue's laughter. "What? You don't think he sounds like that? Watch. I can even make him bow to us." She tipped the cup forward, and sure enough, the image volunteered its obeisance to Blue, who curtsied in return.

A mousy voice spoke up. "There's no chips or dents in it either. Good as new." Grettel had not let go of Blue's hand, using it as an anchor to convince herself that her friend was indeed, right next to her. She had not stopped crying, and no one expected her to. Occasionally Blue would squeeze her fingers, and the tears would start afresh, washing down her cheeks as Elle prattled on about the six spoons they had collected and which restaurant they were sure each came from.

"Do you want to see the bathroom?" Elle asked, though there was not much choice in the matter, once she was on a roll. "Baird found the hairbrush." Elle strode into the bathroom and picked up the wood-handled paddle brush. She twirled it around effortlessly in her palm as though it was a toy top. "He said it came from some Femreaux's garbage. There wasn't even any hair to pick out of it." She gave a vain stroke through her long blonde locks to demonstrate its usefulness, and then placed it on the edge of the sink. "We all use it." She snatched it back up and held it out to Blue, in case she wanted to admire it or put the loved trinket to use.

Blue moved into the tiny bathroom, but threw herself back out, stumbling as she went. "W-What is that?" she stammered, pointing toward the sink, but refusing to look at it again.

Her face. Her ugly, disgusting face shown back at her with too much clarity. The only chances she'd had to see her reflection in The Way was the distorted or foggy images found in a shiny shovel or stainless steel appliance. The sole mirror in the entire facility was in the infirmary, so the only clear images Blue had ever seen of her face were when it was covered in scratch or smeared with her blood. Even though there were no such impurities on her this time, it was all she could see. Brown smudges covering her cheeks. Blood in the shape of her fingerprints dotting her nose or forehead after a thorough beating appeared as she looked at her horrified reflection. She'd been exposed to a lot that morning, but the mirror was a step too far.

"What?" Elle looked around. "Oh, it's a mirror like they had in the infirmary in The Way. So we can look perfect before we start our shifts. All the Vems have them. They're everywhere in the real world."

"No! I don't want to see it!" Blue shouted, wishing she could rein in her overreaction. Her fingers dug into her cheeks, wishing she could claw herself a new face. "I'm disgusting!"

"What? No, sweetie! You're very pretty," Elle assured her.

"Why would you say that?" Grettel squeezed Blue's hand. "You've always been beautiful."

"Stop it!" Blue shook her head, disturbed and beyond comforting. She jerked from Grettel's grip and backed away. "Baird!" she shouted, not bothering to hide the distress from her pinched tone. Though she was in the living room now, it was still too close to that wretched reflective glass. She shut her eyes tight, turned and ran blind out of the hut, not stopping until the cool night air calmed her halfway to the car.

Elle watched as Baird bolted after his sister. The blonde turned to Grettel and shrugged.

Two minutes later, Baird returned, walked straight to the bathroom and took down the mirror. "It's gotta go," he declared.

"What? Why?" Elle protested, dismayed.

Baird did not answer. He removed the glass and took it out back to the garbage, tilting the reflective side down. He came back in and was greeted by Elle's glower, which he ignored as he returned to cleaning the floor.

Grettel gently touched Blue's arm. "Are you okay?"

Blue shuddered, but nodded. "That was awful!"

"What?"

Blue's eyes shut in pain. "My face!"

Grettel and Elle both opened their mouths to protest, but Baird cut them off. "Leave it alone, guys. For your own good. Just let it go."

Elle huffed, but her actions consented. The girls flopped on the couch and spent the next several hours foregoing sleep so they could catch up. Baird was grateful when Lawrence came by an hour later to remove the bodies; the girl talk was starting to wear on him. What was new in The Way, a few of the things Blue needed to know before conversing in the real world, and the latest gossip they'd picked up around the diner kept the three entertained until Baird interrupted, announcing that they should all get ready for work.

Elle showed Blue their uniforms as she and Grettel poked their heads through the light blue shirts with lemon piping down the sleeves that read "Joe's Diner" on the back in black script.

Baird bent down and reached under the couch, which was the only hiding place to speak of. He returned to full height holding a box, which he unceremoniously shoved toward his sister. She took it from him and opened the container with all the hesitation he knew she would exhibit. Inside was two pairs of jean shorts like Grettel and Elle's, one pair of long jeans for colder weather, three pairs of white socks, three sets of underwear, a Joe's Diner sweater and three fresh work shirts that remained untouched. "I've never seen colors this pretty before. I get to wear this? They're really mine?" Blue asked aloud, tracing the perfect stitching.

"Of course, Baby Blue." Elle grinned, bumping her hip against her friend's. "No more orange Wayward jumpsuits for you!"

Baird held his hand up. "Elle gets the new shirt. Blue, you take Elle's that she wore yesterday and Grettel's dirty shorts. That should give you enough *A*-blood scent to last you the day once you wash the scratch stink off of you."

Déjà vu hit the girls all at once. Elle peeled the fitted polo off her white tank top, and handed the uniform to her friend. They had done this routine nearly every day when they were students at The Way to hide Blue's lack of a sulfuric odor from the Vemreaux Supervisors. It was comforting to bring the habit into the real world.

Elle sighed. "Lucky that you don't smell like sulfur to the changed Vemreaux. A few of the snobby ones won't eat at our diner because Waywards serve the food. They think we make it taste bad or something. Losers."

The idea of a Wayward calling the Vemreaux losers was ridiculous, but somehow Elle pulled it off with bravado.

Blue took the new clothes and examined the material with amazement. She had seen jeans before when outsiders would occasionally tour The Way. The navy material had a backing of white to it that she studied like an intricate map. Her eyes were wide as she turned the fabric over in her hands, weighing the difference in weight alone. "Wow! This is so many clothes! Really? They're for me?"

Baird interrupted her musing. "Today, Blue."

Instead of meeting Baird's eyes with frustration, wonder and awe sparked in her as she looked up and nodded. Then, before he could say anything to ruin her bliss, Blue scampered into the bathroom to wash and change.

Blue scrubbed with the harsh Brand *A* soap that guaranteed to keep *A*-blood types fresh all day, hoping that it would remove the odorous stench of scratch that marked her as a new arrival.

She pulled on a white ribbed tank top as a barrier between her skin and the foreign itchy material of the fancy new work uniform. It fit her thin, muscular frame like a glove. Form-fitting clothing was new to Blue, and the difference was shocking. There'd be no hiding it now; the modest curves definitely marked her as a girl.

Blue had never worn shorts. When she walked out of the bathroom, she felt exposed as the air hit her bare calves and the tops of her knees. These were Grettel's shorts, which fell modestly to the small girl's knee. Blue's added height coming mostly from the longer legs she sported took the shorts a good ten centimeters up her thigh. Nothing racy by Femreaux standards, but it was enough to make Blue feel horribly self-conscious. Her bare knees felt as shameful as if they were her furiously covered breasts being exposed to the world.

Elle clapped and let out a sexy whistle. Blue cringed in response and hid one knee behind the other to give it the dignity it now screamed for. Grettel smiled with compassion, understanding the girl's discomfort.

Baird said nothing to his sister's obvious embarrassment, but his upper lip twitched as he bit back a snarky remark.

"And the best part!" Elle flitted over to the kitchen and pulled out a smaller box from one of the cupboards. She handed it to Blue, who did not conceal her concerned look of surprise.

"What is it?" Blue asked without opening the box.

Elle rolled her eyes. "Open it up and see!" Grettel nodded in encouragement at Blue's wary look. She pried the lid off the box slowly. When she peeked inside, she was relieved to find a pair of running shoes.

"Jeez, Blue. It's a present from your new owner, not a snake." Elle pulled out the shoes so Blue could examine them. All footwear in The Way either slipped on or came with a Velcro strap to secure them into place, but there were white ropes on these, which were completely unfamiliar. The ropes were tucked into the mouth of the shoe, and Blue wondered how they worked. She was beginning to think that perhaps accelerating her Vemreaux Studies course had not been so wise. Had she missed an entire section on shoe ropes? Surely Jack should have mentioned something so crucial.

Grettel smiled. "They're called 'shoelaces', and I'll show you how to tie them." She dropped to Blue's side to help her tie the shoes for the first time.

Baird stepped in and stopped her. "She can figure it out, Grettel." He shook his head. "Don't give me that look." Baird crossed his arms over his chest and glared at both girls.

Elle returned his stare with interest. "Oh, it's not just a look you're getting. It's a look and a lecture. Just because she's the Light doesn't mean she's all-knowing. Give the girl a break, Baird!"

"Do you think some Vemreaux's gonna stop and tie her shoes for her? She's got to learn these things."

It took a few minutes of patience as Blue worked on her shoes while Elle and Baird argued, but finally they were tied to her liking. When Blue stood, Baird examined her uniform to make sure she'd put it on correctly.

"Alright, then. The diner's south of the wooded area behind the hut. We usually walk, but you need to get used to the feel of being in a car."

Elle grinned, shoving Baird for good measure. "You ready for the real world, Blue?"

Baird cut off his sister's response, his feet thudding toward the door. "It doesn't much matter if she is. Let's go."

6

FOUND

The hotel was the most expensive one in America's Capital City, so the mattresses were downy soft. The penthouse suite was quiet as the four men slept soundly after their cross-continental flight and night of debauchery.

The shout that woke them was unnerving, but not unexpected. Brody, Liam and Alec each groaned, but Alec was the only one to lift himself from the bed that beckoned him to stay. Instead of moving toward the commotion, Alec went to the kitchen in the suite, filled a glass with cold water, and then made his way to Sam's room where the predictable cries for help sounded.

He turned on the bedroom light and found the man on the mattress with his back arched, writhing against an invisible foe. Sam called out, twitching and flailing to no avail. There was no one to fight with. There never was. In all the times Alec dispatched himself to wake Sam from his night terrors, it was only ever himself he was battling.

"Don't touch me! Get offa me!" Then he began pleading in Italian – a language not spoken publicly since King Sinclair declared the one world language to be English. Many European families still spoke whatever their tongue had been before that in their home.

That was allowed. Just no public shows of disunity. You were permitted as many freedoms as you wanted...in your home. Freedom with strings attached.

Sam pulled at his dark brown hair and kicked at the air, swearing at the top of his lungs as he absorbed whatever attack he was under.

After all the countless times he'd had to wake Sam from his nighttime horrors, Alec was still susceptible to pitying his friend and former co-worker. They'd been a great bodyguard team until Sam resigned. Alec turned the water glass over on Sam's head, but did not act quickly enough in jerking the sheet out from under him to complete the disruption of the dream.

Sam's hand darted out and gripped Alec's throat, squeezing the breath from the guard with unhampered force. "Never again!" Sam shouted, kicking at the air and punching aimlessly with his free hand.

Alec was not a fan of fighting for breath. He cut the flat of his hand through the air to Sam's elbow, knocking the offending limb away. Alec was only permitted a short gasp before Sam landed a fist to Alec's gut, knocking the newly acquired air from him.

"Let me out!" Sam yelled, before spinning off into Italian mutterings.

Once Alec collected enough of his bearings to stand upright again, he grabbed hold of the bed sheet and ripped it out from beneath Sam.

Sam landed with a confused thud on the carpet, breaking him abruptly out of his panic. "What the –?" He blinked the room into focus. "Where am I?"

"Capital City. Americas. Hotel. Any of this ringing a bell?" Alec tried to keep the irritation out of his tone, but being interrupted in the middle of a REM cycle only to be choked and punched did nothing to improve his mood.

Sam scratched his head with his weighted hand. "Oh, yeah. Okay. Sorry I woke you."

"It's fine. You alright?" Alec wanted to check if Sam was physically functional, not emotionally. He knew better than to ask that.

"Yeah, yeah. Kinda hoped sleeping in a different country would..." Sam shook his head. "Not that it's worked any of the other times we've hopped on a plane."

"I know."

Sam reached a shaking hand to his nightstand, fumbling for a cigarette. He dropped the lighter twice before he could indulge in the only thing that calmed him after the appearance of the shadows that chased him nightly.

"It's a non-smoking room," Alec reminded him for the third time since they'd arrived.

"Then they're gonna be really unhappy." Sam's black irises still showed signs he was thinking about his dark dream. "Look at that. It's a smoking room now. It can be a bowling alley for what we paid."

"Do they even help? Maybe you should switch to the old-fashioned plain nicotine cigarettes. Those changed Vemreaux ones, they're supposed to calm you down, right?" Alec observed his friend's anxiety. "I don't think it's working."

Sam's sarcasm came out hollow as he stared lifelessly ahead without blinking. "No. They just look cool."

Alec didn't know why he wanted to know, but that night he found he couldn't stop himself from asking. "So who was it this time? Your dad?"

Sam brought himself back to the present and shook some of the water droplets from his messy hair. "Nah. It was nothing." He cast around for something to give Alec. "A giant chicken trying to peck my eyes out or some shit. I don't remember."

Alec saw the lie, but allowed it. "Alright. I'm going back to bed, then."

Sam took a long drag on his cigarette. "I think I'll go for a run."

He glanced at the alarm clock and groaned after Alec shut the door behind him. Five forty-five. He was never able to sleep past five forty-five, no matter how hard he tried. Medication. Self-medication. Different beds. Different houses. None of it soothed the nightly battles that gripped him in his most vulnerable state.

Today it was memories of his father. Drunk, stumbling and incoherent, Saul Boniface was a man who tolerated no mistakes. Sam made sure none were made, but even that was not a guarantee of an uneventful childhood.

Curdled milk. The one beverage in the house that young Sam usually had to himself was three days past its expiration date. Even now, lying comfortably in the penthouse suite, Sam could smell the decay.

Saul was a changed Vemreaux, which meant that after his dip in the Fountain of Youth, he'd been granted the usual extra one hundred twenty years, hardened bones and unaging organs in exchange for a lesser sense of taste and the ever-common iron deficiency which triggered the thirst for filtered O-type human blood.

The taste for blood usually trumped his father's want for milk, so Sam did not put the beverage high enough on his list of priorities. After all, spoiled milk usually only earned Sam a less enthusiastic breakfast. His father preferred whisky on the rare chance he woke before noon.

That morning the exchange was a quarter cup of chunky milk for a bloody nose and a round with the leather belt. He'd forgotten that the smell would set his father off. Sam was then locked in the bedroom closet with the carton of sour milk to remind him that changed Vemreaux had a heightened sense of smell.

The thing it ended up teaching Sam was to skip breakfast and duck out of the house whenever his father was awake. His father had forgotten he'd locked Sam in the closet and left him there for two days.

Sam flinched and continued to smoke, facing the window. Even though the curtains were shut, he could still detect a faint glow sneaking in to taunt him. Of all the bonuses touted about bathing in the Fountain, sharper sight was never listed as a deterrent. His keen vision could make out shapes in the room, ensuring that going back to sleep would be impossible.

He stood on unsteady feet, pulled on shorts and zipped on a sweatshirt over his bare chest. Sam knew he had to distance himself from the horror he'd endured through his subconscious. He stepped out of the room no one would share with him and found Alec sitting at the table, drinking a bottle of *O*-Negative cola.

Alec was well into his borrowed one hundred twenty years, most of which were spent as security detail for Europe's royal family. He could recall Sam's restlessness even back when Sam was younger and would roam around the mansion on the nights it was unsafe for him to leave his friend and go to his unstable home. He'd been the one to suggest Sam go running if he couldn't fall back asleep, though the demons always managed to catch up.

"Sorry I woke you," Sam offered. It was one thing for him to suffer, but he hated being responsible for anyone else's sleepless nights. He loathed it when his friends witnessed him crying out like that. "Did I...did I attack you?" Sam was unable to look up at his friend as he put out his cigarette on the edge of the kitchen sink and tossed it in the trash.

"No. You just shouted a bit. Same as usual," Alec lied. "Be back before Liam's meeting. They're settling on their final plans for the testing. You're in charge of sobering Liam up so he's presentable for Emperor Anders."

"How'd that fall on me?" Sam whispered as he shoved on his trainers.

"You're the one what suggested that stupid rave last night. You deal with Liam's royal headache when he wakes up. He's your best friend."

"And your charge. Not mine anymore. I'm just here for the sight-seeing." Though Sam was unofficially part of Prince Liam's security, he and the prince were first and foremost best friends. "Shouldn't you be the one getting him up and going?"

"Nope."

"Yeah, alright." Sam stood and stretched, patting his pocket to make sure his room key and phone were there. "Go back to sleep. You're looking old. I'd say you look near on thirty-two with that ugly mug." Of course, Alec had not aged a day since he'd dipped in the Fountain more than a century ago, but Sam missed no opportunity to introduce levity to the grim start of his day.

Alec was not known for smiling. He returned the slight with a rude hand gesture, which Sam answered with a blown kiss before he exited the suite.

The cold air hit Sam like a punch in the face. The hair follicles on his arms were shocked awake, bemoaning the early morning fall weather. Sam jogged through Capital City, admiring the difference from his home country. He'd run to the edge of the capital yesterday, when memories of fights with Liam's older brother kept him from sleep. Today he decided to venture beyond. The tall skyscrapers traded themselves in for trees the further out he ran. The city noise gave way to a few birds and the occasional early commuter.

Endorphins kicked in and chased away his childhood, giving him a fresh perspective for the new day. They had nearly a month and a half to spend in the Americas, and Liam's duties demanded they were near the capital. Sam had heard of some truly wild parties a few cities south, but Emperor Frederick Boniface would not be happy if his son missed his check-ins or failed to be a satisfactory judge in the testing to find the Wayward Light. Frederick was the dad Sam unofficially adopted as his own long before he got a job working for the family. Letting him down was not an option.

Sam was about to turn around when he caught sight of the most obnoxious-colored Humvee he'd ever seen. The large vehicle was neon green with yellow-painted flames engulfing the tail lights. Sam shook his head and smiled, guessing that whoever drove that car was not in the bodyguard profession. The car was parked heading out of town, and the driver's body was slumped over the steering wheel.

Sam neared and saw that the front of the car was caved in around the trunk of a thick oak tree.

His heart rate spiked as his jog broke into a run. He banged his fist on the windshield, hoping to rouse the man sitting inertly in the passenger's seat. When that yielded no results, he yanked out his phone and called the international emergency hotline. The operator assured him she would send police and an ambulance straight away.

Sam was not accustomed to doing nothing. He'd been a bodyguard for the royal family of Europe for several years, and served a term in the King's Royal Army before it was disbanded, due to the successful reign of peace.

Before that, he'd done his fair share of adolescent crime. Sam folded his arms over his chest and let out a short noise of frustration. What he wouldn't give for a crowbar.

7

———

THE WAITRESS

Age of Peace Law 18, Subset 12c
Regarding dining establishments, the menu must be clearly marked for
unchanged Vemreaux and Waywards to limit food poisoning from
consuming changed Vemreaux food.

"Fire hydrants, Elle?" Baird questioned.

"One," Elle proclaimed with a nod as she hopped out of the vehicle.

Blue groaned aloud at the "game" Baird used to make them play in The Way. It was one thing she'd hoped would not make it out into the real world. Perfect recollection was important, sure, but never knowing when the "game" was coming put her on alert at all times.

"Trees?"

"One hundred thirty seven a meter out from where I'm standing," Blue replied, stretching down and touching her toes. Even the pavement was an experience. It was black and smelled odd, unlike the gray concrete walkways in The Way.

Blue fought to keep her smile under wraps, but she was dancing on the inside. She was thrilled to be out of The Way and back with her girlfriends and her brother. She had a new life with just one job and fancy clothes with pretty colors on them to boot.

They entered the kitchen through the back using two of the keys on Baird's sturdy key ring. Baird reached his hand inside the doorway and flipped on the overhead lights. They came in dim at first, the fluorescent bulbs needing time to wake up before they could properly shine.

Her eyes swept once around the kitchen before Baird shut off the lights. "You-See," Baird announced, naming the "game" he had played with Blue since she'd been a child.

Grettel's breath hitched and became uneven. It was the only sound that everyone could hear above the whirring of the refrigerator. "Baird?" she whispered uncertainly.

"It's important, Grettel. Blue has to be able to memorize every room perfectly and be able to use that information at a moment's notice." Baird picked up Grettel's small hand so she could feel his strength and be reassured. "I know how you hate the dark, though. I'm here. Nowhere safer." In the moments he stopped to comfort her, he drew in a stealthy amount of tenderness from the girl he would never admit to needing. Grettel softened him, while Elle kept him on his toes with her smart mouth and lusty looks. There were times he wished he could find the qualities of both women in just one girl.

"Dishwasher." Baird spoke through the quiet, giving his sister a little push forward.

Blue gave him a light shove in return, not caring for the manhandling. Blue's fists rose to four centimeters below her chin, one in front of the other, and clenched there, elbows in. Blue inhaled deeply, separating each scent and assigning it a name and location of origin as best she could. The darkness crowded around her, but she kept her eyes shut to avoid cheating, in case her superior night vision picked up shapes in the void. She moved forward, turning a sharp left three paces in front of her and walking seven more until she reached out and rested her hand on the stainless steel wall of the commercial appliance. "Touch," she confirmed, and then withdrew her hand.

She knew he would have more. He always had more.

"Bring me three clean dinner plates," he instructed.

"She hasn't even seen the kitchen a whole minute, Baird," Elle complained. "Give her a break."

Baird did not answer, but held his hand out expectantly.

Blue weaved around the island in the kitchen, careful not to bump her body to any part of the enclosed space. Resting the plates in Baird's outstretched hand, she knew that he would be smiling because the dark would cover his pride at her ability to be so stealthy.

Wiping the smile from his voice, Baird spoke again. "Elle, put the plates back."

Elle wasted no time in returning the plates to the exact pile they were taken from without making a single sound. Blue was always impressed by her friend's prowess at the "games" they had played for years. Blue's abilities were natural, but Elle's were cultivated through time and lots of practice.

Much to Grettel's relief, Baird dropped her hand and flicked the lights on. "The large fridge's for changed Vemreaux food, and the small one's got fresh things for the unchanged. It's also stocked with food for us." Baird pulled four apples out of the A-blood fridge and passed them around.

"Grettel's the best cook around. We get so many repeat customers because of our little pixie."

Grettel blushed at Elle's compliment. "It's not that. Baird's Green Abby shots keep them coming back. Another bar tried to copy the drink, but it was a total flop." She dipped her head in the man's direction, who acknowledged her praise with a reciprocating nod.

Elle's hand rested on a fancy looking machine with several nozzles and buttons. "This," she explained in her best attempt at a low, creepy voice, "is the blood fountain." She indicated the labels just above the buttons that were faded and spattered grotesquely as her tone changed back to normal. "We've got both the drinkable types here. Filtered *O*-Positive and Negative. It's better than the one in The Way that the professors use with their coffee, isn't it? Newer."

"Vemreaux gotta have their blood," Blue commented bitterly, offering a weak smile. No matter how hard she tried, she could not block out the disturbing image of her own *A*-type blood running through the hoses of the fancy machine, ready to be doled out to any Vemreaux with an appetite or iron deficiency. As miserable as The Way could be, she was glad that drinking *A*-blood repulsed the Vemreaux and made them sick. Work camps were better than blood farms.

Elle showed her the different functions the buttons performed. "This lever flips from Negative to Positive. This switch whisks in flavoring, while this steel grip holds the cup in place. This control blows air into the drink if the customer wants frothy foam on top. This push button here controls the carbonated sweet water to mix in with the blood," she explained, tapping her fingers lightly on the surface of the button. "Don't offer blood drinks to unchanged Vemreaux. They don't drink it because they don't need it. You can tell by looking at their eyes. Black eyes means they've dipped in the Fountain of Youth and gone through the change, so offer them blood. Regular eyes means they drink like Waywards – without hemoglobin."

Blue smiled as she rolled her eyes dramatically. "No kidding. I'm new to the real world, not new to the whole world."

"Baird said to be thorough. Now, of course, this isn't straight blood. That's illegal. It's the same filtered stuff the professors drank in The Way. Enriched with extra iron and vitamins and stuff. *O*-Negative's rarer and more expensive. It's harder to farm, so don't mix them up," she warned, pretending to be serious for a moment. The look didn't suit her, nor could she maintain it, proving so only two seconds later when her pretty lips broke out into a grin of glee at being able to talk to her best friend face-to-face, even if it was about something so gruesome. Elle threw her arms out, lacing them around her friend's neck. "Oh, I missed you so much! This past year's been awful without you."

Grettel joined in the hug from behind and held on tight to both girls, while making sure not to smear any of the apple's juice from her hand onto them.

"We worried about you, like, every second," Elle exaggerated without shame.

"Girl time's over, Blue. Time to learn," Baird insisted without preamble. "Grettel, you can get the kitchen going while I show Blue a few things out here."

Elle threw herself in the doorway, blocking Grettel's path back to the kitchen. "You didn't say please, Baird."

"I wasn't talking to you, Elle."

"I know. You were talking to Grettel, and I don't like you barking out orders to her. Or me, for that matter. Or your sister. New era of manners starts today."

"How's this for manners? Get to work right now."

Elle snarled at Baird, unwilling to move. She ignored Grettel's whimper of confusion at being unwittingly caught in the middle. "Say please." She was always the mother bear, protecting Grettel and Blue as best she could from the harsh winter that was Baird.

"Take my phone and call Master Joe. Let him know how high maintenance you're getting." When Elle gripped the doorjamb more firmly, Baird turned his glower on her. "I don't beg, Elle. Grettel's fine. We're all fine without turning ourselves into beggars. But if you need it, sure. *Please* stop being a pain." He sidestepped Grettel and stood in front of Elle, puffing his chest out to increase his intimidation factor. He placed his hands atop Elle's and pried them off the frame easily. "Now, move. I've got things to do."

Grettel squeaked past the two and made quick work of beginning her morning routine in the kitchen.

"You're being a bully, Baird. Why can't you just be nice?" Elle scowled up at the brusque man.

"I've got better things to do than play your little games, Elle. So do you, in fact." He released her from his grip and turned his back on her. "Blue!" He clicked his fingers twice to summon his sister.

"Yes, Master Baird," Blue answered, stony-faced. When her reply was met with narrowed eyes, Blue grinned. "What? You know, I can never tell if you guys are mad at each other, or if that's just you flirting. Whichever one you're doing, it's not very good."

Baird blanched, and then cringed at Elle's bitter laughter. Elle went about her morning duties on the floor with a slight spring in her step, winking at Blue as she passed by.

"Real cute, Blue. Now, shut up." First Baird showed his sister how to work the register, taking out three coins for her to examine. "Gold, silver and bronze brandishes. Most Vems pay with their bill cards, but some prefer actual cash. I know you learned about them in your Vemreaux Studies class, but I thought you might want a look at the real thing."

She measured the coins' weight and design as Baird handed her one of each paper bill to examine. Waywards had done so much work for such small things. "So the cows make the scratch. The scratch makes the S-bricks. The S-bricks equal currency, which gives the Vemreaux *this* to spend?"

"Yup." Baird did not look up from his pad of paper.

"I've got a question I didn't want to ask Jack."

"Why he didn't pick a different profession?"

"No."

"Why's he so creepy?"

"He's not creepy, Baird." Blue huffed. "So there's three countries, right?"

Baird winced as though her questions were causing him physical pain. "Congratulations. You now have a grade two education."

"And King Sinclair made that law after World War Three when the Age of Peace was issued that all three countries' value had to be equal when it came to currency. So my question is, who keeps track of the three countries to make sure they're playing by the rules and only manufacturing enough money to equal each country's worth?" she asked, handing the coins back to her brother.

"Do I look educated?" Baird was growing frustrated at her string of questions. "I don't know, Blue. King Sin? The honor system? Why? Did you want to trade in all this for a government job counting brandishes and S-bricks? You might be the first *A*-blood type in government employment. That'll keep you under the radar." He gave her a sarcastic thumbs up.

Blue eyed his arrogant thumb, willing herself not to reach out and break it. All the freedom acquired in one day was making her a little unstable as far as controlling her emotions. "Fine. I won't ask questions." *At least not to you.*

"I hate when you explain things halfway and just expect her to connect the dots to make up the difference. Give her a break, Baird." Elle took over to explain the different bill cards, which were not to be confused with paper bills. "They're plastic and act like cash. There are three kinds of cards, and all take funds from a linked bank account. The most common's the green one. It's mainly carried by Vemreaux with enough cash in the bank to afford them a comfortable long life." She sighed wistfully. "The red card's for Vemreaux with barely any money in the bank. We get lots of those in here. Paycheck to paycheck. The third kind of bill card is black. It's reserved for Vemreaux whose money is limitless."

"Elle, there's no such thing as limitless currency." Blue countered with logic.

Elle conceded. "Sure, sure." She waved her hand to indicate that her meaning should have been obvious. "I just mean that a black bill card holder could buy like, anything they wanted, live their one hundred twenty extra years, and still be buried with the thing."

Blue was impressed that anyone could amass that much wealth. "About how many black cards do you get?" she asked out of curiosity.

Elle's eyes sparkled, as if thoughts of someone who could buy an infinite amount of anything danced through her head. "Not many, but next week is Peace Week, so we're bound to get a few loaded dignitaries in here."

Baird chimed in with his dour gong. "Hey, what do you know about the Predator?"

Blue blinked and shook her head. "Hello. Where did that come from?" When her brother offered no explanation, she answered his question. "Just what you've told me on your supervised visits. Six months or so ago, Vemreaux tourists started disappearing off the *O-Blood* island. A couple. Then more. Got them all in a tizzy."

Baird crossed his arms over his chest and faced his sister – a thing he did when he demanded her full attention. "Yeah, well, it's more than that now. They've been finding some of the bodies washed up in the river. Not just dead. Filleted and muscle picked from the bone."

Elle shuddered. "Do you have to be graphic about it? Just say they came back dead."

Baird's frown pronounced itself more at Elle's interruption. "She needs to know what she'll be up against, Elle." He turned back to his sister, who somehow appeared smaller than he would have liked. "An officer was drinking late one night and let it slip that now a couple Vemreaux guards from the blood farm have gone missing. They're trying to keep everything quiet until they can get a handle on it. But they're not doing a great job."

"What does that have to do with me telling her about the black cards?" Elle asked, hands on her hips.

"Peace Week. Dignitaries always come to the capital for Peace Week, and Joe's Diner's just outside of the capital, so we get a lot of foot traffic. America throws a great party. Plus, King Sinclair's coming in for the big parade. Lots of black cards'll be waved around because of that. But they're also here for the testing."

Elle swallowed. "So the date's been set?"

"Some time in the next few weeks. You're not supposed to know, but Lawrence has his ear to the ground. Now that the Predator's been killing more and more Vemreaux, a couple dozen, I think, and they still haven't been able to catch it, they're scrambling for 'the Light to end the tyranny.' That's why I had to get you out as soon as I could manage it, Blue. They're going to take Elle and a lot of other Wayward girls for testing soon. See if any of them's the Light. You have to blend in out here. You have to stay hidden, or they could take you, too."

"Enough!" Elle demanded, slamming her hand flat on the counter. "No one's taking Blue anywhere!"

Blue realized she must have looked as miserable as she felt at mention of the dreaded prophecy, due to Elle stepping in so resolutely on her behalf. *I'll have to be more careful. Can't have her constantly fighting with Baird because of me. I want Baird to be happy someday, if that's even possible.* "Guys, please."

A silky smile transformed Elle's fair face. "It's not been a whole day since she's been bought, and she's seen a robbery, a killing and a whole lot of 'the Light' garbage. Give her some time to be a girl, Baird. Everything else will come when it comes."

"That's naïve, Elle." Baird, it seemed, was the only man partially immune to Elle's feminine beauty. Her appeal was muted when she argued with him so obstinately. He frowned down at Elle in disapproval, hoping that her loud mouth would not rub off on his sister. "She's the Light. Can't change that by ignoring it."

"Yes, I can." Elle grabbed her best friend by the arm and whirled her out into the dining area. "Forget Baird. Let's just talk diner for a while. That's your only concern right now. Waiting tables. Easy as anything."

There were six tables per section, with the restaurant divided into two segments. Booths lined the walls and tables occupied the center space, which Baird informed her were removed for the evening crowd so they could use the space to mingle or dance. He spoke the word "dance" like the word itself was a waste of time. Blue did not miss Elle's pursed lips at his resistance to such things.

Grettel and Elle still fussed that Baird was rushing Blue by making her work on her first day out in the world. Baird answered with a shrug and said that Blue could handle it all, which infuriated Elle. She made her feelings known in the form of prissy hisses and huffs, bestowing the occasional hug on Blue at random to offer her some reassurance that she was still a person, and not just a commodity.

When Baird had everything set up to his liking in the kitchen, he slid a menu over to his sister after motioning for her to take a seat on a tall barstool. She had never sat in a chair with such lengthy legs, and repeatedly checked its strength before finally climbing onto it.

She scanned the menu, memorizing every word on the colorful trifold.

After one minute, Baird retrieved the menu from her view, folded it up and tucked it away. She blinked rapidly, forcing the information to remain plastered to the innards of her eyelids so that each item could be recalled at a moment's notice.

Baird shook his head, not approving of the obvious indicator that she was memorizing something. "Tell," he pointed out. It was their inside language that, with a single word, kept them from falling off their guard. It also made relaxing impossible. "That was sloppy. Anyone can tell that you're not normal by the way you took in the menu. Your eyes are moving too fast. You'll have to work harder to blend in out here."

"Should I put my guard up around you?" Blue raised an eyebrow. "How long did it take you to memorize the menu?" she asked, challenging his authority.

Baird narrowed his eyes at her and lowered his voice. "I'm not the Light with a photographic memory and perfect recall. If you're out of practice, it's on you. Don't blame me for your laziness."

Blue inhaled sharply at his heinous accusation. "Because I want two minutes with the menu, that makes me lazy? You know what I've been doing since you left? Mucking scratch and pressing paper with weights."

"Do you need two minutes?"

"No," Blue admitted sulkily. *I don't need you to be mean to me, either.*

"Pressing paper!" Baird laughed, though there was no kindness in the levity. "Tell me more about your hardships of pressing paper with a bunch of girls. It helps your case if you whine a little more."

Blue scoffed. "You're the one who made me go with the girls! I could've been lugging around bags of fertilizer with Griffin, no problem! You think I'm not as strong as you left me? I'll prove it! I'll take you down right now!" She hopped off the barstool with a sneer.

Baird's finger flew up and pointed in her face. He always towered over his sister, but he puffed his chest out and leaned forward to increase his intimidation factor. "Right there. That's as far as your temper'll ever get with me. Understood? When it's just us, you'll do your best. Memorize the menu in one minute, not two. Carry the heavy stuff for the girls. But when you're visible to the Vemreaux, you're a weak little girl, got it? You're Grettel without the tears."

Without Baird's permission, Blue's hand swooped up and latched onto his outstretched finger. Twisting in a downward motion brought Baird to a rare position of submission on his knees. "Grettel puts up with you every day! That takes a lot more strength than most people can muster. Don't you *ever* call me a weak little girl," Blue ordered in a low tone. "You know who I'm supposed to be."

Baird recovered his surprise and returned his sister's glare from his place on the floor. "I don't think the Light would lose her temper so easily. That makes you weak."

"Who had day one?" Elle called into the kitchen.

"Huh?" Blue questioned, not relinquishing her dominant stance over her brother.

"We were betting on how long it would take for you two to get into it." She lowered her voice. "You might want to cool it, guys. Grettel's already anxious enough." Elle walked over toward the siblings after she finished setting down all of the chairs. She slid into a booth and motioned for her dear friend to join her.

Blue released her brother with a rough shove, but neither seemed to have reached any level of forgiveness. He stalked off to join Grettel in the kitchen.

Elle's smile was a welcome distraction. "Come on, Blue. We've got a little down time before the doors open and you begin your glamorous role as a waitress with sass."

"That's you, Elle. I'm the mumbling invisible one."

"You mean you're the mysterious and gorgeous one?"

"I love you." Blue shivered, shaking out the anxiety that was building up in her body.

"Back at ya, Baby Blue."

"I hate fighting with Baird," Blue admitted quietly. She started to relax when Elle began rubbing the tension out of her forearms.

"Really? I don't get out of bed without the promise of at least one decent brawl with your jerk of a brother."

Elle's soothing touch released Blue's tether to Baird's steep expectations. She thought through all the things she'd wanted to ask Baird, but couldn't, due to his gruff demeanor. "Why haven't I met my owner yet, Elle? Wouldn't he want to know at least that Baird purchased a healthy Wayward? Wouldn't he want to interview me or put me through some sort of testing to make sure I'm the right pick?"

"What's the big deal?" Elle sighed as she examined her nails, wishing she owned a bit of the fancy colored polish the Femreaux wore. "I've never met him, either. Neither has Grettel. He trusts Baird. How could he not? I mean, since Baird took over everything, there've been no customer complaints, the Vemreaux keep coming back for more of his Green Abby shots, and there's been no property damage to speak of." She splayed her fingers up toward her face and gave her friend a doe-eyed expression. "The waitresses keep everyone happy and give the Vemreaux something naturally beautiful to look at."

Blue smiled and nodded. "Obviously. I heard that was what ended world hunger in the first place." She strummed her fingers on the table. "Are we gonna talk about you and my brother? I honestly can never tell if you guys are fighting or flirting."

Elle had a schoolgirl crush on Baird from the time she was old enough to turn her scattered attention to just one boy. It was clear from her beauty and intelligence that she could have her pick of any Wayward she set her affections on, but for some reason, her wandering eye always managed to land on Baird. Even the little tickle she gave his ribs when Blue first reached the hut was a giveaway that they were still doing their discreet dance of attraction and indifference.

"Usually both. One always leads to the other." Elle smiled devilishly. "You know he wants me." She gave a self-satisfied little shrug that suggested he would be crazy not to. Then her confidence drooped perceptibly. "You'd think that being out of The Way and, you know, living together would speed things along, but nothing's changed. I push. He likes it, but won't make a move." She chewed the inside of her lip to keep it from pouting and admitting that the covert flirtations were important to her. She knew that her self-esteem hung entirely too much upon his approval.

Blue interjected quickly. "How could he not like it? I mean, it's you."

Nodding, Elle huffed. "I know, right? It's just a matter of time. Once this testing business is over and they discover I'm not the Light, maybe he'll loosen up. Spotlight won't be on me to divert them from you anymore, which means I won't have to train so hard for a job that's not mine."

Blue's eyes widened as she stared at her friend. "You'll pass whatever test they have for you, no problem. You're the only *A*-blood whose reflexes can compete with a Vemreaux's."

"Not the only one," Elle amended. "But thanks anyway. Well, probably the only one being tested, that's true. Your brother's an idiot."

Throwing her friend an eye roll, the corner of Blue's mouth lifted. "Like that needed to be said. Are you using your mystical deciphering skills as candidate for the Light, or did you realize that the old-fashioned way like the rest of us?"

"Plain old feminine intuition, baby doll," Elle said with a wink.

Blue followed Elle's example of setting rolls of silverware wrapped in napkins on the tables in preparation for patrons. She had never used silverware before. All meals in The Way were eaten with compostable utensils. In a quieter voice, Blue leaned in toward her friend. "How's Baird been?"

Elle sighed. "Truth? He doesn't do well without you. Sometimes it's hard to watch. He's too fixated on my future. He's constantly training me to be seen as candidate for the Light. It was at least balanced in The Way because we didn't want to get caught training. Now that we're on the outside, he doesn't hold back."

"You're one in a million, Elle."

"Agreed."

"It's a good thing you're desperately in love with my brother and would pretty much do whatever he asked."

"Yeah, well, those little agility games like we played in the kitchen? The mind games like counting the trees everywhere we go? I know that's just Baird keeping me sharp." She paused. "Not the kind of games I was hoping for, now that we have a little more freedom."

"Elle, you're in line to be tested soon. Baird would never jeopardize that by distracting you with feelings." Blue contemplated this further. "Of course, he's generally a huge chicken about opening up at all to anyone. You're a very ambitious woman to think you can crack him. But if anyone could, I'd bet it'd be you."

"You know I usually get what I want. I can be patient." Elle made eye contact with her friend as she stood, so Blue could see her sincerity as she spoke. "I'm real glad you're here, Blue. It feels right again, having you with us."

Flipping the sign over to announce to the world they were open, Elle pushed the door wide to allow the customers in.

Blue took a deep breath and braced herself for her first real world interaction with the superior race.

8

BLOCK

"**L**iam!" Sam called into the bedroom. "It's time to get up, princess," he sang annoyingly.

Liam threw something at the closed door that was far heavier than a pillow.

Alec had not been kidding about Sam being the one to wake Liam and get him ready for his luncheon with Emperor Anders. That meant Liam had to be sober, showered, dressed and, well, awake.

Sam's fist pounded on the door. He smiled when Liam groaned. Sam belted out a few lines from an old song he remembered from when he'd gone to summer camp with Liam's older brother, Killian. When he finished with a cheery "Ho-way-ho!" he could hear his friend stumbling out of the bed.

Liam threw open the door wearing nothing but his boxer briefs. "Death to infidels," he groaned, pointing his finger at Sam's chest. The prince's stomach, that in his college years had been toned, was starting to soften with his overindulgent lifestyle. The stylist's choice in haircut for Liam ensured that photographers could appreciate his thick head of brown hair with natural glints of auburn, but was also considerate of the fact that Liam woke up wrecked from some party too many nights to count.

Alec, who had been sitting at the conference table, looked up from his phone as the prince passed him. "Um, I'm thinking the Fem you had last night may want a second date. Or a first, for that matter." He pointed to Liam's backside.

Liam turned, but could not see what Alec was indicating. He ended up twisting himself in two complete circles trying to get a glimpse of his own rear.

"Oh, for crying out loud! Her number, Liam. She wrote her number on your butt in lipstick." Alec shook his head and turned his attention back to his phone, checking the itinerary for the day. "You've got half an hour to get ready for the day and sit your painted backside in the car."

"Ah, Alec," Liam crooned as he shoved the guard. He reached in the refrigerator and pulled out some orange juice, taking a swig without bothering to locate a glass. "Worry, worry, worry. When was the last time you had a 'date'?"

Alec's black eyebrows furrowed while he waited for the page on his phone to load. "You are so high maintenance, I can't imagine adding a woman to my life." He leaned his elbows on the table and frowned up at the prince. Alec was not known for smiling, and this morning proved no different.

"What you mean is, you love me so much, you just don't have room in your heart for another person you'll have to share a bathroom with."

"I'd really rather you had proper clothes on for this conversation." Alec scratched his cheek and flipped to the news on his phone. "Sam. He's still your problem. Your choice in party means you get him going. That means clothing." When Liam made to sit on the upholstered chair beside him, Alec pushed the seat onto its side.

"Well, that was passive aggressive," Liam mumbled, righting the chair. "No royal pardon for you today." He shook his head, pretending to scold his serious guard.

"You can't sit down. One, because you need to get in the shower. And two, because you'll leave her number everywhere you sit." Alec's black eyebrows furrowed together as he grumbled incoherently about the poor choice in women the boys had.

"And what would you have had us do our first night in the Americas?" Sam asked, handing a pile of dress clothes to Liam and shooing him into the bathroom.

"All I wanted was pancakes," Alec muttered with a muted frown.

"That's all you *ever* want," Sam snorted.

"Not true. Some nights I want to stay in and go to bed early."

"Man, you are old."

"And you act like a teenager. You think it's good for Liam to be photographed with that many Fems on his first night here? He's got an image to protect."

Sam bowed. "And I'm perfecting it. Killy's the serious one now. The eldest of the three royal children of Europe claimed his birthright, so that leaves Liam free for clubbing with me." Sam spoke with condescension. "Not sure how Killian will sit on the throne someday with that stick up his ass."

"Very clever. You should write his next speech."

"The people need Killy to feel better about the future of the empire, and they need Liam for the fun of it."

"I thought that's what Suzette was for."

"Nah. Their sister's only good for one thing."

"Wow. You're cynical this morning. You'd think a run would have at least given you an endorphin rush."

Sam banged both fists on the bathroom door ten times to remind Liam of the hour. He spoke to Alec over Liam's protests. "Where's Brody? It might take both bodyguards to get his royal pain up and running this morning."

Liam opened the door and glared at his best friend. "Royal pain, am I? That's just because I haven't turned on the charm, yet. Give me a minute. It takes a while to ramp up the million-bill smile." He gave Sam his best smarmy grin.

Sam shook his head. "I won't be taken in by your charisma. Keep that raw animal magnetism away from me, and march it into the shower. I've got places to be."

Alec spoke up from his place at the table, not batting an eye at the juvenile exchange between the two. "Brody's chatting up the concierge."

"What's she got? Harelip? Wonky eye? One and a half breasts?" Sam inspected his own chest curiously.

"She has a pulse, which is all that seems required for you three to let loose."

Sam straightened at the affront. "Hey, now. I only take home the top tier. Can I help it if they love my European accent?" He walked over to the table once he heard the shower starting, and sat next to Alec. "Saw something on my run."

"A mirror? That why you took so long?"

"Now who's the speech writer," Sam commented acrimoniously. He ran a hand through his messy dark brown hair, leaving a few stray spikes poking out at odd angles. "A car accident. Sort of."

Alec's black eyebrow raised, but he did not look away from his phone. "Everyone okay?"

"Two guys, both dead. Didn't see the accident happen, but I phoned it in. Took off once the cops got there."

"Shame."

"Got a closer look before I phoned it in. Alec, the front of the car was dented into a tree, but I saw bruising around their throats, and one's neck was snapped sideways."

Alec put his phone down and stared at Sam with his full attention. "Meaning?"

"Meaning you both need to go with Liam to the luncheon today. You both need to go with him everywhere. I know you wanted to do tag-team, but if there's a murder cover-up this close to the hotel, I don't think you should risk it."

"You're right. Maybe I should fly out a few extra guards, just in case."

Sam shook his head. "I'm sure he'll be fine. It wasn't too near. Just keep an eye out, is all."

"Thanks, Sam."

"I left before getting too involved. They seemed pretty much set on it being an accident. I didn't stick around to set them right, though, in case cameras showed up."

"Restraint? How unlike you." He held his friend's stare. "I know you say you're happy on Frederick's financial team, but if you ever wanted guard duty again…"

"I resigned for a reason, Alec."

"I know. But no one agrees with your reasons."

"Drop it, old man. I can drink as much as I want now. I can enjoy the local talent with this job. You're the one who should think about switching."

Alec permitted a small smile. "No. I'll leave the royal treasury to you. Had no idea you actually studied in college, but you do a good job. Better than the last guy. Frederick and Harold talk about it all the time."

"The emperor and royal advisor thinking about buying me a birthday present?" Sam smirked. "You fishing to see how big your bonus will be this year? Gotta buy me a beer first."

"It's not even noon yet, Sam. And no, I was simply offering you a compliment."

"Oh. Well, thank you." He took a sip from Alec's *O*-Negative cola. "Speaking of not that, did you do the thing I asked you to do to Liam's phone?"

Alec nodded, frowning at Sam's theft of his beverage. "Last night after he passed out. I wish you could give me a better explanation, though. He and Everest are close friends. *You* and Everest are close, too. I don't get it."

"Blocking all calls from Everest Sinclair is best for now. King Sinclair said he wanted to spend some time alone with Everest, so that's what we'll give him. Time with his son. About time that family did something together besides fight. Don't know how they smile so perfectly for the cameras. Everest hates his dad." Sam looked down at the drink as he thought over the conversation Emperor Frederick conveyed to him before they left for the Americas. "I don't know what Ever's up to, but it's worse than usual. Maybe some time with his dad will do him some good."

"I can only imagine what it is if *you* think it's bad. Come on, Sam. What's Ever mixed up in this time? What's so bad even you won't touch it?"

Sam shook his head and crossed his arms over his chest as he tilted the chair back on two legs. "I don't know for sure, but King Sinclair bought Ever one of the small islands off the *O*-blood mainland just to keep him away from whatever it is."

"So? Everest is always looking for places to disappear. Just a matter of time before he got one of his own."

"It was mostly quarantined for radiation. Just became available for sale from the government, and King Sinclair swoops in and buys this almost uninhabitable piece of land for his son that he's never gotten on with?" Sam waved his hand to move on. "And not just that. Ever keeps calling me, leaving messages asking for Liam and me to come down to rescue him. Sounded pretty desperate. I don't think Liam would be able to resist."

"Alright. It's just odd."

Sam scratched his cheek. "The king and Ever spending time together? Yeah."

"No. Well, yeah, that. Sinclair's a great king, but an average father. Of course, Everest isn't exactly a model son." Alec shook his head. "But no. I meant that it's odd. You're turning down partying with the king's son? Since when?"

"Since I know for a fact his dealer's not doling it out for him like usual. Ever's been cutting back on the hard stuff big time."

"And you're disappointed the party won't be up to your caliber of wastefulness?"

Sam huffed. "You know, the more you try to finish my thoughts, the more I'm finding out what you really think of me."

"That's no secret, Sam."

"Normally, I'd be there in a hot second."

"I was going to say," Alec commented in confusion.

"But he's not getting anything from his dealer because his dad's cut him off from Mike for a while. Getting him clean again. Since King Sinclair asked for us to give E some space, that's what we're going to do. Blocking his calls to Liam keeps Li from hearing the desperate messages and running off after him."

"Probably best. Liam can't help himself. He's not changed yet, but he always wants to try the things you, Everest and Brody are doing, even when he shouldn't."

"Not just that." Sam grasped around for the right words. "Lately when Ever leaves me messages, he sounds…not right."

"How is one supposed to sound 'right' when their mind is chemically altered, or best-case scenario, detoxing?"

"Look, Alec. I've seen Ever on every kind of high there is, but this? This is different. He begs me to come and get him. Tells me his dad's torturing him. I might actually believe him if he was anyone else. He's always been a little theatrical."

"I'd imagine a few days sober would be torture for Everest Sinclair."

Sam snorted. "Just doesn't sound like himself. I'm half-tempted to fly over there and get him." He traced the label on the cola drink. "Remember the guy who helped me light Killian's car on fire when we were having our little row? Didn't hear a trace of that guy in the messages. Just scared and real upset."

"For the record, I don't know anything about that." Alec glared at Sam with much disapproval. "I'm glad Killian backed down. You two…but yes, I know how Everest can be."

"Ever talks and talks, just like his dad, and before you know it, he's lit the match, and you're the one holding it." Sam slammed his chair back down on all fours. "I'm not saying I regret it. Killy deserved that and worse for what he did to me. I'm just saying I don't think I would've gotten there on my own. Ever's pretty persuasive when he wants something bad enough. Best to block his calls from Liam, who's…"

"Easily persuaded?" Alec scratched the nape of his neck as he thought over Sam's explanation. "Still not enough to really go on, but a little extra caution won't hurt. Are you still talking to Everest?"

"Of course. He's my friend. But you know how he is. Too many resources. Too few things on his plate. We both fall off his radar and he'll get antsy."

"Fair enough." Alec went back to his phone, rearranging a few items on the itinerary to reflect extra caution.

Just then, the door popped open and Brody strolled into the room, boasting his success in the form of a big grin. His blond hair had a slight wave to it that bounced when he was particularly cheerful. "Got her number! Meeting her tonight when I'm off my shift. Literally? She's a ten. A golden ten!"

Sam tried to look apologetic, but his smirk was too easy to access. "Ah, Brode. You might have to reschedule."

9

PASSING THE BATON

Griffin tried to ignore Marxus. He tried to ignore the shovel, but there it sat, the only unused tool in the yard. Since Baird had been bought, the shovel was unofficially retired. Every day when the labor crew went out to muck the scratch, Marxus carried out two instruments: his and Baird's. Marxus worked alone now, next to the shovel he thrust down into the earth next to him. If a fight got out of hand, Marxus took his tool and banged it to Baird's, reminding everyone who was in charge. Baird's tool was a beacon, a symbol to all Waywards that the Vemreaux did not keep them in line – they kept themselves working hard. They were not cattle, corralled in feed lots to serve the superior blood types. They were people. The distinction was small, but some days, it made all the difference.

Baird had cowered to no one, not even the Vemreaux Supervisors. They regarded him with respect, for he made their days easier by putting a stop to most yard fights before they got out of hand, which would have made for more paperwork. Though he knew he would never see Baird again, Marxus made sure that no one forgot who was in charge.

Even though they were separated now, Griffin still felt Baird's shadow weighing on his shoulders. Baird was the older brother whose shoes he could never fill, and the man he hoped he could both never be and someday be.

George worked next to Griffin, soothing some of the angst that had been building since Blue had left The Way. "I don't know about you, but I could eat my weight in mashed potatoes tonight. Krish is on kitchen detail, and I hope he does like last time and 'accidentally' knocks in too much butter." When Griffin did not speak, George prattled on. "He got docked a point for it, but it was worth it. Man, I'd donate one of my points to the cause if it gets the potatoes tasting like they did that day."

Griffin nodded and tried to force a smile, but it would not come. His brother was gone, and his sister was under Baird's thumb somewhere out in the real world. Baird's job was to turn Blue into a monster. Blue's duty was to obey and become the killing machine she'd need to be to fight the tyranny. Griffin's position was not as glamorous, but it was every bit as necessary as the others. The youngest offered up a buffer between the two machines, softening them both. Well, softening Blue, and occasionally staying Baird's stream of constant discipline. After Baird left, she, George and Griffin laughed a lot together. They worked hard, but they also took moments to play – a thing Baird never approved of. Now that Blue was gone, Griffin's ability to play seemed to have left The Way, as well.

"...then it exploded and sent little bits of poop everywhere!" George exclaimed, laughing at his own story as he unwittingly smeared scratch across his forehead.

"Huh? I missed it. What happened?" Griffin asked. He forced memories of his sister out of his head as he turned to George, but was immediately reminded of her again when he observed the line of scratch on George's face. Blue was always marked up, much worse than that, but the small reminders were everywhere.

George's shovel stilled as he took in his friend's state. "You're thinking about Blue again, aren't you?"

Griffin looked away and focused on the pile of scratch that

needed to be moved by the hour's end. "I just didn't hear part of your story, George. I'm fine."

"Fine, eh? Griff, you're not eating. You toss all night. Fine? Really? You even missed a great exploding toilet story. I'm starting to get worried."

"I said I'm fine, George. I don't need anyone watching me. You're not..." He was about to say "my sister", but the words stuck in his throat. "You don't need to worry about me. Blasting toilets. I'm there. Who was it? Dug? Nickulus?"

George sighed. "It was Vickee."

"Vickee? Huh. Girl's got some moxie. Maybe you should go for her."

Blanching, George resumed scooping the scratch into the wheelbarrow. "Blowing things up? Getting into trouble? That's your kinda girl, not mine. Knock yourself out, Griff. The girl who plays in poop isn't spoken for, if you can believe it."

Griffin chuckled, making a mental note to flirt with Vickee the next time he saw her. Sure, she was three years older than him, but Griffin was big for his age, just like Baird had been. The shocking cerulean eyes and naturally good looks were only made more attractive by his easy smile. Unfortunately, his grin was harder to locate since Blue had been purchased. Now he looked more and more like his surly brother.

In the distance, Griffin heard the beginnings of a scuffle. He ignored it and continued shoveling scratch.

"When do you think Blue'll come back to visit you?"

"If Baird has any say in it? Never."

"Come on, Griff. You know that's not true. You'll see her again. Baird always visits you once a month. They'll probably come together."

Griffin said nothing to this, but he still had his doubts. On the visits, Baird mostly drilled Blue while Griffin made curt comments under his breath. Baird had always been very controlling, and acted as if he was afraid that if Blue spent too much time with Griffin, she'd turn soft. Griffin made it a point to spar with his sister regularly, so Baird could say nothing disparaging about Griffin's masculinity.

Marxus banged on Baird's shovel, sending a resounding gong of authority out over the vast expanse of the yard. The brawling paused, but picked back up seconds later.

"Great. It's Androo running his mouth again. Baird's shovel's losing some of its power, I think," George remarked. "I'm kinda surprised Marxus has been able to hold down the fort this long."

Griffin watched Joodas and Denny wrestle around, landing blows while Androo jeered from the sidelines.

"Knock it off!" Marxus commanded, pausing his work to snarl at the upset. When the two continued their duel without adhering to Marxus' demand, the towering Wayward turned his scarred face to the quarrelers. The shovel in his hand was no longer a tool, but a weapon. Marxus stalked over to the fight, now doubly mad because not only had they interrupted his work, but they also disrespected Baird, and the whole system the two worked so hard to set up. Marxus had scars on his hands, arms and legs, but it was the gouges on his face from his many yard fights that gave him the edge of foreboding. "End it, guys."

"Oh, no," George murmured. His eyes drifted to three guys coming up behind Marxus with looks of menace.

Griffin followed his best friend's line of vision, his eyes widening. "It's a setup!" Griffin called to Marxus, but the bulldog was in battle mode, focused only on the conquest ahead of him. "Marxus!"

The dull nothing that muted Griffin's mind since Blue had left lifted in an instant. His five senses heightened as his muscles reawakened. He took in a deep, cleansing breath that pushed life back into him. Baird's life. A growl started in Griffin's belly and echoed up his chest until it birthed out of his mouth.

"Griffin, don't!" George pleaded, but it was too late.

Griffin jolted into action, forsaking his tool and sprinting for the center of the yard. Five guys were on Marxus, but Griffin was not deterred. Before the Vemreaux Supervisor could lend his baton of reason to the mix, Griffin yanked his brother's shovel out of the ground. He charged toward the fight, his vision cutting out a terrified George, a confused Androo, the yard and all sense of caution.

Griffin snarled as he raised his arms to attack. He turned in a circle to gain momentum, as Baird had taught him. Then Griffin leaped toward his target, and cracked the shovel hard on the back of Joodas' head.

Baird's weapon sliced through the air with inbred expertise. The sound of metal on bone echoed through the yard. Griffin grunted with each blow that tried to stay his assault, but the shovel never ceased. Five on one hadn't been a fair fight. Five on two? If Griffin was involved, that leveled the playing field. He was wild, and fought without restraint, spit flying and anger flaring beyond control.

Marxus reclaimed his bearings and thrust Denny off of him. He punched, pummeled and punished, ducking away from Griffin's crazy swings. The two fought without mercy, taking the men down, one after the other, until they were the only ones who stood, chests heaving. Their knuckles were white with tension and red with blood.

When he was sure the others would not rise to fight them again, Marxus nodded to the nearest Vemreaux Supervisor. Supervisor Smith preferred to let the Waywards settle their own battles whenever possible. When Baird had been there, fights occurred far less often, so Smith interfered only to sweep away the offenders or offer his baton when a matter got out of hand.

"Looks like you found yourself a replacement," Supervisor Smith commented to Marxus as he nudged one of the felled Waywards with the toe of his boot. "Next time, try not to kill them. More paperwork for me."

Griffin's chin jerked down to look at the bodies at his feet. "I didn't kill anybody! I was just stopping them from jumping Marxus."

Supervisor Smith requested a few stretchers on his Talkie-Comm. He chuckled and shook his head. "I know, kid. I saw the whole thing."

Then why didn't you do something? Don't you know how easy Marxus makes your job? Griffin grumbled to himself. He dropped the shovel and bent down to feel Joodas' pulse, willing it to stir beneath his fingertips. "I...I...I didn't mean to, Supervisor Smith. I didn't kill anyone! That's not real! It can't be!"

The Supervisor sniggered, pulling out a pad of paper from his back pocket. "What'd you think was going to happen? You smack someone's skull with a shovel as hard as you did, they don't stand much of a chance." He shook his head.

Griffin looked down at Joodas' motionless body in horror. His stomach clenched, and before he could stop it, Griffin turned and vomited on the nearest pile of scratch.

Smith pushed Griffin to the side, mid-hurl. "You know you can't go puking on scratch, boy. That pile there? It's worth more than you are. Aim your sick the other way."

Griffin's stomach and throat constricted simultaneously, making it difficult to catch his breath. *Calm it down!* Griffin commanded himself in Baird's voice. *Blue does this kind of thing all the time. She's just out of her mind when she does it. It's your first kill, is all. Joodas was asking for it, jumping Marxus. Exactly what Baird would've done.* Griffin panted on all fours, spitting out the last of his regurgitated lunch. "I didn't mean to," Griffin confessed to Supervisor Smith.

"Relax. I'm just giving you solitary for the rest of the day after the post."

"The post? But I stopped the fight!" Griffin clambered to his unsteady feet.

Supervisor Smith's light demeanor turned sharp. He whipped out his baton and cracked Griffin on the shoulder with it, sending the Wayward back to the ground. "That sounds like questioning a Supervisor! Is that what you're doing?"

"No, sir!"

"All you rats'll get the same punishment. Except poor Joodas." He lifted the dead Wayward's chin with the toe of his boot. "Solitary'll give you all a chance to cool off." He nodded to Marxus with respect reserved only for the Wayward Baird left behind to run the yard. "Marxus."

"Sir." Marxus offered Griffin a hand up. Then he picked up Baird's shovel and handed it to Griffin, who took it with hands that shook from nerves. "Griff, you'll work with me from now on. Help me keep the peace. Baird's shovel belongs to you."

Griffin's mouth fell open. "What? Me? I...I don't think Baird would want that."

Marxus postured. "It's my call. You saved my life today. I could use a second man to help me run the yard."

"But..."

Marxus shook his head. "You picked up Baird's shovel. It's been waiting for you. We all have."

Griffin mumbled a modest reply, but was coming down from the adrenaline rush, so it was mostly unintelligible. He followed on rubbery legs after Marxus, who led the boy to take his beatings like a man.

10

BROTHER BAIRD

"I need you to open the diner early for me today," Baird mumbled.

The sun had barely risen, and Blue knew that she was expected home from her nightly runs at dawn. Since Blue lost the ability to sleep some time in her childhood, she was permitted to run to Capital City and back while the rest of the country dreamt of their next party. In The Way, she'd had to lie on her cot, pretending to sleep for merciless hours to keep this particular fulfillment of prophecy a secret. She flopped on the hard floor of the hut and stretched out her burning legs, happy that she could be herself, if only in the privacy of their home.

"What for?" asked Blue. "Where are you going?"

"Correct response is, 'That's fine, Baird.'"

"That's fine, Baird." *Sometimes I want to punch you in the face, Baird.*

Baird sat up, his short auburn hair rumpled from the awkward angle of resting on the couch. "Lunch special is aged liver with three-month Hollandaise sauce and a side of pickled limes and turnips over mustard greens."

Her nose wrinkled. The changed Vemreaux's lessened sense of

taste lent to unsavory meal choices just so they registered a modicum of flavor. "And for the unchanged?"

"Rosemary chicken with a spinach salad."

"I'll write it on the board." She kept her voice low so as to not wake her best friends. Elle slept with a frown on her pouting lips, daring anyone to wake her before she was ready. Her blonde hair was strewn over the pillow, long legs reaching the foot of the worn mattress, and right arm draped around Grettel.

Grettel's fearful eyes were closed, but her mouth hung open, permitting a soft snore to pass through her lips. Blue glanced down at them maternally, and for the third time that morning, was thankful that she was reunited with them. "Baird, where are you going?"

"I'll be back before the lunch rush, but not much before. We got a request from the Peace Day committee to hold their morning meetings at the diner for the next couple days. Favor to Lawrence, really. They need a rehearsal space for whatever stupid parties are going on in Capital City next week for Peace Week."

"They need any special setup?" she asked, refraining from asking him yet again where he was going.

"Dunno. You can handle it, though. Mayor's gonna be there, someone from the University, Lawrence of course, and a few other important Vemreaux, so, you know, make sure Elle shines and you look...regular." He pulled on his light blue work polo. "I told them they could have the diner from seven till we open today and tomorrow."

"You know Lawrence scares Grettel. You sure she'll be okay without you there?"

Baird glanced down at the girls on the mattress, and Blue saw a shadow of softness sweep his features, and then disappear. "I'll be back around noon or so. She'll be fine in the kitchen. Too busy to be scared."

"You sure about that?"

"What's with all the questions today?"

"What's with all the secrecy?"

Baird sighed as he pulled out a tin can of Grade *V* rations and peeled back the foil top. "It's the first of the month, Blue. I haven't been back to check on Griff since Master Joe bought you."

She'd forgotten about his monthly visits. Only family on the outside were allowed visitation with Waywards. Since most *A*-bloods didn't have freed siblings or parents, there usually weren't many appointments set. Blue and Griffin had been envied that they were allowed to see someone from the real world. The fact that it was Baird, whose name still held high respect in The Way, was icing on the cake.

Blue's heart leapt. "Can I come? Please, Baird, please! I need to make sure he's okay." Words tumbled out of her faster than she could censor them. "I don't know how controlled he is without me there. I just want to make sure he's not getting into fights or anything. Please, Baird!"

Her earnest voice woke Elle, which in turn, roused Grettel. "Ugh!" Elle exclaimed, resting her hand across her eyes. "It's not even really morning yet, guys. I'm sleeping, here!"

"Time to get up, girls." Baird shuffled over to the mattress and tapped Elle's bare foot with his, grinning mischievously.

"Ah!" Elle cried, now irrevocably awake. She sat up, her foot recoiling from his. "Don't touch me with your gross bare man feet. That's disgusting!" He chuckled as he touched her cheek with his toe, relishing her choked exclamation of revulsion. "Sick! Get off me!"

"Baird, I need to see Griffin. I'm better with him. I can tell just by looking how he's doing."

Baird shook his head as he returned to the table, satisfied that Elle was finally awake. She had flown into the bathroom to scrub at her cheek. "I can't send the girls to open the diner by themselves. Not safe."

"It's barely morning! Who's out at this hour? Most lowlifes aren't early risers."

Uninterested in arguing with her, Baird turned and scooped the last of the mashed gray congealment into his mouth. "You've got about forty minutes or so to get there and get it all up and running.

I'm using the car, so you can take the path through the woods." He slipped on his socks and shoes without looking at his sister.

"No!" Blue searched for new arguments to throw at him. "He doesn't talk to you the way he opens up to me. He tries to be all tough to impress you so you know he's a man, but he'll be honest with me. I need to know he's okay!" Beads of sweat from her run dripped down her cheeks, the perfect imposters of tears.

Baird continued to ignore her, which infuriated her all the more, adding flame to her increasing irrationality. Blue's livid eyes glowed like cerulean pools of fleeting madness as she yanked open the nearest drawer and pulled out a butter knife. Without hesitation or calculation, she launched the weapon across the small home, sinking the tip into the door just above the handle that Baird's fist was choking.

Baird froze. Blue seethed. Grettel screamed.

Baird turned his feral eyes on his sister, daring her anger to be bigger than his. "Take this knife out now."

"I will *not* be invisible here!" Blue shouted, fists squeezed tight to tether her temper. "I did everything you said in The Way! I kept my head down, eyes hidden, mouth shut. I hid myself from practically everyone so you didn't make them disappear!" She swallowed the lump that rose in her throat. "I've been in the real world almost a month now, and I've done everything you've asked. I want one thing, and you treat me like I'm invisible. Well, I'm not! Everywhere else in the world, maybe, but not in this house! Let me be a person here!"

Emotions were easy for Baird to dominate. He stared into her, control and superiority winning out over her youthful outburst. "I'll ask you one more time because I underestimated how immature you are." His voice grew dangerously low, and could barely be heard over Grettel's whimpers. "Take...this...knife...out...now."

"I hate you!" Blue screamed into the dawn.

And there it was. The worst thing she could ever say to the person she loved most in the world, and she'd yelled it like a child. Once the words were out, she was lost, all at once untied to her beacon of reason and strength. Her fists wrapped around her middle, trying to hold herself together.

One determined step at a time, Baird moved toward his sister, the hurtful words bouncing off of his well-hidden heart like a girlish slap on the wrist.

Elle was the only other rational one in the hut. She scooped up fresh clothes for her and Grettel, pulled up the petrified pixie and locked them both in the bathroom.

Baird wrapped his long fingers around her fist and led her to the front door. Molding her hand around the knife, they pulled the utensil out together. Just as the tip was freed, Baird surprised his sister by ramming it hard into the door, breaking through to the other side. Slamming her up against the wood, he pinned her neck with his forearm. Beneath the anger, he was glad that the fight went out of her and she did not struggle against him.

"I don't care that you hate me. I don't care what you want. Fact is, you are not a person." Baird's words seethed through clenched teeth. "You're a weapon. The Vemreaux are going to use you to end the predator, and it *will* kill you. Seeing Griffin today won't change that. Fighting me about it all won't make your life longer." His self-loathing peaked, but he kept his tone even. "Say it. Say, 'I am not a person.'"

All traces of struggle left her eyes as the blue orbs dulled to duty. "I am not a person. I'm a weapon."

The whispered mantra nearly broke him, but he held her firmly. "Again."

She obeyed.

"Good girl. Now, can you handle walking the girls to the diner, opening it up and waiting on a table of Vemreaux until I get back?"

She mouthed her agreement, her soulless eyes staring vacantly ahead. Baird released his sister and exited the hut without hesitation. He knew that any weakness or kindness shown to her right now would not help build her into being the Light she would have to be. If there was any chance the prophecy could be beat, it would not be by coddling her. He would take all her hatred and tantrums if it meant she might return to him.

Each kilometer he passed on the freeway brought to mind a new way he'd failed her, or another reason he wished he could be anyone else. He'd seen the conviction in her eyes as she screamed at him.

The 4x4 vehicle pulled into the parking lot of The Way. The enormous facility loomed ahead, reminding Baird of a thousand things all at once as the scent of processed scratch hit him. His eyes swept the lot, noting three unfamiliar vehicles. Two were average commuter cars, but the third was an enlarged black SUV with tinted windows.

There were four check points Baird passed through, each earning him a stamp on his green visitor's pass. He was ushered to the waiting room, which, thanks to the fact that not many Waywards in the real world knew if they had family or not, usually remained empty.

Baird was surprised when the sight of four men greeted him. Two rose up from their chairs at his entry and gave Baird a visual once-over, one of them sitting back down when he was satisfied that the newcomer did not present a threat to the man who sat with his head tilted back and sunglasses on.

The fourth man was lying on his back, stretched out across three chairs. He carried on the conversation as if there'd been no interruption. "I told Ever we're stuck here till the end of Peace Week. All he had to do was pick up a paper to find out you're here filling in for the emperor at the testing, Liam. He's out of it." His dark brown hair did what it pleased, not conforming to any sort of order.

Liam did not open his eyes behind the sunglasses. "Since when is he sober enough to be 'in it'?"

"Since never. I told him to give Killian a call since we're out of the country."

Brody huffed. "Yeah, I can just see the two of them hanging out. I don't care how he plays it, Killy doesn't like Everest anymore. Now that Kill's sober and doesn't need Ever's pharmacy, they have nothing in common."

"Hey, if it'd get him off my continent by the time I get back, I'd be grateful."

Liam groaned. "Could you stop it already? Killian deserves a holiday. I hope he does take Ever up on his offer. I'll call him later and tell him so. He works too hard."

Alec grumbled, "Got to compensate for you not working at all."

Sam stretched out one of his legs. "I tell you what, I'm going to French kiss Josephine straight away when we get home. No one cooks like my girl."

Liam moaned. "Stop lusting after my elderly housekeeper just because she keeps you in pot roast." His face soured. "Bad visual."

Sam chuckled. "Aw! You thinking about me naked again?"

When the waiting room door opened and Jack came out, Baird groaned inwardly. He took it as his payback for being so harsh with Blue.

"Ah, my favorite nephew!" exclaimed the Vemreaux Supervisor Baird most loathed. Baird noticed that Jack's accent slipped into the unfamiliar cadence he often donned when he got too upset or forgot himself in a particularly cheerful moment.

Liam winced at Jack's volume, but pulled on as genuine a smile as he could. "Hey, Uncle Jack. I see the Fountain's been good to you."

Jack grinned at the typical greeting. "When's it your turn?" His eye caught the only ones that did not look happy at his arrival. "Oh, Baird. I'm sorry. I didn't see you there. This is my nephew, Prince Liam Boniface." He grabbed Liam's shoulder with enthusiasm and introduced him to the one Wayward he'd never been able to win over with his charming smile. Jack recovered his Western inflection. "Baird's one of our best, come back to visit his brother. I'll see if Griffin's in the holding room for you."

"Uncle Jack, you sound like a Yank," Liam teased.

Baird didn't need the prince's last name. He could tell by their accent that all four men would have the last name of Boniface. All Americans had the surname Anders, Europeans shared Boniface, and China had Cho. Sinclair was the only name that stood on its own, so the king and his family would not be given to favoritism by sharing a last name with a particular country's people.

Liam tucked his sunglasses into his shirt pocket and stretched out his hand, smiling at the stranger. "Nice to meet you."

"Sir," Baird responded, grasping the prince's proffered hand. The gesture was ordinary, but Baird's intake of breath could not be masked. His own shockingly blue eyes stared back at him from Prince Liam's smiling face. They were unworried, unhurried and kind. Baird had never seen his own eyes look like that before. Somewhere in the back of Baird's mind, pieces of a puzzle began to surface. He instantly felt a surge of trust toward the man – which, of course, made him trust Liam even less on principle. He could not shake the feeling of significance as he released the prince's grip.

"So, you used to work here? I thought it was sort of a lifetime commitment." Liam spoke with a hinted meaning that Baird did not understand.

"No. I'm a Wayward. Bought for work at a diner a few years back, sir."

"Oh." Baird could tell that Liam was holding back his true feelings about the explanation. With features so similar to his own, Baird did not have a hard time reading the prince. He was impressed at the breezy grin that coasted over the hiccup. Liam continued, "I just thought because of your eyes that you were Vemreaux. Never seen a Wayward with Original Vemreaux eyes before."

"No, sir. Your changed friends here can probably tell I'm A-blood."

The more serious, alert guard nodded.

Liam clapped Baird on the shoulder. "None of that 'sir' business. We're like, the same age probably."

"Yes, your majesty," Baird responded without blinking. He did not correct the man by informing him that he was only twenty-one, while the prince looked nearer to his thirties.

Liam exhaled, deflating at the impenetrable man. "Wow, they sure raise 'em right here, eh Alec?"

Alec nodded, but cracked a miniscule smile at Baird's feigned submission.

"What do you think, Sam?" Liam asked the man who'd just hung up his phone.

"Nice and robotic. Just like we ordered," Sam agreed.

"Do they have to make the lights this bright?" Liam rubbed his temples.

Baird moved over to the wall and turned off half the lights. "Robotic *and* able to operate light switches. Just like a real Vemreaux."

Sam sized up the Wayward, and then sniggered. "I like you," he declared.

"Glad to hear it," Baird mumbled.

"Know of any good clubs around here? We hit Sit Seven and Headway, but I'm thinking something with less trance music and more local flavor for tonight."

Alec glared at the man. "Sam."

"What? He's from around here. Good looking bloke. And Liam's right, you could pass for Original Vemreaux if it weren't for the smell. Have you tried cologne? Come on, Brody." He turned his attention to the other guard. "You telling me that's all you got in you?"

Brody shoved Sam. "You know I could've taken that Fem back to the hotel last night if I wasn't on duty. And you blocked me with the concierge, jerk."

"It's okay to be impotent, Brode," Sam kidded.

"Fifty bills says I land a hotter Fem than you at whatever club this Wayward picks for tonight," challenged Brody.

"Deal." Sam addressed Baird. "Alright, Wayward. Think. I need a club where the women appreciate men who can work with what little they've got. Give Brody a fighting chance."

Alec shook his head at Liam. "I used to guard your father, you know. Wasn't subjected to this kind of inane chatter. May need a flu shot to keep from vomiting."

"Staying in Capital City?" Baird asked curtly.

"Of course."

"Try Crowd. It's on 147th and Freedom Way. I hear the Femreaux aren't at all picky there. Wave your bills around, tell them you know a real, live celebrity. They'll come crawling. Plus, country music. Not trance."

Liam laughed. "Not country."

"And no more clubs," warned Alec. "I can't take anymore non-music."

Brody scratched his dirty blond hair. "Trance is music. Techno is music."

Alec frowned. "No, *music* is music, and I miss it. Raise your hand if you don't have a headache right now." He was satisfied to see no hands go up. "Then we go to a normal place tonight. A place with chairs and a reasonable amount of exits to keep an eye on." He crossed his arms over his chest. "Anyway, it doesn't matter what you all vote on, because I've got the keys, and I'm driving tonight."

"What?" Sam protested, sitting up.

"You drive like a lunatic."

"You drive like you're carrying a baby in the back seat."

"Not a baby, just a few grown-ass men who drink so much they almost throw up every time I turn a corner." Alec tapped his phone and stared down Liam. "Your father's team caught a few pictures online, and well, he's asked for you to tone it down."

"What for?" Liam whined. "It's not me what's next in line for the throne. Killian's on the straight and narrow now. I've agreed to no such thing."

"Father's orders," Alec sang, cracking a smile. "Chairs. Chairs and food. I'm tired of appetizers." He turned to Baird. "You said you work at a diner? Do you serve pancakes?"

Baird nodded and pulled out the order pad in his pocket and a pen. He scribbled down the address of the diner and handed it to Alec. "Chairs, food, and a jukebox from the 1980s. Plenty of women with low standards for them, as well. I'm the bartender, so stop by and I'll set you up with a few drinks. 'Bout twenty minutes outside Capital City. Enough out of the way that you won't be bothered by press following this one around." He glanced toward Liam, whose shockingly blue eyes stared into his.

"Perfect. Thank you. Reservations for four at eight."

"Yes," Sam deadpanned. "Thanks for the PG fun."

Baird rolled his eyes. "I'm sure you'll find a way to declass the joint."

Liam shook his head, and then regretted the painful action. "Not tonight. Not tomorrow, either. I got interviews tonight with Emperor Anders. Then all day golf with Emperor Cho tomorrow. Gotta at least pretend to look over the Wayward profiles they're gonna be testing."

Alec raised an eyebrow. "Two whole nights to recover from a hangover? This is a sign you should slow down, old man."

Liam snorted. "Look who's talking. You're like, a hundred or something."

"Actual reason we can't go to a real place tonight?" Alec asked.

"I'm meeting up with the redhead from that bar at some club tonight. I think it had fighting or fists in the name."

Baird spoke up when no one filled in the blanks. "Fisticuffs."

"Yeah. That one. Her tonight and that brunette tester. What's her name? Anyway, she's taking me out tomorrow night." When Alec glowered at him, Liam shrugged innocently. "What? I'm adorable." Then he ramped up his accent to the level of a caricature. "Plus, they love me accent here, mate."

Alec rolled his eyes and turned to Baird. "Fine. Reservations for four at eight on Friday, then."

"I'll be sure to roll out the red carpet for your monkey." Baird jerked his thumb in Liam's direction.

Liam laughed loudly, and then winced. "Hey, you're funny. Like I'm the monkey! I get it!" He grinned, happy to be in on the gag. "No one jokes about me like that to my face except this lot. Everyone's always so proper around me. You made my morning, mate."

He had not counted on being taken in by the prince's charm, but despite himself, Baird cracked a smile.

Jack reentered the room, chasing the levity from Baird's face. "Whoa," Liam commented, still smiling. "This one does *not* like you, Uncle Jack."

Jack did his best to keep a pleasant expression plastered in place. "Baird? Your brother's waiting in Holding Room Two."

Baird nodded to Liam as he moved toward the door.

Jack raised his hand to give him a paternal pat on the back, but Baird stopped to turn and glare at him, unleashing every bit of his most terrible intimidation on Jack. Jack's hand froze, not daring to touch the man who so obviously did not wish it.

"Good to s-see you, Baird," Jack said, his voice wavering under Baird's strength.

Baird did not respond, but nodded respectfully to the other Alpha male in the room, Alec, and exited down the hallway.

It was the same amount of time he'd spent with Griffin on his previous visits, but this one felt immeasurably longer. Baird remained impassive as he endured his younger brother's temper. Griffin was prone to fits. One of the many regrets Baird had in leaving The Way when he did was that he was not able to toughen the tantrums out of his brother.

Griffin's left eye was swollen shut from a yard fight that he insisted "was nothing like his fault." His good, cerulean eye leaked the occasional tear, which it always did when he got angry with Baird or Blue.

"You shouldn'ta taken her yet!" Griffin raged, revisiting his initial argument. He pounded his fist on the table with unnatural strength for a fifteen-year-old. "It's driving me crazy to be stuck in here when I know any minute she could be discovered or figure out her calling. I mean, '*end the tyranny*'? What does that actually mean? What tyranny are the Vemreaux even suffering from? And then what? She goes out, kills whatever the Vemreaux are so afraid of, and dies? That's a steaming pile of scratch, that is! And how can you stand for it? Don't you care about us?"

This was the part where Griffin took a long enough breath in hopes that Baird would chime in a plea for his pardon. How he wished he didn't need his brother's approval.

Instead Baird chose silence, as it suited him well for most occasions.

"I've still got almost four years left in here before I can be purchased. Four years! You think my sister's still gonna be alive when I get out?"

"I can't help that, Griffin. And it's closer to three years. You'll be sixteen in a couple months."

Griffin's nostrils flared as he wiped at his wet cheeks. The tip of his peaked ear turned pink with anger. "Bring her with you next time! Bring her here so I can at least see her before she dies! I need to know you haven't completely erased her. You with your lessons. She was funny when she left! She laughed a lot! How long till you groom that outta her? Bring her back here so I can make sure she's still her! You owe me at least that much."

I owe you? Baird argued silently. Of course, he said nothing, refusing to engage with a child in pointless arguments. Despite the fact that Griffin was the largest and most well-built Wayward in his year, and two years above him, Griffin would always be a child to the brother who raised him. Baird kept his face impassive and remained seated, arms crossed over his heart to make sure his brother's tears did not make their way into it.

"Any message you want me to give to her?" Baird asked, loathing the way his brother looked at him, a mixture of hatred and hurt.

"Yeah. Tell her that her older brother's an ass. A message," Griffin scoffed. "Anything I want to tell her, you'd never repeat. I'd tell her that it's not the same without her here. That I don't want to be the only one of us in The Way. That we kept each other sane, and now I don't have that! No one's here to calm me down. No one's out there to calm her down, either!"

"She's fine. She's got the girls."

"Bring her with you next time, Baird!"

Baird stared at his brother, stony faced. "Alright. I'll tell her you miss her."

"You're a terrible messenger. We both know you'll tell her whatever'll keep her under control. Your control." Griffin swore to himself that when he grew to be as big as Baird, he would not be as cold. They looked so alike, just separated by a few years of experience.

Griffin quieted, since his arguing was getting him nowhere. He swiped at his nose as he searched out any tells from his brother. "Is she happy?"

"Are any of us?" When this did not satisfy Griffin, Baird softened. "No. She's not happy with me right now. She wanted to come see you, but it wouldn't work with our job this time. She laughs a lot with the girls, who all miss you."

"They said that? They told you they miss me?"

Baird rolled his eyes. "Elle said to tell you that you're the hottest piece in your year, and she wishes she could be there to hit on you and make all the other girls your year jealous."

Griffin laughed whole-heartedly. Baird thought it looked good on him, and told himself that jocularity would not happen if the two men lived together.

"And Grettel? She still jumping at shadows?"

"Yeah. She told me to give you a hug from her." He looked to his kid brother awkwardly. "You can imagine one, can't you?"

Griffin scoffed. "Been a while, but yeah."

"How's George?"

"Like you care about my friends."

"How's the yard?"

Griffin pointed to his bruised eye. "Keeps me on my toes."

"Who did that to you?"

"Just some guys mouthing off about Blue again. Saying she was only picked for one thing." Griffin swallowed, looking like he might be sick. "Lotsa rumors going around about that, Baird. Promise me there's no truth to it. It's…just wondering about it's making me a little crazy."

Baird's eyes bored into Griffin. "I promise I will never let that happen to any of the girls in my care. The Vemreaux we work around generally don't pay attention to the wait staff. For the most part, they leave the girls alone. You don't have to worry about that, Griff. And you don't have to fight about it, either." He leaned forward. "Now tell me who blacked your eye."

"I broke his rib, so we're even."

"A name, Griffin."

"This time? Danyul got one over on me. But like I said, I broke his rib, so he knows he can't mess with me or talk about Blue like that. I got solitary for a day and a decent beating from Supervisor Tum, and he got the infirmary for a week. So, yeah. I won."

"Let them think whatever they want, Griff. Fact is, there *are* bad masters out there who do buy Wayward girls for one thing. Stories like that keep girls from signing their lives away on the dotted line when it comes to it."

"I won't let them talk about my sister like that. You should hear the things they say."

"I don't care what they say, and *you* should only care what *I* say." Baird took out a pen and spare bit of order paper from his pocket and scribbled "Danyul" on it, then drew a thin, ominous line through the center of the name. He'd used this signal to Marxus on more occasions than he would have liked. "Give this to Marxus from me. He'll take care of it."

Griffin refused to touch the paper. "I can take care of things myself. It was just a yard fight. I'm Marxus' second, now." Griffin dared Baird with his eyes to object to the new regime. "Like I said, I laid Danyul out. He won't be a problem anymore."

"That black eye reads like weakness, Griff. The others'll spot it and pounce. Won't matter you won one fight. Another'll find you."

"I'm not having him killed, Baird. It's a stupid yard fight. I'm not like you."

"No." Baird shook his head disapprovingly as he stood. "You're not. Take care of yourself, Griff. I'll be back in a month."

"Promise me you'll bring her next time?"

"If I can."

The two did not hug or shake hands; they never did on these visits. Baird swallowed the advice he wanted to give, and Griffin choked down his need for approval. The two communicated all this through a single parting look before Baird left the holding room.

11

A BRIEF HISTORY

"Are you sure you're okay?" Blue asked Grettel for the fifth time that morning. The kitchen was humming with the various machines and simmering that was going on, but Grettel was a shadow, cloaked in fear.

"I'm okay," she replied as she reached for a heavy stock pot.

"Let me," Blue offered, lifting the pot with ease and pushing it onto the burner, noticing that Grettel flinched. "I know I freaked you out with the whole knife thing. I'm sorry."

Grettel put on a meek smile. "You said that already. There's nothing to apologize to *me* for. You didn't do anything to *me*," she hinted.

Elle sauntered in and flopped onto the only stool gracelessly. "That girl reading the poem is terrible. So boring. And she actually clicked her fingers at me like I'm her pet or something. You mind waiting on the table for a bit, Blue? There's nothing to do, and I'm tired. Would you miss me too badly if I took a little nap back here?"

"Go for it," Blue agreed, still feeling guilty. "And I'm sorry for waking you guys up like that. I shouldn'ta lost my temper."

"Make it up to me by letting me sleep till we're open for real."

"Done."

Blue picked up a water pitcher and entered the dining area behind Elle, the blonde's million kilowatt smile ever at the ready. "Hello, gentlemen. This is Blue, and she'll be taking over for a while. Blue, this is the Mayor of Capital City, David Anders," she motioned to a Vemreaux in a gray suit. "Then the Dean of Students at Capital University, Professor Standwicke Anders."

The sandy-haired man smiled at the new waitress who hid behind her hair.

Elle introduced her to the rest of the table, which consisted of the Assistant to the American Emperor, the head of the Non-Profits of America Group, the Peace Week Coordinator, and Lawrence, who was the leader of the Businesses of Capital City Committee.

Tables had been cleared away so the theatre troupe could have the space to perform for the Peace Week Committee. Blue refilled their water glasses and took inventory of the table. Six men sat, displaying varying degrees of interest in the show.

"Poem's fine, Beth," the mayor insisted when the actress asked for their opinion.

"Thank you, Mayor David," Beth cooed as she checked her itinerary. All the actors wore a different color scarf, except for Beth, who donned a red brooch on her low-cut black top, marking her as the leader. "English playwright John Bailey wrote *A Bloodthirsty Conqueror and a Peace-Loving Blood Drinker*. His account of Francis David Vemreaux's split from the greedy Juan Ponce de León is one of the scenes our troupe will be performing on the main stage at the Peace Day festivities."

The Assistant to the American Emperor looked mildly impressed as he speared a forkful of haggis. "Can't say no to a skit honoring our founding father."

Lawrence spoke for the group. "That's fine, Beth. It's all fine. You guys want something to eat or drink before you carry on?"

Beth looked to the petite waitress and snapped her fingers twice.

"May I help you?" Blue asked. She tilted her head forward, obscuring her eyes with her hair.

"I should hope so. I'll take your most aged meat with the foulest smelling sauce you have. Anything that would kill an *A*-word," Beth instructed, nose in the air.

Pink Scarf and Purple Scarf gave the cocky Fem disapproving looks, but said nothing.

"Now, now," Professor Standwicke protested, his eyes taking in the young waitress' submissive stance. "There's no need to speak to her like that."

Lawrence's fist gripped his fork more tightly. "I'll thank you not to use that kind of language, Beth. We haven't given you the green light, yet. Peace Week's about harmony, not bigotry."

Beth shut her mouth tight, ignoring the frustrated looks her group shot her. The men in the troupe placed their requests more respectfully, given Lawrence's glower.

Blue left quickly to put in the orders. The kitchen door swung shut behind her, giving her new freedom to breathe. "Hey Grettel, do people call us *A*-words a lot? Or is it just the ones who want their food sneezed on?" Blue handed the order sheet to the girl.

Grettel smiled. The thought of such a devious act was so unbelievably delicious, the mere prospect scared her. "Not all the time, but I've heard it from the ones you'd expect. It's not a nice word. The good Vemreaux don't talk like that."

"That's what I thought." Blue pressed her ear to the door, and could hear the rehearsal picking back up. She knew Baird would not approve of her being so visible, but her brother was kilometers away. Blue exited the kitchen and plastered herself to the wall inconspicuously to find out what the actors had yet to say about the world she still knew so little about.

Beth twirled a lock of black hair on the end of her red-painted fingernail as she began her speech, using it to hone in the men's attention. "After World War Three, when those ruling the world unleashed dozens of nuclear bombs at each other, destroying the lands they so viciously fought to protect, the increasing number of Vemreaux decided to reveal themselves. The Middle East, much of Asia, Central and North America had been decimated overnight.

Asia endured significant land damage that still has not been smoothed over in rural areas."

The Assistant to the American Emperor interrupted Beth with a raised finger. "Please strike that last sentence from the speech. I'm fairly certain that King Sinclair will not want mention of any lack of progress."

Beth nodded and continued. "Much of the land that was historically fit for inhabiting was permanently damaged with radiation from the blasts. Homes were lost, family lines ended. It was no wonder the inferior blood types didn't put up much of a fight when we came into power. The rulers who commanded the launch of these horrendous bombs were quickly slaughtered."

The assistant raised his finger again, this time earning a frown from Beth. "Slaughtered implies that we were inhumane or acted in a way that was not to keep the greater peace. Can we agree on 'disposed of'?"

Beth nodded, making a note. "Most of the countries in the world were in disarray and in desperate need of order and an honest face to look up to. The Vemreaux gave them that. Politicians used to be untrustworthy. Now we all love our leaders." She beamed at the mayor and the emperor's assistant.

Blue felt like vomiting. Or laughing. She couldn't decide which.

Daniel stood next to Beth and joined in. "Automatic weapons were immediately destroyed. Bombs and all the guns in the world were sought out with our keen senses and immediately done away with."

Beth brought the focus back to her, annoyed at having to split the attention. "The number of our superior race was such that we now possessed the power to corral all humans of inferior blood types into prison camps, so they could pay for their war crimes. That's when King Sinclair and his team of scientists discovered that filtered O-type blood could stave off anemia in the changed Vemreaux. The O-blood types' payment for having their basic necessities met is a reasonable donation of half a pint of blood every eight weeks. The work camps became happy places of education and personal fulfillment, most people volunteering to lock themselves in there for the promise of food, water, shelter and a life away from war and radiation. The O-bloods who refused to leave their war-torn homes were killed and used to feed the need of the Vemreaux. Their blood was filtered and dispersed to the war heroes."

"Strike that whole last part from the speech," the assistant instructed. "No need to dwell on unpleasantness at a worldwide celebration. And they're not prison camps. They're schools. Big difference, young lady."

Blue soaked in every syllable, memorizing how the Vemreaux rationalized their own war crimes to themselves. She did not even realize that her feet carried her slowly closer to the action.

Beth droned on. "A-blood types were separated from the other mortals and placed in areas that would later be called The Way. The superior Vemreaux could have done away with the useless blood type altogether, as we had when we purged out the rarer types that held less ability to quench our thirst for iron. However, we pride ourselves on being fairer than the mixed bloods that ran governments before we came to power, so even though their blood makes us ill, the A-bloods were permitted life, just like the other inferior O-types. They serve their purpose by providing cheap labor and the occasional human test subjects that are always filled with volunteers."

Lawrence gestured to Beth with his mug of coffee. "You give that long of a speech without mention of the predator, people'll boo you off the stage. I don't care how short you wear your skirt."

Beth rolled her eyes. "That's all anyone wants to talk about anymore."

Pink Scarf took his index fingers and put them to his lips like fangs and hissed, earning a disapproving scowl from Beth.

Daniel's part of the speech meant that Beth had to stand there patiently and wait, which she could not do without conveying her annoyance. She puffed out her cleavage to silently take back some of the attention.

Daniel projected his voice without having to command it to do so.

"Beginning its plot of terror, the predator began stealthily snatching a few of the local Vemreaux, but not returning them for months. The deaths were first listed as missing person's reports, but then their bodies were discovered later with vital organs gone, skin torn to shreds or removed, and their bodies drained of blood. The numbers are still increasing. Though the *O*-blood island contains many smaller vacation islands famed for their beauty, tourism has slowed to the area. None have seen the predator with their own eyes and lived to tell the tale."

"I don't like where this is going," Mayor David protested. "This is supposed to be a celebration of our history, not a time to scare people. Give them a day without the predator splashing the headlines."

"No predator talk at all? That seems disingenuous. It's all people gossip about these days," commented Lawrence.

"Fine, but shorten it a bit. I don't want to hear about filleted bodies while I'm drinking my martini, and I'm guessing I won't be the only one."

Daniel nodded while Beth scowled. His male voice carried through the quiet establishment, captivating Blue and the diners. "More than a decade ago, a Vemreaux named Hank Manneclaken Cho readied himself to go into the everlasting waters. When Hank came out of the Fountain of Youth with his twelve decade life extension, it was not with the same black eyes and heightened senses we all enjoy. He was struck with blindness when his foot left the waters. His green eyes turned to the beloved Lucinda Vemreaux's vivid blue as others watched him in horror fumble around for a writing implement and scrawl on the nearest wall."

Blue's heart dropped into her stomach, as it often did when people quoted the prophecy around her. The tiny hairs on her arms rose to attention as she stood unnaturally still and straight.

Pink Scarf lurked at Daniel's side, breaking out his theatrically deep voice and rolling his eyes back as if he was possessed. "*There is a Light born who will put an end to the tyranny. The Light will not rest until the world has been brought to peace. The Vemreaux will bow before the*

Wayward who leads them into battle for the sake of harmony. She will strike down the predator and make the ultimate sacrifice."

And there it was. Blue swallowed hard. The bitterness of the prophecy brought a bad taste to her mouth and threatened to choke the life from her. She shouldered the gall with grace, standing in the background as they unknowingly talked about her.

Beth shoved Pink Scarf and resumed the speech, which was now beginning to lose the attention of the important men. "As soon as he finished writing on the wall, Hank's eyes immediately turned to black. His sight came back to him, but he was unaware of his actions that produced what would now be the prophecy all Vemreaux hang their hopes on. It was said that Hank was blessed with the spirit of Francis David Vemreaux's now deceased wife, Lucinda, who lived out her days in blindness even after her blue eyes turned to black." She still held Blue's attention, demonstrated by the gasp that the waitress emitted at Beth's words.

Mayor David Anders stood, drawing the attention of the thespians. "That's why Peace Day is that much more important this year. The parades in the past have sometimes lasted for days, bringing out the crowds like nothing else can. Add finding the Light to that, and you've got yourself a party that'll last maybe weeks."

Lawrence nodded. "Lot of businesses around here need that kind of boost."

Mayor David agreed. "It would really help my approval ratings to find the Light on my watch. The Way West guaranteed me five decent candidates from their facility. Testing's starting tomorrow."

Professor Standwicke looked up from the worn textbooks that captured his attention several minutes ago. "I thought that was happening Friday."

"No element of surprise if the Light has time to prepare. The real Light should be ready at a moment's notice if she's to go up against the predator."

Blue swallowed and took a meek step back, dipping her chin again to obscure her face. She was always ready to fulfill her destiny, but would never be ready at the same time. Even as she served the actors their meals, her mind did not wander from the testing other Wayward girls would be subjected to because she could not come forward. She was nearly invisible to the diners, which was exactly how she knew Baird preferred it.

The one patron who did notice her motioned her to his side. Professor Leander Standwicke Anders scarcely had room for his plate with all the textbooks that surrounded him. "Would you mind giving me a hand with some of these? It looks like we're just about out of time, and I'd like to spread these on a table, if I could."

"Yes, sir, professor." Blue gingerly lifted the large stack of books, thrilling at how close she was to the new knowledge. She wondered why the books were so thick, and what undiscovered treasures could possibly be hiding inside.

"Stand. I go by Stand. Leander Standwicke Anders is a mouthful."

"Yes, sir, Professor Stand."

"Now, it's just us here. I don't know about you, but all this 'sir' nonsense that some Vemreaux require doesn't work for me. How about I call you..." He looked at her nametag. "Blue? Is that right? And you call me Stand." He hoped to get some sort of a reaction, but she merely nodded. He'd never intimidated anyone before. The very notion made Stand uncomfortable. When this particular Vemreaux was nervous, he found it impossible to keep his mouth from running.

Blue stood silently, staring at her feet as he told her the history of the University down to the moldings, listed each of the school's presidents that he'd taught under, his favorite subjects to teach, and a few memorable students. He laughed to himself at one particular story that had a newly changed Vemreaux running around to seven different classrooms until he sat down in Stand's Logic class, only to stand up an hour into the session and ask in a confused voice, "This isn't Biology?" Blue found the story amusing, but she would not offer up more than a simple smile, which he could not see through her thick hair.

"Did you catch the speeches and the play?" he asked, realizing that the woman had been completely silent for five minutes.

Blue nodded.

"It's a lot to take in."

She made sure her stance was perfectly submissive.

"I imagine that's a lot more detail than you got in The Way. Do you have any questions? Sit down, please."

Blue shook her head silently, wondering why the professor was being so nice. The tall, light-haired Vemreaux had a studious build to him that suggested book study as opposed to outdoor sports. He'd chosen to be frozen at thirty, which made him look far more experienced than she.

Her gaze lifted to the half dozen books he had stacked up on the table. She debated the wisdom of lingering out in the open with a diner, but they were largely ignored by the other men, who were still discussing the details of Beth's speech. She'd witnessed Elle sitting with a table occasionally, laughing and joking with her sparkle that was always on. Blue didn't see any real harm in permitting a one-way conversation with the nice man.

Stand motioned to the books. "I'm also the head of the Math department, and we're getting new curricula in for a few of the classes. I'm reviewing some of the old textbooks to see if any are still usable with the new lesson plans." He took in her timid demeanor and softened further, smile faltering at her training. "Are you a student at the University?"

Blue's brow furrowed. "No, professor, sir. I'm Wayward."

"Then you don't have to call me 'professor'. I'm just Stand here." He sipped his water carefully. "And being Wayward doesn't mean that you can't attend University."

Blue raised her eyebrow as he set his glass down. "How many Waywards are enrolled?"

Stand chuckled. "She speaks!" he exclaimed, but immediately regretted it. He watched her wince and bury her face behind her hair even more. "You got me there. We don't have any yet, but it's still open to anyone. Do you want to go to University?"

Blue had never been asked that question before. His words

pounded around inside of her until she forced them to quiet. "I was bought for the diner. I'm a waitress, sir."

"Stand," he corrected. "And please sit. Unless you have something else to do. Keep an old man company for a minute."

Blue looked around, making sure absolutely nothing needed to be tended to. Drinks were all full, the Vemreaux were barely beginning their meals, and the rest of the diner was ready for the day's crowd. The real kicker was that Baird was still gone. She knew he would not approve of her silently sinking down into the chair opposite Stand, but she did so anyway, relishing the rush of rebellion.

"Thank you." Stand looked relieved to have drawn her so thoroughly in. "And we have plenty of waitresses who attend. You're presuming that cleaning up and feeding people isn't as important as being a student, but I highly disagree. Without a tidy space, learning is difficult. Cleaning is the precursor to learning for a lot of people. What you're doing is, to some, more important than how many times I go over my notes that I've taught twelve times already."

"Are you seriously telling me that taking out the trash is more important than knowledge?"

Stand's obsidian eyes sparked with the thrill of a new debate. He further pushed his opinion about the nobility of taking pride in a clean building, but Blue was not convinced.

"Well," she responded, realizing she'd been baited into having a conversation with the Vemreaux, "no one's gonna give you a diploma for serving drinks."

"Is that what you want, Blue?" His voice softened as her name rolled through his lips. "Do you want to earn a diploma?"

Her brow furrowed, the questions confusing her. "I didn't say anything like that. I'm *A*-blood. I'm not going to go to a Vemreaux school."

"People fear possibilities more than impossibilities. Possibility means there's something to be risked. Impossibility means it's not their fault things never change."

The words hung in the air between them.

"Your owner can't forbid you from going to school, Blue. It's against the law. Emperor Anders is a good leader. His rules make more possibilities for *A*-bloods." Blue did not respond, so Stand continued. "My father told me that if I wanted to go to school, I'd have to get a job and pay for it myself. When I was nineteen, that seemed impossible, but I got a job and slowly chipped away at an education." He paused solemnly. "This diner isn't all the real world has to offer."

"I thought you said waitressing was noble work." The corner of Blue's mouth lifted when he didn't have an immediate response.

Caught in his own logic, Stand put his hands up in surrender. "You got me," he admitted.

His need for her to look at him was so obvious that Blue almost lifted her head to acknowledge him, but thought better of it. She was there to work, not to make friends. Stand was making it difficult to be invisible, and if she paid him more attention, she was sure others would take notice of her presence, as well.

"So how do you like working at Joe's?" he asked, hoping a change of topic to a lighter subject would loosen her up.

She shrugged. "S'okay." Her generic answer was multi-purpose and applied to almost anything. She used the succinct response whenever possible.

Her brief answers did not deter conversation as she intended, but rather spurred on Stand's verbose nature. "It must be nice to work with your brother."

"How'd you know Baird's my brother?" she questioned cautiously.

"I come in here every now and then. Baird runs a good restaurant. Asked him who he was getting to replace Valerie, and he said his master was buying his sister."

"Oh."

"So are you glad you get to work with him?"

"S'okay."

"I have three sisters, all older. You wouldn't know it to look at me, but I'm the baby of the family. We're all blonds, not with pretty hair like yours."

Blue hid her grimace at his compliment. No one referred to her as pretty except for Elle and Grettel, and she was positive they only said those nice things to be kind. Blue judged that Stand must also be unnecessarily sweet to the point of fibbing.

Stand chatted on about his family unit, and Blue learned that his parents divorced forty years ago, but remarried recently. This time they opted for a five-year marriage instead of the traditional kind. His sisters were all married, but he was, as he put it, the "eternal bachelor".

His family story lasted until it was nearly time to open the diner. By the time she pushed back her chair to stand, Blue realized she'd participated in an actual conversation with a Vemreaux that went beyond regular dining basics. "I've got to get back to work."

"Thank you for keeping me company. Best conversation I've had in a while."

Blue did not correct him with the fact that he'd done most of the talking. "I'll get you some more water."

"Would you mind taking this book for me?" Stand suddenly recalled that he had an entire plate of nearly untouched food before him.

"Yes, sir."

"Stand," he corrected.

"Yes, Stand," she amended. "I can hold it in the kitchen for you until you're done."

"Oh, no. I mean throw it out. It's much too old for use."

Blue froze. "Throw it out? Like, in the trash can?"

"You can always recycle."

Blue bit her lip as she gathered the text to her. Even though it was being discarded, Baird might view it as stealing if she did not ask for permission. She stood uncomfortably, looking down at the book in her arms and hoping the right words would come to her. "Um, I um, would it be against the rules if I, um, read through it before throwing it away?" The moment the words were out of her mouth, her eyes darted around to make sure no one else heard her indiscretion.

Hope welled in Stand's black eyes. "Of course, I wouldn't mind. Keep it as long as you'd like."

"You won't get in any trouble?"

"I am the only one who will scold myself. I should be giving you new books, not second-hand ones like that. The cover's barely holding on."

Blue's voice was small. "I really...I get to read all this? As much as I want?"

Stand's breath caught behind his Adam's apple when she lifted her chin and gave him a genuine, no-holds-barred smile. He immediately chastised himself for the attraction that swelled. He nodded, recalling the decades of age difference between them that, to her race, would certainly matter. Big, beautiful blue orbs sparkled, tying his tongue as he became entranced by her gaze.

Unable to contain her enthusiasm, Blue carefully opened up the first page, the second and then the third, finally getting past the beginning, and at last reaching the content. She could add, subtract, multiply, divide, and figure percentages, but not much else was taught in The Way beyond the basic skills.

Once more she looked up at Stand and chose to allow a measure of emotion to come forth from her. Gratefulness wrapped around her tongue as she spoke quietly. "Thank you! I've never owned a book before."

Hand flying up to his chest, Stand grasped the fabric there as though he was trying to slow the engorging of his heart. He wanted to reach out and touch her shoulder, but knew how inappropriate that would be. The logic still left in his brain screamed out at him. The innocence of her deep eyes was overwhelming.

"I'll go one better," he offered, lecturing himself silently at his gumption. "If you want, I'll teach you what's inside."

Her stunning eyes expanded into saucers as they stared at him. "Thank you!" Her face gave way to an unbridled grin. "Really? You'll teach me how to learn Vemreaux math?" The captivating and rare public smile fell as quickly as it came. "But Stand, I can't pay you. You should be paid for teaching someone."

It was his turn to avoid her eyes as he averted his attention to the texts left on the table. "I don't just teach when I'm on the clock, you know. I can't help myself. Besides, I teach logic now, mostly. It's been decades since I picked up a math book. I may not be all that great a teacher." He paused. "Do you want my help?" He forced his voice to be casual, as if it truly did not matter to him when or if they did this.

"Of course!" she exclaimed at the ridiculous question. "I didn't even know there was more math I *could* learn."

This earned an incredulous look from the professor. "Are you serious?"

It was the wrong thing to say, for her chin dropped and her eyes hid behind her hair purposefully. "I can only be expected to know what they tell us, Stand. If they don't offer it in The Way, chances are I've never heard of it."

"I was planning on stopping by the diner tomorrow afternoon between my classes. I have a little break midday." Stand wished Blue would look up at him. "Start with chapter one. That's Geometry you have there, and it might get a little confusing. If you have any questions, write them down and I'll help you go over them while I have my lunch. Can you take your break then?" He chided himself for being so obvious.

"Sure. But do you really want to teach on your break from teaching? You don't have to, you know. I'm sure I can figure it out."

He smiled, but he did not think she saw it with her humble posture. "I'm sure you can, but I really don't mind. I eat by myself most days. It'd be nice to have the company."

The kitchen door swung open, distracting Blue and reminding her of the time. She excused herself, and rose up out of her chair at the sight of her best friend moving to open the front door.

Seventeen diners were waiting outside, ready for lunch. Blue shot her friend an apologetic smile, which Elle waved off. The girls sat the hungry patrons, took drink orders and met back in the kitchen.

"So, I saw you talking with Stand. Isn't he nice?" Elle tried to conceal her hinting.

"Yup," Blue responded succinctly. "Busy day today. When do you think Baird'll come back?"

Elle shrugged and called over the stove to Grettel. "You ready for a mad rush, pixie?"

Grettel gave a quaking thumbs-up that did little to reassure the girls.

Tray assembled with the necessary drinks, Blue dipped her chin and started taking orders.

"You must be Baird's new girl. Goodness, you're young." The Femreaux at her second table smiled, eyeing her youthful features. Blue did not miss that the diner referred to the place as Baird's and not Joe's, even though it's was Joe's name on her shirt and on the sign outside. She wondered if all the patrons felt this way and how many of them had ever met Joe. "Has Valerie popped yet?"

"No, she's taking some time off before her baby comes, ma'am. I was bought to replace her." Blue tilted her head downward submissively so that her hair covered most of her face.

The Femreaux turned her onyx eyes to her husband's. "She'd better have that baby soon. Her trip to the Fountain's coming up, and beautification won't be quick after what she put her body through. Such a waste. Why doesn't she just hire a surrogate from the blood farm? Hope that baby's worth it," the Femreaux commented as though she meant to say it under her breath, but put a bit too much volume behind it to keep her words private.

Most of the conversation was easy enough for Blue to understand, and she responded with a polite smile. She worried that she would not know how to keep up with current affairs, since she was so sheltered in The Way. "Can I take your order, ma'am?" Blue prodded. She hated speaking obvious statements. They knew what she was there for; she shouldn't have to say it.

"Sure." The Femreaux glanced at the menu, even though she knew what she wanted.

Blue did not understand why people did that, either. *After making a decision, why not stick with it? Does she expect something else to magically appear on the laminated pages?*

"I'll have the soured pork roast with vinegared mashed potatoes instead of fries. Does that also come with pickled trout slaw?" she asked, glancing over the menu again to see if she missed a clue somewhere.

"It comes as a separate side if you order potatoes, ma'am." The Fem nodded. "Sir?" Blue asked the Vemreaux who looked more bored than anything else. Perhaps they came here a bit too often.

"I didn't see Baird at the bar. Is it open yet?" Taking in Blue's youth, he added a justification to his companion and the waitress. "Peace Day isn't until next week, but there's no harm in starting the celebration early." His face looked like it had a sheen of wax covering it. His lips were unnaturally peaked.

"Bar's not open yet. Can I get you something to eat, sir?"

"Just some scrambled three-month eggs and a Green Abby when he starts making 'em." He thwapped his menu down on the table to signify that he was finished ordering.

His Femreaux took a loud slurp from her blood shake and shot him a condescending look. "Honey, don't you think it's a little early to start with that? It's not even noon." She glanced up at Blue for some female camaraderie as though the waitress should lecture her husband on the social faux-pas of the day.

Blue's chin remained down, either focused on her order pad or on the ground respectfully. She swept up the menus and hurried with her chin angled to the ground to the next table and the next. She sat two more tables in her section before walking back to the kitchen and slapping the order forms in the middle of one of the counters for Grettel to tend to.

Grettel poked her head up and gave Blue an encouraging smile. Blue returned it, then surreptitiously flipped open the Geometry book and scanned the first two pages of chapter one, breathing deeply through the rapid processing her brain was performing. It attempted to catch up and catalog the problems, plus all the events of the day, in an order to best serve easy retrieval.

Elle came to stand next to her friend, affectionately knocking her shoulder against Blue's slightly shorter one. "Not so different than

The Way's cafeteria, right? Just a little more frozen faces here." She pulled her face so it looked unnaturally lifted. "Did you see the wax face at table number seven? Yikes. Hate to be stuck with that mug for a hundred twenty years. Gotta wonder how bad the original was."

Before Blue could respond, Elle whistled. "Oo! Where'd you get that?" she asked, leaning over the book curiously.

"Stand was going to throw it out, so I asked if I could keep it."

Elle pressed her finger to her mouth in mock thought. "Hmm. I wonder if your brother'll have a ridiculous problem with that."

12

THE BOOK

Age of Peace Law 27, Subset 3a
Government-owned buildings such as libraries, hospitals, and town halls
are open to Vemreaux and freed Waywards. Owned Waywards are not
citizens, and therefore, are not permitted access, unless escorted by their
master.

"*A* book?" Baird stormed predictably when he saw the treasure his sister was clutching to her chest as he entered the kitchen that afternoon. "Where did you get that, Blue?"

"Stand said I could have it!" she protested. Blue unhappily surrendered the worn hardback to him when he made a grab for it.

"Oh, so now it's good ole' *Stand*, is it? What happened to giving him respect by calling him by his full name? Professor Standwicke too much of a mouthful for you? You two old friends now?" He flipped back the cover and leafed through the pages. "And you can't just take books from a college. You have to pay for them. I thought you wanted to save up with us and pool our money to buy your brother. Is this your grand plan? To waste your money on books and let Griffin rot in The Way until he's sixty?" Grettel shot him a disapproving look, which he chose to ignore. "Did you steal this?"

"No!" she cried, her volume matching his. His head shot up at her insurrection. Immediately she lowered her voice. "Professor Standwicke wanted me to throw it away. I asked him if I could keep it, and he said yes. He even offered to help me learn it all."

Baird had no response to this, but he still searched for a reason to be right.

Elle stood next to Blue to unite herself with the girl, her morning nap reviving her sharp tongue. "I can't believe you just said that to her. How much more do we have to sacrifice for you to be satisfied? You won't even let her own trash?" She shook her head at the man, who she could tell realized that he was quickly losing the argument. "Go take your anger out on a squirrel or something. Leave your sister alone."

The object of much distress felt heavy in his hands. "Fine! Just don't let your reading get in the way of work. I don't know if you've noticed, but we're getting slammed out there."

"When's the help coming that you called Master Joe for? I thought you were going to get us an extra body on the floor this close to Peace Week."

"I don't know what to tell you, Elle. The new waitress should be here already." He turned his attention to Grettel, who was struggling with a pot a third of her size. "What'd I tell you about this pot? Let me lift the big ones."

Grettel shied away from his reach, surrendering the vessel with a miniscule squeak.

Baird's countenance darkened when he realized he was not forgiven for the altercation that morning. He ignored Grettel's fear, hoping it would dissipate. "So what is Geometry, anyway?"

Elle laughed, which only brought back the scowl the man had been nursing for most of the morning. "You don't even know what it is, but you forbade it? Ladies, I give you our fearless leader." She lifted her hands and clapped in false appreciation.

"What?" He jutted his chin out to the mocking blonde, defending his ignorance. "I know it's some kind of math."

Blue did her best to explain what little she understood from the few minutes she'd been permitted to actually flip through the book. "I don't know yet. It looks like putting numbers to angles and pictures so you can make them more perfectly."

Baird scoffed. "Vemreaux are useless. They go to school to learn how to draw a line correctly?"

"It's more than that. I'm just not good at explaining what I haven't really studied." Blue sucked in her lower lip before she spoke again. "Professor Standwicke said that he would help me through the book. Would you mind if I took a break tomorrow when he comes in? It'll be a short one."

Baird's hesitation made Elle turn to the man murderously. "Oh, give the girl a break. You know she's allowed to take a lunch, Baird. It's not like she's gonna go out drinking with the Vemreaux or something. She's taking a short break at our slowest time of the day to study. Quit being so controlling."

"If you can find time for it, then fine. But work comes first, you hear me?" He reminded her of this as if she was the irresponsible type that needed the extra instruction.

Sometimes Blue got the feeling that he just wanted someone to fight with. She was glad Elle took his grumblings as a coded form of foreplay and didn't mind them so much.

"Nights are only gonna get busier, so I need you all on your game." When Blue shot him a look that suggested he was underestimating her, he explained further. "The dignitaries and heads of military are all coming to Capital City in the next few nights with their entourages. The bar's gonna be packed, so no Geometry at night."

"Okay, Baird," Blue conceded before Elle could start up again.

"Wow, are you two psychically seating people now?" he asked, motioning toward the door.

Elle wanted to argue, but Baird was right. The line at the hostess stand kept growing, and no matter how fast the girls were, and how many tables they turned over, they could barely keep up.

An hour later when the tension between the four dissipated, Elle stalked into the kitchen and thwapped her tray on the counter irritably. "Where is that third waitress? You have to tell Master Joe to find a third person to hostess, at least. I know you don't like complaining to your master, Baird, but I don't care!" Before he could respond, she hurried on. "Between Blue and I, I'm pretty sure we can keep the customers happy. We just can't take the time to seat everyone and bus tables in between."

"Elle, I don't think..." Baird began with his token amount of resistance.

"I'm not asking you to think, Baird. I'm telling you I'm going to hit my limit mid-shift. Is that what you want?"

"So feisty," he commented with a small smirk. Baird sighed. "Fine."

"I don't see you calling him," Elle complained, tapping her foot impatiently.

"I talked to him half an hour ago. He's sending help tomorrow. Something about getting the dates confused."

Elle swore, and for a second, Baird was sure she was going to pick up her tray and throw it at him.

RESPONSIBLE LIAM

"Ronald Cho? That guy is such a snore!" Liam complained. "Why can't we go swimming? That blonde from last night invited me to some lake with her friends."

Alec took a breath and tried to count to ten, but only made it to four as he moved the vehicle to the left lane. "First of all, 'that blonde' isn't all that descriptive. You made out with three last night. And 'some lake'? Which one would that be?" He shook his head, trying to keep his irritation at bay. It was only ten in the morning. He'd have to ration out his frustration if he wanted to make it through the whole day without snapping. "And the owner of Amsteron is an important man that your father wants you to spend some time with. Build relations."

"Not exactly the kind of relations I was hoping to have while on holiday," Liam groaned. "I couldn't have been more clear when I told Dad that I didn't want to become emperor after him. That's Killy's job. I belong at the lake."

"And which lake is that?"

"Quit being a smart alec, Alec." Liam chuckled at his own joke. "Get it? Because your name's Alec! I can't believe I never thought of that one before."

"Hilarious. Frederick knows that you want to waste your life on booze and women, and he's made his peace with it. However, he asked you to do him a favor and keep things good between the royal family and one of the most powerful non-royals in the world. Since you're both in town for the testing, you get to entertain him for the afternoon."

"Ronald's so boring, though! I doubt he's ever had an original thought. Everything he says sounds like a regurgitation of the King. So, yeah, he's powerful, but it's all good investments and business sense. He has zero people skills."

Alec couldn't argue. He'd had the misfortune of sitting in on about a dozen too many meetings with the man. It was rare that he made it through without yawning. "You could always bring up the subject of his cats. He loves talking about those. Probably has lots of original thoughts involving them. What's he up to now, eight?"

"Oh, man! Alec, if he starts talking about his cats again, I'm bailing. I can't take it."

"You're not bailing. You're spending a couple hours working. It won't kill you. Did you know that your brother doesn't even want to celebrate his birthday this year? He scheduled meetings all day long. I wouldn't complain about a business lunch."

Liam's brow furrowed. "What? That's not right." He pulled his phone out of his pocket and pressed the fourth speed dial. "Killian? What's this about you not celebrating your birthday this year?"

Killian's voice came through with a note of surprise. "Good evening to you, too, Li."

"Evening? I call too late? What time is it there?"

"Only six. I'm on my way to meet with Harold, though. What's going on?"

"Alec said you're not doing anything for your birthday. Please tell me that's not true. Tell me there's something left of the brother who broke into the school in the middle of the night to throw me the best sixteenth birthday bash ever. Took them forever to get that desk out of the tree!"

Liam could hear the smile in Killian's voice. "Well, that brother got suspended, and read the riot act by Josephine. And it's not like I did it alone. It was Sam's idea." Killian's levity died when he mentioned his former best friend's name. "I don't really feel like celebrating my birthday this year."

Liam gave the pause that lingered its proper respect before continuing. "You never feel like celebrating anymore. I don't like how all about work you are, Kill. It's not right. When are you going to have any fun?"

"Fun?" Liam heard Killian take a bite of something and continue speaking with a mouthful of food. "Who says my life isn't fun? I get to sit down with Harold as soon as Isaac drives me home, and get briefed about Amsteron's proposal to move the O-blood facility to Asia. See? I get to talk about Amsteron while you're meeting with the head of Amsteron. It's almost like we're hanging out, Li. I can feel the fun already."

Liam sighed. "No, you can't. You haven't been fun since you and Sam...broke up?" He couldn't think of the right words.

Killian laughed, choking on his sandwich. "Jeez, Liam. Sam wasn't my boyfriend. It's okay that people stop being mates. It happens. Besides, now you two hang out more. He's a much better fit for you, anyway. We got into way too much trouble."

"I wish it could be how it was."

Killian's voice sobered. "Well, it can't. I made my bed, now let me lie in it. I don't mind working on my birthday, Liam. After the change, they all sort of run together anyway. You'll see. It's just another day."

"Please, Kill. Please do something fun. I'm stuck over here, and can't take you out to celebrate properly."

"I love that your definition of 'proper' probably includes strippers or clowns and massive amounts of liquor."

"Well, liquor's required when you set out to watch a striptease put on by a brothel of clowns."

"Yikes. Now that's in my head."

"Sorry. I'll fix it. You think Harold would make a good clown stripper? You think Isaac's got a few loose bills on him to wave around and make Dad's royal advisor dance?"

Killian laughed again, and Liam could tell his brother hadn't participated in such cheekiness in a while. "Man! America's a lucky country to get your humor for a few weeks."

"Yes, and it's wasted on Ronald Cho and his cats." Liam fiddled with his seatbelt. "Killian, please do something fun for your birthday."

"I'll think about it. Everest called me yesterday and invited me to his new island. Thought I'd fallen off his radar."

Liam smiled. "I thought you didn't party anymore."

"I don't, but there aren't any cameras on his off-island. Honestly, I could use a break from campaigning. I don't know how Dad keeps up."

"Good! Do it! Go see Ever, and he'll fix you up. Just don't drink anything without a sealed cap."

Killian chuckled. "I won't. I actually kinda miss Ever. Haven't seen him in a while. Said he needed me to come rescue him from his father. He was all theatrical. Kinda funny."

Liam grinned, glad to hear a little life in his older brother's voice. "Run, Killy! Run! Go hang with E for your birthday. Take that fiancée of yours with you and go topless surfing till she's tanned in all the right places."

Killian's voice turned to scolding. "Bernice isn't the topless surfing type, which is exactly why I chose her."

You mean why Harold chose her for you, Liam thought bitterly. He would never voice his true feelings aloud to his brother, though. "Alright. You go and have a laugh with Ever. Don't be old."

"I love you, too," Killian said before ending the call.

Liam turned his attention to Alec. "I like sitting in the front seat for a change. Can't do this back home, but since not as many people recognize me here, I get to do all the cool stuff." Liam pressed a few buttons on the dashboard.

"I'm so glad," Alec replied in monotone. "Really. I love it when you mess with the radio."

Liam wished Sam was in the car with them. He could distract from Ronald's boring chatter and liven up the afternoon. Alec was great, but he was always a little testy when they kept him out too late for too many nights in a row.

Liam cast around for something to talk about with his bodyguard. "So, what do you think about Bernice?"

"She's fine."

Liam snorted. "Wow. You hate her!"

Alec raised his eyebrow. "It's not my job to think. It's my job to keep Killian and you all alive. Bernice is fine. She doesn't pose a threat, so I have no opinion."

"Come on!" Liam urged, bordering on whining. "Don't be Adult Alec. Be Fun Alec! Entertain me, darn it!"

"Are you thinking I'm a bodyguard-slash-clown stripper?"

Liam howled. "Now that's all I see when I look at you! That's wicked!"

Alec grumbled as he exited the freeway, glad that, at the very least, he'd unwittingly provided Liam with a pleasant visual distraction from Ronald Cho and his tiresome cats.

14

THE STORM CELLAR

The Waywards were worn out as Baird drove them back to the hut that night at one-thirty in the morning. Grettel was so exhausted that her eyelids drooped, but she fought with them when Baird announced that they would be going to the storm cellar before their bed.

The soft moonlight barely illuminated the creepy contents of the storm cellar, but Blue didn't need the light to recall everything that was down there. There were seven different dulled knives that had been discarded from Master Joe's kitchen and various Vemreaux garbage bins, four pool sticks, two wooden baseball bats and eight pieces of strong wood that were comparable in size, a 2x4 set up as a balance beam, five bowling balls, two unmatching chairs, a chart on the wall marking the rotation of training, a dartboard, several boxing gloves and a punching bag that stood upright rather than hanging from the ceiling.

Baird made the conscious choice to allow his sister's personality to come out in the storm cellar. He figured it was the safest place she had to be somewhat herself. He smirked at the life that revived in her as she looked around at their family secret. "Alright, then. See what damage you can do in two minutes."

A tired Elle picked up one of the pool sticks and moseyed over to the 2x4, willing her body to gear up for the sparring session with her friend. Rolling her shoulders and cracking a stiff bone in her neck, Elle hopped up on the beam, holding her broken pool stick up at the ready. Blue lifted a second stick off the floor and joined her friend, standing at the opposite end.

Baird pulled out the two chairs, lining them up together so he and Grettel could more comfortably watch the fight. "Have a seat, shorty." He patted the chair next to him. "I don't want any marks left on Elle because she's got the testing tomorrow, so make sure you don't aim to wound. First one off the beam loses." He eyed his sister speculatively. "Try it one-handed, Blue." When she made to dip her left hand behind her back, Baird amended his command. "Use your left."

She sighed, but obliged by tucking her dominant hand to the base of her spine, taking care that it did not tense up into a fist. It would serve as her focal point. If her hand remained limp back there, then she was in control of the fight. Even if she won the duel, she would know that she had lost if her fingers curled into an unbidden fist.

"Alright, two minutes. None of this sweet little best friend waste of time. Go!" His raised voice coerced a squeak from Grettel, who was now more awake. Her eyes were painted with unease as she watched a scene she had viewed different versions of many times before.

Immediately, Blue struck out at her friend. She and Elle sparred often enough that the forward point of Elle's left toe told Blue everything she needed to know to win. Elle countered with her stick, blocking the sudden blow. Instantly, Blue came at the base of Elle's shoe with the weapon, knocking the outer sole just hard enough to distract from her actual plan. Elle's attention was successfully diverted as she moved her left foot out of the way, so Blue shoved her right shoulder backwards, throwing her off balance and spinning her slightly sideways. Blue smiled as she lightly struck her friend's fleshy backside just enough to make her fumble on the beam. Anticipating Elle's exceptional balance, instead of waiting for her to pitch forward, Blue placed her hand on Elle's chest and shoved her back and downward. In only eighteen seconds, Blue successfully knocked Elle completely off the beam without leaving a mark.

Elle stood, rubbing the sting from her backside as she tried to work the furrow out of her brow. "Were you sparring with anyone in The Way while we were gone?" she asked, confused as to how she had been taken down so quickly.

Blue swung the stick in front of her through the air, aiming at an imaginary foe. "You test soon. Tomorrow, in fact. I just thought you'd like to be as sharp as you can. No point in toying with you, right?"

Elle's lips pursed, and all the play went out of her. Suddenly she felt foolish, their plan laughable in its simplicity. "I won't make the first round. I've been practicing five days a week, and I can't even last a stinking minute? There's no way they'll choose me." Her shoulders slumped as defeat mingled with regret on her face.

Before her brother or Grettel could speak, Blue held up her hand. "I don't think it matters anymore. I've been thinking about it and, I mean, I'm out now, right? Baird's my boss. No one's watching me to see if I'll be the Wayward Light. Even when I talk to the Vemreaux and take their orders, they don't notice me enough to really remember me." Her eyes darted to Baird, who looked wary. "I say you purposely do bad on round one so they won't ask you back. You don't have to be the diversion anymore, Elle." She dropped to the ground and gently took the stick away from her friend. "You can just be you."

Grettel stopped breathing with the suggestion.

Blue's words so staggered Elle that she couldn't wrap her mind around the concept. Elle looked to Baird for confirmation.

Baird dashed the newly formed hope by shaking his head. "As soon as they figure out none of these candidates are actually the Light, do you think they'll just stop looking? Elle's been considered since they started the search. Even if she did stop parading around as the potential Light, her name's still down in their books." He stood up and collected the sticks from his sister. "Blue, important people from all three countries'll be in town for this first test. They'll want to get to know the players. Everyone around here knows she's likely to be chosen. We can't just all of a sudden drop the act and expect them to buy it. Some of 'em will probably come to the bar to meet Elle before and after the big day."

"How far does this go, then?" Blue asked petulantly. The stale underground air filled her nostrils as she crossed her arms. "How long do we have to keep this up?"

Posturing at her attitude, he stood in front of his sister to fully confront her. "Until you get your calling. Until you figure out how you're going to destroy the predator and put an end to the tyranny. Isn't that how the prophecy goes? As long as we wait for it, Elle needs to be the diversion. No one even looks at you when she's around. We can't quit now."

His comment made her voluntary stealth feel like a joke. Like anyone would want to look at her when her gorgeous best friend was around. Inwardly she cringed at the insinuation, but outwardly she held her head up. She swallowed and leveled her voice to iron out any hurt she might otherwise betray. "Okay. Let's say she makes it past round one, which we all know she will." Elle's chest lifted with the vote of confidence. "Let's say she makes it through all the testing and is declared the big, bad Light. Then what? What if I still don't know what I'm supposed to do? Is she supposed to go off and get herself killed so my identity can be secret?" She shook her auburn hair. "Where do we draw the line, Baird?"

Despite his constant quest for control, an emotion that looked shockingly like pain surfaced on his face before he could flush it away. "Okay. Fair point. Let's think it through. The predator's on the O-blood island, right?"

"I heard a table talking about it today," Elle chimed in. "They're thinking of moving the O-bloods from the island because they're having trouble finding Vemreaux to replace the ones working the blood farms that've been disappearing."

"Okay." Baird processed this new information quickly. "So, that's where you need to go, Blue." He thought through a few different possibilities, each one putting his sister in more danger than he would've liked. "The only thing I can think of is buying you a plane ticket and letting you go off and kill the predator."

Elle and Grettel both spoke out at once against the idea. Words like "insane" and "cruel" were piled atop phrases like "she can't do this alone", "she'll be a criminal" and "won't allow a Wayward without an escort overseas". The latter complaint stuck, and he had to admit that it was a hindrance.

Waywards who were bought as opposed to freed were not truly people as far as the law went. They were property. Joe owned Blue, and although she had never met him, none of them felt that he would be too keen on letting her go after just putting out five hundred thousand bills for her purchase.

Grettel timidly suggested, "Couldn't we just tell Joe that Blue's the Light? Maybe he'd give her up at least temporarily if she could put an end to the predator."

Baird and Elle immediately vetoed the motion. Baird spoke louder. "No one can know about Blue's identity for her own safety's sake. If whatever this predator is has time and the mental capacity to study her, it would make her chances of survival that much worse."

"I'm not banking on survival, guys. The prophecy says that the Light will have to make the ultimate sacrifice. You guys all turn a deaf ear to the last part, explaining it away whenever you can, but it's going to happen." Blue had long since accepted this. Baird took a little longer. He tried many different approaches to give her a way out, but with so little information known about the predator, his efforts grew lax over time.

After much speculation (that, because of the late hour, mutated quickly into arguments), it was decided that they would follow on the path they'd set out on with a few alterations.

Baird ran his hands over his face as he spoke. "Elle will compete as the Light during the first round. During the second round, I want you to fail out. Can you do that?"

"Did you see how quickly I hit the ground tonight? I don't think that'll be a problem," Elle joked.

"Fine. Blue stays here under Joe's ownership for now. We'll think of some way to get you over to the *O*-blood island covertly so you can put an end to the predator once and for all."

"Sounds good to me," Blue nodded.

Elle breathed with new life. "Really? One round and then I can drop the act?"

"That work for you?" he asked.

"Yes, Baird! Yes. That's perfect!" She nearly choked on her happiness.

Blue looked at her brother and caught the elation that hit him when Elle was truly joyful. She immediately made plans to get them alone so Elle could capitalize on her window of opportunity. "You look tired, Grettel. Why don't you go on to bed? I'm gonna go for a run, guys. See you in the morning."

"Subtle," Baird criticized, rolling his eyes at his sister.

"You saying eighteen seconds on the beam is enough training for her for the night?" Blue challenged. She dodged his punch of gratitude and followed Grettel up the stairs.

15

ALL THE EFFORT

Baird took every available moment to practice with Elle, so as soon as she was awake the next morning, he beckoned her to meet him in the storm cellar again before Grettel woke. He ignored his sister's knowing look and swallowed anything that might turn into a fight between them.

Elle was good at attacking, but slightly less than amazing at blocking on the beam. The third time he tapped her shin with the toe of his shoe, he knew that her head was elsewhere. "Hey, where are you?" he asked.

Elle did not lower her hands, but took his distraction as an opportunity to throw out a jab to his stomach, which missed completely. "I'm here. I'm on the beam. I'm in the fight."

"Is that a fact?" It was the second time he'd got a light jab to her chin. With accuracy akin to his sister's, he was always careful not to hurt her or leave any marks. Usually his fist started out balled up, but by the time it reached her pretty face, it ended up a light slap. Baird was adamant that hand-to-hand combat with her should only happen on the beam.

"Yeah. I'm just a little nervous. That's all."

"Then you're not on the beam, Elle. You're at the testing." He swung for her face, but she shifted backward to miss the punch by centimeters. "One step at a time. Right now, you're just fighting me. No one else. Only me."

Elle lifted her leg to kick his thigh, but he pushed her knee down before it was able to gain any real force. Baird smirked. "Come on, now. It's your big chance. Fighting with each other's the thing we do best." He stilled his attack so she could catch up. "Your left elbow's about two centimeters too low to be useful for anything other than fanning me. Come to think of it, it is getting a little warm down here. Never mind. You can keep doing it like that. Feels nice," he teased.

"How does this feel?" She steamed at his correction. Elle tried to throw him off balance with a swift uppercut, but Baird grabbed onto her fist and held it in his much larger hand. Her left arm cut the air to jab him in the jaw, but he caught that as well.

"Relaxing. It feels like you're blowing a breeze at me. I am pretty hot."

"You're the only one who thinks so."

"Is that why I pull in more tips tending bar than you do all day? Pity because I'm so ugly? Wow. I always thought it was because the Fems all wish they could have me." He held tight to her fists until Elle conceded defeat.

"Fine. You win."

"Thanks for putting me out of my misery."

"Shut up. I've got a lot on my mind," Elle complained. Baird released her fists and the two hopped down in step.

On any other day, there may have been sexual tension that produced witty banter, but Elle was quiet. It really dawned on her the previous night what she was about to get herself into. This was the plan the whole time, but it wasn't until now that her flawless smile began to crack under the pressure.

"You're not focused, Elle. There's no point in practicing if you're not going to keep your head in it," Baird lectured disapprovingly.

"Sorry. Let's go again."

They stepped back up on the beam together and faced each

other. It took only twenty more seconds before he landed another touch on her cheek.

Groaning loudly, she cast her useless fists down to her sides in defeat. The stale air of the storm cellar felt as though it would choke her if she stayed down there much longer. Never before had she felt the creeping fear of claustrophobia – especially in a place that was not all that small. The stress of her fate felt heavy on her chest as she struggled not to hyperventilate.

"I'm gonna flunk out of the first round, aren't I?" Elle tried to keep the panic out of her voice.

Baird softened. He knew that she was not built for this much pressure. No one short of he and his sister were, but Elle fought to keep up with them all the same.

"If you were going up against me, yes. But you won't be. You'll be up against other *A*-blood types who hope they're the Light. You've actually fought with the real Light hundreds of times. There's no way that you won't make it to round two." He'd saved his most reassuring speech for that morning and hoped she wouldn't need more than that.

Elle nodded, her breathing beginning to slow. She did not look entirely convinced, but he didn't see a point in carrying on about it.

Baird stepped down and stared at her hesitantly. With her still on the beam, they were at eye level. Her concern bore deep into him, threatening to weaken his cold demeanor that usually served him well. Her confident smile had no place in the room anymore, and he found that he missed its reassuring presence.

He knew what she needed, but was reluctant to give it to her. Each time he held her, it only served to soothe her aching heart for the exact measure of time that his arms wrapped around her body. After the release, she was even more addicted to the feeling than before, her eyes imploring him for another embrace and another. He did not want to set a precedent as a hugger or a source of comfort for her. They were already too flirtatious, given the gravity of their lives.

His sister would be leaving at some point to fight the greatest battle of the decade single-handedly. He was charged with running a business that only grew more difficult to handle. Elle was going to be tested in ways they could only imagine. His chest tightened as he imagined someone striking out at Elle with the intention to hurt her.

"Baird?" she whispered, fear creeping into her voice and destroying her poise. She took half a step closer to him and lifted her hand to touch his cheek.

Before she could make contact, Baird reached up and caught her hand, holding her by the wrist. He stared into her eyes, willing sense to reach his brain so he did not fall prey to the emotions the beautiful blonde emanated. "No. You deserve more."

Elle's eyes sharpened with the same determination that kept her from wilting amongst the more polished Femreaux. "I deserve to get what I want."

Knowing his fearlessness did not extend to relationships, Elle sucked in the desire to be loved and tucked it away with her increasing libido.

THE LEAVES WERE TURNED TO OUTLANDISH SHADES OF CONTRASTING colors. As handfuls of foliage fell around them on their walk to the diner, the four did their best to pull their minds out of their preoccupations and enjoy the scenery.

Blue and Grettel held both of Elle's hands, for Baird would not step up and be what she needed. Blue clutched her book in her other hand possessively. She was on chapter eight now, and was determined to comprehend the entire book as quickly as she could devour it. She feared that Baird would soon come up with a valid reason to keep her from diverting her attention from the predator and Elle to Geometry.

As they walked, Blue began to see the world in angles that desperately needed bisecting. She did not possess the tools the book demanded, but she could draw lines and circles without a compass or a protractor and still get the accuracy described in the book. She was always excited to learn a new bit of knowledge that could prove to be useful in her preparation for fighting the unknown. She voiced to Baird that she was grateful it was a Geometry book that she found and not something tedious.

Groaning, Baird trudged ahead of them.

"He's downright cheerful this morning," Blue muttered indignantly.

Grettel's small voice spoke from Elle's other side. "I hope you get help out on the floor soon. I don't know how you're going to handle it tonight, go to the testing and still get enough rest for your shift tomorrow."

"Don't you know?" Elle grinned. "I'm amazing."

When they reached the diner, Baird pulled out several large packages from the kitchen that Joe put there for them. They contained canvas and poles that were tied in a bundle. There were also many more tables and chairs littering the dining area that were now supposed to be put up outside. Another box stored decorations in the form of fancy lights strung together.

As usual, Baird took charge. "You two work on setting up inside for lunch. Grettel, get the kitchen going, and Elle can do the dining area." He pursed his lips as he tried to make sense of the sheet of directions that was packed inside one of the boxes. "Blue, help me set this up."

Elle set the chairs down from the tables, wiping everything off and putting out the baskets of condiments and napkins. When Grettel had bouts of downtime in between thawing things in the oven or waiting for water to boil, she sat and helped Elle roll the silverware inside napkins. The two girls talked about unimportant things as they sat together. Elle found that it was the inconsequential chatter she valued most in providing a salve for her nerves. If Grettel could still be normal around her, then perhaps it wouldn't be as bad as she was anticipating.

When Blue and Baird came in from outside, it was nearly time to open.

"How's it look?" Elle asked, setting the massive pile of finished silverware aside.

"Go see for yourself." Baird wiped his brow as he leaned against the countertop to rest a moment before going into cooking mode. Blue, also sweating from the heat of the day, got him a glass of water, which he took unhappily.

"You look tired," she commented with pity in her eyes as she leaned over to look at him more closely. "Maybe you should lie down."

"Oh, shut up," he snapped, bringing out a silly grin in his sister. He was the only one she gloated to about her superior...everything. He was the only one who seemed to think he could fairly compete with her.

The girls came back in with awed expressions. "It's the most beautiful thing that's ever happened to this diner!" Elle exclaimed, a fresh spring in her step. "I love the taller tables and chairs. They look so fancy!"

Grettel's gushing was not as loud, but it was just as genuine. "I love the lights. I can't wait to see them twinkling tonight. Whose idea was it to hang them like that? I thought they'd just be along the edges of the tent, but they're covering the whole roof of the canvas. I love it!" She clapped her hands together under her chin as her brown eyes danced with the romance of happiness.

It was the pick-me-up the four needed. Elle flirted with the customers with new playfulness, and Grettel actually hummed under her breath as she cooked with Baird in the kitchen.

Blue even caught her brother purposefully grazing his hand across Elle's smiling cheek when he thought no one was around. She thought Elle might jump forward and finally kiss him, but was disappointed that her brother dropped his hand and turned to chop up chunks of molded lamb to throw into the sickeningly thick mint and radish stew. Of all the things they were forced to prepare for, it seemed her brother would never be ready for Elle.

16

LUCINDA

Age of Peace Law 2, Subset 1a
A Wayward attacking a Vemreaux forfeits his right to a trial by jury and is
subject to the swiftest punishment under the law.

Daniel eyed the novel Beth was clutching in her hand as she spoke. "I can't believe you love that book so much," he interrupted. "It's so sappy."

"What? Donald Smith's novel was much better received than your bizarre play. Come on, Daniel. I'll read the narration and Lucinda's parts, and you read Francis."

Blue's pen was poised, but she absolutely refused to ask them a third time what they were going to order. Daniel, Beth, Brown Scarf and Purple Scarf took up residence at a table in the center of the diner, and for the past half hour, had ordered only drinks.

"Buy me a shot?" Daniel raised an eyebrow to Beth.

"Fine," she sighed, clicking her fingers to assure the waitress was paying attention. Blue willed herself not to reach out and crush the small bones. That would definitely not be laying low. Luckily, the crowd was thinning, transitioning between the lunch and dinner rushes. "We'll have another round, then." Beth held up the book between them and began to read, projecting her voice so it carried throughout the diner. "Francis David Vemreaux in all of his glorious might journeyed as far from the greedy Juan Ponce de Leon as his illustrious legs would carry him. The first community he came across was located in Richmond, Virginia."

Blue waited on a nearby table, keeping a curious eye, and ear, on Beth's story as it unfolded.

Daniel read in a sweeping, dramatic voice. "'Kind sirs, I am a sailor who survived a shipwreck. I have wandered many sleepless nights in search of honest work so I can earn a place of respite,' Francis said to the men who were hauling in lumber."

Beth jumped in, "'What skill have you with an axe, sailor?' One of them asked."

Daniel flexed his bicep, and a few onlookers whistled appreciatively. "'Skill enough to be called woodsman instead of sailor,' he replied."

The actors relished the attention and stood, quieting the commotion around them to a dull mumbling.

Beth batted away Daniel's bicep. "'If you can help us build our homes as fortresses from the harsh winters, we will no longer call you sailor nor woodsman, but friend.'

"The people there worked hard. They took him in as one of their own, and he returned the favor of the peace-loving group by working with the men, adding his strong hands and heightened senses to their workforce. His tireless toil alongside them earned him a place of respect in the tight-knit community.

"One particular woman in the area struck his fancy by sewing up the tears that gaped in his clothing. 'Good sir,' Lucinda smiled up at him, revealing eyes bluer than any water he'd ever seen. 'This is the fourth pair of britches you've brought me this week. You'll have to take more care how you swing that axe you're so handy with.' Her eyesight was said to be so keen that her stitching was tighter than a loom's."

"Oh, I love this part!" a woman exclaimed when Blue asked her what she'd like to order. There was no point in working at the moment; everyone was being entertained by Beth and her minions.

Daniel continued. "'Mi'lady,' Francis replied, 'then what excuse shall I bring next time to gain the privilege of seeing your beauty?'"

Blue had never been wooed before, and desperately hoped it was nothing like that in real life.

Beth continued, clearly wishing she was the lovely subject in the book. "One look from her cerulean irises did most men in, though she did not take her advantage often. Lucinda caught his attention and never gave it back. The two began spending stolen moments by the butter churn, and he went out of his way to help her with her regular tasks. Lucinda's cherry lips and peaceful smile tamed his warrior's heart into that of a man who sought no greater adventure than capturing the love of a woman.

"It was a late summer's eve spent in the company of wildflowers and thick grass that brought Francis to the hut where the women dipped candles. Lucinda's diligent arms did not tire, and her lips never complained that the work seemed endless. 'I can hear you,' she sang as she hung two candles connected by their shared wick over a line to dry. 'Have you come for more darning, Francis? I'll not be able to get to it until the morning.'"

Daniel read, "His silence drew her to the door of the small work hut, where she found him on his knees with the entire village gathered behind him." At this, Daniel tossed his chair over and threw himself onto the ground before Beth, drawing every eye. "No, Lucinda. I've come for your heart!'"

Elle laughed aloud, earning a few annoyed looks from nearby patrons. Blue shrugged at her friend, who had given up waiting on people who obviously were happy to be hungry, so long as they were entertained.

Beth grinned. "'Oh, Francis!'"

Daniel placed his hands over his heart. "'Lucinda, my love. Make me the happiest man in the world and marry me tonight.'"

Purple Scarf took the book from Beth's hand and commandeered the narration. "Throwing her candles and caution to the wind, Lucinda wrapped her arms around his strong neck in the company of many excited eyes."

Beth's actions followed the narrator's commands, and she found herself sitting on Daniel's bended knee. "'Yes, Francis Vemreaux! Yes!'" The kiss that connected her lips to Daniel's was sloppy and filled with makeup-laced saliva that the man did not seem to mind. "Oh, Daniel!" Beth cried. His tongue connected with hers, increasing the shared moisture to a level that made Blue gag. Her normally composed face could not hide her horror at such a crude display.

Purple Scarf cleared his voice above the cacophony of cat-calls from other tables. He read, "She leaned down and placed a chaste kiss on his forehead, causing many women to shield their eyes to respect propriety." At this, many Vemreaux laughed, including Beth and Daniel, who finally followed along appropriately.

"The two married with the town's fervent blessing, though neither she nor the village knew anything of his extended life or the blessed fount. After their marriage, he tried many times to convince her to head south with him, but she would not dare to leave the community she so loved for a journey he would not explain the importance of. They were fruitful and multiplied, and the urging from him ceased as fatherhood distracted him. The years slowly etched themselves into her smooth face while leaving her husband's untouched. Francis and his beloved wife gave birth to their fifth and final child, each of whom was born with their *B*-type blood.

"When her fortieth year came about, the woman was taken ill with a fever."

Beth hopped up onto the long table and laid down on it dramatically, drawing every male eye in the vicinity. She crooned, "'Leave me, Francis!'"

Purple scarf kept on reading, holding the book out for Daniel to catch glimpses of the part Beth had clearly committed to memory. "Her hand was thinned with sickness and heated beyond comfort."

Beth cried out, arching her back seductively to gain the most possible attention. "'Take me and leave me in the woods away from you, the children and the village. I will not spread my disease! It will die with me!'" Beth began coughing.

Daniel threw himself over her form in a way that did not erase their disgusting kiss from everyone's mind. "'Then my heart shall die with you, as well! Will you not hearken to my urgings to travel south with me? I know of a way that might save your life! Do you not want to see your sons grow to be strong, strapping men like their father? Do you not want to see your daughters on their wedding day?'"

"'I may not live to see them age but a few more days. If your journey will remove me from the village and save my children from this death, then I will suffer you to take me wherever your heart desires.'"

"'Very well, my love. I will leave the children in the care of Silvester's wife, Naomi. We will come back to them with no trace of this vile sickness.'"

"'What good is life if I cannot see your handsome face? My eyesight is fading!'" Beth's legs parted ominously, inviting Daniel to mount her in the presence of the entire bar. The diners were fervent with encouragement. Catcalls, whistles and whoops filled the diner.

Blue's mouth fell open, and she found that even though she wanted to, she could not look away. She had never seen the seat of panties that were not white. The difference was shocking.

"'I will make your life worth living. Our children's laughter will fill your ears and bring you joy. I will take you broken, and bring you back whole!'" Daniel lifted Beth's leg and looped it around his back, revealing her bright red underwear to the waitress and now several others.

"With little medicine to help her, the illness took her eyesight only one day after they left camp." Purple scarf finished the passage just as Baird came over to break up the two that were acting out the birds and the bees for his sister.

Baird nodded to Lawrence, who'd been enjoying the view from his table. Since Baird was *A*-blood, he had to be careful around Vemreaux and not overstep his bounds. Joe put him in a precarious position when he left him with no *B*-blood reinforcement to help manage things. While Baird was more than capable of physically dominating the situation, he could be in real trouble if a Vemreaux pressed charges against him. Lawrence rose from his seat and accompanied Baird over to the copulating two. "Get off my table," Baird ordered.

Beth merely laughed at the Wayward's gall.

Lawrence had little patience for their disrespect of the man who controlled the Green Abby shots and helped him end the degenerates that sullied his many businesses. Lawrence grabbed Daniel by the scruff of the neck and yanked him off of Beth, who squealed with shock. "Hey!"

"Get off my table or get out of my bar." Baird stared her in the face, though her skirt was less than decent and served as the focal point for many.

Beth complied, blushing with false propriety as she sank back down into her chair. Daniel was shaking his head at Lawrence in what was clearly a deferential fear. "No, sir," he muttered. "Never again." When the tall, bald man released Daniel, the skinnier Vemreaux lifted up his chair with hands that Blue noticed were shaking, despite his forced calm smile at his friends.

Lawrence was intimidating, even in a suit. He glared at Daniel. "Finish the story."

"What?"

"Stand up here and finish the story with some respect for your people."

It was clear that Daniel wanted to argue, but would not dare to further incur the wrath of this man. He snatched up the book and read so quickly, the words were barely intelligible. "Francis David Vemreaux carried Lucinda's heated body through state lines that had yet to be drawn, down to the small fountain in Florida that blessed his body so long ago. It was his last attempt to save the life that had become more precious to him than his own.

"Gently and tenderly he bathed her." Daniel looked uncomfortably toward Lawrence. "Then there's some stuff here about that...ah, here we go." His eyes coasted over the fabricated eroticism and searched for something less racy. "Once he tipped the water down her throat, he could feel the change rolling through her. When she opened her sightless eyes, they had turned from the perfect and purest blue to a pitch black that matched her husband's."

Brown Scarf chimed in as soon as Daniel flopped down in his seat. "Thus the Vemreaux race began, and here we are today." He stood and addressed the diners. "Come see our troupe perform on the main stage at three o'clock sharp on Peace Day in Capital City!" He was gratified when his words were greeted with polite applause.

Lawrence clapped Daniel on the shoulder, causing the actor to wince. "There. Was that so hard? As you were, people," he announced to the restaurant.

Baird caught his sister's eye and motioned for her to join him in the kitchen. He tried to put on a calm expression for Grettel. "Hey, midget, could you give us a minute?"

Grettel obliged and stepped out the back entrance into the parking lot for a much-needed break.

As soon as the door closed, he stared his sister down. "How many shots have they had?"

"The couple making babies on the table?" Blue inquired.

"Real cute, Blue. How many?"

"Two rounds, is all. Couple blood drinks, too. No food yet. Too busy with other things, I imagine."

Baird held his finger up in front of Blue's face, and she knew that all humor was to cease. "You listen to me. That girl is trashy. She'll be pulling stuff like that for the rest of her life to get attention from Vemreaux who're too stupid to notice she's using them to feed her own ego." He watched his sister nod submissively. Baird ran his hand over his face to gear up for the uncomfortable thing he needed to say. "Do you...do you have any questions about what you saw out there?"

Blue thought that she would rather face the predator with one hand tied behind her back than discuss sex with her brother. She mashed her lips together in thought. "Just one."

Baird crossed his arms over his chest and set his feet shoulder-width apart, squaring off to face her dreaded question. "Alright. Out with it."

"How long does Elle have to wait before you throw her down on a table like that?" she teased with a grin. Before Baird could shut his mouth that had fallen open, Blue snickered. "I'm nineteen, Baird. I took sex education in The Way. I was starting to wonder if you ever took the course, though."

He responded by playfully lunging at her to catch her head in a lock, which she artfully ducked out of. Blue laughed, and the sound did his heart good, lifting his mood from the terrifying conversation he'd been psyching himself up for five minutes to have with her. "Is this conversation over, then?" he asked, smiling with relief.

"Please, yes. And forever."

17

STAND TOO CLOSE

Elle flitted into the kitchen wearing a secretive smile. She fixed a fresh glass to make a second blood shake for her customer. "Someone's a popular girl today," she commented, filling the air that Baird was determined to make tense with his honed-in hostility.

"Oh, yeah?" Blue replied without looking up from her book. There was a lull in the hectic rush as the lunch crowd thinned and the dinner diners were just realizing their appetites. "How much did the mouth breather tip you?"

"Not me." Elle tapered her smile to appear as if she knew something that Blue did not. "Someone's asked to sit in your section."

At this, Baird slammed his knife down on the cutting board and stomped over to the door, peering through the hole in the upper half that revealed the restaurant. "Who is it?" he demanded.

Grettel flinched and busied herself with a boiling pot of potatoes to avoid Baird's wrath.

"Will you calm it down, Baird?" Elle put her hands on her hips and stared at the back of his head. He could feel her eyes on him, so he made sure not to turn around. "Man alive! It's just Stand. You act like the predator itself's gonna come up and order hisself a blood smoothie or something. Get a grip!"

He did feel a little foolish, but wouldn't admit his overreaction. Instead, he turned away from the door, still avoiding Elle, and returned to the cutting board.

Blue jumped down from the island and skipped to the door, knowing it would agitate her brother. "Oo! My first fan!" Baird most hated it when she acted like a child, so she made sure to behave as such when he was being particularly insufferable. She contemplated whistling just to push him further, but decided against it. Grettel looked like she was about to climb into the pot of potatoes just to escape the man.

Blue's skipping ceased when she emerged from the kitchen. She resumed the subservient body language she was beginning to find restrictive. She had only two other tables that were occupied, and they were both enjoying their meals without need for her, so she did not mind that Stand took his time ordering a haggis sandwich on pumpernickel with a side of trout slaw.

"How has your afternoon been?" Stand asked politely as he handed her the menu.

"I've been studying that Geometry book you gave me." She spoke conspiratorially, unsure they should be talking of such things out in the open.

His smile danced in his eyes. "That's great! Have you gotten to any of the homework sections?" Stand straightened his tie to have something to do with his hands.

"Yes. Though, there's one thing that I don't understand yet."

"Yet? That's a very healthy attitude. I'm sure a smart girl like yourself can do anything you put your mind to."

Blue's head shot up and she stared at him warily, her eyes holding him in a near trance. "You don't know that I'm smart." What she really wanted to say was, "how do you know that I'm smart?" but she knew that would be too much of a tell.

"If you don't believe in yourself..." Stand began awkwardly, but then switched tracks halfway through. "Smart people want to learn."

The statement was almost a compliment, which made her feel exposed and uncomfortable. Blue did the only thing she could think of. She walked away.

Blue slapped the order form down on the ledge for Grettel, who was nearest, but Baird swooped in and snatched it up. His temper was on a gradual decrescendo after having been put in his place by Elle. He worked on filling the order while Blue brought the professor a glass of water.

Stand looked up, hoping to catch her eye, but Blue remained veiled behind her scrim of hair. "Are you busy right now?" he asked after thanking her for the water. She shook her head in lieu of opening her mouth. "Why don't you bring out your textbook? I can help you with the things that don't make sense *yet*." His emphasis on the last word sounded like teasing, so Blue relaxed.

"Really? That'd be so great. I'll be right back."

She stopped on her way back to the kitchen to check on her other two tables, one of which was doing fine. The other requested an *O*-Positive blood shake refill with a shot of lemon flavor this time instead of chai.

Blue mixed the shake quickly and grabbed her book off of the island where she'd left it. Baird was eyeing the text, looking like he would very much enjoy stabbing it with the knife he was holding. The sharp utensil was supposed to be used for cutting Stand's haggis before plopping it into the pot. Baird wagered it would do just fine on the book.

Blue dropped off the freshly made shake to her nearest table before heading to Stand. Though she'd seen Elle lean on the edge of people's tables and occasionally sit down in a booth as she took an order, Blue felt awkward making such assumptions of other people's spatial preferences. She stood behind the chair opposite the professor. "May I?" she requested in a small voice.

"Please. So where are we at?"

Blue noticed that Stand's casual use of the word "we" was not common. None of the other patrons included her like he did. "I'm stuck at noncoplanar lines. I know I'm supposed to know what that means, but I just don't." She opened the book to the page that had several noncoplanar line problems on it and frowned.

Stand mimicked her expression without meaning to. "Oh, well it's been a while. Let me see for a minute." As he flipped through the chapter, he shook his head. "You'll make this a lot easier on yourself if you start at chapter one. This is chapter eight."

"I did start at chapter one," Blue responded, defending herself. They'd had textbooks in The Way. She knew how to read a book properly. "That part I understood. It's these noncoplanar lines. I don't want to go much further until I understand them."

Stand looked up at her with a baffled expression. "You mean to tell me that you taught yourself eight chapters of Geometry in a day?"

"No," she corrected him patiently. "I *can't* make it through chapter eight because of the noncoplanar lines. They came out of nowhere without an explanation. I'm sure it's something all the Vemreaux know."

"Apparently not, since I can't remember what they are and I actually completed the course. It was decades ago, but still." Stand caught himself too late. He hadn't meant to reveal his age to her. Though to most Vemreaux, age was not an issue once you were frozen, he had not spent much time around perpetually aging people. He wondered if the fact that he was far older than her would matter. She did not appear as though anything odd had registered to her. This relieved him, until he realized that his age didn't matter to her because she did not consider him in the way he was hoping she might.

He looked down at the page she'd given him and turned to the previous one. Sighing, he pointed to the binding. "Well, here's your problem. Someone tore the page out right before it."

Blue gasped and placed her hand over her mouth. The idea of checking for such a heinous crime had not occurred to her. "Who would do something so awful?"

Her innocence endeared him to her. Stand chuckled, flipping to the back of the book. "More people than you'd think. Let's see what the glossary has to say. Hmm. Noncoplanar's not in here," he muttered aloud. He thumbed through the pages until he found the right one. "Now, here's coplanar. It means 'within the same plane'." His blond brow furrowed. "Well, what does that mean?"

Blue let out a light laugh and took the book back from Stand, judging correctly that he was perhaps not the best tutor for the subject. "Never mind. I get it now. I didn't know math books had glossaries. I wouldn't have bothered you."

"You're not bothering me."

It was at that moment that Baird decided not to wait for his sister to come back for the order, and he refused to let Elle deliver it. He stalked out of the kitchen after removing his stained apron, striding toward Stand's table. Blue had her back to him, but she could smell her brother's scent on the air. Abruptly she stood, but Baird's heavy hand pushed her back down.

"Here you are, Stand. On the house for showing my kid sister Geometry." His facial features were carefully knit into a pleasant expression, but Blue knew better. "Can I get you a blood shake to go with your meal?"

"No, thanks. And it was no trouble, Baird. She's a very smart girl."

"Is that so?" Baird commented jovially, but Blue could hear his teeth clicking together as he spoke.

"I'll leave you to your meal." Blue made to stand, but the professor held up his hand.

"You're going to leave me to eat this whole meal by myself? You know, some people think it's pathetic to dine alone."

Baird chewed on the inside of his lower lip and excused himself.

Blue knew he'd let loose on his feelings about her eating with the Vemreaux soon enough. For the time being, she decided to take Stand up on his offer to sit with him while he ate, hoping to avoid Baird's inevitable confrontation.

Blue did not know nearly half of the things Stand shared with her. She knew that Christopher Columbus discovered North America, but she did not know that he thought he was in some place that used to be called India at the time. She could list all of the presidents and their vice presidents in order before the switch was made to emperors, but she had no idea that some of them had been Vemreaux. She was surprised to find that Abraham Lincoln and John F. Kennedy were of the superior blood type.

"Why did they die so young, then?" Blue asked, letting her curiosity direct her tongue.

"Just because someone's *B*-blood doesn't mean they bathed in the Fountain. Abraham Lincoln bathed in it, but Kennedy didn't. And Kennedy was Original Vemreaux, too. There are Vemreaux today who choose not to bathe in the Fountain, for whatever reason." He took a bite of his haggis on pumpernickel, making sure to swallow before continuing. "Tough skin and bones or not, bullets are bullets, especially ones fired to the head. Neither man would've survived either way." He took a sip of his water. "That's one of the reasons the guns were all destroyed when we entered the Age of Peace."

Blue looked down for a moment before building up the gumption to ask a frank question. "Stand, can I ask you something not about Geometry?"

"Of course. You can ask me anything," he said kindly.

Blue permitted a small smile at his benevolence. "Baird said that scratch backs the Vemreaux currency. But I know that it wasn't always that way. Scratch has only been big since World War Three, after they rounded us up by blood type." She watched Stand squirm in his seat slightly. "What backed the currency before that?"

Stand exhaled pointedly that this simple query was the one she wanted to address. "Well, before the world unified under King Sinclair, there were many countries, far more than three. The most popular backing used to be gold. Then when countries borrowed more from each other or their own banks than they could possibly pay back, they began to back their currency with debt."

"I'm sorry? Did you say debt?" she asked, leaning in curiously.

"Yes. The more they borrowed, the more money was printed. It was basically a house of cards that was built up so high, into the trillions, in fact. All it took was for one large country with a solid military force to call in what was owed to them for it all to collapse.

When the other countries couldn't pay what they owed, they went to war, which eventually became World War Three."

"In The Way, they told us that World War Three happened because of the violent nature of us lesser blood types."

Stand thought over his response. "Well, violence certainly played a part in that, *B*-blood or not. But that wasn't the start of it. Now we have one world currency that's backed by a renewable and regulated resource. Waywards have an important job, tending to the cows and making S-bricks. S-bricks took the place of gold bricks. How would we fuel our houses without the methane gas put out by your facilities?" He took a bite of his meal and chewed thoughtfully. "Before World War Three, they mostly used finite resources. Oil, coal, what have you. Wars were fought over the resources over and over again. Now King Sinclair regulates everything, so all three countries are treated the same. This way, there's no cause for war."

"Still," Blue spoke up, "I don't understand how they thought backing their currency with debt would be a good idea. That sounds...like a disaster waiting to happen."

"I wonder what practices we hold to now that in one hundred years would be considered barbaric?" Stand lowered his voice. "I'm sure you can think of a few."

Each time their conversation was interrupted by the demands of other customers, Blue found that she was irritated. There was so much about the world that she did not know, so much that was kept from them in The Way. "I'll be right back," she promised.

"Until then," he said politely, tipping his head to her like a gentleman. This thoroughly embarrassed her.

"Can I get you anything new to drink? We've got more than just water."

"Water's fine."

Blue took two other tables' orders before freshening Stand's drink. When she delivered the beverage he'd requested, she finally decided she knew him well enough to risk conversing more personally.

"Do you not like blood shakes or smoothies? We've got a good selection." It was rare that a Vemreaux did not order either blood or a Green Abby at Joe's.

Stand fidgeted, and Blue thought to herself with a wry smile that he'd be terrible under interrogation. Looking up at her uncomfortably, Stand fumbled through his response. "I, uh, I just don't think it's appropriate to drink blood in the company of a Wayward. Bad taste and all."

Blue was surprised at his answer. "Huh. Well, you don't have to hold back. I mean, I'm probably not gonna be able to sit with you anymore today. Crowd's picking back up, and we're supposed to be super busy tonight, so you don't have to drink water. Blood doesn't make me squeamish or anything. I mean, I'm the one who serves it."

"Well, it made me squeamish before I changed, and I guess old habits die hard." He lifted the water to his lips and sipped, pretending with the worst sincerity that water was what he preferred. "I'm so glad that you –"

But Blue did not get to hear what he was so glad about, for the table next to him chose that moment to spill their blood smoothie across the table and onto the ground. "Excuse me, sir," she murmured as she quickly moved over to the table. Blue righted the tall glass and began moving the plates containing the diners' food so that their meals would not be ruined.

"Ew! What a mess!" the Femreaux yelped as she moved away from the spill.

"You. Girl. Clean this up," the Vemreaux that dropped the smoothie barked at Blue in his embarrassment. "On my new pants!" He groaned as if it was Blue's fault that blood stained clothing.

Elle trotted over to the scene, offering up several rags from the kitchen, club soda and a spray bottle of vinegar and water. Blue quickly wiped up the table while Elle moved the disgruntled diners to a clean one so they'd be more comfortable. Elle rejoined her kneeling friend to sop up the mess with a mop before the red puddle could spread out even more.

The sight was too much for the sensitive Professor Standwicke. He soothed his conscience by pushing his chair back and helping the girls. He scooted the dirtied table to the side so they could clean underneath it. The snotty couple that made the mess sneered at Stand as though he was judging their bad behavior.

Elle took a mental note of Stand's benevolence, but she did not say anything.

Blue was not too surprised that he offered help to them. She wished Elle could fall for a guy like Stand. He didn't seem like he'd have any trouble giving himself over to niceties, but that was simply not her friend's taste. She preferred the challenge and someone to fight with. In that respect, Baird was perfect for her.

"Thanks, Stand," Blue spoke from under the table.

Elle put the mop back in the bucket when they were finished, only to find that the professor had already sprayed down the table for them. "Oh! Thank you, Stand." She was baffled by his kindness, for this was the first time a Vemreaux had ever helped her clean up a spill. Elle's stomach churned as she recalled the slivers of dried scratch bricks she'd had to eat off the floor in The Way if anything fell and broke.

"It's no trouble." He waved his hand to say that she should expect no less from a gentleman.

Elle noticed Stand's eyes were fixated on Blue as she sprayed and wiped the floor with a clean rag. Clutching onto the grotesquely soiled ones, Elle bit back a smirk as she turned away from the two and went back to the kitchen to put her cleaning tool away.

"Someone's got a crush!" she sang happily when she reached the privacy of the kitchen. Both Baird and Grettel looked up at her in confusion.

"Did you knock something over?" Baird asked with one eyebrow cocked. Part of their constant training was to never drop anything, trip or bump into a table or person by accident. In fact, accidents were really just not tolerated.

Rolling her eyes, Elle dropped the pile of soiled rags into the dirty laundry bin. "No, but thanks for the vote of confidence. Honestly, it's so helpful. Some Vemreaux in Blue's section knocked his drink over. Can we focus, please?" She turned the hot water on with her elbow and began washing away the remains of blood that clung to her hands and wrists.

"Who's got a crush?" Grettel helped her out by getting them back on topic.

"Thank you." Elle nodded to her shortest friend. "I think Stand's got it bad for our favorite color. You should see him talk to her. He's acting all nervous, like he's on a first date! When the drink spilled, he actually helped us clean it up."

Grettel's eyes widened in time with her smile. "Really? That's great! Stand is so nice." She had met the Vemreaux only once, but heard him conversing cordially with Baird a few times.

"Yep," Elle agreed, drying her hands off on a slightly damp towel.

Baird did not share in their enthusiasm. His movements went from fluid to abrupt as he tried to rein in his temper. Without commenting, he made his way over to the door and looked through the porthole out into the dining area. Sure enough, there was his sister, cleaning the table while Stand stood next to her. Baird watched for more ammunition he could use to throw at his sister when he forbade her to get involved with a Vemreaux.

When she came back into the kitchen almost a minute later to dispose of the dirty rags and fetch a new blood shake to replace the one that spilled, Baird's arms were crossed over his chest. "What do you think you're doing?" he barked threateningly. "You're a Wayward!"

Blue looked up at him with a furrowed brow that showed her complete ignorance. "What did I do?" she asked innocently as she began washing her hands. The water was already hot and felt good in the temperature-controlled building that Blue thought was always a little too chilly.

"You're...you're *flirting* with the Vem! Don't think I don't see the way he looks at you." Baird cringed at the thought. He'd never had to call his sister out on flirting before. In fact, when the words hit the air, he began to doubt their veracity. Elle was the flirtatious one. Blue always tried to avoid people, knowing that her eyes made her too memorable.

Taken aback, she looked him straight in the face so he could see she didn't know what he was talking about. "Who am I supposed to be flirting with?"

Sighing dramatically, Elle placed her hand on her hip and spoke up before Grettel became too affected by the tension. "Gimme a break, Baird. *She* wasn't flirting. Honestly, have you lost your mind?" She turned her attention to Blue, gearing up to explain something delicate. "Honey, I'm pretty sure Stand has a little crush on you. I saw him watching you while you were cleaning up the blood. When he's talking to you, sometimes he fumbles over his words like he's all nervous. What did you ask him about, anyway? Sex?"

At this, Baird whirled around at the blonde, flabbergasted.

Blue was horrified as the water continued to run over her fingers, heating them to an almost painful point. When Baird turned a murderous gaze on Blue, she stammered under the pressure.

"N-No!" she nearly shouted. Somehow she managed to keep the blush out of her cheeks. "I was just asking him about Geometry! He's a Vemreaux, Elle. He doesn't like me. He knows I'm A-blood. That's crazy!" As the words came forth, she wondered if she was wrong. Had she missed signals that were obvious to others? Was her guard really that flimsy? "I didn't do anything like that, Baird! I swear!" Blue suspected that she really did not know all that much about the world. Despite her intelligence, she began to feel inept.

"Sweetie," Elle cooed soothingly, wishing now that she had said nothing at all. "It's okay if a guy thinks you're good looking. Frankly, it's about time. Either those Wayward boys are backwards, or you're just too good at hiding."

Nerves not used to being touched began churning uneasily in Blue's stomach, giving off the telltale muscle twitches that started in her belly and crept up to her shoulders. Blue's eyes darted anxiously around the kitchen and landed on a set of kitchen shears sticking out of the knife block. Quickly turning off the water, she all but dove for the scissors.

"Blue, what the –" Elle began, but gasped when she saw the scissors opening around a lock of the thick, shoulder-length auburn hair.

"Blue, don't!" she exclaimed, her frightened expression matching Grettel's.

It was Baird who acted fast, coming back to himself upon witnessing his sister's innocence. Before she could clamp the scissors down on more than a couple stray hairs, he moved quickly over to her and stilled her hand. "Don't move," he warned, his fingers tightening on her wrist.

"It's *my* hair!" she protested. "It's my hair and maybe it's the thing that's making him look at me like he shouldn't!" She glared up at him with the same vibrant eyes, but hers possessed the steel of resolve he'd bred into her. "Baird!" she almost pleaded. The steel slowly melted with the fear that her brother rarely saw. "It has to go! I want it gone!"

"It can't go," Baird countered simply. He saw in her eyes the honest shock at the insinuation that Stand was anything more than a helpful Vemreaux. Pity for her ignorance calmed his temper. Immediately he blamed himself for not teaching her how to tell friendship from male affection.

"Why not? If I look like a boy, then we'll never have this problem again!"

He knew that she was strong and would cut off her hair if she wanted to, so he resorted to reason instead of force. "If you cut your hair off, you won't be able to hide your eyes as well. There aren't any piles of scratch to cover your face with here."

Elle hissed in disgust that this tactical approach was the one he chose, refusing to address the deeper-rooted personal issues that Blue clearly needed guidance for.

The next command came out slowly, each word sounding like a whole sentence. "Put...the...scissors...down."

The two stared at each other, and Grettel thought it looked like they were having a silent conversation. Tension twisted her tummy as their intimidating glares hopped around in her stomach like a soured buttermilk pancake as it anticipated the trepidation of the flip.

The siblings' wild and determined faces were a mirror of the other. At the same time, they both grew sad, the fury dissipating from the room. Blue's voice was barely a whisper. "I didn't ask Stand about...you know. I swear."

"I know. Sometimes Vemreaux just get confused. All they think about is sex, money and blood. You have to make things clearer to him."

Blue's hand loosened enough that Baird could untangle her fingers from the handles. Without another word, Blue decided the conversation with her brother was over, and ducked out from in front of him to fill up a glass with blood and lemon before exiting the kitchen in silence.

"Don't," Baird shot out a warning to Elle before she could open her mouth.

Grettel turned her focus back to the stove, but the soup did not crave her attention as her body language suggested.

"I hate you for making her smear that awful scratch all over her face in The Way! She's allowed to be a woman, Baird," Elle spat venomously.

Turning away from them, he picked up his knife and began slicing into a chunk of vinegar and horseradish-cured beef. "No, Elle. She's not." Heat fled from his body. He felt cold inside and out as the knife grazed the flesh in uneven strokes. "She's the Light who's gonna end the tyranny. She's the Light who's gotta make the ultimate sacrifice," he paraphrased the familiar prophecy. "She can't be making new friends like Stand who'll remember her when she's gone to the island. No one can care about her, Elle. You know that." His voice quieted, giving away his greatest source of fear and worry.

With deliberate steps, Elle walked over to the counter he was standing at. "You make me sick!" Abruptly she raised her hand and slapped him hard across his cheek.

Though it did not hurt, Baird's head snapped up. He stared at her in shock. "What was that for?"

"That's for you to remember your bad behavior by." Tears threatened her composure, but she held them back. Elle knew how he hated it when she cried. "Don't you *ever* say that again. You're just as bad as the Vemreaux, using the Light as a means to an end instead of letting her be a person along the way. I'll see to it that someday Blue's treated like a woman. I don't care that she's never had a role model of a decent man in her life. Good men exist, and if it's the last thing I do, I'll make sure you can't ruin that for her!"

"You don't know what you're talking about," he argued, though he was not sure why.

Elle laughed humorlessly. "You know what? You're right. How would I be able to spot a decent man when I've only had eyes for you?" She spun on her heel and left the kitchen.

Grettel slowly stepped down from her stool. She sniffed back her tears that fell uncontrolled like hot lava down the side of a volcano. Instead of going to Elle for comfort, she simply stood next to Baird at the chopping counter while he tried to ignore all three women in his life.

In the privacy of the kitchen, Grettel placed her dainty hand on the small of his back and began rubbing soothing circles into the fabric of his uniform. Her hands were rough from working so diligently in the kitchen, but the compassion transcended her cracked skin.

Baird's shoulders slumped. His knife faltered, dropping to the cutting board as Grettel wrapped her short arms around his waist in a private hug that was meant to bring him back to himself, no matter how hopeless that man might be.

"I'm sorry," he whispered as he leaned his chin on the top of her head. "I didn't mean it, you know. Blue's gonna be fine. She'll kill whatever's out there and come back to you with no one the wiser." He tried to pull out the most reassuring words he could muster, knowing that Grettel's hope for Blue rested largely on his and Elle's optimism. "Maybe after all of it, Stand'll still be around." As Baird spoke the words, he grimaced. Stand wasn't right for his sister. She needed someone who could be more assertive and keep her on her toes.

Baird shook his head, releasing Grettel from her duty of calming him down. He squeezed out a tight smile devoid of joy, and then shooed her away before her tear-filled eyes became contagious. "Thanks, midget."

BLUE DELIVERED THE NEW DRINK TO THE TABLE THAT HAD SPILLED IT, and then turned to Stand. He looked up at her from his seated position with such kindness in his eyes that her chest tightened as she opened her mouth.

"Thank you for all of your help, and for being so nice to me, Professor Standwicke, sir."

The formal address caught him off guard. "Blue, you know you don't have to call me that. I'm not your professor. I'm your friend."

Blue's eyes focused on the toes of her shoes. Her ten members squirmed around inside of them as she forced herself to be someone she despised. Regret bubbled in her heart at the thought of so easily destroying the first Vemreaux friendship she'd managed to make in the real world. However, Baird was the law, and he was right. Stand paid her too much attention.

Once again, it was time for her amazing disappearing act.

Blue swallowed the lump in her throat, refusing to look up. The subservient posture of her head tilted downward hid any sign that she lamented her next words. She did not want to push him away. She rather enjoyed Stand's company. But if Elle was right and he was thinking that she was a woman with choices, he needed to be cut out before his imagination ran away with him.

"I'll do the rest of my studying alone from now on. It's not appropriate for you to be seen helping an *A*-blood. I'm grateful for everything you've taught me, but I can't..." The lump threatened to choke her, and for one second, she wanted to take it all back. He was so kind.

Blue took a deep breath and recalled all that her family had already sacrificed to get her here, and everything they would still have to endure to get her over to the island.

In the end, it was not as difficult to sever the tie as she'd been anticipating. It was simply choosing Baird over a Vemreaux.

She inhaled another breath and continued on with less hesitation. "I just can't. I'm not a good person for you to be seen with. I'm nineteen, Stand." She turned on her heel and left his company before he had a chance to collect his shock.

Sadness hit Elle almost as deep as it did Blue as she watched the scene play out. She followed after Blue and saw not an emotionally shaken girl, but a robot, operating on autopilot as she sat down to roll silverware. Glaring at Baird, she filled up a glass of water to bring to Stand. He looked stunned and, indeed, very hurt.

"She's young," Elle explained quietly so that the other tables wouldn't hear. "Trust me. It's really got nothing to do with you, Stand. You're a great Vemreaux. One of the nicest that come in here. She's still new to the world."

Stand nodded in thanks, but pushed his meal aside. He slid too many bills onto the table and left with only his embarrassment intact.

18

GRETTEL'S GROWTH

At around three o'clock in the afternoon when they had a rare moment of downtime, Blue sat on the counter and opened her Geometry book with less enthusiasm than she'd had that morning.

"Learning anything good?" Baird asked as Grettel left for a bathroom break.

Instead of having the conversation her brother initiated, she started her own. "We don't have to pretend that I'm coming back after I leave here." Her eyes stayed focused on the numbers and words in front of her. "I mean, we have to fake it for the girls, but you and I?" She motioned her hand between them. "We don't have to do this. I'm not naïve."

Baird swallowed before responding, wishing for one second that someone would lie to him to protect him from the inevitabilities of their harsh life. "Good." He continued chopping.

"We need a better plan for when I figure out what my next move is. I mean, how do I leave without Master Joe sending out the search party?"

"I don't know."

"I mean, I could just run for it. I'd find a way over to the island.

I'm not betting on returning, so what does it matter if they send out the warrants?" She shrugged as if they were speaking of table arrangements instead of her death.

Baird shook his head. "I don't like it. Too public. Too risky. They'll find out that the money for your plane ticket came from my account. That information's not exactly private for Waywards. If they execute me or put me in prison, who'll look after the girls?" He sighed. "You know they'd probably just off me. I don't exactly have a forgivable face." He was joking, but there was legitimacy to the offhanded statement.

"True," she agreed churlishly.

He pretended to be affronted, but the joviality didn't last.

"I got rid of Stand."

This was information he'd assumed by the daggers Elle shot at him that afternoon, but it was nice to have it confirmed.

"I don't think he'll be back to the diner anytime soon."

"Were you at least nice to him?" Baird pretended to care, thinking it might absolve him for wanting her to never speak to the Vemreaux ever again.

"No," she stated simply, not needing to lie for reputation's sake. "He wouldn't stay away if I was nice. You wanna know the worst part?"

"Do I ever!"

"He tipped me the price of his meal. He's a good person."

"That sucks," Baird offered in what he hoped was a helpful tone. He could picture Elle grimacing.

At that moment, an interruption came in the form of the back door opening and a bored looking Femreaux strolling into the kitchen. Before Baird could shoo her out and lock the door, she waved him off as the cook Joe sent over to help out.

Gratitude was quickly replaced with confusion.

"Cook? You mean you're not a waitress?"

"No, honey. I'm not a waitress." Her crinkled nose suggested that he'd insulted her. "I'm one of the cooks at Little European?" She spoke it as a question to see if anyone had heard of it. "It's the bistro at 7th and Union Way?" She flipped her blonde locks that were streaked with sporadic pink chunks throughout and sized up the kitchen, unimpressed at what she had to work with. "I'm Stephanie."

No look of comprehension dawned on Baird or Grettel as they stared at her, still surprised at the predicament. "Hold on a minute. Just let me figure this out." Baird pinched the bridge of his nose as he tried to puzzle out just how a third cook would benefit them with their limited wait staff.

He pulled the phone out of his pocket and called Joe, leaving through the back door for privacy. The recorded message came on, and for once, he wished his owner would pick up. "Joe, it's Baird, sir. Thank you for sending over the cook, but we're still short a waitress or two. We need more help on the floor, or I can't see how we're going to handle all the customers tonight."

He hung up abruptly before he could start to whine, which was exactly what he felt like doing. When he reentered, he found the blonde Femreaux rearranging the kitchen more to her liking, telling Grettel to move things for her so that she could see how they looked in their new spaces. Grettel's eyes darted to Baird unhappily as her compliant nature obeyed.

"Grettel, can I talk to you for a minute?" he asked, holding the back door open for her as she walked outside.

"What are we going to do, Baird? Is Joe sending someone to help Elle and Blue?"

"I don't know," he groaned, wishing his brain would hurry up and find a better solution. "Grettel, do you think you can waitress tonight?" His words caused her eyes to widen and panic to hit her features, just as he knew it would. "I would do it myself, but I have to be at the bar making drinks."

"But Baird, I don't know. I mean, I'm…I can't! I don't know how to be a waitress! You mean I would have to talk to the Vemreaux and bring them their food on those big trays?" Her eyes darted around the parking lot as if a better reason than "this is a bad idea" would come to her. "But what if I drop the tray and the food goes all over? What if Emperor Anders comes into the bar and I spill his drink on him? He could have me killed, Baird! I don't want to die!" The moisture in her eyes was always so close to the surface. It gathered and spilled out in droplets onto the tops of her pale cheeks.

"Shh." He tried to calm her through his amusement at her wild exaggerations. Reaching out, he held her head to his chest and patted her hair. Immediately she calmed down and snuggled into the warmth. "The great Emperor Tom Holloway Anders has never been to the bar, but I'll tell the girls to take the important tables if we get any, okay? You can make more than one trip to the tables when you drop off the food, so the tray won't be as heavy as you think. The girls'll show you."

"But Baird, I...I don't know how to be a waitress! Some of the Vemreaux are not nice at all! I just want to be in the kitchen with you!" Her tears sprang afresh and dampened his uniform as she squeaked out her fears. Her greatest ambition in life since she'd left The Way was to hide in the background behind the strength of Baird.

"Do you think I'd ask you if there was any other way?" He rested his chin on the top of her head.

"Why won't that Femreaux do it? Can't you make her go out there?"

"She's here to help out Joe, and she won't waitress. We don't have another option." He released her from the hug as soon as it hit fifteen seconds. He wasn't big into showing affection, but occasionally bent for Grettel in private. "Now let's go back in and let Blue and Elle run you through everything. It won't be as bad as you're thinking." He tried his best to reassure her, but she only cried more consistently.

"Can I...can I just have a minute out here?" she asked through her condensation.

How any man could say no to her was beyond him. She was so small and unassuming. "Of course, short stuff. I'll send one of the girls out in a few minutes."

When Baird went back into the kitchen, Grettel's tears flowed more freely.

So blinded by emotion was she, that Grettel didn't even notice the figure approaching until it was standing in front of her. She gasped in surprise at the sight of a gritty-toothed man. She recognized him as the pimp Baird hated so much. She couldn't recall his name, but she knew that he helped run a nearby Wayward prostitution ring. She'd only seen him in passing, but each time, Baird snarled at him and his practices. His fingernails were crusty, and his teeth were the shade of cheddar cheese.

"Hi, beautiful."

Grettel did not respond, but merely wiped her tears away. He was the first man to ever call her beautiful, and it felt dirty. She trembled.

He looked down at her welcomingly. "I saw you crying." He breathed his foul breath in her face. "I don't like to see pretty girls so sad."

"I'm not supposed to talk to you. You're a bad man." Grettel sniffled, not able to look up at him.

"Who told you that I'm a bad man? Is that guy you're always with your owner? I thought he was A-blood."

His breath made her blanch, but she braved the unpleasant odor to answer. "Baird's not Vemreaux. And Joe's my owner."

"You look unhappy with them. You have options, you know. You don't have to stay with someone who makes you so miserable. Is he your boyfriend?" His words fell like smooth silk from the disgusting mouth.

Grettel guffawed and blushed. She did not have options, and Baird was not her boyfriend, nor did he make her miserable. "I don't have a boyfriend. And I'm not unhappy with Baird. He takes care of us."

The man reached out and wiped a tear from Grettel's cheek with his filthy hand, taking in her skittish flinch. "Is this how he takes care of you? He leaves you alone to cry?"

Grettel cringed at the contact, but could not move any further back against the concrete of the wall. She let out a whine of distress.

"I think he doesn't take very good care of you."

"I...I..."

His words upset her, and she refused to believe them. Though Grettel's mind was firmly set against him, her body was too scared to move. Her frightened eyes met his as he lifted his hand to hold her face. "My family's got room for you if you ever decide that there's more for you out there than what Baird has to offer."

No sooner did the words come out of his mouth than the back door to the diner opened, introducing Blue to the unwelcome scene. She froze only for a second, wishing she could thrash the guy herself.

"Baird!" Blue shouted urgently over her shoulder before the black had a chance to creep in on her vision.

Her brother dropped the knife and radish that he held and bolted for his sister immediately. He knew that she would never raise her voice and draw such attention to herself if it was not vital.

The unwelcome man dropped Grettel's face and held his hands up in surrender. This claim of innocence had no affect on Baird, and upon seeing the pimp, his charging footsteps did not slow.

"Get outta here!" Baird shouted in his deep, commanding voice.

"Just having a conversation," the man defended himself coolly.

"There's nothing for you here, so go!" Baird watched every retreating step. He stalked back purposefully, ignoring his sister's disgruntled stare and glaring at Grettel.

New tears bathed Grettel's cheeks as she pressed herself to the wall to escape the wrath that she was sure would now be pointed at her.

"What was he doing?" he asked accusatorially.

Grettel sobbed pitifully. "I don't kn-know! He just came over here after you went inside and started t-talking to me!" Grettel recounted the conversation to the two, and as Baird's anger subsided, her sobs calmed down to hiccups. "That's all that happened! I promise!"

Baird sent his sister back inside so he could have a word with Grettel. He moved from standing confrontationally across from the dainty girl to standing beside her. "Do you want to leave, Grettel?" he asked quietly. "Do you want to go with that guy?"

Grettel shook her head quickly, but Baird waited before continuing.

"I wish you could do whatever you wanted, but you can't leave. Joe bought you, which means you have to stay where he puts you."

He sighed, letting his shoulders lose some of their tension. "Even if it were possible for you to leave without being hunted down, you can't go because of what you know about Blue. I know it sucks sometimes, but we're all we've got, and we need to stay together." He kicked at the dirt sadly. "We need you, Grettel. Who's gonna keep me from going off on Elle when she runs her mouth? The girls need you. Blue only just got you back. You know how many friends she has? Two. Oh, and that George kid, who doesn't know her secret, and who she'll never see again."

Grettel buried her head in her hands.

Baird looked over at her to make sure she'd stopped crying and was actually hearing him. "You can't go making friends with dangerous people like that guy. He's a fisher. An *A*-blood pimp. Do you know what he does with girls like you? He convinces you he's got something better, but all that happens is he takes you to the commune, then he makes money off of you selling your body to desperate unchanged Vemreaux. You get rescued by the cops? They throw you in jail or off you for running out on your master. Trust me, squirt. You don't want that life." The thought made him angry and sick at the same time, twisting his mouth into a bitter expression. It wasn't just any girl, it was Grettel. *His* Grettel.

Grettel looked up at him, her chocolate eyes swimming with emotion. "Baird, I would never leave you. Not for that guy or anyone. You keep me safe."

Baird gave her a small smile, shaking off any unnecessary emotion that threatened to shake his worldview. "And I always will, shorty. Come here." Baird wrapped one arm around her head, mussing her hair gently. "Let's go, midget. Today's the first day of the rest of your life and all that. Your new career as a waitress awaits!" He laughed as she groaned, allowing him to pull her back inside.

By the look on Elle's face, they both guessed correctly that Blue had filled her in on what transpired outside. "What's wrong with you?" she sneered. Though the question was directed at Baird, Grettel shrank off to the side. She took off her long white apron to exchange it for a short black one the waitresses wore.

"What?" He went back to cutting the radish he'd left on the island.

"What? Why didn't you tear his kidneys out and feed 'em to him? He'd take her as soon as look at her, and you know it! He's a degenerate loser who'll keep fishing for Wayward girls to add to his collection! Do you think Joe'd be fine with letting that scumbag put his filthy hands on his property like that?"

The Femreaux who'd joined them for the week was trying to ignore them as she studied the recipes before starting out cooking.

"I think it might be time to switch you from Grade *A* rations to Grade *V*," Baird mentioned with a raised eyebrow. "You're getting a little aggressive." Baird motioned with the knife for Elle to walk away. He did not want to discuss anything in front of the Femreaux.

Elle looked like she wanted to argue, but surprised him (and herself) by biting her tongue and stalking out of the kitchen.

Blue filled up a glass with a strawberry-flavored *O*-Negative smoothie, exchanging a silent look with Baird that told him she agreed with Elle. Instead of speaking her feelings, she simply put a straw in the glass and motioned for Grettel to follow.

The small girl obeyed, but she possessed no poker face. Fear contorted Grettel's features and caused her to loop her fingers together in nervous knots when she followed Blue out into the dining area. She kept her eyes trained on Blue's shoes, counting the little venture a success if she made it out of the kitchen and back without having a nervous breakdown.

She watched with a lump in her throat as Blue took the table's order, jotted it down on a pad and dismissed herself from their presence. Grettel was surprised to find that her friend did this all while looking either at her shoes or at her order pad. Blue had a superior memory to anyone Grettel had ever met, but she was relieved that her friend still used the order pad to appear normal, forgetful even. Grettel breathed easier when they moved back into the kitchen.

The Femreaux still had not started cooking at all. Baird looked as if he wanted to use the knife in his hand on something other than the radishes rolling around on the cutting board in front of him.

As sorry as they felt for Grettel, they began to see the long night ahead for Baird, as well. Elle twirled a lock of gold hair in her fingers, as was her custom when she went about plan-making. "One of my tables is mostly older Vemreaux changed in their forties, I'd guess. Grettel, you can take them. I already brought them their drinks. They'll be a good first table."

Blue agreed, but Grettel wasn't sure that any table would be a good first one for her.

Elle kept prattling on to make her more comfortable. "In my experience, the older they make the change, the nicer they are. Something about their more mature appearance makes them seem, well, more mature." She cast around for the proper word, but it escaped her. "You'll do fine, Grettel. Honestly, it won't be as bad as you're thinking. I mean, Blue here barely looks up at the customers and still manages. You don't have to impress them or anything. Just take their orders, bring them out, refresh their drinks. No biggie, right?"

"I don't know," Grettel said nervously. She twisted the fabric of her shirt in her fingers.

Elle kissed her forehead and filled up another blood smoothie. "Now, go on out there to table three in my section and say, 'May I take your order, sirs?' Write down whatever they say and come back to the kitchen. We'll watch you from here." Grettel looked like she might cry again. "Go on, honey. I've already told them to be easy on you."

Swallowing, Grettel double checked that she had everything in her short waitress apron. The black material left her feeling completely exposed as she took her first step obediently forward.

Just then, someone pounded loudly on the back door to the kitchen, causing Grettel to yelp.

Baird wiped his hands off and moved over to open the door. The Vemreaux standing in front of him looked bored and unimpressed as he strolled past the Wayward.

"Joe said I'd make more in tips than I usually do at Olive's. Is that true?"

Baird grumbled, "You're late," but the Vemreaux did not seem to notice.

Grettel spun around to look at the new Vemreaux. "You're a waiter?" she squeaked. It was the first time she'd initiated a conversation with a stranger of the superior race. The relief on her face and in her voice lit up the room.

"Uh-huh. Tips good here?" he asked, unsure if he was actually going to stay and work.

"Decent," Elle confirmed, sliding a straw into the drinks she filled. "You'll pull in over a hundred bills easy by the end of the night."

He did not look impressed, but he slid off his jacket to indicate that he would bless them with his presence. "I'm Steve. How late do you stay open?"

As he spoke to the girls, Blue could tell that he was trying not to breathe the scent of sulfur that all changed Vemreaux could smell on the skin of A-bloods. His nose wrinkled in disgust.

Grettel's waitress apron was already off, as was the weight of the world. She almost skipped over to the hook that held the cooking aprons and twirled the strings of the white covering into a happy bow. Then she picked up an order from the nail the waitresses placed them on and started filling it.

"Happy about something, midget?" Baird asked with a smirk. He was almost as relieved as she was that she did not have to go out and smile amongst the wolves.

"Oh, you know me," she almost sang. "Just glad to be at work." Her grin was giddy.

Baird laughed, drawing the eyes of the wait staff. The Femreaux, Stephanie, still did not look up from the stack of recipes, making them all wonder how much help she'd be to them at this rate.

Though all Vemreaux had beautification available to them to partake of before their appearance was frozen for one hundred twenty years, it did more for some than for others. Steve had brown greasy hair and a smattering of freckles that almost changed his skin tone from pale white to a spotted brown. His black eyes were set beneath one eyebrow that really should have been two, and he had so much dirt under his fingernails that Elle was glad he wasn't bringing her any food or drink. She was just as disgusted with him as he was with them.

The girls took him out into the dining area to show him how the tables should be divided. It was decided that when the outdoor vicinity opened, Elle would take that and leave Blue and Steve to tend to the two sections inside. Though Blue was not thrilled with this idea, she kept it to herself, knowing that she could better handle Steve than Elle. The two had already descended from a veiled dislike to out and out criticism.

"I'm just saying, you could've at least washed that gunk out from under your fingernails, since you're going to be serving food and all. You think people want to see the nature center you're growing under there?" She snapped when her third hint that he should wash his hands went over his head.

"Yeah, well all the soap in the world wouldn't do a thing for that stink coming offa you. Ever hear of perfume? I wouldn't want my food brought to me with the cloud of rotten eggs you'd bring along with it."

Elle fumed at this socially inappropriate insult.

Blue excused herself to go check on her tables and seat a new group of Vemreaux waiting at the hostess stand. She sensed it would be a long night with the two of them going back and forth, and she was right.

19

STONE BONIFACE

*B*rody could tell Liam was trying to say something, but the fifth downed shot was beginning to affect the prince's speech. That, or the techno had addled his brain, as Alec was fond of warning them.

"What?" Brody shouted.

"Where's Sam?" Liam repeated.

"Sam?" Brody clarified. "In the bathroom with some Fem."

"Sweet! Then we can stay a little longer?"

"What?"

Liam tired of yelling to his friend and motioned for Brody to move away from the speaker. The club was packed, so weaving through the crowd with his guard took a little strategy. Eventually, they found their way to the bar where Alec was sitting.

Alec tapped his watch, not bothering to speak the words that would only provoke whining requests from the prince to stay longer. Alec had consumed what he hoped was his last mozzarella stick ever, and wiped the grease from his hands onto a napkin.

Brody shook his head when Alec made to stand. "Sam's not ready."

Alec pulled out his phone and texted his friend. "What's he doing?"

"Who. Who's he doing." Liam winked, unable to stop bopping just because he left the dance floor.

"Oh, brother. I'm not waiting around for that." Alec punched in another irritated message to Sam. "We have to get you to the testing in a little bit. First round starts in a few hours. Plus, you've got golf in the morning with Ronald Cho."

"Push it back!" Liam exclaimed, fist in the air. His swaying hips moved closer to Alec as he indulged in a suggestive groove, happy to annoy his guard.

"Owner of Amsteron doesn't push things back, Li. And get off me," Alec grumbled, elbowing his charge back a few paces. "If Sam's not out here in five, I'm going in there, and it won't be pretty."

"Five minutes?" Liam confirmed. "That's a whole song! See ya!" The prince escaped back to the crowd of partiers before Alec could protest.

Alec waved for Brody to follow Liam. Wrangling the prince took at least twenty minutes at every attempt, and only made Alec surlier each time. He drank the rest of his water and tried to flag down the bartender for a refill, but the employee was swamped with people ordering more costly drinks. Alec sighed, wishing for pancakes and a chair that had an actual back to it. He was tired of barstools and bar food and barflies. And even though it was only slightly past dinnertime, Alec was just plain tired.

He was about to go looking for Sam when he spotted the messy dark brown hair approaching. Alec flagged him down, noting the disheveled appearance that left little mystery as to what he'd been up to. "Time to go," Alec stated when Sam reached him at the bar.

"Need me to grab Liam?"

"Yeah. You coming back to the hotel with us?"

"Of course. We finished."

Alec sighed. "Did this one at least give you her name?"

"You mean did she give 'Stone Boniface' her name? I dunno. Probably. I didn't think to ask."

"You know that your fake name makes you sound dumb as a rock, right?"

Sam's expression drew up in confusion. "What? No, it doesn't. Stone sounds cool. Badass from Europe." He shook his head. "Stone didn't call you back? Must be because he's tearing it up overseas on his motorbike."

"Or because he's waiting for his best friend's nanny to make him a cup of tea."

"Stone doesn't drink tea. He drinks beer. American beer!" Sam pushed his fists together at his stomach and flexed. "Then he crushes the can on his head!"

"Stone, Brick, Pan, Sam...whatever you're calling yourself these days, go get Liam. I'll bring the car around."

Sam tried to flag down Brody, but with all the jumping bodies and waving hands, it was near impossible to be seen. He had no choice; he simply had to go back onto the dance floor.

Instead of forging his way through the crowd, Sam picked the most scantily-clad Femreaux in easy reach and made his way to her. She had dyed blonde hair with brown streaks, teased into a do that Sam was positive would start on fire with all the product she'd put in it. She was dancing with four girlfriends, who all smiled flirtatiously when Sam approached.

"Wow," he commented appreciatively to the one with the skimpiest outfit. "You look amazing."

"Thanks! Not so bad yourself. I'm Penny."

Sam smirked. "Stone. Stone Boniface. You also look like you want to help me find my friend. Ladies, mind if I borrow your queen for a minute?" Sam explained his plan in as few sentences as possible. He'd done this no less than once a week ever since he'd started bar-hopping with Liam. It was more effective than going to the prince. Best make the prince come to him.

Penny fell for the devious smirk. She fell for the handsome features and the alluring European accent. She fell for the eye contact that made her feel the special one to garner such a sexy Vemreaux's attention. Before she knew it, she was agreeing to his hands on her hips as he turned her around. Penny shrieked as Sam tossed her in the air, catching her deftly on her way down.

The buxom beauty's barely covered bosoms bounced, catching the eye of most men in the vicinity, some of whom cheered. Liam's finger shot up from the sea of faces, indicating to Sam that he'd received the signal and was on his way over.

Penny giggled as Sam spun her around. Her arms flew around his neck as Sam indulged the flushed woman in a few beats of a dance while he waited for Liam and Brody.

Penny's tongue was in Sam's mouth by the time Liam's fingers slowly crept up Sam's side. "Ah! Liam, get off!" Sam protested, pulling away from the kiss.

If Sam had his way of breaking Liam from the crowd, Liam had his own manner of pulling Sam away from his lust-filled trysts. "Whoa!" the prince commented. "She looks exactly like your mum, Stone! Amazing!" Liam turned to Penny. "Do me a favor and say, 'Stone! Eight-year-olds don't need to breastfeed!' in that exact voice!"

Penny pulled back, horrified. "Um, thanks for the dance," she said as she ran back to her friends.

"Thanks for that," Sam muttered. "And you know my mum's a brunette and looks nothing like that one."

"Yeah, but she doesn't know that. I got your signal. We gotta go, yeah?"

"You know…" Sam ran his hands through his hair, searching for a jab good enough to toss at his best friend.

"You love me?" Liam suggested, finishing Sam's sentence to his own liking.

"Not right now, no."

Liam's grin was unabashed as he bopped toward the exit, grabbing a discarded drink from the bar and downing the dregs as they left.

20

GRETTEL'S CONFESSION

Though Grettel's anxiety spiked at being alone with the Femreaux in the kitchen when Baird left to tend bar, she was grateful for the help. Compared with what she thought would be her position for the rest of the week, her relief smoothed over the ridges of fear that usually etched into her forehead.

More drinks were ordered than meals, and the two cooks had some downtime to contend with, though not enough for the Femreaux to go home. Grettel began turning over things in the kitchen that she rarely had the time to clean and gave them a good scrubbing while the Femreaux talked on her phone to just about everyone she knew as she prepped food for the next day.

When it seemed she reached the end of her lengthy call list, Stephanie turned to make the best of the night by conversing with the shy Grettel. She pulled up a photo album on her phone and waved the small girl over. "Come look at my pictures of Asia. Went their last year on vacation. Pretty, right?" She flipped through the photos quickly, adding a short commentary here and there.

Grettel was enthralled; she'd never seen pictures from another country.

"Do you live around here?"

Grettel nodded, but didn't know if she was allowed to tell her exactly where. Baird so coveted their privacy. Her shyness often kept her from saying things he'd rather she didn't.

"I live about twenty-five kilometers north in Capital City." She said as she shut her phone. "Are you going to see the parade when it starts out?"

Grettel nodded, the childlike gleam in her eyes conveying her interest in being there in person. "I want to see the jugglers," she confessed with very little volume to her voice.

"What's that?" Stephanie asked for some amplification as she pulled a basket of potato wedges and turnips from the fryer.

"The jugglers. I want to see them."

Stephanie laughed. "I can't wait to see the Vemreaux on stilts as high as a building. I always secretly want to go up there and push them over, just to see if I can."

Grettel gasped at the scandalous confession.

The Femreaux laughed again. "I wouldn't actually do it. But every time I see them walking around like that, I just get the urge, you know?" She dumped the wire container's fried contents into three napkin-lined woven baskets. "Do you ever feel like that about anything? Like you can see yourself doing something dangerous or bad, but you know you'd never really do it?"

Grettel looked from left to right nervously, as if someone would be there to arrest her upon answering the question. She paused for so long that the Femreaux gave up the hope of occupying their time with a conversation. She hadn't known or worked with many Waywards personally, and she wondered if they were all this skittish around the Vemreaux.

Grettel surprised Stephanie by leaning forward and answering like she might get caught and thrown in prison with such unruly thoughts. "Sometimes," Grettel said, her eyes darting around again like a cornered animal. "Sometimes I can see myself knocking over that tray of straws over there. I think about it every day at least once." Quickly, she held her hands up before the Femreaux could judge her too harshly. "I've never ever done it, but," she looked wistfully at the tall pile of clear straws with red lines down the sides, "I think they'd look pretty all messy on the floor." She put her hand over her mouth to keep her from speaking anything more outrageous. Grettel hoped that the Femreaux wouldn't tell on her for it.

Stephanie stared at the girl in confusion for a moment before letting out the loudest laugh she'd permitted in quite a while.

Grettel jumped back at the eruption, but then slowly relaxed and shared in the levity when it died down into a giggle. Tears peppered Stephanie's cheeks with the joy at hearing such an inoffensive confession.

"You act like you're talking about committing a murder or something. I'll tell you what, if you knock over that pile of straws, I'll help you pick them up so quick that no one will ever know."

Grettel gasped and shook her head so fast that Stephanie was surprised her eyes did not rattle.

"Go on. I think it'd be good for you." When Grettel still didn't look convinced, Stephanie whined. "Oh, come on! I can never do mine in real life. That'll always be something I think about. But you can do yours and no one'll get hurt! Please, Grettel? I swear, no one will ever know. We can even put down napkins on the floor so that they won't have to be thrown out." This slowed Grettel's resistance. "Come on! I'd do it myself, but I think it'd be good for you to be a little reckless. It wouldn't be the same if I did it. I don't think it would even count."

Grettel paused in the throes of her existential crisis. The debate in her head was so furious that she feared she might lose her mind if she did not make a decision soon. "You'll help me pick them up?"

Stephanie nodded vigorously, her black eyes twinkling with glee. "So fast, no one'll ever know. It'll be our little secret."

After another moment's pause, Grettel finally moved toward the pile, eyeing it with trepidation.

Stephanie practically danced over to the container of napkins and pulled out a few, opening them up and placing them on the ground to make a wide area for Grettel to do her damage.

With trembling fingers, Grettel reached toward the small silver bin they were piled high in, but stopped short of touching it. "In my imagination, it's really more of an accident," she explained, her brow furrowed.

"Okay." Stephanie would not be deterred from the only fun thing that had happened that day. "So, you and I are having a conversation about cute men and we're talking with our hands a lot. I say something like, 'Isn't Baird hot for an A-blood?' And you say…"

"Um, can we pretend to talk about something else?" Grettel was uncomfortable thinking of the safe and steady man that way.

"Sure. Let's talk about the sexual tension between him and that blonde waitress. What's her name?" she asked. Stephanie looked up at the ceiling as if the name might be written up there.

"Elle." Grettel smiled, her eyes already gearing up to beam her amusement at the new topic. "She's got a big crush on him," she confessed, placing a finger across her lips to indicate that it was supposed to be a secret.

"Talk with your hands. Remember, it has to look like an accident."

"Oh, yeah." Grettel shook her head. This time spreading her hands wide, she repeated, "Elle's got a *big* crush on Baird."

"How big?" Stephanie pointed to the shiny bin, encouraging Grettel to go for the gold.

"Huge!" Grettel laughed and then sucked in her breath as her hand landed on the silver tray, knocking it to the ground.

Straws flew everywhere, soaring to heights they never imagined possible. Most of the plastic cylinders never even hoped for the independence she granted them, and they fell immediately to the floor with barely a clatter. A few practically jumped out of the bin as if they'd waited since the day they were formed for the chance to fly higher than their lifespan would allow. They all but leapt out into the air, some gracefully, and some spiraling with no thought of control. Each one parted atoms and changed the air current, no matter how unnoticeable. Those brave straws hit the floor, reveling in the reverberation that echoed up their bodies, doing justice to the exuberance they put forth for their once-in-a-lifetime adventure.

The contained pile looked much smaller in the bin than when gravity allowed them to spread out wherever they chose on the floor. The lengthy sticks danced to their freedom, rolling as far out as they could to escape the prison of the silver tray that held them perfectly in place. A few more audacious ones rolled off of the napkin barrier and dared to sully themselves on the floor in their escape for liberty. They coveted each centimeter that belonged, for the moment, only to them.

Grettel squealed in shock, horror and delight as they fell like matchsticks in unruly piles, strewn about at her feet like a pack of cards with no chain of command.

All of a sudden, Grettel felt very tall and powerful. The straws, though they were free, seemed to bow to her and kiss the tops of her shoes for granting them this one moment of liberty. Some were grateful to lay flat in a place other than their silver prison, but others used those around them to stand up almost straight in the air, bragging to the world that they would not be pushed down, crushed to the ground without resistance. Grettel reached below her and lifted one such straw up, examining its beauty. Then she tucked it into the pocket of her apron with dainty hands that never possessed the strength that solitary straw did.

Stephanie did not move to pick up the mess at first because she was so captivated by the striking difference this one act of rebellion had on the submissive girl. Grettel did not look like the same young woman she'd met when she arrived earlier that day. She appeared strong and confident, with an edge of feistiness to her that was unexpected. Stephanie watched as the girl fingered the single straw, holding onto it as a memento of the day. Stephanie knelt not to clean up, but to do the same, carefully choosing a straw that stood erect in the pile of fallen soldiers and placing it in her pocket, as well.

"Oh, the mess!" Grettel exclaimed, snapping out of her reverie and falling to her knees to scoop up the straws in handfuls.

Just like that, the timid girl was back, but Stephanie felt privileged that she was one of the few people in the world who got to see the girl step out boldly for once in her life, if only for a moment.

"That was incredible!" Stephanie squealed as she hurriedly gripped the straws and stashed them back in their place. She moved quickly because the look on Grettel's face suggested she may succumb to a panic attack at any moment for all the chaos she caused. "Really, amazing! I mean, I don't really know you, but I'm so proud of you! Who knows? I may follow in your footsteps and kick the stilts out from one of those clowns on Peace Day after all!"

Her giddy grin made Grettel grimace. "No! Don't do that!" she insisted before she realized that Stephanie was joking. She looked down sheepishly, making sure they'd retrieved all of the straws.

What their searching eyes failed to notice were two rebellious straws hiding underneath the island in the center of the kitchen, waiting for the proper time to escape out into the world.

ELLE'S SPONTANEOUS COMBUSTION

The bar was packed so tightly that the outdoor area was a relief for the overflow. The evening was a bit colder than most would have preferred, but at the very least, it kept jackets clutched over the bare arms of the scantily clad Femreaux that frequented the place in search of a drink, a dance and possibly a date for the evening.

Joe had a contractor come in that afternoon. The Vemreaux fit the sound system and jukebox with speakers that piped the music to the outdoor dining area. Everyone was impressed with the clarity of the sound. Elle could hear every song perfectly as more and more brandishes were dropped into the slot. Tunes that were much harsher than the government-approved ones brought out the drinker and dancer in nearly every Vemreaux in attendance.

It was almost nine o'clock when Elle noticed the very important Secretary Graham Anders and his one-man entourage walk from their black car slowly toward her, each step taken methodically and purposefully in the direction of the waitress. Just like his posters that hung in shop windows to announce his many accomplishments, Secretary Graham's smile appeared forced.

The wave of fear that echoed up through her spine like an electric shock was quickly suppressed before it shown in the eyes that caught his. Amidst the many tables that demanded her attention, Elle paused to nod at him, acknowledging the official's presence. Attempting to ignore him as he walked straight toward her was a wasted effort. Wherever else she tried to look, she found her eyes being drawn back to him in his expensive, hand-crafted black suit with gold trim.

"Eloise Louise Anders?" Secretary Graham inquired when he reached her.

A few diners looked up in surprise, whispering with both fear and excitement that it looked like a Wayward might get taken in for either testing, or for incarceration.

"Sir," Elle responded briefly, the busyness of the night not allowing for lengthy conversations. "You can sit anywhere that's open out here, or you can wait for a table inside."

Each movement she made down to wiping off one of the few vacated tables was watched by the two as they mentally took notes of everything she did. "May we speak to your owner, Eloise Louise Anders?" Secretary Graham asked evenly.

"My owner isn't here, but Baird speaks for him when he's gone. He's inside at the bar." Her thumb jerked over her shoulder toward the diner behind her. Flashing them a parting smile that suggested more levity than she felt at the moment, she turned her back on them to tend to a not-so-patiently waiting table. Being referred to as "excuse me" or "waitress" did nothing to bolster her self-esteem. She took it all in stride though, knowing that soon enough, the testing would be over, and she could stop the training and the covering for Blue.

As she gathered up orders to turn into Baird and the kitchen, her trepidation changed into curiosity as her eyes fell upon the Secretary of the Militia for the Americas speaking to Baird privately over the bar. Baird was nodding stiffly, as if he did not really want to say yes to the men, but for some reason had to. Elle wondered idly what Baird's world would be like if he permitted a voice to his own opinions in public. She was surprised when Baird took a business card from the

Secretary and abandoned the bar to disappear into the kitchen. Her prying eyes being what they were, Elle decided her orders needed to be personally handed to the cooks, so she entered the kitchen a few steps behind him.

The phone was already pressed to the side of Baird's grim face as he muttered a rushed message into the mouthpiece. She thought she heard her name and decided to put her tables on hold for the moment and wait for an explanation. She hadn't eaten in a while, so she took a bite of the sandwich Grettel made for her that she'd only been able to nibble on once in the past two hours.

Once Baird pressed the red button to end the call, his eyes fell on hers. The mixture of dread and resolve was an odd wash on his face, and she did not know what to make of it. "What's going on?" Elle inquired through her masticated food.

Baird did not answer at first, but only stared. Elle's unease grew as he sifted through the words he wanted to say, choosing carefully the ones he was required to. "The Secretary of the Militia for the Americas is out at the bar right now."

"I know. I saw him walk in."

"Well, he just told me that he's here for the testing. They'll collect you tonight and take you with them to Capital City. They'll bring you back tomorrow before your next shift." He glanced down at the phone in his hand. "I just have to get the okay from Joe first, who never picks up when I call."

Elle froze with her bite of sandwich still in her mouth as she processed his words with a wave of nausea.

Grettel gasped, while Stephanie did not understand what was going on.

Without looking at any of the women, Baird spoke. "Stephanie, would you mind taking a break for a few minutes? I need to talk with the girls real quick."

Stephanie obliged, glancing once more at Grettel for an explanation before exiting out the back door.

When Elle still didn't make any move to reply, Baird tried to soothe her. "The way Secretary Graham was talking, I think they're going to try to test the 'won't rest until the tyranny is put to an end' part by making sure that you don't sleep. Why else would they show up with no warning and take you all night? They'd probably keep you all week if you weren't owned by Joe. I'm thinking the ones that still live in The Way'll be kept and observed the whole time."

"But Baird, I do sleep! And after a day like today, I'll need to sleep a lot!" As soon as she broke her silence, the words started flowing out of her quickly. She rejected the rest of her sandwich and placed the plate on the counter. Grettel ran over to Elle and hugged her fiercely, trembling for her friend.

With more grace than he usually cared to access, Baird moved to Elle and lifted her hand, detaching Grettel and pulling Elle to him. This contact was very different. The trepidation in his eyes made his arms wrap not around her shoulders, as they usually did during the infrequent times he'd been forced to show affection. Instead, they draped around her waist. The ease with which he held her as he ran his thumb up and down her spine slowly relaxed her posture. He smiled as an involuntary shudder ripped through her.

The apprehension in Baird gave way to a gentler tone than his usual gruff cadence. "Grettel, will you stand outside the door for a minute and keep Blue and Steve out? We need some time."

Grettel's mouth fell open, but she quickly obeyed, braving her dread of being in such close contact with the Vemreaux to give Elle her long-awaited moment.

As soon as the door shut behind her, his face moved forward to place his cheek to Elle's, rubbing the rough stubble against her smooth cheek.

Elle's breath came in short bursts as her mind raced to verify that this was, in fact, happening. That she hadn't grown so tired waiting for him to make a move that she was hallucinating the contact. Her fingers rose from her side and brushed across the back of his neck to give him the green light for anything else he wanted to do.

Baird had long pictured this moment, and as he kissed her cheek to gear up for what they both wanted, he savored the softness of her creamy skin. He whispered in her ear, his breath tickling her and causing goosebumps to erupt down her arms. "Do you want something to think about tonight to keep you from falling asleep?" He moved his hand to the back of her hip.

Of all the times Elle had imagined him making his move on her, she always had some witty reply that served as their foreplay. In the reality of being awake and finally in his arms, Elle could scarcely remember her own name as he breathed onto her skin so seductively. Her brain pushed out a muddled sound of affirmation that her mouth garbled.

That was all that Baird needed. Years of unrequited sexual tension came to a climax as his kiss moved to her chin, his fingers tracing her throat, and then finally, at long last, to her patient lips.

Heat washed through them both like a warm river current, never calming as it continued to stir and crash in waves over their bodies. Elle's lips parted to allow more of the kiss to invade her senses. Her mind flitted so fast over the sensation that she found coherent thought impossible. She let out a soft moan, drawing a throaty rumble from Baird as he deepened the kiss. With no practice, their lips moved in mashed synchronicity. The urgency of their years spent abstaining from such pleasure finally came to an explosive end.

Baird kissed Elle over and over, doing justice to the many times he'd seen himself take her in his strong arms and press her beautiful body to his. She bent to his will easily, molding her limbs around him in ways he wanted, but would never ask for. Her fingers traced the back of his neck, his jaw, his shoulder and his waist. It was as if they had a mind of their own.

Each stroke of Elle's hand brought a grateful kiss that Baird couldn't rein in. It was when he pulled away from her mouth to lay urgent kisses on her throat that words found her. "I love you, Baird," Elle whispered with so much emotion that Baird had to close his eyes.

He wished she hadn't said it, but there it was, out in the open air, threatening to choke the life out of him as his lips touched on her collarbone. Too many responses rushed past him, making it difficult to pick out the right one. He knew what she wanted to hear, but it simply wasn't in his nature to say it. Instead, he went for the most he could give her, which was a huge leap for him. "You know you're the only one I want."

This was clearly not an "I love you", but Elle made do, glad that the kiss did not end with him shutting down on her because of her admission in the moment of weakness.

Baird brought his lips back to hers before she could say anything else that would push him in deeper than he was ready to go. "Tonight," he began, changing the subject, "when you're in Capital City..." Baird blessed her mouth urgently again and again, building up the passion a second time. "I want you to think about how good and bad we are together." His lips muffled any response she could make. "I want you to think about how much I want you." His hand grabbed her hip and squeezed, drawing a yelp from her. "How much I've always wanted you." Over and over they drank from each other's fervor, relishing the taste of such closeness and closure from years of attraction.

With the punch of a gong, the phone in Baird's pocket rang. A frustrated growl expelled from Baird as the never-ending duties of his life tapped him on the shoulder. Before he spoke, he ran his hand over his face to regain some semblance of composure, and let his fingers rest on the back of his neck.

"Yes, sir?" he answered.

Elle touched her fingers to her lips and closed her eyes as she savored the sensation of his lips tasting hers. Taking a step back, she leaned against the countertop to steady herself until she could trust her legs to stop shaking. As Baird mumbled into the phone one- or two-word answers, Elle tried to convince herself that this was not just another of her plentiful daydreams. Baird had really kissed her.

Before he even hung up, his left forearm decided that it had been far too long without her and pulled her forward into a one-armed embrace as he spoke with his owner. When the presence of Joe was gone from the room, Baird leaned in, gently this time, and placed a barely-there kiss on her malleable lips.

"Joe gave you the okay to go with them. He just got off the phone with Secretary Anders to make sure he sends you back in the morning before your next shift. Joe wished you luck." There were too many words to say without breaking them up with another kiss.

His finger curled under her chin and lifted it slightly to place another light command to her willing lips. "You can leave with them after we close up. Joe said that they'll just have to wait." He brushed his lips back and forth across hers slowly without landing on them and stopping to savor another kiss.

Her eyes fluttered shut again as she enjoyed his teasing caress.

"What am I going to do without you?" The last kiss he laid on her lips was so tender that a whimper escaped her mouth as he pulled away. Her tough resolve had forsaken her, leaving her a puddle of lovey goo that could barely keep its eyes open.

Unable to keep the cocky grin from taking over, Baird patted her cheek twice in satisfaction. "Don't you leave without saying goodbye, Elle." With that, Baird left her to gather her bearings in the privacy of the abandoned kitchen.

2 2

ONE NIGHT AWAY

The night rushed by, and all too soon the Secretary and his assistant were ushering Elle out of the bar. With her game face fixed firmly in place, Elle marched out of the building in desperate need of a shower and sleep. Baird knew that she would not receive either.

Steve sat down to count his tips, but Baird leaned the chair forward. "Get up and clean or get out. You're not getting paid an hourly wage on top of those tips to count your money."

Steve grumbled, but muffled the more offensive words due to Baird's menacing presence. Baird frowned when Steve still had not made a decision. "I'll make it simple for you. Get out. Tomorrow when you decide to come to work, make sure it's on time."

"Whatever," Steve mumbled as he left the building.

All through their cleanup of the diner, Baird tried not to notice Grettel's and even Blue's knowing looks regarding the advance he finally made with Elle. "Would you two stop it?" He forced the frown to pronounce itself more prominently on his features.

"I have no idea what you're talking about," Blue said as she lifted the chairs to sit atop the tables. "Then again, I might know something about a blonde Wayward who burst into flames in the kitchen."

She caught the rag that he threw at her head. "Rumors. I'm sure it's not true."

Grettel giggled, breaking Baird out of his false pout. "I bet she stays awake all night for sure," the small brunette supposed happily. "Good timing." Taking in Baird's scolding smile, she grinned at him before skipping back into the kitchen to help Stephanie put the clean dishes away.

Baird's face fell once he did not have to pretend for Grettel anymore. It barely registered with him that his sister moved before he felt her hand on his.

"Hey." Blue spoke in a soothing tone with eyes that held too much understanding. "She'll be fine."

"You act like I'm worried. I'm okay."

"You act like I don't know when you're putting on a front," she countered. "You raised us right. She'll be fine." Blue watched her brother try to appear unaffected. "Baird, it's just one night away from us. Have some faith in yourself. You're a good teacher."

Guilt crept in over his shoulder like an eight-legged nuisance when his conscience reminded him that Blue could not date or get romantically involved with anyone. Yet here he was, callously making out with a woman in the kitchen.

"I shouldn'ta kissed her," he admitted.

"Maybe the dumbest thing you've said all year."

Baird looked up at his sister in mild surprise at her attitude. "If you can't be with anyone, I shouldn't either. It's not right."

"Who do you imagine I'd ever get involved with?" Blue sighed. "Look, kiss or no kiss, you've been with Elle for like, a decade. I'm glad for you." She glanced down at the rag in her hand. "Do you think I want to die knowing my brother's a chicken?" Baird opened his mouth to protest, but Blue held up her hand. "I want to see you happy with Elle. Do us all a favor and just go for it."

"You don't know anything about it," he sulked, sour at being told such wise words from someone with no experience in the matter.

Blue's voice was steady and quiet. "I know everything about you, Baird. Raising me tears you apart, bit by bit, day by day. I'm not an idiot. You've made too many sacrifices." She ran her hand through her wavy hair that was the same color as her brother's. "Elle? She's the one who can put you back together after I'm gone. Of course, that's only if you can learn to let her. You've always been a little bit slow with that sort of thing."

She moved away from him to put three meters of distance between them. The two continued cleaning up the dining area together, enjoying a few moments of silence.

Unbidden, a private smile found its way onto Baird's lips as he lifted up the chairs and placed them on the table. "I can't believe you called me a chicken."

"I can't believe that's the worst insult I could think of. Give me another hour. I'll come up with something better."

"Can't wait," he replied tonelessly.

"We're done in the kitchen," Stephanie announced, emerging from her work station with her purse. "Good working with you, Baird." She extended her hand to him, and he acknowledged her gesture of respect. "Nice to meet you, Blue. Good luck to Elle, and really, really good working with you, Grettel." There was no mention of Steve before she waved goodbye and left.

IT WAS ONE-THIRTY IN THE MORNING WHEN GRETTEL TOOK OFF HER shoes and uniform shirt, placing them on the side of her bed. When she turned to eye the empty space that should hold Elle, her face was so pitiful that Blue frowned along with her.

"Don't worry, Grettel. She'll be fine. They'll send her back for her shift tomorrow." Blue tried to reassure the girl, but Baird was looking down unhappily at the half-empty mattress, as well. She pulled off her uniform shirt to take her nightly run in her jean shorts and white tank top. Stretching out her muscles, Blue turned out the light once the two were in place and ready for bed.

Before she could touch the handle on the front door to make her exit, Baird's low voice caught her. "Hey, Blue?"

"Yeah?" she answered, glad that his voice sounded too tired for a lengthy conversation.

"If you could figure out your calling like, tomorrow or something, that'd be real helpful."

She glared at him, but in the dark and with his eyes closed, it was a wasted effort. "Okay. Hey, I thought of a better insult for you."

"I'm too tired to hear it. Save it for a time that I'm being a real jerk."

"Just one time?"

"Get!" Baird shouted at Blue as she ran out the door.

THE TWO WERE STILL IN THEIR RESPECTIVE "BEDS" WHEN BLUE reentered the hut after her night-long run. She was a little surprised that Baird hadn't woken up at ten on the dot.

She reached for the uniform shirt that Grettel had worn the night before and some clean shorts, socks and undergarments before locking herself in the bathroom to shower and dress for the day.

By the time she finished brushing the kinks out of her hair, she could hear movement in the living room. Grettel and Baird were eating their Grade *V* rations silently at the table. Grettel's drooping eyes suggesting she had missed Elle's presence in the night.

Without a word, Baird motioned for Grettel to take the bathroom next. She stood obediently and went to collect her change of clothes.

Baird had already set out Blue's rations, and she thanked him as she pulled open the tab. "Thanks. You look kinda terrible."

Baird responded by roughly shoving her with one hand. She

grinned. No sooner had she righted herself, than the noise of an approaching vehicle interrupted their breakfast.

Baird stiffened. "Get behind the couch."

"It's Elle," she informed him, judging by the cadence of the walker's steps. Sure enough, the front door opened to reveal her bedraggled friend.

"Elle!" Blue exclaimed, jumping up from the table and closing the distance between them.

The woman looked positively exhausted, but true to her nature, she offered up a cocky grin. "I made it to round two," she whispered, her voice not wanting to be the one to tell her body that it wasn't nighttime anymore.

Blue hugged her friend, but only briefly.

Baird nudged his sister out of the way so that he could be closer to Elle. Foregoing propriety, he placed a yearning kiss on her lips as he held her cheek with his palm.

Blue's mouth dropped open at the display after years of veiled flirtation. Elle melted under his touch, thrilling that there was an actual witness to it this time.

"I didn't dream it, then?" she asked breathlessly.

Shaking his head, Baird kissed her again after letting out a short laugh. "Do you usually dream about me?"

"All the time," Elle admitted, not bothering to straighten her posture after he pulled away. "Must sleep." She kicked off her shoes and discarded her thoroughly worn work shirt. "I'll tell you guys everything later, though there's not much to it. Can you handle a few hours of the lunch shift without me?"

Elle yawned as she collapsed on the mattress. Her eyes were already closed, and Blue doubted that an answer was necessary.

23

A SLIGHT SHIFT OF EVERYTHING

"Steve's still not here yet?" Grettel inquired as Blue dropped off four orders.

"Not here, but everything's okay. I can handle the lunch tables by myself. The Vems will just have to be patient. I'd rather Elle be sleeping right now."

"I'd rather that useless Vemreaux show up for his shift," Baird grumbled.

"Careful what you wish for," Blue warned.

Steve did not grace the diner with his presence until one in the afternoon, leaving Blue to wait on all the lunch tables by herself. "Is there a reason you're late?" Baird asked, whipping out his phone and hitting the sole preset speed dial. Without waiting for Steve to answer, Baird spoke into the device. "Joe, sir. It's one o'clock and the waiter you sent us only just arrived. We appreciate that you've hired us help, sir, but if he shows up late again, I'm going to have to ask you to find us another waiter to replace him. Someone who's worth what you're paying." He hung up the phone and eyed Steve, who had the decency to look mildly abashed.

"Yeah, yeah. Sorry or whatever." Despite the mumbled apology, Steve moved as slow as he did the day before. He moseyed out onto the floor and took whatever section he wanted without asking Blue or thanking her for handling it all on her own.

Though she wanted to glare at him, it was more pertinent that she remain forgettable, so she kept her frustration to herself and allowed him to view her as a doormat. She thought of Elle working so hard and carrying more than she should of her burden. When she compared her friend's massive efforts to Steve's inability to show up on time, she cringed.

"Just one swift punch in the face," she pleaded with her brother privately while he was setting out shot glasses in the bar to prepare for the night rush.

"No, Blue."

"I could probably sneak up behind him and punch him out so fast, he wouldn't even know it was me that did it."

"I'll let you know when we can test that theory."

Steve sauntered past them and dropped his tray on the bar, speaking lazily to the waitress who'd been picking up his slack all afternoon. "I'm going out for an hour. You can handle it, Blue."

Baird frowned as his sister tilted her chin to the ground and nodded with her mouth shut. Though he'd been the one who insisted she do so, there were times he hated seeing such a powerful creature so tethered. He knew eventually she'd have to let off some steam so that she did not randomly explode and cause some real damage. He made a note to spar with her personally that night after the diner closed so he could take the brunt of her frustration.

When her friend showed up at four-thirty, Blue was grateful for the help. Elle took the outdoor section after she helped Blue tear down the tables that covered the dancing area. Steve pretended to be doing something in the kitchen for ten minutes that kept him from being of any use.

Though Elle looked a little tired, none of her sparkle was gone. Every new table she greeted received a brilliant smile, and each attractive Vemreaux got a flirtatious look or remark to up her tip.

Though it was still light outside, Baird turned on the twinkling tent lights before switching from the kitchen to the bar. A few

Vemreaux even cheered when Baird started making the first batch of Green Abby shots.

"Finally!" Lawrence called to Baird. "I'll take two for starters." Instead of a bill, Lawrence slid a folded napkin across the bar to the Wayward.

Baird dropped it out of sight onto a few glasses, reading the scrawl as it opened.

Cops checking out a business next to one of mine. Gotta lay low. No more deliveries for a week or two.

Baird nodded covertly, tearing up the napkin and throwing it in the trash as Lawrence pounded back two of his favorite shots.

Before long, the tables filled up, leaving people to wait at the bar or enjoy the night in the outdoor area, which was also becoming more and more populated. The fresh air served as a powerful upper for Elle after the sleepless night. The breeze was only slight, but it was cool and stung her nose if she inhaled for too long. The fifth table in a row that she waited on wanted the same thing as the previous four: a round of Baird's specialty. A few patrons ordered an actual meal, but most requested drinks and appetizers. After all, it was Friday night. Everyone knew that the testing had begun to find the Light. It was all that most of the tables prattled on about as Elle doled out the little glasses of green happiness.

"See that guy, Blue?" Elle asked her friend on one of the rare times that their busy paths crossed. They were patiently waiting for Baird to make more shots for them to take out to their anxiously awaiting tables.

Blue followed Elle's focus and saw a man sitting with his two buddies. "Sure. What about him?"

"I bet he's got a green bill card. See how relaxed his shoulders are? He's comfortable enough. Judging by the flannel, though, my guess is he's single and will be for quite some time."

Blue raised an eyebrow at being let into Elle's game. "What's his name?" she asked, playing along.

"Probably Russell or something like that. Yeah, his name's Russell and he makes a living selling outdoor equipment for Vemreaux yards."

"Why's he single?"

"Oh, he broke up with his last girlfriend because she didn't like to go camping. Said she did when they started dating, but the big reveal came three months in. It was all downhill from there."

"Women," Blue complained, shaking her head in mock disappointment at her gender.

"I know. Anyone interesting in your section?"

"Well, there's this Fem over here that's got an aversion to wearing underwear." Blue pointed to a brunette with bright red artificial streaks coloring her hair. "That's Lulu. She's a college student studying...the art of staring at the wall. She has great ambitions in life to work in a piercing parlor. There's just one problem, though."

"What's that?" Elle pretended to pout in concern for the fictional plight.

"She's deathly afraid of needles."

Elle snorted. "Good one."

"It goes back to a childhood trauma when her rich Vemreaux parents didn't buy her a castle for Christmas. She threw herself on the floor and accidentally rolled over one of the Wayward servant's sewing needles."

"Those lazy Waywards." Elle shook her head in disapproval.

"I know. It's like, get a job already."

Elle sniggered. "Know what other game I like to play?"

"What?"

"I like to count how many pairs of underwear I see. Most of them are Fems just showing off their goods 'accidentally'." Elle rolled her eyes. "You'd be surprised how many Vems are in desperate need of belts."

Blue laughed aloud. "Well, they've got to budget, Elle. I mean, Green Abby shots aren't free, you know. Belts don't always rank high on the list when you've got your priorities straight." She tapped her temple to indicate the superior reasoning. "Hey. How are you holding up for real?"

Elle sighed. "I've got a table outside with two judges I met at the testing. They were introduced to us with a bunch of other important Vemreaux, but that's it. None of them really spoke to us. I guess they were watching us somehow like on a camera or something." She scowled. "I hope they stayed up all night watching us do nothing and trying to stay awake after our physicals. I hope they're real tired today. Now I have to go pretend I'm not sleepy at all." She put on her best fake smile. Baird loaded up her tray with shots, and Blue did not miss that when he leaned in to supposedly whisper something in her ear, Elle's knees nearly gave out beneath her.

Just then, two very good looking and sharply dressed Vemreaux caught Blue's eye as they walked into the diner.

Elle hefted the tray onto her shoulder once she reclaimed her bearings. "Those guys definitely aren't from around here. For real." She nudged her best friend as she imparted the knowledge. "See the upright walk and the perfectly tailored clothing? They're important, all right, but they're not from Capital City. Probably good tippers. You take 'em before Steve does. My section's full."

A scantily clad Femreaux walked in front of the girls, sporting a skimpy lime green pair of panties that Blue could not understand the mechanics nor the practicality of.

"That makes forty-seven panties so far, and counting!" Elle smiled and winked at her friend.

"I need more shots, Baird," Blue insisted.

"Go seat them," he called over his shoulder as he turned away from her. "I'll try to have your tray filled up when you come back." He looked up and saw how many people his sister was waiting on. Steve moved so slowly that Baird wanted to make a beeline to the idiot and test out Blue's stealth knockout theory. Blue's section, which was supposed to be exactly half the inside of the diner, had magically morphed due to his laziness into two thirds of the tables.

Blue reached the hostess stand, refusing to look up as she addressed the men. "Two?"

"We'll be four eventually. Got reservations under Brody." Brody was average height with blond wavy hair that insisted upon tickling his forehead whenever possible. His body language was jerky instead of fluid, and the smile that hit his lips when he caught the eye of a nearby Fem had entirely too much agenda to it. "That one's mine, Sam," he informed his friend.

Blue checked the list. "Nothing under that name, sir."

Brody frowned and rolled his eyes glumly. "Check under Alec, then."

Blue found Baird's indication and picked up four menus. "Right this way." She led the two to a table near the center of the diner.

"No, not here," Sam spoke up. He reached forward and touched Blue's arm to get her attention. A static shock leapt from him to her, and she jumped, dropping the menus on the floor.

Blue was appalled she'd made the mistake, and hoped her brother would not catch her rare human moment. "Excuse me, sirs. I'm sorry!"

Sam dropped to his knees next to her and scooped up the nearest menu. She'd not looked at him properly yet, but froze as his strikingly handsome face filled her vision. Messy dark chocolate-colored hair, easy crooked smile, and black eyes that missed hers as she hid her face before he could really see it made her blush.

He turned to hand her the menu, and his knees knocked into hers. Blue tried to avoid the contact from the gorgeous man and ended up losing her perfect balance, toppling over onto her rear.

Her mouth hung open. She'd never fallen down, except on purpose to throw a fight or appear weaker than she was. The action dazed her, and she took four seconds to ponder the cause of her displacement.

Sam's hand reached out to her after he stood and brushed himself off. "Sorry about that."

She hesitated, and then took his hand, absorbing a second shock while trying not to absorb his good looks. "I'm so sorry, sir."

"Up you go," he grinned, confused when she kept her face from him. "Um, this table's not going to work for us. Do you have a corner booth? The guys meeting us need it."

His voice was strangely accented in a way she'd never heard

before. She wanted to think of something clever to draw out more words from his slanted smile, but only nervous ramblings came to mind. "They're occupied, but I can seat you here for now, and then move you when one b-becomes a-available." Her hand flew over her mouth at the blatant stutter.

Brody's focus was still on the Fem he'd seen at the door. "That's fine. Liam won't be here for a bit. Can't imagine they'll have an easy time finding a cab this hour, either."

She sat them at the open table and handed off the menus with a shaky hand, scolding herself harshly for the sudden breakdown in control. Things she never cared about before suddenly flooded into her brain. There was a stain on her shirt. *Ugly*. The shorts were too short for her liking. *Ugly*. Her knuckles were rough from outdoor Wayward work. *Ugly*. Her hair was not doing a perfect job of hiding her blush. *Ugly*.

"Ten bills says I take that Fem back to the hotel tonight," Brody said to Sam.

"I'm not taking that bet. She looks plenty desperate."

"I thought betting was your job."

Sam gave Brody an annoyed frown. "There's more to managing finances than betting. Skill. Pure skill."

The two flipped open their menus lazily. Brody spoke to Blue without looking at her. "What's your best drink?" There was an accent to his cadence that matched Sam's.

"A Green Abby," she replied without looking up.

Sam grumbled. "Oh, joy. Another one of those cryptic labels that tells you nothing. What's in it?" He appeared studious as he took in the menu's contents like a map. His slouch suggested that he spent many luxurious days with little troubles, but the no-nonsense expression that darkened the sunshine of his striking face threw her off in her assessment of his personality, which she was usually fairly good at. In that moment, before Blue could stop herself, she thought that Sam was the best looking Vemreaux she'd ever seen. Nervous, unfamiliar butterflies birthed themselves in her belly and hammered around like they were trying to escape out her navel. She made sure to keep him only in her periphery, so as not to stare.

"It's the bartender's invention. The main ingredient's absinthe. Would you like to try one, sir?" she asked him, still not looking up.

"What else's in it?"

Blue shook her head. "No one knows except the bartender, sir, but once a Vemreaux tries it, they don't order anything else." She tried to maintain even breathing and concentrated on fading into the background.

"I'll just grab one from the bar," said Brody, his attention and body following his prey.

"Leave some Fems for me, Brode," Sam called to his friend. Then he turned his attention to the seemingly timid waitress and raised an eyebrow. "Are you kidding me? You really expect us to order a drink without knowing what's in it?" His gaze was now fully on her like a beam of hot light that made her finger twitch and her breathing hitch.

It was simply too much. The sound of his voice was enticing beyond what her superior strength could endure. Though his words were nothing to smile at, Blue's head lost the battle with her brain and lifted up at the sound of his alluring voice. Unbidden, her shocking eyes bored into him, begging the man to continue speaking. Of all the many voices she'd heard in her life, his was the only one that drew her in and held her captive. With wide eyes, as though he'd said something off-color, she stared at the newcomer, forgetting his question and herself.

Slowly, everything else began to fade into the background. The loud music, the gyrating Vemreaux, the smelly food and the logic in her brain all fled from her awareness. It wasn't black that clouded the edges of her vision, but a hazy gold blur that perfectly framed Sam's face. The longer her eyes met his, the more unsteady her breathing became.

"I, um," Sam began awkwardly.

Blue registered the equal amount of shock coming from the face she was staring into. He looked at her as if he was seeing a ghost, his gaze familiar, yet fearful. Patrons at the next table called out for her, but she could not see or hear them. She only took in the black eyes of the Vemreaux across from her, staring right back with the same blazing intensity.

His chestnut hair had flecks of black in it, setting off the comfortably tanned skin nicely. His angular jaw did not betray a smile, only a stunned expression as he continued to stare wordlessly. Three small freckles dotted his left cheek close to his eye, setting off the symmetry of his face. When Blue's brain processed his full lips, it was not in the calculating manner she would usually take in someone's appearance. The way she memorized his curved mouth brought a blush to her complexion – something she'd never had difficulty suppressing until that very moment. The embarrassing heat flashed up her face and down her chest, rattling her usually unmoved heart. Her blush made her feel naked, exposed, and yet she did not run, but presented herself to his scrutiny.

The sounds and faces surrounding her crashed back over her all at once, clueing her in to her odd behavior. Blue's breath came in shallow pants as she broke her stare from the stranger and turned as much attention as she could back to her order pad.

"Can I..." She ran out of breath and had to steady herself to finish the simple sentence. "...drink, sir?" She could feel the onyx eyes on her. Blue fought with every instinct that told her to take another glance in his direction.

"Um, yeah. I'll have a basket of chips for the table." He folded up his menu and slid it over to her.

"I'm sorry. We, uh, we don't serve chips here, sir. Only fries. Will that do?" The red in her cheeks was embarrassing, and she wondered if from his place at the bar, Baird was watching her fall to pieces like Grettel would.

"Yes, that's fine." He looked like he wanted to correct her about something, but decided not to.

Instead of gazing into those deep, dark eyes that held her for far too long, she stared fixedly down at her shoes, tilting her head so that her hair safely covered large sections of her face. "Drink, sir?" was all she could manage to squeak out.

Brody came back, tie loosened as he dropped his jacket on his chair. "She wasn't kidding about those Green Abby shots. Amazing! I'll have another, miss."

Again Sam's clean voice came, drowning out all other noise. Her heart tugged in her chest to hear him speak for hours, even if it was just to read the menu aloud to her in his fantastic accent. "Just a beer for me, thanks. Pick your favorite."

"Come on, Sam. Try a shot," Brody encouraged.

"I don't drink things from foreign bars I've never heard of," Sam stated flatly. "Got any dipping sauces?"

Her cheeks and chest continued to heat. Blue did not trust her voice to speak. Instead, she abruptly turned and walked to the kitchen, willing her feet not to run every step of the way.

By the time the doors closed behind her, she could barely take in a full breath. Grettel and Stephanie were actually laughing together, and beneath her panic, Blue was happy that Grettel could be so at ease in the presence of a Femreaux. For the moment, it seemed Blue had switched roles with the timid pixie, and she did not like the shift.

Grettel paused in the middle of her giggle and gasped. "What's wrong?" She dropped her knife on the cutting board and ran over to the hyperventilating girl.

Blue immediately regretted using the kitchen to hide in when she saw the short woman's laughter snatched away and replaced by her usual fear.

Grettel called over her shoulder to the Femreaux. "Stephanie, could you go get Baird?"

Blue shook her head, but still couldn't find the right words. The Vemreaux's haunting face kept surfacing and tying her tongue whenever she tried to speak. Finally she forced out a breathy, "No, Stephanie. I'm fine. I'm just a little tired." Blue was glad that the Femreaux seemed to accept this explanation and did not leave the kitchen for the bar.

"You're tired?" Grettel's alarm only heightened at Blue's words.

"*You're* tired?" she repeated slowly, the simple words confusing her. "Sit down, Blue. You're all flushed. What's going on?"

Before she could answer, Stephanie chimed in. "It's that Steve. He's such a waste of the immortal waters. They should really raise the IQ minimum for bathing in the Fountain of Youth. Having his kind of idiocy lingering around for a hundred and twenty more years is just a punishment to the rest of us." Stephanie continued on her rant while she wet down a washcloth and rang it out in the sink.

Blue permitted her head to tilt all the way forward and rest on Grettel's shoulder. She felt her hair being lifted off of her now sweating skin and a cool cloth gently placed on her neck by fingers that she judged correctly to be Stephanie's. The cold sensation counteracted the heat in her cheeks, and as the warmth dissipated, her breathing returned to normal. An uncomfortable itch crept up her spine at being taken care of so thoroughly by the two women. Baird would not approve at the display of weakness. Blue stood up straight, with new bearings, and removed the cold cloth. "I'm sorry, guys. I don't know what got into me. I'm fine now. Thanks."

Stephanie was already accepting the gratitude with a smile, but Grettel was not convinced. Never before had she seen her friend shaken like that. Her frightened eyes asked Blue if they were safe.

Blue sighed, heaving out more tension than she realized she'd been building up. "Everything's fine, Grettel. Really. I just overreacted out there. Nothing's wrong at all." She looked up at Stephanie. "I do need a basket of fries, though. Few different dipping sauces, too, I think."

"You *think*?" Grettel clarified with a wary gaze.

"Coming right up," Stephanie sang as she dumped a bowl of already cut potato and turnip wedges into the fryer and listened to them sizzle and pop deliciously.

Before Grettel could say anything else, Blue stepped away from her, fixing a false smile on her face. "Really, Grettel. Don't worry about it." Then her eyes darted to the door to indicate Baird. "Please just drop it for now."

Blue exited the kitchen and let herself into the bar with Baird, being sure to keep her face hidden from him. He knew her too well, and would surely be able to scout out the flaws in her armor. Blue lifted a shot glass from the counter behind him and placed it on her tray. He tried to keep that counter stocked with the coveted shots for the wait staff to continuously take out to the diners.

"Baird?" she asked from behind him. "I never really thought much about this wall of beers before. What's a good one?" If she was to truly pick her favorite, that would mean she would have tried at least one or two to make that decision. As it was, she had never sipped alcohol before in her life.

The hustle of the evening still hadn't completely darkened Baird's sunshine that came from finally making out with Elle. "Thinking of trying your hand at a drinking game?" he teased over his shoulder as he flipped a bottle of clear liquid in the air to dazzle the nearest drinkers.

"Ha," Blue commented tonelessly, glad to be getting her veiled personality back. "A table asked for my favorite beer. What's my favorite beer?" she asked, taking in all the different labels.

"Which Vem?" he inquired, his eyes scanning the room.

For a moment, Blue debated pointing Sam out to her brother, fearing that he would see her finger shake when she lifted it. The worry was unnecessary, for she overestimated her brother's observational skills. She nodded toward Sam without looking directly at him, though in her periphery, she could see that his black eyes were on her. The blush crept up to heat her cheeks once again.

"Ah, the dignitaries. His friend ordered my shots, but he wants a beer? He's a paranoid control freak," he guessed. "Get him a Boddingtons if you want a good tip."

Blue blinked as she flipped through the various labels she'd just scanned in her head, resting after three seconds on a yellow can taller than most of the others. Setting the drink with a chilled tall glass on the tray next to the shot, she added eight more shots she knew another table would want on her way. She then stopped by the kitchen to add the basket of fries to the light load along with the limburger cheeseburger and trout slaw a different table requested.

She dropped off the burger and slaw quickly; she detested the strong smell. As she passed the shots around the table of three Vemreaux and three Femreaux, she could still feel the black eyes staring at her. Summoning up her inner Elle that she pulled out in extreme circumstances, Blue relaxed her shoulders and erased her discomfort as she approached the man that made her knees weak.

Though Elle would have said something witty and given them a dazzling smile, Blue was satisfied keeping her eyes on her tray or down at the table top as she unburdened herself by setting down the food and drinks. Inwardly she cursed her nerves as her hand shook slightly while setting the beer and glass in front of the captivating Vemreaux. Despite their relaxed conversation and smiles, something about the men seemed unnaturally cold, like they were capable of unthinkable cruelty at the drop of a hat.

"*This* is your favorite beer?" Sam questioned her with disbelief.

She had not predicted being spoken to on her selection, and for a second, her brain froze at being caught. Quickly she thought of Elle and tried to mimic her attitude. "No, it's your favorite, sir," she insisted, still not meeting his eyes. "W-Would you gentleman like anything off the menu tonight?" she inquired politely, masking the slight tremble in her fingers as a cramped muscle that needed to be flexed.

"I'll have the haggis with the grapefruit gravy," Brody said as he handed her the menu.

"This isn't what I ordered." Sam held up the can of Boddingtons as a visual to his complaint. "I asked for *your* favorite beer, not mine."

Blue kept her eyes averted to her order pad and shook her head. "Um, I'll get you what I drink, sir, but you won't like it." She was amazed at how even her voice sounded and how confident the words seemed. Elle would have been proud. "Anything to eat while you don't drink your favorite beer, s-sir?" she asked, a traitor crack breaking up her cool tone.

Sam continued to stare into her, silently begging her to meet his gaze one more time, but she refused. She was not willing to be so shaken again in the presence of so many witnesses. "The fettuccini with the clam sauce. How long is that aged? Menu didn't say."

Brody rolled his black eyes. "Really? Does it matter? Every time we go anywhere, you have to be so picky." He folded his forearms over his chest and sighed with frustration. "Josephine can't cook you every meal, you know."

"The clams are aged three months, sir."

Sam scoured the description on the menu. "What about the cream?"

"That's only aged to curdling, thinned with fresh buttermilk."

He set his menu down and eyed her. "What does it come with?"

"It comes with a side of either trout slaw or fries."

Sam touched his index finger across the crest of his lower lip, drawing her eyes like a beacon. "What can you tell me about the trout slaw?" he asked, now combing the menu for any other questions he could throw at her.

"I'm literally dying over here," Brody complained. "Barely ate lunch, and that was hours ago. I'm starving! Quit being a woman and pick something!"

Blue had to take a deep breath before answering. She did not want his effect on her to be known. "The trout's aged only a month, but in the sun, so it speeds the process along. The mayonnaise isn't aged at all." She was impressed that she could regurgitate the bits of information she'd gained from food packages and passing through the kitchen so speedily.

The two Vemreaux stared at her with their mouths open. Finally Brody turned to Sam and jerked his thumb in Blue's direction. "Marry her." Then he looked up at Blue, whose face was still hidden. "Thank you! Thank you!" he praised her, hands pressed together. "Usually takes literally ten trips back and forth from the kitchen before this one gets all his questions answered." Brody downed the liquid in the tiny glass in front of him. "Oh, man! That's an amazing shot. Whoa! See ya, Sam. I'll be dancing with the Fem I'm taking back to the hotel tonight."

The unbidden blush swept over her body again as Sam looked up at her. She cursed her fallibility at not being able to control such a simple reaction. She was grateful for the lower lights, but knew that some of her vulnerability had to be visible to Sam's unrelenting stare. Her legs felt like jelly, and the butterflies turned vicious in her stomach. She wished he would order so that she could escape, but he seemed to be purposefully drawing out the answer she already knew he'd give.

"I think I'll have...hmm...yeah, that sounds good. With the trout slaw." He held his menu by the side instead of the base, and Blue did not look up as she took it from him. Her hand reached out to retrieve the menu, and as she did so, the tips of her pointer and middle fingers barely brushed up against his.

Though this was the third time, she did not predict the jolt of unmistakable electricity that shot up her arm and rippled through her body at his whisper of a touch. The shock produced a tiny yelp from her lips that sounded so like Grettel, she was instantly ashamed.

They both dropped the menu on the table as they stared at each other in surprise. Her eyes locked on his. She watched as he drank in every crevice and curve of her face, all pretense of confidence and superiority gone.

24

VIOLENT BUTTERFLIES

Maintaining composure was now a wasted effort if he was going to play games like this, she steamed, jumping to the only logical conclusion. Narrowing her gaze into a glare, Blue snatched up the menu and stomped off, not caring that he looked stunned and not at all guilty, as she thought he should.

As she disappeared into the kitchen, she shook her head angrily that some Vemreaux played such tricks on Waywards. She wondered how small the device was that he'd used to give her the shock. It escaped her keen vision completely, but explained why she'd been off-kilter ever since the first electrified contact.

Slapping the order on the hook for the cooks, she examined the fingers that received the charge to add up the damage. Surely if there were marks left on her fingers, Baird would notice immediately and scold her for being careless. How could she have known about such a mechanism? None of the others ever mentioned it to her. Perhaps it was a foreign weapon or something still in the trial phases. Luckily, her fingers appeared unscathed. Blue fumed, her sheepishness gone as she exited the kitchen to wait on other tables.

Though she tried not to, her eyes darted up of their own accord to the dreaded table. The two Vemreaux were joined by a pair of overly made-up Femreaux that Blue had seen in the bar before. One was fawning over Sam and the other was tossing her hair and laughing at something apparently hilarious that Brody said. Blue's anger increased at the stupidity of these women. There they were, throwing themselves at the dignitaries all because they were rich and good looking. Very good looking. The jerk.

The tousle-haired Sam looked away from the flirting Fem and turned his head to stare at Blue, his gaze questioning her sudden mood change. Insecurity washed through her as she sized up his expression. It certainly didn't match what she expected of an evil man. He appeared confused and concerned. The corner of his mouth lifted into a small, slanted smile directed only at her, completely bypassing the Femreaux hanging on his arm and whispering in his ear.

Blue almost cursed aloud as the blush betrayed her once again. Hurriedly, she ducked her head and waited on the next table, taking the glower she wanted to point toward Sam and using it to scold herself instead.

A growing line at the hostess stand left Blue to believe that Steve was taking yet another break. Spiting him by seating them in his section was just a bonus; there really were no empty tables in her section, and she didn't know how long they'd have to wait for Steve to seat them.

"Where's that lazy Vemreaux?" she asked the girls in the kitchen with more of an edge in her voice than she usually allowed. "Steve's not on the floor again and he's got tables waiting for him."

Stephanie tattled on him by jerking her thumb over her shoulder to the back door, indicating that he was, in fact, taking yet another break. Blue wanted desperately to march out the door and drag him back in by the collar of his shirt to give him a good thrashing, but she knew that might be slightly conspicuous.

Instead, she settled for going out through the dining area to the bar to summon her brother. So many Vemreaux were crowding the long bar. She felt bad for bothering him. Lifting up the table top barrier on the end that separated him from the drinkers, Blue skirted in next to Baird.

"Hey. Steve's on his, like, fiftieth break and he's got tables. Will you just deal with him? If I do, it'll be ugly, and I'm itching for ugly right about now."

"Alright, but you have to make the shots. Do you know how?"

She nodded, surprised that he would hand over the legacy so easily.

Baird leaned on the bar and dried off his hands. "Don't get too excited. I'm not gonna tell you what's in the bottles. Let me watch you make a round so I know you can do it right."

Five Vemreaux signaled that they wanted another, but Blue still took the time to throw her brother a withering look at being observed in this juvenile way. Of course she knew how to make them. She reasoned that anyone with a steady hand could figure it out after watching Baird go back and forth with the liquid as many times as he did each night. It was what was in the bottles that escaped her knowledge.

Elle walked quickly to the bar. The only sign of sleeplessness came from her eyes and lack of smile. She leaned on the edge and shouted over the noise to her friend. "Hey, I need twenty-five shots for the patio." She propped her tray up on her hip. "Since when does Baird let anyone make his shots? I thought he'd die with the secret."

"He still might. He didn't tell me what's in the bottles." She held up a labelless glass container as a visual aid. "He's out back dealing with Steve."

"That idiot still giving you problems?" Elle asked as she ducked under the divider. She joined Blue behind the bar so they didn't have to shout.

"He's still breathing, isn't he?"

"Yeah. For now." Elle helped Blue load the many shots onto her tray before bumping her hip against her friend's. "You're a cute bartender, you know. I can tell the Vemreaux like the switch." Her head jerked to the barflies who were watching Blue every bit as much as the attractive blonde.

"Great," she muttered, shaking her head. "So much for being invisible."

Elle shrugged. "You can't help how gorgeous you are. I should know." Lifting the tray to her shoulder, she flipped up the divider and let herself out of the bar.

"'Nother Abby over here," an accented male voice called from the other end.

"Make that two," beckoned his female companion.

Blue did not look up as she set the shots down in front of them. Brody sized up the new bartender whom he deemed to be too small for the task of holding her own behind the bar.

The Fem led him onto the dance floor, parading around her short skirt and midriff-baring shirt. Blue wondered if she would ever be drunk enough to dance publicly like the Fem did, not that she would dare compromise her prowess with alcohol to begin with.

"Hit me, Baird," demanded Lawrence, good-naturedly. He made to sit down on the stool and nearly fell off of it.

Blue quirked an eyebrow at him, but said nothing by way of a correction. She made a separate shot for him, only instead of the clear bottles, she used carbonated water.

Baird tapped his sister on the shoulder to relieve her, but instead of leaving, she stood on her toes to speak privately to him.

Baird leaned down to compensate for her small stature. "What?"

"I think Lawrence should be cut off, Baird. He can barely sit upright. I watered down his shot, but he should really go home."

Baird observed the Vemreaux he so often did business with and nodded. "Yeah, okay. I'll call a cab."

"Thanks," Blue muttered as she moved around her brother to resume waiting on her tables.

"Look at you, caring about the customers." Baird ruffled her hair affectionately. He wasn't one for hugs or public displays, but a quick hair muss was a multi-purpose response. It served as "I love you", "you're welcome", "thank you", and the occasional "you got me". She shoved him playfully in response.

The corner booth had just become available, so Blue made quick work of clearing it off and wiping it down. She geared up to address the handsome Vemreaux before moving toward his table, but when she turned around, he was right behind her.

Her hand flew to her chest in surprise, her hair falling from her face as she looked up at the man who was standing a little too close. "You scared me!" she accused. Her eyes darted guiltily to the bar to be sure Baird had not seen someone succeed in sneaking up on her. Then she ducked her head down to hide her face again, doing her best to ignore Sam's playful smirk that melted into a frown. "I, um, your table. You wanted the b-booth?"

"I did," he said, not moving from in front of her. "Who…"

At that moment, the person behind Blue decided to back away from their table abruptly, knocking the waitress forward into the man she was trying to escape.

Sam's strong arms flew around her, catching her with a laugh meant for charming. "Falling for me already, are you?"

For one tiny moment, the world slowed. The firm chest. The alluring scent of his cologne. The perfect home for her cheek to rest, just over the beautiful stranger's heart. Blue's own heart pounded erratically, and for two seconds too long, she forgot to pull away. She forgot her brother. She forgot the diner. In that smallest of moments, Blue forgot herself.

The world with all of its needs crashed down on her, refusing to be ignored. Blue was mortified at her clumsy display. "Oh! I'm sorry, s-sir," she stammered as she righted herself, her skin burning where he'd touched her. Sam smelled as good as he looked, and Blue had to fight to keep herself from looking up at him again. Before she could make a bigger fool of herself, she slipped from his near embrace and moved the contents of his table to the booth as quickly as she could, then all but ran back to the kitchen.

Grettel gave Blue a wary look, which she ignored. She shook off all thoughts of the Vemreaux, putting out of her mind his scent, his lips, his touch, his hard chest, and all the other things about him that proved a horrid distraction to her superior control. *Just another customer. No big deal. People trip all the time. It would've been weird if I hadn't fallen forward.* Before she stacked the hot, smelly food onto her tray, she filled a tall glass with water and added it to the load. She kept her face from her brother as she stacked fifteen shots on her tray, balancing it with care as she walked back onto the floor.

With her head firmly tilted downward, she delivered the shots to various tables, and then placed the plates of food and water in front of the intimidating Vemreaux. Sam's new acquaintance was making herself at home next to him by pressing her shoulder into his chest so he had a full shot of her cleavage. Blue couldn't place the uncomfortable feeling this gave her. She kept her eyes from finding their way over to Sam. He had been on his phone, but ended the call when she slid his food and fresh beverage over to him.

"Thank you." He looked to her name tag. "Blue? Your name's Blue?"

The Fem next to him echoed his tone with a twist of snobbery. "What kind of a name is Blue? Your momma pick that out for you?" She lazily reached her hand over to pick up a cherry tomato from Sam's plate.

So quick that only Blue saw it coming, Sam batted her hand out of the way. "If you want food, you can order something all by your little self. Don't go snaking stuff off my plate. Not unless you want to lose one of those greedy fingers."

The Femreaux produced a sassy face to hide her embarrassment, and withdrew her hand.

"You don't know me," he concluded, making it clear that she was not privileged enough to be granted the lofty place of the woman he shared food with. The daring of her wandering hands suggested that she knew him intimately, or at the very least, that her sneaky fingers wanted to.

"Can I get you anything?" Blue asked quietly to the Femreaux. In her peripheral vision, she tried to see if there was a device anywhere on Sam that could deliver the shock he'd given her earlier.

"No, thanks. I don't start drinking until after ten."

Blue always found it odd that people offered personal information up like it was nothing. With no urging whatsoever, everyone at the table now knew that the woman drank after ten o'clock. It was as if she was desperate to be known in some small way. It was currently half past eight, and Blue wondered if the distinction of time made her feel like a lady with limits rather than the girl who was running her fingers up and down the crass Vemreaux's thigh while he tried to eat.

"Do you wanna dance, Stone?" she asked Sam in what Blue was sure was supposed to be a seductive voice.

"No." Sam geared up for sarcasm. "See this food on my fork? I'm eating, here. Odd, I know. Eating in a restaurant. Why don't you go pretend it's ten or something. Prince Liam's on his way, and I've got to make a few phone calls. Official business and all. You understand."

The Femreaux wore a disgruntled expression that her seduction proved unsuccessful as she left the booth.

Blue turned on her heel to walk away, but froze mid-step when the voice she could now recognize anywhere pulled her back. "You forgot the beer." He tapped the open Boddingtons with the butt of his fork before lifting the noodles to his mouth.

"No, I didn't, sir. Y-You asked for what I drink." Her eyes lifted only to indicate the tall glass of water that now had beads of condensation running down the sides as the glass frosted over. "I'm sorry, sir, but I don't drink beer."

Sam stared up at her like he'd never seen such a strange puzzle. Lifting the glass to his lips, he took a sip, but jerked the drink away immediately. "Oh, you've got to take this back. It's much too strong for me."

A dainty smirk played on her lips, giving way to the blush that she'd never had to wrestle so hard with. He didn't seem like a kind man to the Fem who obviously wanted his attention. Why was she smiling for him? "Enjoy your meal, sir," Blue mumbled as she quickly walked away from the table.

"Hey, wait! Blue?" Sam called after her.

Blue did not turn around. As fast as she could while still being discreet, she headed in the direction of the kitchen instead of checking on her other tables. When she reached the door, she decided that Grettel could probably go without seeing her so shaken twice in one day. The hallway that contained the restrooms was usually deserted, so she went there instead to catch her breath.

Pushing the door open to the ladies' room, Blue was grateful that it was empty. She leaned against the wall next to the door and placed her hand on her chest, hoping that might slow her heart's rapid jumps.

When her eyes closed, she was disappointed to find that the self-imposed darkness did not offer the comfort she hoped it would. She could not escape the mental image of his eyes boring into her, watching her every move in a way that made her subconsciously straighten her hair.

Upon opening her eyes, Blue was confronted with the tall mirrors over the sink, aimed to point out every flaw, of which she could name hundreds. She shuddered at the sight, let out a pathetic whine, and pointed her head down so that there would be no chance she could accidentally see her reflection.

In that moment, she missed the simplicity of The Way. None of the boys there made her feel like this. She could be covered in pure scratch and not think twice about how she looked to others back then. Over and over, she chided herself on the ridiculous behavior, making sure that she would punish herself later by hanging out less with Grettel. It seemed her shy friend's demeanor was rubbing off on her.

Eventually Blue's breathing returned to normal, and she ran out of reasons not to check on her other tables. Her hand gripped the long metal handle and pulled the door open. Not expecting anyone to be standing there, her eyes locked in on the black pools that she was trying so hard to avoid. Startled, her breath caught in her throat. Her hand flew to her mouth to stifle her second girlish yelp of the evening. "C-Can I help you, s-sir?" She was unable to look away from his intense stare.

"Where are you from?" Sam questioned, not backing up to give her space.

Blue wasn't sure what exactly she'd been expecting him to say, but it certainly wasn't that. "Why?"

"I just want to know."

"Around here," she answered as generically as she could.

Not deterred by her evasion, the Vemreaux took a step forward. "Do you have relatives in Europe?"

Confusion took over for surprise. "How would I know that?" Her eyebrows wrinkled as she considered the question. "I'm A-blood. I'm a W-Wayward." Inwardly she berated herself for the embarrassing new development of stuttering that she couldn't help in his presence.

Sam's face fell slightly, but he continued to study her. "Your eyes. Do you wear contact lenses?"

"Huh? N-No, sir. These are just my eyes." Upon receiving such focused attention, her gaze darted to his polished shoes uncomfortably, shrinking back behind her hair.

Compassion softened Sam's tone. "Why do you hide your face like that?"

"I'm not hiding anything," Blue retorted a little too forcefully. "I'm sorry, sir. I have t-tables to wait on." Her leaden feet tried to move her body away from him, but he stepped in her path. "Excuse me, sir." She flattened her body to the cool wall to slide past him, but his fingers caught her elbow.

The moment their skin touched, the same thing happened again. Electricity shot up her arm and heated her body in an instant.

Blue gasped at the audacity of the man to shock her yet again. Her eyes flared, and without thinking of the consequences, she grabbed onto his knuckles with speed that was not thought to exist in a Wayward. Blue twisted Sam's hand behind his back faster than he could react, and slammed the front of his body firmly against the concrete wall.

25

CAUGHT IN THE ACT

"What're you trying to do?" Blue whispered, fear polluting her threat.

"Let me go!" Sam growled. "How...how are you doing this?" His surprise mutated to concern when he realized he could not break free from the dainty woman's hold.

"How do you keep shocking me like that?" Blue's meticulously refined temper began to trickle through the carefully constructed dam that Baird had worked so hard to instill in her.

The Vemreaux's surprise heightened while his fruitless struggle against her ceased. With the side of his head pressed up against the wall, his becoming mouth barely moved as he spoke in the same hushed whisper. "You felt that?"

"Of course I did! You...you shocked me! How'd you do it? Why are you experimenting on A-bloods? You need our consent for that." She gave a little more volume to her voice, but still spoke through gritted teeth. One hand held his firmly in place against the base of his spine, separating his thumb from his fist so she could jerk it backward to inflict pain if he tried to escape. Her other forearm was pressed to his neck to keep his head against the wall. Just a little more pressure and she could choke him out. A little more thrust and she could crush his skull. A little closer and she could smell his delicious scent more fully.

"Experimenting? What are you talking about? *You* shocked *me!*" Sam accused vehemently.

"I did not!" Blue pressed harder against his neck, his skin warming hers and sending a thrill through her. She could feel the foreign pulse running through his neck, and now that she was this close, she could see his face more clearly. A short scar hid beneath the hair on the back of his neck. The loose dark brown spiky waves stuck up at odd angles, begging to be combed or straightened. The three freckles decorating his cheek caught her eye once again and proved to be an utter distraction to her anger.

"I don't experiment on Waywards, and I didn't do anything to you. Now, you should probably back down before someone sees this and you really get in trouble."

It was only a matter of time before the altercation was noticed. Blue could only hope that it would be Baird or Elle that interrupted them. Her jaw clenched as she took in the face of Brody strolling down the hallway.

"Aw, how cute. Can't say I ever pictured you taking it from behind, Pan. But now that I think about it..." His voice trailed off lightly, as if he'd caught his friend making out with a girl in the hallway.

"Brody, would you get her off me?"

"Come on now, little girl. We don't want to hurt you."

The hand that clenched her shoulder suggested that his words were false.

Wisps of black crept into the edges of her sight. Blue exhaled, trying to force the darkness to stay away, but she could not ignore Brody's firm grip. She responded by stomping back hard on his instep with her heel and letting go of Sam's neck temporarily to fling a well-aimed elbow back, popping Brody squarely in the nose. She didn't want to break it, just get him to back off so the dark would retreat.

A string of expletives poured from Brody as quickly as the blood flowed forth from his nose. "Who is she, Sam?"

"Her face, Brody!" Sam gasped as Blue leaned on his windpipe again, this time with more force. His words choked out from him slowly. "Look at her eyes." He struggled harder, but realized with confusion and dread that he could not overpower the petite waitress.

Brody tried to look Blue in the face through his watery vision, but every time he moved in front of her, she jerked her head out of the way defiantly. She didn't know why they wanted to see her eyes, but she refused to give them anything.

"Alec!" Brody shouted, his words garbled due to the blood and mucus. "Get Liam out of here!"

Before Blue could turn to see the third body she'd need to incapacitate, he was on her. Arms with more strength than Brody and more cruelty than Sam's ripped her from her prey and threw her back against the wall. Her head knocked against the concrete and bobbed twice before she could blink her world back into focus.

"Oh, no. That was not good," she warned. The black rims were back, and she whimpered pitifully as she tried to blink them away. Baird would tell her to breathe and run. Baird would tell her to get control.

Baird was not there, though.

Brody was disoriented, but he managed to pull his charge into the men's room, locking the door behind the prince until his vision cleared up.

On the other side of the door, Alec had Blue by the hair and yanked her up by her auburn locks. Her eyes remained closed so Sam wouldn't have whatever it was that he needed to see them for. She refused to make a noise of irritation as she was jerked roughly to her feet.

"Stop!" Sam yelled at his friend. "Don't hurt her! It's a misunderstanding or something. I just want you to look at her eyes." The hand that gripped her hair did not loosen. "Could you just show them your eyes? Nothing bad's gonna happen, I swear. You just look an awful lot like someone we used to know." He rubbed his neck. "How did you pin me like that? I couldn't budge!"

Blue kept her lids firmly shut as she calculated what would be her best move. Alec pulled her by the hair so her temple was pressed to his mouth. He whispered his hot breath in her ear. "If you don't open your eyes, I'll tear them out of your pretty little head so we can look at them whenever we want."

His bluff was hard to call, but she figured she couldn't really be in any more trouble if she refused him. One way or another, she'd kill the predator. Did she really need eyes for the task? She was already in deep as it was.

With her lashes shut tight, the black ceased its mission to bring Blue down to the land of no return. Matching his hushed voice, she cooed, "I bet they'd make nice earrings for your mommy."

She heard a movement in the air and raised her fist to punch Alec, but Sam's voice stopped her. "Alec, don't! She's just a girl! Let her go."

Alec surprisingly consented, releasing her hair. However, he made sure Blue was surrounded on both sides as they backed her up to the wall behind her. Alec slowly covered her fist with his and shook it. "What exactly were you going to do with this? You smell Wayward." He frowned and leaned in closer, sniffing her shoulder. "Sort of," he amended.

Blue shoved Alec harder than he'd been expecting. "Get off of me!" she sneered.

Alec resumed his close proximity, crossing his arms over his chest. His head cocked to the side as he sized up the disproportionate amount of force that came from the slight girl. "You were going to punch me a second ago. What good would a blow from a Wayward do against a Vemreaux?" It was clear to Blue that Alec was not mocking her; he was trying to fit the pieces together. "Did you give Brody that bloody nose?"

"Please," Blue whispered. "Please don't touch me. Alec, is it? Sam? Stone? Pan? Whoever you are, just leave me alone. It...it'll be very bad for you if you don't let me go."

Alec's tone turned dark. "That so? It'll be bad for you if you don't tell me what's going on."

The pregnant pause that filled the hallway waited for Sam to put words of sense into it, but all he did was stare at her face, breathing unsteadily. He drank in her appearance, and even through her clenched shut eyelids, she could feel his stare boring through her skin that seemed remarkably unclothed, despite its appropriate coverings.

Brody reentered the hallway, keeping Liam shut in the bathroom at his back. His eyes were venomous and his nose was still bleeding, despite the paper towel he pressed to it. "Dude, who exactly is she supposed to look like? Some Fem you scored with back in your prime?"

Sam muttered something about still being in his prime, but his gaze did not leave Blue's face.

Deciding that things needed to be moving along if she was going to keep Baird from getting himself involved, Blue sighed. "If I show you my eyes, will you let me go back to work and leave me alone?"

"Not a chance," Brody sneered beneath the blood.

"I wasn't asking you, useless. I'm talking to eyeball snatcher." Her chin jutted to the side to turn her face from the three as best she could. With her eyes closed, she waited for any sign of a tell from Alec.

Sam and Alec silently conversed before Alec answered. "If you show us your eyes, we'll let you go back to work." She noticed that he left out the "and leave you alone" part. It was the best offer she'd get, and she knew it.

Before she gave them what they wanted, Brody protested, his hand still covering his face where the blood stained it. "Dude, she literally broke my nose!"

"I did not, you big baby! But grab me again and I'll break your arm," she warned. The heat of the snarl building up in her felt remarkably good, a sweet relief from the bottling up she'd done her whole life. The match was all she needed to ignite the flame of controlled violence she'd kept in the dark for far too long.

Brody laughed, but Alec did not.

"She's Wayward, Brode. As much as she may want to, she can't break Vemreaux bones," Sam corrected him.

Alec stared at Blue, eyes widening. "Sam, you might just be wrong about that."

"Show us your eyes." The sweetness in Sam's tone was gone with his patience. Blue caught wind of the same annoyance with which he'd shooed away the Femreaux's hand from his food at the table.

As quick as she could, Blue's lashes fluttered open and shut again to fulfill her side of the bargain. When her foot lifted to leave the space blind, Alec grabbed her chin like a vice.

"I warned you not to touch me!" She was only just in control of herself, but feared losing all sanity to the black if Alec was not dealt with. So many people were in the diner. Even Baird couldn't cover up a massacre.

Eyes closed, Blue held Alec's shoulder, snatched his belt buckle and used the leverage to launch Alec into the air. The wall stopped him mid-flight with a crack.

"Holy!" Brody exclaimed, backing against the bathroom door to protect the prince from whatever or whoever could best Alec so completely.

From his dazed spot on the floor, Alec looked up at the girl. "Nobody touch her!" he cautioned. "She's…"

Blue's eyes remained closed, but her voice was clearly panicked. "You shouldn'ta put your hands on me! I-I didn't want to do that!"

Sam was just as stunned as Alec to see the impenetrable man on the floor. His hands were up in a defensive fighting position, even though he was too bewildered to attack properly. "Brody, go get the bartender."

Immediately Blue's eyes flew open and locked on Sam's. "Don't you touch him!" she choked out, fear replacing the fury in her fists. She was unable to harness the vulnerability that shown through as she silently begged him to leave Baird alone.

Though Sam and Alec were sufficiently shaken as they took in her unveiled appearance, it was Brody who had the strongest reaction. Gasping aloud, he froze. Pain shot across his face that Blue did not expect. Pain mingled with disbelief, and disbelief gave way to rage. Before his friends could react, Brody flew at the girl, grabbing her face in his bloody hands and pulling her forward roughly. "Who are you?" he demanded as he examined her.

Control, she reminded herself as the shadows threatened her vision once again. Blue could have ducked under his amateur grip easily, but the sudden agony in his expression stopped her from following through with her earlier threat. "I'm no one!" she promised.

Brody's wrath was tempered with such immediate misery that Blue took pity on the stranger and allowed him to yank her into brighter light. "Sam? Who is she?" Brody's voice broke as he spoke. Blue wasn't sure if he was going to cry or haul off and hit her.

"Easy, Brody. I don't know. She's just a waitress." Sam paused, his voice softening. "She does look an awful lot like Julia."

Brody's hands tightened around her cheeks, and she wondered if she'd have bruises in the morning to hide from Baird. "Don't you say her name to me!" he roared, shaking Blue's head as he raged. "Who are your parents?" he demanded of the girl, liking how it felt to shake her roughly. He'd never jostled a Wayward woman in such a manner, and his temper found its release in the malicious action.

"What did I say about putting your hands on me?" Blue reminded him evenly. *Control!* she screamed at the black vapors as she fought to keep her head.

Sam stepped forward, but Blue was faster. Her fists shot up between Brody's and spread out, knocking his hands off of her face. She grabbed onto his right arm deftly, but before she could break it, Alec was up on his feet. His arm on her shoulder stayed her movements.

Still gripping Brody's struggling limb, Blue murmured to Alec through her teeth, "I know you don't want another lesson about putting your hands on me, Vemreaux. I owe him a broken arm."

Sam brought reason to the scuffle. His arms crossed over his chest as though the men held all the cards. "You break his arm, we break your boyfriend's." He spoke the last word with mild disdain.

Confusion loosened Blue's grip, and she consented to dropping

Brody's arm for the moment. "Go right ahead. Who do you imagine's my boyfriend? 'Cause I'd love to meet him myself."

It was Sam's turn to look confused. His hand lifted and gestured to the crowded diner. "That bartender who watches you like a crazy stalker."

"*That bartender* is my brother, and he doesn't appreciate Vemreaux putting their filthy hands on me." She wiped the small smear of Brody's blood from her chin.

Sam looked as if the conversation had turned a corner.

Blue angled her head to the left to speak to Alec, who was now behind her. "I showed you my eyes, now let me go." When his grip on her shoulder did not give, she clenched her fists at her sides. "You wanna be a man that lies to little girls, corners them in dark hallways and beats on them?"

This did something to Alec's conscience, but still he waited for Sam to give the okay.

Her fists longed to plunge into Alec's seasoned stomach. "Vemreaux are pathetic. Please don't make me hurt you again. I really hate doing it."

"We have some questions for you." Sam nodded for Alec to release the girl. Seeing his friend's hand on her like that made him uncomfortable.

The darkness faded away completely, and Blue stood taller with confidence that she'd bested the blackout. "Good for you, but it really doesn't matter. See, you're not my owner. My owner tells me what I have to do, which is wait on those tables. Leave me alone!" Blue made sure Alec was never out of her periphery. Brody's instability was grating on her. Sam's unrelenting study of every movement made her heart flutter in an unsettling way that she could not control.

"Where's your owner?" Sam asked, as if they were having a casual conversation about breakfast cereal. He rubbed the fresh crease above his eyebrow, and then withdrew a pack of cigarettes from his pocket.

"He's not here. My brother acts on his behalf. That's why he watches us so closely."

Alec turned and walked steadily down the hallway, back into the clusters of partying Vemreaux. "What's he doing?" she asked warily.

"He's just going to get something."

She watched Alec turn right at the end of the hallway. "No!" she shouted, lunging to run after him.

Sam stuck his leg out and tripped her, satisfied when she tumbled to the ground. His cigarettes fell as he wrenched her arms to her back and knelt on top of her, pinning her roughly to the ground. She struggled against him much harder than a girl her size (or a full-grown man) should have been able to.

"Leave my brother alone!" she cried, wondering how to get him off of her without seriously injuring him.

"Stop!" Sam insisted, using his full strength to secure her arms. She yanked one free, but he jerked it back quickly. "How are you this strong? Calm down!"

"Let me go!" she seethed. "I don't want to hurt you, too."

"Do you think I want to hurt you?" He bent down and spoke quietly in her ear, causing her to stop struggling and breathing all at once. "We just want to ask you a few questions. If you want your owner or your brother there for it, that's fine. That's all he's doing. He's just telling your brother to come back here so we can talk to you." When she stilled, Sam continued. "Now, can I let you up?"

Blue gulped as she nodded. She was grateful when he released her arms and shifted his body so he sat at her side. She rolled onto her back, humiliation washing over her at the violence she'd been a part of and the doom she would now have to answer to. She covered her face with her hands as she slowly sat up next to Sam, hugging her knees. "I'm in big t-trouble, aren't I?"

"I think we're all just trying to catch up, here." Sam's hand rose to stroke her cheek, but thought better of it. Instead, his palm landed on her shoulder to soothe her.

The touch sent shivers down her spine, and chased away all shadows with the same dreamy golden haze she experienced earlier in his presence.

Blue did not resist as Sam brought her head to rest on his chest.

Goosebumps broke out on her flesh as her body loosened like buckets and buckets of jelly. She desperately clutched his shirt, making sure she had something to hold onto before she lost herself completely to the tender moment. She could smell his cologne-scented deodorant that wasn't too strong and could only be noticed when you were close to him, as she was in that moment. His forearms were muscular as they pressed into her. Without willing her muscles to do so, she relaxed against his sturdy frame as she closed her eyes, trusting this stranger to ward off the world for a few moments. "There you go," she heard Sam whisper.

Brody eyed his friend warily, unwilling to label Sam's odd behavior and the tender embrace. "Pan, what the–?"

Sam's chin turned to Brody. "You look like a horror flick extra. Go wash up before her brother sees you like that. Check on Liam while you're at it. I got this."

"Why shouldn't he see? She did it," Brody accused, but consented to washing up in the restroom behind them.

The moment the bathroom door closed and left them in the hallway alone, Sam's thumb rubbed a circle slowly on her back, relaxing her further without her knowledge. Blue could not recall ever being held like this by a man, and definitely not by a handsome Vemreaux. Despite Baird's voice screaming in her head, she yearned for more – needed more of whatever this was.

Blue shivered as Sam's words tickled her ear softly. "I thought *you* shocked *me* back there." He paused, but continued on when it became clear she was not going to speak. "I shouldn't have followed you, though. You probably thought I was stalking you or something." He exhaled. "Man, that's creepy. I waited for you outside the bathroom!" The admission was painful to recall. "I don't know what my deal is. You just look like Julia so much with those crazy eyes of yours. Younger, of course, but still a lot like her." He shook his head when he realized that he was rambling. "I didn't mean to scare you, or for all this to happen, yeah?"

He seemed to be asking for absolution, which Blue could not give him. "O-Okay."

Sam's hand stilled on her back. "Is it okay, or are you just saying that?"

Blue knew he asked a question, but answering was not top priority. He smelled too good, felt too perfect. She soaked up the embrace greedily, her mind unwilling to process much of anything else.

"Blue?"

Her name on his lips brought her back to reality. His accent was turning her brain to mush. "W-What?"

"Are you okay?"

Blue summoned herself back from the bliss her body dared to run off into. She spoke slowly, still under his spell. "Just don't let them touch me. It...it sets me off in a bad way. I don't want to hurt anybody!" she insisted desperately.

"Shh. You don't have to worry about that anymore. I won't let them touch you. It's okay, love."

"Th-The only way that this'll be okay is if your questions and my answers stay in this bar, which I don't think you or your boys can do." Blue swallowed, lowering her voice to a whisper to cover the tremble that happened when she inhaled his sweet breath. "I-I don't know who your Julia is, but I'm not her. There's n-nothing I can tell you about someone I don't know."

The movement of his thumb on her spine was so slow that it had already enticed her into a malleable conglomeration of gelatin in his arms. "Then I guess we'll just have to stick together till we figure this out. Alright, little Wayward?" When his fingers began tracing up the back of her arm, she let out a gasp that melted into a sigh as she trembled.

"Okay, Stone."

"Sam," he corrected, swallowing as he confessed to the pretty woman in his arms his real name. "My name's Sam."

Sam gave her an appraising look before making a decision. She stilled as he bent even closer to her, leaning his face to her neck. Blue tilted her head back involuntarily, giving him further access to her vulnerable throat. Normally she would never allow her defenses to crumble so easily, but she found that the instinct to fight and protect herself was fleeing her limbs in his presence. Her eyes closed and her back arched as Sam inhaled the scent of her skin, the gold fog clouding what was left of her focus with its twinkling allure. They both moaned softly when Sam brushed the tip of his nose up and down her neck seductively, taking all question of innocence out of the debate.

"Hmm. You don't smell Wayward."

When a mildly concerned Baird rounded the corner with Alec and his eyes fell on his sister with a Vemreaux's face buried in her neck, he snapped. His feet pounded toward them like rain piercing the earth while his finger pointed at Sam. "You don't touch my sister!"

Sam dropped his hands immediately, his palms raised in surrender as he distanced himself from Blue.

Blue woke from her trance with a jolt, red flashing in her cheeks as she clambered to her feet. She moved guiltily away from Sam and met her brother halfway, forsaking the golden temptation.

Baird caught his sister's arm and shoved her behind him, sandwiching her between himself and the wall to shield her. He turned to Alec, but he was really addressing Sam. "Whatever you want, the answer's no! No questions. No nothing! She's not your property."

Sam opened his mouth to answer, but Alec held up his hand. "If you don't answer our questions, we'll just have the testers come here and take her in with the rest of the candidates. One way or another, she'll answer us. It's up to you how far it goes."

Baird glanced over his shoulder at his sister's guilty expression. He watched as she lowered her head in shame. "After everything we've done," he whispered accusatorially. "What did you do?"

It seemed Blue would buckle under her brother's disappointment, and finally Sam decided he could take no more. "She didn't do anything. She just looks like someone we used to know. All we want is to ask her a couple questions about it."

Without breaking his fixed stare at his sister, Baird lifted his finger and jabbed it at Sam. "I wasn't asking you, Vem. You don't speak for her." When Blue shot Sam a look of concern, Baird went from angry to furious. "I catch your hands on my sister again, I rip 'em off and hang them over the bar as a souvenir. You got that?" He turned to his sister. "Blue!" Baird shouted, bringing her out of her silence as he moved her out from behind him.

Blue's voice was steady, but the stress was obvious. "I got confused and accidentally punched one of 'em. I'm sorry!"

Baird looked from Alec to Sam, appraising the damage. His mood lightened when he saw no evidence of her using real strength. It was then that the bathroom door swung open to reveal Brody's face, which was now pink from scrubbing the blood off it. Despite the Vemreaux's usual put-together demeanor, he sacrificed fashion to shove toilet paper up his nose to stem the flow.

Baird's jaw tightened. "Confused, eh?" He turned to Alec. "I'll see that she's dealt with."

"That's really not necessary, officer," Sam mocked the *A*-blood's stern tone as he scooped up the discarded pack of cigarettes and pulled one out. He lit it and took a puff, hoping it would calm his perception of the situation. It did not.

Alec addressed Baird with authority. "We can ask our questions officially or unofficially. It's up to you. If you prefer, we can come back here with the testers so the conversation can be documented." Alec knew exactly which strings to pull to make them dance.

Blue wondered just how dangerous the man could be.

Baird closed his eyes as if the dim light pained them. When they finally opened, they landed on his sister who was looking like she wanted to melt into the floor. Only his superior control kept his anger from boiling over as he looked down at the regret weighting Blue's shoulders. "No, sir. We won't need the testers. If you wait until we close up tonight around one, you can stick around and ask her your questions." His voice went too soft for his liking, so he allowed his anger to spike again. "But you're not to talk to her without me there, and anything you learn stays in the bar, you hear?"

Sam nodded, but Alec did not. "That's fine."

"Phones, then," Baird demanded, his hand extended to them. "And you're not to leave the diner for any reason."

"Come again?" Sam asked.

Brody scoffed. "Man, this Wayward's got balls. Who do you think you are, barkeep?"

Baird turned to Brody darkly. "I'm *her* keeper. You think a busted nose from a little girl's a problem? Keep it up, and I'll really give you something to cry about."

Alec sized up Baird appreciatively. "Look, Baird. I get it. I get who she is, and I get that you don't want the testers exploiting her. We just want more information so we can lend a hand. We work for the Emperor of Europe. We may be able to get you two some help. Believe me, we *want* to help you." He shook his head at the prince when Liam opened the bathroom door and joined them. "We can't put Prince Liam in danger, though. One of us'll have to leave with him."

"I can guarantee your prince's safety. I'll keep Blue under control. She won't go near him till we all meet up after closing." When he could see that Alec was still hesitant, Baird added, "That's the best offer you're gonna get, Alec. One of you steps foot outside the bar, we run. We've kept hidden this long. How easy do you think it'll be to find us when we're *really* trying to lay low?"

The men sized each other up for ten seconds before Alec conceded. "This is probably the one thing that might trump protocol for the prince's safety. It's for the good of the world."

"Your prince is one of the testers, right? He can't leave to go there tonight," Baird commanded.

Liam finally spoke up, the laughter that never really left his eyes dancing beneath the surface, despite the gravity of the situation. "I'm just supposed to be there to put my royal stamp of approval on whoever they choose at the end of it. I wasn't going in tonight, anyway. I'm too handsome. Nearly started a riot last night. They could use a break from my good looks."

"She starts a fight again, and deal's off. You'll have more to worry about than testers if she attacks anyone near Liam. I won't put the prince in danger any more than I already am," warned Alec.

Liam rolled his eyes. "Francis' grave, I'm not that delicate."

"I won't touch him," Blue promised.

"There. Now hand over your phones. If you really get it, you know what a bad idea the testing is, and why she needs to be kept hidden for now."

Alec sighed. "Yeah, I know." He pulled out his phone, detached the battery and handed it to Baird. "Go on, guys."

Sam and Brody followed suit, but Baird was not satisfied until he retrieved Liam's battery, as well. "Now, keep your mouths shut till after we close, you hear? And you, Vemreaux," he glared at Sam, "there's no smoking in here."

"Seriously?" Sam questioned, making light of the tense situation. "I think you've got bigger problems than me, chief."

"Doubt it," Baird mumbled angrily, then turned on his sister. "You didn't black out, did you? Is this the worst of the damage?"

"I didn't black out," she confirmed quietly. Though Baird started moving back to the bar, Blue did not follow. She scowled up at the men. "If there's any more fighting tonight, I won't talk at all – testers or not. I don't care who started it, no one puts their hands on me again. You keep away from mine and I'll keep away from yours," she promised, directing her offer to Alec.

Alec agreed and allowed Baird to pass.

Baird gripped his sister's thin wrist firmly as they exited. Instead of going back to the eager customers, Baird practically dragged Blue into the kitchen. He looked as if he wanted to shout at her, but thought better of it. Fighting to keep his voice low, he growled, "Run."

"Baird, I don't think..." she began uncomfortably.

"It's my job to keep you safe, and it's not safe here anymore. Run and don't come back. I'll find you when they're gone."

Grettel and Stephanie were chatting animatedly on the other side of the kitchen. While Grettel took notice of the two siblings speaking in hushed harshness, Stephanie was too interested in her own story to analyze the situation.

Shaking her head, Blue stood firm. "I'm not running. Let them ask their questions. They already know enough. They won't just let it go and accept that I'm gone. You want this to go public? That's the quickest way, and you know it."

Baird's anger competed with his fear for first place on his face. Upon considering her words, the anxiety won out. "I don't trust them." Before Blue could agree or disagree, Baird held up his hand. "I don't want you saying a word to them. One of them talks to you, you walk away. I want you either in the kitchen or on the floor where I can see you. Don't you dare test me on this, Blue." Baird considered all the angles as his eyes darted around to see if he'd missed anything. "And I want you and Steve to switch sections."

Not waiting for a response, Baird turned and exited the kitchen. Blue thought about calling after him, but knew that her brother would not answer.

2 6

CLOSING

*D*read coursed through Blue's veins like ice as she waited on her tables. Each new Vemreaux represented a possible threat to their secret now, and she was unable to push away the fear. It was nearly impossible to do her usual act of meek invisibility by hiding behind her hair or moving out of people's way. Everywhere she moved, she could feel eyes boring into her. If by some miracle the four Vemreaux looked away from her for a moment, she could still feel her brother monitoring her steadily as she worked.

About three minutes after they sat back down at their table, several Femreaux tried their hands at seducing the wealthy foreigners. This time, however, Sam waved each of them away. They continued to observe Blue, cataloging her every move.

When he caught Blue glancing up at Sam from across the diner and blushing, Baird made a beeline for the quartet that was none too subtle. Leaning his fist on the table, he growled. "You want to be a little more subtle, you idiots? You're drawing attention to her with all your staring."

Brody leaned back and lazily kicked his feet up on the seat next to him. "You might want to watch your tone with us, barkeep. We're literally the ones holding the cards here."

Baird looked very much like he would enjoy throttling the Vemreaux until the smug smile was choked from his face, and guessed that he was not the first whose fingers itched with the desire. "Every Fem in the place is watching your table. You think no one's gonna catch on who you're gawking at? Her job is to fade into the background, which she can't do with all the attention. She gets made, we say nothing and you look like the jokers you are." He addressed Brody. "I don't think anyone'd have trouble believing that someone came up and kicked your face in just 'cause they didn't like the look of it."

"Ladies, how about we save the arm-wrestling match for a little later." When Sam's mirth evoked a deadly glower from Baird, he smartened up. "Look, we've got to keep an eye on her because she's a threat to the throne." He jerked his thumb to Prince Liam, who smiled apologetically. "We'll be less obvious, though."

"Glad to hear it," Baird muttered. He stalked back to the bar. Every time he left it for any reason, the drinkers and diners grew panicky for more shots. Though he was glad for the business, that night all he wanted was to close up and get to whatever was coming.

As Baird made drinks, he did not add any flair to the job. There was no more bottle juggling, no feigned friendliness to the flirting Femreaux who were attracted to his glowing eyes. Everywhere his sister went, his stealthy gaze followed to make sure she did not go near the dreaded booth.

Steve waited on her tables as she tended to his. As the night wore on, Steve began to forget how much he needed the money and that he was there to work, not take breaks or sit down with the diners at his leisure.

Every time Blue tended to one of the tables Steve was supposed to be taking, Baird envisioned grabbing Steve and tossing him out the back door.

Many times Baird's eyes coasted over to the booth, and without fail there was a different cluster of Femreaux clamoring for attention from the rich and powerful Vemreaux. Brody's nose was beginning to return back to a less conspicuous puffy shape. Baird was glad to see that his sister probably had not broken it. Perhaps there was hope that they could deny her true identity after all, though he doubted it. He watched as Brody left the booth a few times to dance or make out with a Femreaux he'd just met.

Alec did not leave his seat, but did welcome women into the booth to keep him company. They entertained with their roving hands and overdone laughter. Baird could not imagine the serious and deadly Vemreaux cracking a joke, but the Fems ate whatever he was saying right up, not caring that they were the ninth or twentieth woman to hang on him that night. Sam and Alec sat on either side of the prince, serving as barriers to keep the women from touching Liam without a thorough check for any danger.

Every time Baird caught Sam's eye, he glared. Just as Liam had pick of the litter, Sam was even more handsome and attracted the drunken women in droves. Fem after Fem whispered in his uninterested ear, touched his arm and scooted so close that Baird did not have to guess at what the women wanted from him. Sam kept glancing covertly in Blue's direction, waving off the Fems almost as quick as they came over to him.

Though his attention to Blue did not seem perverted, it also was not as coldly medical or observational as Alec's was. Every time Sam stared at his sister with a curious or forlorn gaze, Baird wanted to punch him, just once, good and hard. Well, maybe twice.

Elle trotted over to the bar to collect more shots several times during the remainder of the night, but Baird hardly noticed her flirting. When he finally turned his attention to her, he noticed bags under her eyes. Her movements were slower and contained more deliberate thought behind them. He turned toward her, resting the bottles down on the shelf below the bar so that he had both hands free and less to keep him from focusing on her.

"It's almost one," she commented. He could not tell if she sounded hopeful or dismal about the time. "I'll help tear down and come say goodbye before I go."

Nodding, Baird loaded the rest of the shots atop her tray. Before she picked it up, he caught her hand and held onto it for a few fleeting seconds. "Be careful tonight. Just fall asleep fast and I'll come get you."

"Really? In the car?" she asked tiredly. "May not be much of an act. I might fall asleep on the way to the testing."

"Find someone with a phone and call me." Baird's fingers clutched hers to remind himself of where he was and that nothing terrible had actually happened yet. "You don't have to tear down. We can do that. Just come see me before you go." He squeezed her hand to savor the contact, hoping it would bring back some sense to the night.

Elle smiled, getting a little life back in her face as she lifted the tray and finished waiting on the last of her tables. Baird made another dozen shots and set them behind him for the stragglers who couldn't seem to get it into their heads that they did not live at the bar.

The Vemreaux paid their tabs down, slowly filtering out in groups or in couples. At last, the only table in the place that still contained people was the booth that would soon demand his attention.

Not wanting to make their night any better, he took his time scrubbing down the bar while the minutes ticked by. Usually he'd kick out anyone sitting on the wooden stools after one in the morning, but he permitted one of his usual customers to indulge in his last drink as long as he pleased. Martin could be trusted to consume alcohol as long as he was still upright, which, judging by his exaggerated sway to the last song still blaring on the jukebox, would not be much longer.

Steve's last table exited, but instead of helping tear down, the lazy Vemreaux sat down in a chair in the middle of the diner and began counting his tips. Blue diligently bussed the rest of her tables and then moved on to his.

The stress of the day needed an outlet, and Baird was grateful for the target that the slovenly waiter presented. He cracked open the kitchen door and did his best to appear friendly. "Stephanie, thanks for all your hard work. You can go on home. The kitchen looks great."

It was true. With the two women to clean it, they were nearly finished.

"Alright, Baird. And you, you little elf, I'll dig up the picture of that house in Asia I was telling you about. Wish Elle good luck for me."

As soon as the door closed behind him, Baird disregarded the four Vemreaux he'd eventually have to acknowledge and walked over to the chair where Steve sat. Very quietly, he bent down and breathed over Steve's shoulder. "You."

Steve sat erect for the first time in Baird's memory. He tried to turn to look at Baird, but the Wayward moved his face so close to the back of Steve's head that he could not turn fast enough to see him. "What do you want, Baird?" he asked irritably.

Baird spoke into the back of the Vemreaux's head, breathing heavily to make him squirm. "Have you seen how small my sister is?"

"So?" Steve rubbed the hot breath off the back of his neck, but Baird was not deterred.

"Do you know how many of your tables she's had to take?"

"Yeah, so?"

Baird paused, knowing the Vemreaux at the booth could probably hear him. "Do you know that I know where you live?"

Steve stopped breathing, fear lighting his nerves. "I was just going to help her clear off the rest of the tables."

"Those are your tables, useless. She's bussing *your* tables." Baird breathed one last time on the waiter, catching Alec's amusement out of the corner of his eye. "Do you know how it feels to watch your family be taken advantage of? It makes me...less than happy. Do you know what I do when I'm less than happy?" Now he was just taunting the Vemreaux. It felt good to have some small amount of control still. "Do you know how many Waywards die every year because they fall into the scratch pit and get buried alive in it? How many bodies do you think I've seen disappear?" Then, just to toy with him, Baird lowered his voice. "How many do you think I've *made* disappear?"

Steve shot up from his chair like he had been shocked. Without looking behind him, he immediately began cleaning off the rest of the tables in the dining area. Baird saw Blue's raised eyebrow at his actions. He responded by shrugging innocently, catching a muffled laugh from Alec.

THE TABLES WERE TO BE LEFT OUT TO WEATHER THE ELEMENTS, BUT JOE wanted the chairs inside after closing. Elle was moving slowly as she wiped down the last of her tables under the dark sky. The brilliant smile that pulled in so many tips was faltering as her thoughts gave way to whatever was in store for her that night at the testing.

When Baird could take it no longer, he pulled out a chair and motioned for her to sit in it and rest her tired feet. "When's the tester coming to pick you up?" he asked quietly.

"I told him one-thirty, so any minute, really." She leaned her head on her hand and allowed her eyes to drift shut for the moment. "What's going on with you and Blue? I've never seen her so distracted. And you're so mad. Why? What'd I miss?"

Baird considered informing her, but thought better of it. "I'll tell you tomorrow when you're awake." He watched her yawn without covering her mouth, her chin tilting up to enjoy the full body of it. Baird smiled at her cuteness. "You ready for tonight?"

She shrugged, her lips puckered from exhaustion. "Bring it," she joked, her head still on her hand.

Baird began to pull the chairs out from the tables and move them to the entrance. It would have been more effective to bring them all the way in, but he wanted to prolong his time outside with Elle.

"Don't kill yourself trying tonight. Just get in and get out. For what it's worth, I'm impressed you made it this far." Even though he saw Elle nod, he couldn't tell if he was really getting through to her. "She'd never have been able to stay hidden this long without you."

"That's because I'm amazing."

"Did my distraction help you last night? Give you something to keep you awake thinking about?" he teased her.

Elle's lips pulled up into a dreamy smile as her head bobbed slowly. Baird ignored the rest of the chairs to stand in front of her and lean over for another kiss. Her eyes were closed, so she wasn't expecting it, and gasped when his lips moved on hers. Her hands flew to his face and his wrapped under her arms, pulling her up to standing. The warmth was comforting as she pressed into him, exploiting every curve to his notice. He clutched onto the fabric of her shirt that was dampened from clinging to her back with sweat. She hummed under her breath a little purr of enjoyment, giving new life to his passion.

Deeper he drove the kiss until they were both out of breath and had to pull away. Her eyes were definitely open when she touched her cheeks to calm herself. "You're supposed to distract me, not give me a heart attack." She watched him crack a smile before he pressed his lips to hers gently once more. "Baird," she murmured as her mouth began to move with his once again.

"I love that you say my name when I kiss you," he admitted, lightly nipping at her lower lip.

"Baird," she inhaled languorously, "the tester."

"That's not exactly the sexy talk I was hoping for," he murmured. It took a full two seconds before he understood that the tester was now there to collect her. He drew out the process of pulling away, so as not to end the closeness too abruptly.

Elle looked around Baird's tall shoulder and waved to acknowledge the tester. "Do you want me to stay and finish up?" she asked, still coming out of the bliss.

"Nah, you go on ahead. Maybe Steve'll actually do some work tonight. Say goodnight to the girls first, though. I'm sure Grettel's had quite the day worrying about you. She doesn't like sleeping alone, either. Little thing tossed all night."

He lifted the chair Elle had been sitting on and carried it over to the others near where the tester stood. "Evening, sir," he greeted the man respectfully.

The Vemreaux official nodded, but kept his attention on Elle as she walked toward him.

"I just have to say goodnight to the others. I'll be ready in a minute." She floated past him before he could remind her of the time.

Elle grabbed two chairs and dragged them inside behind her, stacking them up to the right of the entrance so they'd be easy to get to the next day. Her eyes flew to the only booth still containing diners, surprised at the company. Baird never allowed people to stay this late. She thought of going over and finding out what they were still doing there, but decided she'd better make use of the time and say her goodbyes to the girls.

Elle drew her hand into her apron to remove the thick wad of tips and handed the money to Blue. "Give this to Baird, will you?"

"No problem. You taking off?"

"Yes, and I deserve a decent hug. It's my last night pretending to be you," she whispered, "so make it a good one." She extended her arms with a grin that the finish line was at last in sight.

"Hey, don't overdo it tonight. Baird'll come get you as soon as they kick you out. It'll all be over soon."

"You sound like your brother." Elle squeezed the girl tight. "I'll be back in a little bit, and you'll all wonder how I got to be so awesome." Blue pulled away and smiled, but Elle noticed the force with which the corners of her lips twisted up just enough to pass as believable. "What's wrong?" she asked, though she knew the response that would come.

"Nothing, Elle. Everything's fine. You concentrate on you tonight." Blue searched her brain for a distraction. "I can't believe all it took was this whole testing ordeal for my brother to finally make his move."

"I know, right? Had I known it would be that easy..." Elle blew her a farewell kiss and sauntered off.

Blue shoved Elle's wad of tips into her apron and went back into the dining area to help her brother tear down the rest of the tables and chairs. She grabbed a table and hefted it onto one shoulder, using the lip under the edge for leverage. She strolled out of the hallway onto the deserted dancing area that she'd already swept up.

As soon as her brother saw her, he abandoned his chairs and trotted over to help her.

"I got it," she assured him. He'd never offered her assistance before.

"Could you at least pretend to struggle a little? We're not alone here." His voice was quiet as he took the table from her and helped her set it back up.

"Okay." She didn't see much of a point. The Vemreaux at the booth already knew she had more strength than the average girl...or body builder. Baird went straight for the kitchen while Blue finished the exaggerated labor of dragging the chairs inside.

Alec spoke up from his seat. "You don't have to put on a show for us. We know you can lift chairs without making that face."

"Okay," she offered, though she changed nothing for the Vemreaux, sticking to her brother's instruction. She felt Sam's penetrating eyes on her, but she did not look in the direction of the booth. So adamant was her need to keep away from the magnet that unthinkingly drew her in, that she treated their whole section of the restaurant as if it were the sun – too overwhelming to look at.

Baird finally emerged with the two girls. Grettel was hesitant, but stuck next to Elle and behind Baird to shield herself from view. She shot a quick look of panic at Blue, who did her best to smile comfortingly.

The three exited the building, and Blue could see through one of the tall windows that Baird was talking with the tester as he took the key to the hut off the ring and handed it to Grettel. It was probably wise to ask the tester to drop Grettel off at home under the guise of Elle desperately needing something from the hut. There was no need for Grettel to stick around in the diner for what would no doubt be a lengthy conversation that would just upset her. Blue wished she could retreat for the shelter, as well.

CARDS ON THE TABLE

Sam was smoking to calm his nerves as the four went to a table in the middle of the floor. He moved to sit next to the chair Blue was headed for, but was intercepted. "No, Blue. Sit here," Baird instructed, indicating the seat at the end of the table on his right side. Usually the two siblings sat opposite each other so they could keep watch behind the other person's back, just in case. It was an old habit he'd engrained into her in The Way.

"Okay," she consented, and obediently sat down next to her brother. She pulled out two separate stacks of bills. "These are Elle's," she handed him the thicker one as the Vemreaux settled in around them. "These are mine."

He nodded and bent the top bill of Elle's in half before placing Blue's money over it to combine them into one easily foldable stack that he slid into the pocket of his jeans. Sam's eyebrows wrinkled in confusion, but he said nothing.

The shots Baird placed in the middle of the table as a peace offering caught Brody's eye. He reached over and downed the first one.

"You okay, little Wayward?" Sam asked casually.

Blue kept her chin down and nodded submissively. Sam frowned.

Baird made no indication that Sam had spoken, but crossed his arms over his chest and leaned back in his chair to make himself more comfortable for the interrogation he was sure was coming.

Liam was never one for awkward situations, so he set to rectifying the tension. "Good to see you again, Baird. And we haven't met yet." He extended his hand to Blue, grinning jovially and naturally, as if his face were given to smiling often.

"This is the ever-impressive Liam," Sam explained. "Just ask him."

"Sir." Blue took his hand for one shake, and then dropped it immediately, shrinking yet further back into her chair.

"Show him your eyes, *A-word*," Brody ordered as he fiddled with the shot glass.

Sam hissed at the offensive slur and kicked his friend under the table.

Before she consented to revealing the window to her soul, Baird spoke up. "We're agreed to keep everything private?"

"I'm great with privates," Liam joked, dismayed when no one laughed with him. "What? No? Well, I thought it was funny."

"Are we going to go through this all over again?" Alec leaned threateningly toward the girl seated at his left. "We keep our mouths shut, you open yours." Alec grew impatient and stood to confront Blue.

Alec's arm rose to force the girl to look at Liam, but Baird held up his palm. "You'll not put your hands on my owner's property."

Liam was uncomfortable as he shifted in his chair. "Seriously, guys. You suck at getting information from people you can't beat it out of. Why is everyone still so tense?"

Brody guffawed. "Why? Ninja Barbie got the drop on Sam and popped me in the face. That's why. Smug little brat."

"She's like fifteen, Brody," Liam chided, his disdain plainly communicated. "You can't talk to kids like that."

At this, Blue opened her eyes to correct the affront. "I'm nineteen," she said indignantly.

She had a remark stored up to toss at Brody, but the words failed her. Staring back at her were the eyes she tried for so long to hide. Her mouth fell open as she struggled to make sense of the bluest irises she'd seen apart from hers and her brothers'. "What...who are you?" she stammered, all of a sudden unsure of herself. Still, she could not look away. Something inside of Blue shifted, but she did not know what or why. For whatever reason, Blue's subconscious latched onto Liam.

It seemed the feeling was mutual. Liam's response came several beats later as he tried to collect himself. When he spoke again, the jocularity was forced. Liam tried to push away the confusion that seeing her face brought him. He leaned back in his chair. "See, that's why I love the Americas. No one knows who I am here." Deciding he could no longer resist the temptation, Liam finished the shot in his hand in one gulp, shivering as it slid through him.

Baird held up a hand to Liam. "You'll want to go easy on those. That's absinthe. Meant for changed Vemreaux." He noticed Liam eyeing the other glasses as if they presented a challenge. "Mind answering my sister's question?"

"Oh, yeah. My dad's the ruler of Europe. I'm Liam Boniface. My dad's Frederick." When Blue made no noise of surprise or admiration, he added, "The emperor what came to power about two decades ago? That one."

Though Baird already knew this, the weight of their plight pressed down on him afresh. He closed his eyes to keep from scolding her and shook his head as he covered his face with his hand.

Blue's eyes darted to the exit, calculating how far she could get without being apprehended. As if reading her mind, Alec stood behind her chair, resting his hand heavily on the wood at her back.

"I'm sorry, Baird," she whispered.

Baird surprised her by addressing something entirely different. "Are you going for a run tonight?"

"Probably." Blue shrugged, confused at his off-topic question. Baird did not explain himself, but stood and walked toward the kitchen.

"We just gonna keep being uncomfortable, then?" Liam asked,

clearly disappointed. When no one responded, he sighed. "Guess so."

A minute later, Baird returned with a plate of leftover noodles decorated with red sauce. He rested it in front of his sister with a roll of silverware and a look that demanded she eat.

Liam spoke to Baird, since Blue was not willing to glance up at him. "The Fems here tonight were sure happier than that. You're not a fan of my dad, then?"

Instead of waiting for Baird or Blue to speak, Sam explained the situation. "They're concerned with anonymity. You're a public figure. Not exactly easy to sneak by unnoticed."

Liam itched the back of his arm and huffed. "Seriously, guys. Could someone just say whatever it is we're all afraid to say? Because it's going on two in the morning, and I'm getting tired." His lips pursed as if the next few words pained him. "I get it. She looks like Julia. But she's not my sister, Brode. She's not Julia. Julia's dead, guys. Leave the poor kid alone."

Alec was the brave voice that broke through all the carefully constructed walls and shields with the blunt edge of truth. "We think she's the Light, Liam."

Baird stiffened at the declaration that was now out in the open.

"I don't know, Alec. Sure, she caught you guys off-guard, but maybe she's just been trained well. Some of those Waywards at the testing were pretty tough. Her blonde friend? Saw her at the testing. Impressive file they had on her physical examination. They probably just trained together or something." He glanced down at Blue. "Look at her. I mean, she's just a little thing. How's she going to end the tyranny and kill the predator? You could knock her over with a stiff breeze."

Blue jerked her head up at the insinuation that she was anything less than four meters tall and built like an oak tree. Unrolling her napkin, she picked up the silver-colored knife and flung it across the length of the diner without turning her head to verify the target's location. The utensil soared to the dart board that hung on the wall near the bar. The point of the dulled butter knife blade sunk straight into the red bull's eye.

Brody swore loudly and got up to make sure that it did, indeed, hit the middle. Liam made an unintelligible noise of surprise, while Alec's reaction of staggering silence rang out from behind the girl.

Sam's mouth fell open. He coughed out a mouthful of smoke to cover over the nervous laughter. "You were saying?"

Baird shook his head and rested his forehead in his hand. "Was that really necessary?"

Blue shrugged in lieu of a response.

"Do it with the spoon and I'll be impressed."

"Can't. The angle's all wrong from here." She tapped her head three times smartly. "Geometry."

Baird groaned at her smirk of vindication.

"Why am I eating two dinners? I finished the sandwich Grettel made me earlier."

Glancing around at the unwelcome audience, Baird sighed. "Since it's all out in the open now anyway," he grumbled. "In The Way, you laid in your bed at night and pretended to sleep. Now that you're running all night, you're not taking in enough calories." He glanced over at Liam. "You're gonna need two dinners from now on if you don't want to get knocked down by 'a stiff breeze'."

"Okay." She leaned her elbow on the table and rested her head on her hand as she twirled the cold noodles on her fork.

The first Vemreaux to get his words back was Sam. "You don't sleep, then? The prophecy's true?" He watched her take a bite from the glob of noodles and sauce on her fork instead of sucking the whole messy mass into her mouth.

"Yep." Her lips curled around the "p" while she chewed.

"What's that like?" Sam inquired, taking another puff.

"Boring."

"You'd think the Vemreaux working in The Way's nursery would've figured that one out and reported it," Brody commented from across the room. He pulled the knife out of the dart board and examined it for signs of falsity, unable to mask his astonishment. "How did you do that?"

Shrugging was what Blue was most comfortable with, so she stuck with it. "Baird can do it, too." She excused her behavior, writing it off as no big deal.

"No, I can't," Baird corrected her. "Not from this angle. You know I have to be straight in front of it."

"I meant you can hit a bull's eye with a kitchen knife," she amended, licking a stray bit of sauce from her lower lip.

"Look," Baird said, placing his hands on the table to draw Sam's eyes from his sister's mouth. "No one can know she's the Light. This whole testing thing's a terrible idea. If anyone was to find out it's Blue, her face'd be everywhere. How much of a chance do you think she'd have against the predator then? Surprise is a handy weapon." He glanced over at Blue. "Even better than a butter knife, if you can imagine."

"Agreed. We're here because Dad needed someone to represent Europe at the ceremony on Peace Day, and someone to sit in on the first day of testing." Liam's hands subconsciously mimicked Baird's. "It's all photo ops and diplomacy nonsense. I'm great with the nonsense. Camera loves me." Liam eyed Blue's food, looking like he very much wanted to finish it for her. "So what happens now? What's your plan for the predator?"

This time Blue spoke for herself, which surprised them. "There is no plan yet. I can't get over to the O-blood island to kill it. I only got bought last month."

Liam's face fell. "Who owns her?"

"The same guy who owns me and this diner. Name's on the logo." He jerked his thumb over his shoulder to indicate the back of his uniform. "Joe Anders."

Liam addressed only Baird. "So let me get this straight, we have the Light who can end all the Vemreaux disappearances and deaths, but she can't do it because she's gotta work in a bar? Who is this guy?" He reached for his phone, but recalled the missing battery unhappily.

Sam sighed, the early morning hour creeping up on him. "This Joe guy doesn't know she's the Light, Liam. He just thinks he bought himself a pretty little waitress." He leaned back into his chair and puffed, examining Blue through the translucent wisps of smoke.

"Americans," Liam murmured with a bad taste in his mouth. "Don't you know what you're doing to your economy in the long run by buying slaves instead of freeing them? He doesn't have to pay you two as much as he'd have to pay a Vemreaux or a freed Wayward. I'm sure there are plenty of Vemreaux who'd like a steady job at a diner."

"Are you one of those people?" Baird asked snidely, leaning forward to look at the man more directly. "Do you want to work in a bar, Prince Liam? It's a great job. Only fourteen-hour days six days a week for tips and A-blood minimum wage."

Liam looked uncomfortable as his eyes darted to the girl who so looked like his sister. She ate without reacting to their political conversation, and he wondered if she also was required to work such excruciating hours. Julia never worked a fourteen-hour week when she was alive.

It was Brody who got them back on track. "So she literally can't fly to old world Australia because her owner doesn't know she's the Light, yeah?"

Baird nodded once. Blue was losing her steam with the food, her fork resting on the plate while she eyed the rest of the noodles, debating if she should stay in the storm cellar and finish her Geometry book instead of going for a jog.

"Well, this is stupid. Just go on the run. Buy a plane ticket and fly to the island." Liam shrugged like it was no big deal.

"We're not free, we're owned. If an owned Wayward runs from his master, you know what'll happen. Face splashed everywhere, and if we're found, it'll be either death or prison, if they're feeling generous. We'd never make it to the island. We wouldn't make it past airport security."

It was Blue who spoke up before the others could interject their pointless arguments. "We?" she inquired, sitting back from her food to stare at him.

"You heard me."

"You're not going with me, Baird." It was the first time he'd said anything about going out on the death mission together. The very thought surprised and scared her.

"That's not your decision."

"How'm I supposed to kill anything if I'm worrying about it ripping you apart first? No, Baird. I won't watch you die." She pushed her spaghetti away obstinately.

"The prophecy doesn't say –"

"The prophecy says that I'll be the one dying. What chance do you think you'll have against it if it gets me?" She looked up at him with regretful eyes. "If you try to follow me, I'll run. Police'll find you before you catch up to me and they'll kill you. Is that what you want? You don't exactly have a face that stirs up mercy in people. No, Baird. You have to stay here and watch over Elle and Grettel. That's the deal. I get to die, and you get to babysit. No trading."

In that little exchange, the men at the table witnessed a short power shift where Blue was briefly in charge of making the rules. No one spoke for a moment while the two ironed things out.

"This isn't over, Blue. It's not up to you. The prophecy was written without considering that you'd have help with you. You might not die if you have me there." His voice took on a pleading tone instead of argumentative.

Blue glared up at him as if it was the cruelest thing he could have said to her. "Don't you put that in my head! Don't make me hope things could be different. You're staying here, and that's that. It doesn't matter, because I can't leave the diner anyway. People can just keep on getting slaughtered out there while we sit here and argue about whether or not you'll be stupid enough to die with me."

"Don't be a child about this."

Her eyes flashed dangerously, but she held her tongue. Blue stood, pushing her chair backward into Alec. "Excuse me." She turned to walk from the table. When the intimidating Alec moved to block her path, her anger shifted its focus to him. "Move!" Blue tried to sneer menacingly, but knew that she still looked like an unimposing girl. All the submissiveness was starting to grate on her. The 'yes, sirs' and 'right away, sirs' were far from what she wanted to say. She'd wrestled with her control for too long and under too many eyes. Blue could feel her discipline begin to wear thin.

Alec had no intention of obeying. He pointed to her chair. "Sit."

So quick that no one really saw all of it, Blue's shoe swept behind Alec's feet and pushed them out from under him as one small hand shoved his chest straight downward with unnatural force. The Vemreaux all gasped in horror and amazement as the immovable Alec fell to the floor with what seemed like barely an effort on her part. With the wind temporarily knocked out of Alec, Blue stepped all of her dainty weight on his chest as she walked over the guard toward the bathroom.

Liam broke the silence. "Whoa! I've never seen anyone take you down before."

Alec did not answer, and the others knew better than to tease him about it.

Sam looked as if he'd like to say something, but thought better of it. He shifted in his chair before picking more appropriate words. "Can she buy her freedom?"

Shaking his head, Baird eyed Blue's spaghetti. "Waywards can't just up and free themselves. Their owner has to do it. We don't know if Joe'd keep her secret. It's too big of a risk to tell him she's the Light. How much more money do you think he could make if he advertised that you could get your blood shakes brought to you by the Light? He doesn't exactly put our health and safety first as it is. Like I said, fourteen hour days, six days a week."

Brody sat down in the chair next to Baird, turning it around so that he straddled it backward. "Why don't you just buy her, Liam? Offer more than he paid for her. Pretend you desperately need some reliable American slave to carry around your tiara or something, and you just happened to literally stumble into the bar and find her. Then we can go over to old world Australia on holiday or on assignment after we get back home. Frederick'll okay it. Killian's thinking of taking his guards over there to get away for a while anyway. The safer parts, of course. Alec, Sam and I can take her with us, or you can go on official business from the emperor."

Liam churned over the details of Brody's plan. "My dad can't know she's the Light. He wouldn't exploit her or anything, but he'd have an obligation to the people to announce it. If I buy her as a servant, she's got to play the part in front of people. Would she really be able to do that without, you know, throwing us to the ground every chance she got?"

Baird's spirit lifted as new possibility shone on their formerly unsolvable problem. His mind raced over any hiccups that might thwart the perfect plan. "She'd be fine. You should see the way some of these Vemreaux in the diner order her around. Blue's strong willed, but she'll submit if it's for the greater good." He considered this further. "Well, maybe not to you." He indicated Brody, who put on his best mock surprise face. Baird took a deep breath and trudged on to the issue he was less comfortable with. "Alright. Let's talk money. We've been saving every brandish to buy our younger brother when he comes of age. We still have to find the right Vemreaux to make the transaction for us, since technically we're not citizens. We're shy on the money, though. We can kick in just under two hundred thousand bills. We also can't free Blue ourselves because we're not Vemreaux."

Liam looked insulted. "I don't need money. My dad's the emperor, remember? I just don't have a servant on principle, but my family employs a few.

Sam threw his head back. "I'm totally telling Josephine you called her a servant."

"Don't you dare, Sam. She'd kill me! Baird, give me your owner's number and I'll call him first thing in the morning, yeah?"

"Wait." Baird held his hands up to slow the quickly progressing conversation. "We need to lay down a few ground rules first. You don't want any money from us? That seems off."

"Not a brandish. I think her ending the predator makes us square," said Liam.

"And you're buying her only so she can kill the predator. You're not making money off of her any other way?"

"Are you implying something, *A-word*?" Brody interrupted.

"Brody, shut it," Liam insisted, correcting his friend's inappropriate comment. "We won't use her for anything other than killing the predator. Same thing you're using her for. She'll have to act like a servant, though. If someone in my family tells her to get me a drink or clean my room, she's got to do it, or she'll draw attention to herself."

"Agreed." Baird's wary stare flickered between Alec and Sam. "And you all keep your hands off my sister. If she doesn't want to show people her eyes, you respect that." Alec did not nod, but he did not argue either. Baird figured that was as good a response as any from the quiet Vemreaux. "You grab her face, it'll be on you when she rips your hand off. Don't think she can't do it. If she's the Light who can kill the predator, you won't stand a chance. And you," he turned his attention to Sam, who'd been uncharacteristically quiet.

Before Baird could get out the threat Sam knew was coming, the Vemreaux stood from his chair and strolled casually to the bathroom. "I'll go check on the warrior."

Not willing to let Sam off without a warning, Baird called after him, "I catch your arms around my sister again, and I'll break them myself. Her blood's the same as mine, and I can do it, Vemreaux!"

Liam and Brody both snapped their heads to gawk at Sam, who kept a steady pace toward the restroom hallway.

"She's nineteen, perv!" Baird shouted.

2 8

THE TRUTH

Sam cringed as he stood outside of the ladies' restroom for the second time that day. He could hear her feet shuffling around inside and hoped that her brother's voice had not carried this far.

As he stared at the bathroom door, he questioned his motives. Why was he waiting for her? The faint hope of another quiet moment alone with the girl was marred by the fact that his friends and her brother sat just a few meters away in the dining area. Who was she to him? Aside from being the Light, she was just a Wayward. A pretty Wayward who threw him up against the wall, besting his strength in a way that both confused and excited him. Beneath the feigned submission to her brother was a fistful of moxie that drew him in. He'd never met anyone who held his attention the way she did.

He never followed a Femreaux to the bathroom to make sure she was okay. He was usually the one they went to the restroom to cry in private over after he'd cast them aside when he'd lost interest. He leaned against the concrete wall and shoved his hand in his pockets as he waited for the beautiful stranger. He sucked on the end of his cigarette, hoping the familiar action would bring him back to normal.

The bathroom door flew open to reveal Blue's carefully composed face, which fell into surprise when she saw that he was waiting for her again. Her hand rose to her chest to indicate that he'd startled her.

"You okay?" Sam asked, immediately berating himself for not coming up with something smoother.

Blue nodded in response.

"They're coming up with a pretty good plan out there. One that involves your brother staying here and you going to the O-blood island without a parade of police behind you." He placed his free hand behind him at the base of his spine and pressed it between his backside and the wall to keep from fidgeting. "Do you want to go back out there? Throw in your brandish before it's decided?"

"Okay," she replied lamely, her blue eyes meeting his black ones without the usual curtain of hair between them.

Something about her noncommittal response caused him to stiffen, the subtle muscles in his face tightening. "You don't have to, you know. I asked you if you want to." He blew a mouthful of smoke away from her.

Blue's face scrunched, not understanding the distinction.

Sam shook his head. "Never mind. Come on."

Without thinking, he pushed himself off of the wall and took a step toward her like he wanted to hold her hand on the short stroll back to the table. Before his fingers could act out their desired insanity, he shoved them into his pocket to keep them from causing further damage. All the while, his hand itched to be free of the expensive black material and touch her, having acquired the addiction in that very hallway from the restraint that turned into a tender hold.

"I'm sorry about earlier." He caught himself and rolled his eyes. "And for waiting for you outside the bathroom like a stalker twice now." His full lips tightened with embarrassment.

She walked next to him with less distance than she would

normally put between herself and another, though she was careful not to brush against him. When she inhaled his subtle cologne, she tripped over her own two feet, stumbling before righting herself with chagrin.

"You alright?" he asked, his hand touching her back kindly.

"Yeah. Just clumsy tonight." When they were visible to the others, she tilted her head down to avoid eye contact with her brother, certain that her near fall and her desire to walk closer to the Vemreaux was somehow visible on her face.

Alec was sitting in her chair, so she decided it was fitting to take his instead of making him stand back up. She'd knocked the wind out of him pretty easily, and thought he probably needed the extra comfort of a chair while he reassembled his bearings and whatever could be salvaged of his pride. The vacant seat that had been Alec's was across the table from Baird, to the left of Liam. When she reached it, it magically pulled out for her. She looked up in confusion, thinking perhaps Sam wanted to claim the chair as his, but he motioned for her to sit in it.

"What?" Sam questioned when his friends' bewilderment mirrored hers. "I'm being nice."

Brody stared at his friend in astonishment. "It's literally like watching a baby giraffe take his first steps."

Blue consented with wide eyes, and Sam slid the chair smoothly under her. Unable to hide her surprise at being treated so sweetly, the dreaded blush crept into her cheeks and trickled down her neck.

"Tell," Baird grumbled, allowing his expression to dip into grave unhappiness.

When Blue did not say anything, Brody spoke up. "Tell what?"

Baird shook his head. "Nothing. I just caught one of her tells. That's a new one, Blue. You'll want to iron that out quickly."

She offered no biting retort, but shrunk in her seat, wishing the frame would swallow her whole. She was relieved when Baird said nothing more of the embarrassing pink in her cheeks. Liam, Alec and Brody all stared at her to see what he was talking about, but they noticed nothing except for the small bit of color that lingered.

"Dude." Brody turned to Sam uneasily. "She's *A*-blood. She literally reeks like rotten eggs."

"And you, Brody," Sam cut him off before he could make it worse, "don't exactly smell like a summer breeze." He did not know what possessed him to pull Blue's seat out for her. Never in his life had he done something so chivalrous. Even the promise of a satisfying night with an experienced Femreaux could not evoke such manners from him. Though he did not regret his actions, he did wish they had not been witnessed by those who knew his wanton behavior best. He reclaimed his seat and tried to disappear behind the smoke.

"Okay." Liam interrupted the quarrel he was sure would erupt. The girl next to him squirmed in her chair, invoking his compassion toward her when he saw her discomfort at being in the spotlight. "Your brother and I figured out a way to get you to old world Australia without too many people being involved."

Her ears perked, but her head remained downward.

"How would you feel about me buying you from your master? You'd have to pretend to be my servant and come with me on holiday or on assignment to the island, but I could get you there, no problem." He draped his hand lazily on the back of her chair, causing Blue to stiffen.

She looked up at Baird across the table, ignoring everyone's study of her every movement. Blue's eyes moved rapidly back and forth as she processed the new information, trying to bring to light any possible problems with the plan.

"If Joe doesn't put up much of a fight, we can have the paperwork done early next week. I have to stay for the Peace Day parade, and I've got to stop by The Way West to see my Uncle Jack again at some point, but we can leave the day after that if everything's in place."

Blue looked up at the prince, breaking out of her silence. "Your Uncle Jack? Is he a professor in The Way West?"

Liam cracked his knuckles. "Yeah. You know him?"

"Yes!" For the first time, Blue allowed her smile to seep through her control. "He was my favorite. Great guy."

Baird nodded grimly as he stared into the two sets of identical blue eyes across the table. So much about himself and Blue looked similar to Liam. The tanned complexion, rare Original Vemreaux eyes, and about half a dozen other small things finally clicked in Baird's mind. He watched his sister smile up at Liam, showing off their similarities. It was the last piece that he needed to fall into place to complete the puzzle he had been doing without consciously thinking about it. His breath quickened, but he fought to suppress the tell before his sister could notice it.

"Well, he's my favorite uncle, so we have something in common after all. What do you think about the plan?" Liam asked, put off by her prolonged silence at what he thought was a great idea.

"Okay," she replied simply and went back to staring at the table in front of her.

Sam exhaled like he would very much like to say something, but shoved a fresh cigarette between his lips to keep himself from talking.

"What?" Baird asked her, noticing that her eyes were still processing the new plan.

Her voice was so quiet that Brody had to lean in to hear her. "Do we have that kind of money? I thought we were saving to buy Griffin when he's old enough. I don't want to be the reason he's still in The Way when he's sixty."

"We'll still keep saving for Griffin, Blue. And we're not paying for you. Liam is. He wants to buy you like a real servant and take you with him so it's legal and no one asks any questions. They're all ex-military and Liam's royalty. They'll be able to take you where the Vemreaux've been disappearing from. Just tag along and stay out of their way until they get you there."

"Okay."

"When we go, you'll have to do enough work to blend in. I'll keep you as a personal servant, so you can stay closer to us." Liam swallowed in distaste. "I've actually never had one before, so this'll be new to me, too. It won't be long before we can get over to the island and sort this predator out."

"I still don't feel comfortable not paying you. It doesn't seem right." Baird frowned.

Liam waved his hand to say that it was the least he could do to end the predator's reign of terror. "I'll tell you what. You teach your sister here to make these, and we'll call it even." Liam eyed the other shots on the table that sat there like twinkling green glasses of happiness, begging to become a part of him. The first shot was already doing its part to impair his judgment. He'd spent many a drunken night trying to build up resistance to the powerful alcohol's hallucinogenic effects, and could usually down five shots before losing himself to the euphoria.

"When you call Joe tomorrow, wait until after ten o'clock in the morning. He doesn't like being bothered before then." Baird patted his jeans pocket before looking over at his sister. "Blue? You got a pen and paper?"

Blue obediently pulled out a pen and an order sheet from her apron and slid them across the table.

Baird scribbled on the back of the paper and handed it to Liam. "This is his number. Blue's his newest waitress, so he probably won't be too attached yet. Start the bidding a little over the buying price. You might get lucky." Recalling his sister, he slid the plate of spaghetti across the table to her. "Finish it."

"Okay." She sighed as she picked up the fork and slowly resumed eating her second dinner.

Sam murmured something under his breath sarcastically, pulling Baird's eyes over to him. "Something you want to say, Vemreaux?" he challenged.

After considering the question for a moment, Sam sat up straighter in his chair. "Actually, yeah." A dark look from Alec and Liam told him to push the more nasty things he wanted to say out of his mind and focus on the actual issue. "If she says 'okay' one more time, this isn't going to work. How are we supposed to know what she needs if she won't speak up?"

Baird considered this and dropped the abrasive lilt in his voice. "What do you need to know?"

"Oh, I don't know. We've never spent much time with an *A*-blood. What does she eat? How often? Apparently she doesn't sleep. That's something we should know." Sam bit back the other much more personal things he wanted to discover, but would never ask her brother. "Stuff like that."

"Alright." Baird answered for his sister, as he was accustomed to doing. "The prophecy's true. As soon as it was written, she stopped sleeping. No naps, nothing. She had to pretend to sleep in The Way to keep the professors from noticing her, but she doesn't like it." Baird noticed his sister moving the noodles around on her plate nervously. He knew that she did not like all of her secrets being poured out for the Vemreaux to analyze.

"She eats Grade *V* rations in the morning, a regular lunch and a normal dinner. Stuff Liam probably eats since he's not changed yet. If she goes running in the night like she's been doing since she got out of The Way, she'll need a second dinner, like the one she's pretending to eat right now." He threatened his sister with a glance.

Blue stopped fiddling with the food and ate it. Like a puppet on a string, she danced for him, doing whatever he asked without the resistance she wanted to put up.

Alec was amazed at Baird's level of control over the occasionally willful girl. He studied the Wayward's movements so he could repeat them and achieve the same subservient results in the potential killer.

"Guys, she was only bought a few weeks ago. There's a lot she doesn't know about the world. She studied everything she could in The Way, but the Vemreaux don't like Waywards knowing too much." He directed the next command to Liam. "Don't send her out alone in public. She can run by herself if it's a safe area that you live in, but only in the middle of the night when there's not so many people around."

Brody scoffed. "You really afraid someone's gonna jump her?"

Baird folded his arms and crooked his neck to stare at him. "No, I'm afraid she'll get spooked, attack some Vemreaux and cause a scene like she did tonight. She's my sister, and I won't let her go somewhere she's not going to be watched over. Either you do it, or the deal's off. She's not to be alone during the day."

Blue's mouth pursed like she wanted to defend herself, but she kept her eyes down.

Liam shrugged. "That's fine. We won't be in Europe long. Couple weeks, a month or so. Just enough time to set up a flight and pack for the fight."

"No," Blue said with just enough volume to change the flow of conversation. Her eyes were still fixed on the plate in front of her as she spoke. "Pack for the fight? None of you'll be fighting. I'm the Light, not any of you. This thing abducts Vemreaux and kills them. You can take me there because owned A-bloods can't fly unaccompanied, but that's it. You can't fight with me."

All of the guys except for Baird put up a protest, their voices clashing and drowning out each other's words. Baird finally spoke above the din, holding his hand up as he addressed Sam. "You're the one who wanted her to speak up and tell you what she needs. You can't have it both ways."

Her spaghetti forgotten, Blue lifted her chin to meet Alec's fixed stare. "If any of you try to come with me, you'll be one more thing I have to watch out for. I won't be able to kill the predator if I'm responsible for making sure he doesn't off one of you. Just let me go in and put an end to it." She knew that even though Liam held the black bill card and the blood line, Alec was the one to appeal to.

Liam still looked uncomfortable with this plan, but tried to find some compromise. He turned to her and immediately regretted it. Blue met his gaze with those signature blue eyes and so looked like the sister he'd lost, that his words nearly stuck in his throat. "But how will we know when to come get you? What if you need help and we're too far away?"

Baird snorted. "What help do you imagine you can give her?"

It was Brody who answered. "Look, asshole. Alec and I are bodyguards for the royal family. That means we're the best. Sam used to be one, too. We're all three ex-military. We're not exactly dead weight here."

"Yeah? Well Blue just tossed your dead weight around like it was nothing, and you think she'll need help from you? This is what she was born to do. If you tag along, she's right. You'll make yourself a target for the predator and she'll sacrifice the kill to rescue your worthless hide. Don't know if you've noticed, but the predator snacks on military the same as it does civilians." He tilted his head, considering Brody. "Or she'll do the smart thing and let the monster take you before she kills it. Give it a last meal. You all have to stop thinking of her like she's a woman or a person. She's not. She's the Light who's going to end the tyranny for all of you in control of the planet."

The statement marring her femininity stung Blue, but she suppressed the words she wouldn't defend herself with. She swallowed the unexpected lump in her throat as she stared down at the hands clasped in her lap. They looked almost feminine, but Blue could imagine them coated in blood, as they had been so many times throughout her life. Baird and Liam traded political theories while Blue tried to become invisible, so her sore spot would not be so exposed.

When it was agreed that they would take her as far as they could and leave her to the fight, Baird ruled that the night was getting late. "I've got to do this all over again tomorrow, and unlike some people, I need sleep." He glanced over at his sister and the six bites of food disregarded on her plate as she stared at her fingers in her lap. "Finish up, Blue."

Her unwilling hand lifted and grasped the oddly weighted utensil, scooping another bite into her mouth. She knew that she was exhibiting at least two different tells that were not missed by Baird.

"What?" Baird asked her, stretching to make a show of how tired he was.

Blue shook her head in response, not trusting that there were words to describe all that was wrong.

Liam's heavy arm patted her back, causing her to stiffen. The prince did not notice her discomfort. "There'll be more to talk about after I make the deal with Joe. Same time tomorrow night?"

Baird nodded and stood, ending his participation in the conversation. Blue swallowed the last bite and picked up her plate, carrying it into the kitchen with her head down. She could feel Sam's eyes on her, but her pride hurt too much to enjoy the thrill of it as she had before. She imagined him looking at her as a Vemreaux Supervisor would gauge a cow's usefulness. She wished that she could disappear into the ground.

Blue began to adopt her brother's point of view by telling herself as she rinsed her plate in the industrial sink that, in fact, she was not a girl, though she possessed the raw mechanics for the gender. *Useless breasts,* she chided her body angrily. *Stupid, stupid, stupid. Just because I wish I was a normal girl, doesn't make it true. Normal girls don't do inverted one-handed push-ups. Normal guys don't, either. Baird's right. I'm not a person. I'm a weapon. Stupid, stupid, stupid.* She glanced down at her body. *Ugly.* Elle and Grettel were better examples of girls. *I'll never be pretty, like Elle. She's obviously a woman. And Grettel's so sweet, everyone knows she's a girl. I'm not beautiful. Ugly. Ugly. Ugly. Grettel never would've attacked someone like I did out there.*

Blue took a deep, steadying breath. *I'm a machine, built for one purpose: ending the tyranny. I'm not meant for love and silly girl things. That's why I'm ugly. That's why I'm terrible at everything besides fighting. That's why I only have two friends, and Baird chose them for me. I wonder if he threatened them into the job? I wonder if they really love me?* Blue shook her head. *No, they love me. I can tell when people are lying.* She heaved a sigh of relief, glad that she still had Elle and Grettel, and that Baird had not scared them off.

Why did Baird have to tell them I'm not a girl? Why'd he have to say it in front of those guys? Something in her sunk at Sam not viewing her as female. *How could Sam think of me as a woman? I threw him up against the wall and pinned him there.* She shuddered at the memory. *No point in trying my hand at flirting now.*

It doesn't matter. She chided the swell of emotion in her chest. *I'm dying soon anyway. Will it really matter if I'm a girl when I'm dead?*

THE ART OF RECEIVING HELP

*B*aird and Blue ran home in silence, both of their uniform shirts removed and tucked into the waist of their jeans. Blue's shoulders slumped and her feet swept over the ground dejectedly.

"What's got you dragging?" Baird asked, not unkindly.

"I'm not allowed to drag? Are you testing me right now? Sorry I'm not performing like you want. It's been a day," she sassed him.

"Oh, so you're in one of *those* moods."

"What moods?"

"Immature. Sulky. Don't take it out on me. This is all your doing, you know."

"Now you're monitoring my temperament? Leave me alone, Baird."

"Hey, don't take it out on me that you got caught. Just lucky it was those guys, I guess. Or unlucky. Can't decide which."

"Are you allergic to silence all of a sudden? I said to leave me alone."

"Stop being a baby. This is the situation. Deal with it."

"What makes you think I'm not? I sat there and listened while you told them everything about me. I dealt. Doesn't mean I have to be all smiles and sunshine about it."

"If you're wishing things could be different, they can't. Like it or not, this is a good thing, what happened tonight. We're one step closer to you ending the tyranny."

"And me dying!" she exclaimed. "You always forget that part. Man! You're so happy to be one step closer to getting rid of me. You can go off and never give me another thought. I'll just be rotting away on some island, vultures pecking at what's left of my body while you tell yourself how glad you are that the precious Vems are safe. I was never a girl, so who cares if I die?"

Baird stopped running to gawk at his sister, mouth agape. "Is that what you really think of me?"

Blue turned to look at her brother, foregoing her jog. "I'm only going by the words coming out of your mouth, Baird. Couldn't be clearer how much you hate me. Thursday! Next Thursday, and I'm out of your life for good! Maybe a little less peace about it all on your part would make me feel not so much such a steaming pile of scratch."

"You selfish brat!" Baird shouted, and before he knew it, his fist was flinging out at her. "You have no idea what I've gone through to get you here!"

Blue ducked, and answered his aggression with a blow of her own that connected with his jaw. "Now who needs to learn control? You're failing the test, Baird!" she taunted him.

Baird fumed, landing a kick to her hip. "Do you have any idea how hard I worked to get you out of The Way?"

"So you can what?" She kicked his thigh, knowing she left a bruise. "Pimp me out to the first people with a plane and a plan?"

"Pimp you out?" Baird raged, punching her shoulder.

Blue shook off the sting. "Then why? You get me out so you can spend some time with me? Educate me on the real world? Take me to see the cool buildings? You know how much I wanted to see the tall ones! I've been out for weeks, and you've done nothing but train me!" She spun and hit her brother's ribcage with her flat palm.

"I got you out so you could end the tyranny! You think I like it anymore than you do? This is what we were built for!"

"No!" Blue screamed. "This is what *I* was built for! You were supposed to be my brother who loves me! You were supposed to give me a life before I have to give mine away. Well, Baird, you failed that test. Now you've found a way to get rid of me. Good job! I'll be somebody else's problem."

"Stop it!" Baird tugged at his hair, looking like one more word from her might push him over the edge of sanity.

Blue took off, far faster than she'd been going to escape the man who might always be incapable of being the brother she needed.

What did you expect? She chided herself as she ran for the hut. *Did you really think you'd have years left to live? Ending the predator is the right thing to do. Did you really think you'd get to just live in the diner like the girls and giggle about everyday gossip, spending your time waiting on tables?* Life expectancy for an *A*-blood in The Way was sixty. After that, they were put to sleep. At this rate, she would not even reach her twentieth year.

Grettel's cry of horror broke through Blue's silent tirade. "Baird!" Blue called, not bothering to cover over her alarm. Her steps quickened, and she could feel her brother charging behind her, their squabble discarded with the threat of danger. "It's Grettel!"

At a dead run, the two dashed down the path, up the three steps and into the shabby front door to find not just Grettel, but Elle on the mattress. Elle's tears fell as she lay on her side, but Grettel's exploded out of her in panic like tiny, wet punches that punctuated her pain.

Elle's shirt was pulled up to her ribs, revealing a large angry red smear on her side that wrapped from her abdomen around to a few centimeters over the back of her hip.

Baird swore. "What did they do to you?"

The composure that Elle had been holding onto broke when Baird bent down next to her and touched her skin. Grabbing onto the front of his undershirt like it was her last hope for a breath of air, Elle's quiet tears broke out into loud sobs. Baird pulled her to him.

Elle buried her face in his chest as he cradled her and rubbed her back.

"It's fine. I can barely feel it. I'm just so happy that it's over!" Elle blubbered.

"What happened?" he asked again in a voice he hoped was kind, but sounded a bit too severe.

"I didn't make it to the next round," she cried. "We sparred tonight against each other, and I got there last, so I didn't get the good weapons."

At this, Baird was furious. "Why on earth would they think that the Light would need weapons? Stupid Vemreaux!"

"It's over! It's over! It's finally over!" Elle wailed. Pain mixed with joy and formed into tears that ran down her face. "I can just be myself now, Baird!"

Baird yanked his keys from his jeans pocket and shoved them into his sister's hand. "There's a first aid kit in the kitchen in the utility closet. Grab it and a few rags." When Blue shot up too slow for his liking, he barked. "Hurry!"

Blue tore out of the hut and leaped past the steps. The branches whipping past her did nothing to deter her speed or focus. The only thing that could derail her attention was the vehicle still occupying the parking lot when she reached the diner.

She fiddled with the keys until she pulled out the two she recalled Baird using to get into the diner every morning. Though she heard Liam calling her from the parking lot, she did not turn to acknowledge him. Baird would not tolerate wasting time, and his temper was already stretched thin at this late hour.

Blue ran to the kitchen and threw open the utility closet, scanning the contents for something that could look like a first aid kit. On the top shelf rested a small white box with a protruding handle. It was much too high for her to reach, but before she could grab a chair or hoist herself up the shelves to grab it, a tall body appeared behind her.

"What's going on?" Liam asked, the teasing tone never leaving his voice.

"Could you grab that box for me, sir?" Blue requested, not bothering to divert her eyes from his.

Liam paused for a moment to absorb her appearance. Then he reached over her slight frame and pulled down the white box with "First Aid" written in red block letters on the front.

Blue sighed with relief. "Thanks." She took it from him and moved out of the closet, shutting the door behind them. There were clean rags in the drawer nearest the sinks. To be on the safe side, she snatched up four of them. Without offering an explanation, she moved quickly out of the kitchen and smacked right into Sam, nearly knocking him back.

"Oh!" she exclaimed, steadying herself as he held onto her shoulders to keep himself from falling over. "I'm sorry, sir!"

Words came to him only when he saw what it was that Blue was clinging to. "What's wrong? Is your brother hurt or something?" He did not retract his hands from her arms.

Blue shook her head, unable to calculate how much time she was wasting by standing mutely in front of the most attractive Vemreaux she'd ever seen. She was suddenly aware of her exposed skin covered only by shorts and a tank top.

"No, it's Elle. She's one of the candidates for the Light and she got injured in the testing. They sent her home a mess."

Sam released her, but then pressed his hand to her back, walking beside her toward the exit. "We'll give you a ride, then. It'll be faster."

"Okay," she agreed. Her response caused him to stiffen.

"You don't have to, you know. I'm not going to make you come with us. We'll drive you home only if you want us to." His pace slowed and Blue worried at the wasted time.

"Okay," she consented again, not understanding his quandary.

Sam groaned at her reply.

Never had a man other than her brother led her with his palm pressed to her like that. It was equally gentle and firm. Through the contact she could tell that, despite his slacked demeanor, hard muscle lurked beneath the surface. Though she would have shrugged away from the contact were it anyone else, she thrilled at the touch and allowed him to direct her.

Until she tripped again. The box fell to the ground as the toe of her shoe caught on the floor. She pitched forward and would have landed on her face if Sam's hands hadn't righted her. "Ugh!" she groaned. "What is my deal today?"

Sam shrugged. "You impervious to tripping?"

"Usually? Yeah."

Sam knew there was a pickup line that perfectly fitted the situation, but he bit his tongue as she moved forward. Though Sam dropped his hand from her as she locked the diner back up, he stayed close, not permitting more than an arm's length to come between them even as they jogged in the parking lot out to the car. "Alec, keys." When Alec did not comply, Sam insisted further. "Your old lady speed isn't going to cut it right now. You don't like it, you and Liam can call a cab again."

Blue eyed the vehicle warily as she slid into the back seat between Alec and Brody. When the vehicle glided forward instead of jolting like Baird's 4x4 did, her eyes darted around to make sure that they were, indeed, moving. Her hand gripped the back of her seat and reached out to hold onto the center console before her. She tried unsuccessfully to keep her face from displaying its inner turbulence.

Sam took his gaze off the road to stare at her wide eyes and tensed body. "Are you okay, little Wayward?" he asked.

Blue wished he would focus on the road. "I'm fine. I just don't ride in cars much. Left up ahead."

"What, do you take the bus?" Liam asked conversationally, turning to look at the wild-eyed woman.

Blue shook her head, tightening her hold as they rounded a corner. She fought down the vomit that threatened to explode out of her with the unnatural rocking. "No, I run. And there aren't cars in The Way. This is like the fifth time I can remember ever being in a car," she admitted. "They go so fast."

Sam eased his foot off the accelerator. "Sorry. I was just trying to get to your friend quicker."

"No. Go fast. It's fine. I'm just not used to it. I'll get over it," she assured him through gritted teeth. "Baird'll be mad if we go slow because of me."

"Baird'll get over it," Sam grumbled, not speeding up at all.

"Here," Alec offered, reaching around her and placing his hand on her shoulder. "Let me anchor you."

Sam watched in the rearview mirror, regretting his insistence on driving. He followed her directions and ended at a shabby hut that had probably stood prouder before World War Three. Many bricks were chipped, the roof was barely hanging on and there was no railing for the stoop. The roof was missing a few shingles, and the missing bricks on the outside showed different layers of color and raw material beneath the sub-par construction.

Sam stopped the car. Blue's heart thudded when she reached over Alec and tried the handle, but the door did not open. For the briefest of moments, she thought that perhaps it had all been one elaborate hoax, and they were going to kidnap her. Fear swarmed up in her and trapped the shout to the walls of her throat, so it did not give her away. Before trying to break the glass, the locks popped up of their own accord. When she tried the handle again, it opened easily. She chided herself for being so paranoid.

Alec eyed her curiously as she stepped out, clutching the white box and the four rags. "What? Did you think we were going to lock you in or something?"

Not knowing if she should respond with the truth, Blue kept her mouth shut.

Liam followed behind her. "Aw, come on, kitten. Why would I go through the trouble of buying you if I was just going to kidnap you?" He pretended to consider this as a viable option. "Wait. On second thought, hop in the trunk for me. It's cheaper your way."

Blue permitted a small smile to brush her lips at his joke as she rushed past him up the stairs. She opened the door and tossed the first aid kit to her brother, who had Elle still clinging to his shirt. Her side was no longer bleeding, but there was nothing clean to get the blood off with besides their only bath towel, which Elle categorically refused to sully.

Baird opened the white box and pulled out several things that Blue did not recognize.

"Get a rag wet, Blue, and hand it to Grettel." Then, as an afterthought, he added snidely, "So you decided to show the prince our palace?"

Rarely was it wise to converse with Baird when he delved into the depths of sarcasm, so Blue kept her mouth shut as she ran water over one of the long rags.

"These are the guys I was telling you about. The ones who know Blue's secret now, and are gonna try to help get her over to the island," Baird explained.

The stench of fresh A-type blood was a little overwhelming for Sam, but he kept his thoughts to himself and tried not to wrinkle his nose.

"What happened?" Liam asked. "Your sister said she got hurt at the testing?"

"I know you," Elle commented. "You were there yesterday to see if anyone slept."

"Liam." He made to stick his hand out for her to shake, but realized the folly of this. The beautiful woman was on the floor nursing a very fresh wound and should not be bothered with niceties. He stepped back to stand next to Sam at the entrance.

"I'm not the Light, Liam. I'm not her!" she confessed, tears rolling down her face.

Alec eyed the gash. "Baird, do you know how to do stitches? It looks like she might need them."

Baird shrugged as if he couldn't be bothered with such things as knowledge at present. "I'll figure it out." He watched as Grettel wiped away the blood and revealed not one, but many cuts.

"I can't, Baird!" Grettel cried. "I never learned stitches! Nurse K-K-K-Kalista n-n-never..."

Baird reached out and touched Grettel's hand to calm the stuttering that always came about when she thought of the nurse who abused her so long ago. "Shh, Grettel. I know. Don't worry about it." He squeezed Elle. "Hold still, Elle."

Brody, Alec, Sam and Liam stood inside the entryway at a complete loss. The hut looked small from the outside, but being inside of it, they felt positively cramped. Guilt washed over them when they compared the hut to their privileged living quarters.

Liam eyed the mattress on the floor. "Makes me feel like a jerk for complaining about the softness of the hotel bed two nights ago."

"You are pretty high maintenance," Sam agreed as he pulled out a cigarette and lit it up.

Liam guffawed. "You're one to talk."

Sam could not wrap his mind around the quaint hut until Blue passed in front of his frozen vision to exchange Grettel's soiled rag for a fresh one. Being alerted to her presence snapped him back to the matter at hand.

"Let me," Sam offered, stepping toward the huddle across from Baird where there was an extra bit of room.

Baird sized up the Vemreaux warily.

Sam rolled his eyes. "I was a bodyguard, remember? You don't want to know how many times I stitched this one up." He jerked his thumb at Liam, who beamed with pride at having accumulated numerous injuries.

Baird did not look impressed. "You know, actual medical experience would be more assuring."

Sam's helpfulness was obscured by an unsettling, crazy look that swept over him. He unbuttoned his cuff and rolled up his sleeve to show Baird the many marks on his arm. Blue gasped at the long, angry scars. Most Vemreaux had theirs removed before they dipped in the Fountain.

"If I can stitch myself up, I can handle little cuts like hers. Trust me, I can help you." He smiled at the marred skin paternally, fire lighting beneath his black eyes and revealing his volatile nature.

"Sam," cautioned Liam warily, bringing his best friend back to reality.

"Yeah, well her skin's Wayward, not Vemreaux. Don't make it worse," Baird threatened as Sam washed his hands.

"No pressure," Liam added, winking conspiratorially at Blue. Blue looked down at the floor when her smile betrayed her.

After looking around for any other place to sit, Sam knelt down on the mattress next to Elle. He pulled out his lighter and heated the needle retrieved from the first aid kit to disinfect it. Cigarette in hand, he threaded the needle and examined the lesion. The only spot too deep to heal on its own was about nine centimeters long and stretched between her abdomen and the front of her hipbone. "Blue?" Sam glanced up toward her, hoping to see her face without a veil of hair between them.

"Sir?" Blue replied without looking up.

"Could you get a fresh rag and wipe off the wound? It's still a little bloody."

Blue obeyed, leaving Grettel to scurry over to Baird while still trying to keep a safe distance from the three at the entrance.

Blue sat down right next to Sam so she could study what he was doing. His usual edge of sarcasm or just plain aggression melted into sweetness as the heat from her body connected with his. "So, first I'm pouring this on the open area," he showed her the bottle. "It disinfects the cut, and it's already diluted. No point in sewing it up if it's all infected, yeah?" He was not sure why he hoped she would respond verbally, but when she did not, it brought about a small amount of frustration. Like a hesitant animal, he had to lure Blue to him with the promise of work and usefulness. "Elle, is it?" Sam asked, turning his attention to the patient. "This is going to sting a little." Before Elle could ready herself for the oncoming pain, Sam squirted a healthy amount of the clear liquid onto the wound and watched Blue as she observed it seethe and bubble angrily.

To her credit, Elle only expressed her discomfort through choppy breathing and did not complain or cry out. The stench of her blood was beginning to get to Sam, so he made quick work of sewing up the tear.

"Think you could not smoke all over her, nurse?" Baird

commented as Elle coughed.

"Good luck prying those away from him," Brody said with a snort.

"Smoking soothes me. You want me tense and unfocused for this?" Sam protested, stick protruding from his lips. When Elle's coughing became a problem for his sewing, he jutted his chin out to Blue. "Fine. Take it, little Wayward. And put your free hand here to keep the flap closed while I sew it up."

Blue hesitated only a second, but obeyed. Her fingers brushed his lips as she relieved him of his habit for a few seconds, and the blush she knew her brother could see crept up her neck, unbidden. She tried to ignore Baird's incoherent grumbling. Her other hand reached down and pressed the edge of the cut inward. When Sam's fingers met her at the center, she had to summon more strength than usual to keep a controlled face.

"Then you tie a knot at the end of the thread a few times, so it catches." Sam continued instructing her on the mechanics of stitching, feeling like a dunce when Baird pointed out that all Waywards were taught how to sew, and that most of the t-shirts made in the Americas were stitched together by them.

Blue made a good nurse, holding the flap of ripped skin with her steady fingers, and not once getting queasy at the sight of the blood or the needle. Sam laced the few stitches into the skin while Elle tried to stay as still as possible with no anesthetic.

"You're a tough one, Elle," Sam commented. "Better than quite a few Vemreaux I've had to patch up over the years. That one howls like a baby," he joked, smirking up at Liam, who shrugged in his defense. Sam sealed the stitches with a large band-aid that had adhesive on all four edges. "There you are. Good as new."

Elle thanked him, and in the very next breath, allowed her tears to flow once more into Baird's shirt. Now that he could move her without causing more damage to the wound, Baird sat back and leaned against the wall to rest his stiff knees.

Elle did not need the invitation to take her small window of advantage and play the damsel in distress. So rare was she allotted the role that she wasted no time in crawling into his open lap so that her tired blonde head could rest on his firm shoulder. "It's over! It's over!" she repeated.

"I know, Elle. You were amazing." Baird kissed her cheeks so tenderly, that Grettel looked away. It was rare that Baird complimented Elle, and rarer still that he coddled her. Grettel wanted the moment to last as long as possible.

Sam opened his mouth, and Blue placed the cigarette back between his full lips. Before he could utter the flirty comment he'd built up, Blue picked up the tools they used to patch up Elle and stood from the mattress. Sam frowned when it occurred to him that not only could he not get her to look at him or come near him without some sort of nonsexual incentive, but he could not keep her near him once he finally got her there.

Like a puppy, Sam stood and followed her over to the sink to wash his hands with her. He kept expecting to have to breathe through his mouth around Blue, but found that he could stomach the scent of A-blood coming from her.

Blue stopped rinsing her hands so that he could wash his first. Sam scrubbed all the way up past his wrists to insure that all traces of the foul blood were gone before he rinsed the conglomeration of suds away. Seeing no other towel, he picked up a clean rag Blue had taken from the diner and dried his hands off with it.

Unable to put too much distance between them, he turned off the water for her when her hands were clean and began blotting the water from her skin gently, intertwining his arms with hers so that he could feel her body heat once again. Of course, he could have just handed her the towel. He could have placed it on the counter for her to pick up and dry her hands off with, but the high that Sam got from being so near to her was better than any drug he had ever done. Blue was tempting and amazingly addictive. He was glad that she did not seem the type to ask for anything, because if she did, he was pretty sure he would do it, no matter the consequences.

Sam shivered when Blue made the bold move of tracing one of the many scars on his forearm. Her captivating eyes took in the marks, while worry weighed down her expression.

Sam leaned closer to her. "Don't worry. Elle's will heal much better than that one."

Blue did not respond, but looked up at him, face forlorn. There were so many things he wanted to say to her. Usually his turbulent childhood was brushed over with as much bravado as he could muster, but he found that he could not ignore the woman, nor could he manage to distance himself from her.

Blue's eyes were full of gratitude and something that looked a bit like longing. "Thank you," she whispered. The sound of her voice wrapped around him like a hook, pulling him forward against his better judgment.

The urges he normally succumbed to were baser and involved dark corners or very uninhibited Femreaux, but in that moment, his hand reached out and touched the thick waves of auburn that tried to obscure the world's view of her face. His fingers moved her lovely hair and tucked it behind her ear, revealing whole parts of her countenance he'd not seen before. The slope of her soft cheek led down to her jaw, where his thumb decided to take up residence. He watched her eyes flutter shut and noticed her breathing hitch as she was lulled into the same spell that held him so firmly in its clutches. Her beguiling mouth was right there, and his thumb acted on its own as it traced the curve of her full lower lip.

Blue was unaware of the feet that kept her attached to the floor. She could not recall how many Janes were still in The Way, nor the perfect order in which she usually kept their barcodes filed away in her mind. For once in her life, Blue even managed to forget about Baird as her heart rate quickened at Sam's gentle touch. There was one person, one name that took over, and she breathed it without thinking. "Sam."

"What did I say would happen if you put your hands on my sister again, Vem?" Baird interrupted their tender moment with his acute knack for abrasiveness, slamming them both back into reality. He moved Elle off his lap and stalked over to Sam, ripping the Vemreaux from his sister.

Sam whirled on the Wayward and shoved Baird off of him. "No one's hurting anyone, Baird. Lay off."

Blue could see the resolve in her brother's eyes. She knew that he did not back down easily. "Baird!" she shouted. "You can't attack a Vemreaux!"

"I warned him! I promised him a broken arm if he didn't keep his hands off you, Blue!"

"Control, Baird!" Blue yelled. Her fear and anger fought to dominate his rage. "You hurt him, they'll take you away! Think of the girls!"

Baird considered this, but his fury was too fresh. "It's worth it!" He lunged at Sam, fighting until he had the man in a headlock.

Grettel screamed, and Elle stumbled to her feet. "Baird! Stop!"

Alec and Brody stood in front of Liam, unsure how to extricate the prince from the duel when the two bears were brawling so close to the door.

Blue was on the floor, clutching her temples, mentally fighting with a foe they could not see. She looked crazy as her fingers clawed at her face. Alec was not keen on letting Liam too near her insanity, either.

Sam easily gained the upper hand in the scuffle. He tossed an apologetic look at Blue before flipping her brother over his shoulder.

Baird landed hard on the floor, the wind knocking out of him and deflating his fight. Reason crept back in slowly, pushing out the violence that wanted to dictate his actions.

Instead of rushing to Baird, Elle dove for Blue. Her shaking arms went around her friend, hoping to stop the blackout that she could tell was trying to take over. "Shh, baby doll. Quiet now. It's okay. No one's in danger. No one's fighting." Her trembling voice told another story. "Sam's not gonna press charges. He won't take Baird away from us. Right, Sam?"

Sam's anger at Baird softened when he took in Blue's tremors. "No. Of course not. I'm not going to send someone to be killed just because he's stupid." Then he turned to Baird, who brought himself up to sitting, and scowled. "Very stupid. I'd like to know what damage you thought you could do to me, Wayward. You're not the bleeding Light. The only thing you're doing is annoying me. Trust me, that's not what you want. I didn't do anything to your sister."

Baird succeeded in ignoring Sam when he took in his sister's rocking and the telltale signs that a blackout was forthcoming. "No one's fighting, Blue!" he shouted, hoping the night would not end in a slaughter.

"Someone get me the towel!" Elle pleaded.

Grettel was too afraid to move, her sobs obscuring her vision as she held her knees in the corner of the room. Baird was the first to obey, grabbing the towel from the bathroom and draping it over Blue's head.

Elle held the fabric tight over her friend, cutting out any light from getting to her. "See? No black. Just close your eyes, Blue. It's all fine. Nothing's wrong. Just your brother being an ass. Normal day." She fumed silently at Baird, who ignored her jabs. "Baird, tell your sister it's over. Tell her you won't go after Sam anymore."

Baird glared at Elle, wishing there was any other way. He knew that Blue needed to know the threat was diffused, but the urge to throttle the cocky Vem was still too appealing. "I won't break Sam's arm, Blue. No one's getting hurt tonight, so calm yourself down." When his sister whimpered, his voice turned sharp. "I said calm down! This is what it looks like when I care about you, so stop your whining! Do you want to hurt these guys?"

"No!" Blue moaned.

Elle's shoulders relaxed that Blue was lucid enough to speak. The massacre had been avoided. Elle wanted to sob all over again, but knew the job wasn't over yet.

Baird's intensity did not wane. "Then you will get a hold of yourself!" He counted to five, ignoring Sam and Liam, who fired off questions he would not answer. "Are you under control?" He watched his sister nod from inside her makeshift fabric fort, and then pulled the towel off of her. She had pink lines traced down her cheeks – a sign of the stress that pushed her to self-mutilate so she did not have a blackout. His fury lessened, knowing that this was entirely his fault.

"You have to waitress in the morning, Blue. You can't go marking yourself up like this."

Elle hissed at Baird and snatched Blue closer. "Like that's the thing to focus on." Elle could see the worried expressions on the faces of the men staring down at them. "Look, I don't know why we have company tonight, but whatever you all think of us, it could've been a hundred times worse. You should all leave now." She made eye contact with Sam and mouthed, *Be careful.*

"What just happened?" Liam asked Elle.

"Baird almost got you killed," Elle responded. "She doesn't do well when the things she loves are threatened." Then, to challenge anyone who would dare judge her best friend, Elle said, "Do you?"

Sam stepped toward Blue and bent down so he was in her line of vision. "Blue, I wasn't going to hurt your brother. But Baird has to learn that he can't start stuff this close to Liam. It's not safe. I was just defending myself, and now it's over. You don't have to worry." Sam ignored Baird's growl and touched the marks on Blue's cheek, watching her eyes flutter. "And you don't have to do this to yourself. Baird's not in trouble."

"Sam," Alec warned, watching as Baird seethed.

"I don't think she was worried about Baird," Elle commented as Sam rocked back on his heels to stand.

Blue blinked like she was coming out of a trance. That he could pull her into such an unguarded stupor frightened Blue and threatened to squelch the butterflies that were now swarming like killer bees in her stomach.

Baird was not happy. Instead of thanking Sam, he addressed Liam. "Time to go, guys. Freak show's over. We'll see you tomorrow after one when we close. We really need to get some sleep." What he wanted to say was, "If that cocky Vemreaux so much as looks at my sister again, it'll be more bloodshed that he'll have to patch up."

Liam understood, though he was just as baffled at his friend's complete personality shift. "Not a problem. Good to meet you all." He bowed his head, ever the diplomat, and pushed Sam out of the hut while he still recognized him.

30

STOLEN MOMENT

As soon as they reached the safety of the rented vehicle, Brody let loose before Sam turned the key in the ignition. "What was that?"

"Since when do you act all romantic? And with a Wayward? Are you just screwing with her? Because that's not gonna fly if she's going to be living and traveling with us, yeah?" Liam frowned as the car backed out onto the road. Before Sam could spit out his retort, Liam kept going with everything he had been storing up to say once they were away from the Waywards. "I don't know if you've noticed, but her brother hates you. Like, really hates you. You trying to get a rise outta him?"

"Actual hate," Brody agreed.

"Stop slagging me off," Sam grumbled.

"If he's going to trust me with her, you've got to stop pushing him like that. String along the Femreaux who're stupid enough to let you. They should know better, and it's fun as anything to watch, don't get me wrong. But Blue's just a girl, Sam. She doesn't get your short attention span. Plus, she's obviously unbalanced. Did you see that thing they had to do with the towel? Not normal."

"I think we're well passed normal," Alec commented as he

pinched the bridge of his nose. "She didn't do anything, but I can't help thinking she was still a threat to you, Liam. I can't predict her, and that makes her dangerous. And her brother? Pure psychopath. Good thing he's only Wayward."

Liam scoffed. "She's a kitten. Not dangerous, Alec. And you can handle Baird. But Sam, trust me when I say that she's way too much for you to handle. You'd have no idea what to do with a woman like that."

Sam took a corner rather sharply, and Liam consented to buckling his seatbelt after that. "A woman like what?"

"A Wayward. It's a different culture. Leave her be."

Brody stretched in the back seat next to Liam. "We'll pick a different bar for happy hour tomorrow, and you can find some Fem to make it with. Get whatever it is you're up to literally out of your system, Stone."

Alec's arms crossed over his chest as he pushed Liam's point from the passenger's seat. "If I had a sister, no way I'd let her near you. And Baird? He loves his sister. He's insane, but he cares enough about her to not want you pulling your tricks with her. Can't fault him for that."

"Leave it alone, guys," Sam warned. "I didn't do anything. No tricks."

"How many people's sisters do you imagine you've slept with?" Alec prodded further.

Sam's knuckles were clutching the steering wheel so tight that he hoped it would break and bear his frustration. Through his gritted teeth, he summoned up a few choice words that seemed most appropriate to slap on his friend. Before he could spew them out, a moving spot of white caught his eye in the side mirror.

It was Blue in her white tank top. Sam could see the full length of her bare arms in that delicious garment. He expected them to be bigger and bulkier with the force he recalled her smashing him up against the wall with. As it was, she appeared feminine. Swallowing, his brain alerted him to the fact that his eyes were staring at a section of her body that was impolite in all social circles to ogle. It was the first time he was glad she was not looking at him.

"Are you even listening to us?" Brody asked.

The urgency with which she ran to the diner had left her, and it seemed to Sam that she was jogging for the fun of it, chasing away whatever monster told her to claw up her face. She was much like him in that way. Neither of them wanted to be cooped up or contained in one place for too long. Both found ways to deal with the pain.

Blue's hair fell and rose behind her as she jogged past the car which was now stopped at a red light. Her eyes were fixed ahead of her, but Sam could tell that she knew it was them and was making a concerted effort to keep her head from turning in his direction.

Despite the chill of the night air, Sam rolled down the window and called out to her. "Hey! You need a ride, little Wayward?" His was the only vehicle on the road at the late hour, so he ignored the traffic light when it turned green.

The smirk in his voice caused the corner of her mouth to turn up as she slowed and trotted over to the car, stopping a meter from it. Away from the watchful eye of her brother, Blue's tightened tongue loosened. "No, thanks. I have a lot of time to waste while they sleep, sir." Her eyes darted around to make sure that no eavesdroppers could hear her admission.

Sam looked around as well and caught the eye of Liam, whose stare was attempting to bore a hole through the back of his head. "I tell you what, how about you stop calling me sir and start calling me Sam." He waved his hand between them. "You're not just some waitress and I'm not just some Vemreaux. We're friends now." He shuddered at the word, wishing he picked a better one. He never realized how difficult it was to talk to women until she stood outside of the car, waiting for him to say something sensible. "If everything works out, we'll be together a lot. Might as well just drop the formalities, yeah?" He gave her his best crooked grin, which exploded into a full-blown smile when he saw her cheeks darken even in the dim moonlight.

"Okay."

Sam's smile faltered at her immediate compliance. He thought about offering her a ride again, but stopped himself. It was one of the few times he heard her express an opinion. Even if it was not what he wanted to hear, he would accept the faint sting of the miniature rejection if it meant she was speaking for herself instead of spouting out the one word he was beginning to hate. "You and the girls doing alright?"

Again, she glanced in the direction of the hut to be sure Baird was enough kilometers away. "I'm sorry about all that back there. And thanks for not calling the cops. Baird can be...but he doesn't know any better. We're his responsibility, and he takes that seriously. I'm sorry he attacked you, though. He shouldn'ta done that. I'd just fought with him before we found Elle all torn up, so he wasn't thinking clearly. I'll watch him better next time."

"I'm fine, little Wayward. I just don't like seeing your pretty face all scratched up."

Blue touched her heated cheeks. "It's nothing. It'll heal by tomorrow. Always does."

"Then I guess I'll just have to stop by tomorrow to check on you."

Blue tried to rein in her smile, but did not succeed. "Okay."

"Have a good run, little Wayward," he offered lamely. Then as she turned back to the road, he was struck with the uncontrollable urge to see her face one more time. "Hey, aren't you going to wish me sweet dreams or something girly like that?"

The few steps she took away from him were matched by the car he coaxed to crawl forward. It was worth the slow progression, for he caught a rare sight indeed. Blue tilted her head back and let out a quiet laugh that reached out and excited Sam's entire body. "Sweet dreams, Sam."

The sound of her laughter was nothing compared to his name cradled on her tongue, coming out of her pink lips. She leaned down and peeked past the driver to the rest of the passengers. "You too, sirs."

"You can use our names, Blue," Alec muttered.

Liam pushed aside his shock long enough to respond. "You know you can call me Liam." Then considering it, he added, "Or The

Amazing Liam. Prince Liam. Legend with all Fair Femreaux Liam. Whatever suits you."

"Okay." Blue laughed again, the sound of it sparking between her and Sam like crackles of electricity popping in the air. "Sweet dreams, Sam and sweet dreams, guys."

With what Sam deemed as too much ease, she turned and jogged away from them. It was only when Alec cleared his throat that Sam realized he was barely pressing on the gas so that he could remain next to Blue a little while longer as she traversed up the road. He recalled his former self and stepped down on the accelerator to take them into Capital City to their hotel.

Sam cringed as the stare and whistle from his best friend pulled him back down to earth. "Shut it, Li."

"Oh, man!" Liam threw his head back on the headrest. "Baird's gonna kill you dead."

31

THE LAST TEST

Elle was feeling much better after a solid seven hours of sleep. While a day off of work to rest and heal would be beneficial, it was simply not an option. There was too much money to be made, and she wouldn't put all that work on Blue and leave her with the slovenly Steve on a Peace Day weekend.

Life returned to normal as quickly as possible, Baird using his famous method of forbidding talk about the night's events as a tactic to move past it.

Most of the Vemreaux were off work and ready to start celebrating. Happy hour started an hour early at the customers' behest. Most alcohol did not affect them the way it did an *A*-blood or the unchanged *B*-bloods, which was why Baird's Green Abby shots were so coveted. Absinthe was one of the few intoxicants that did them in across the board, and during a stretch like Peace Week, everyone wanted to celebrate a little more freely than the average weekend release.

The jukebox had a line around it, and the backup overhead music only played two light ditties when the restaurant first opened for lunch. Ever since then, the loud and angry celebratory electric guitars rang out triumphant from the vintage red and gold painted box. Every once in a great while, a Femreaux would request a sappy love song that would incur so many boos that the ballad was barely audible.

It was difficult for the wait staff to hear each patron as they placed their order, but as the day drifted into evening, Blue and Elle read their lips as most of them declared "Green Abby" as their choice for the night.

Baird flagged his sister over to the bar around midnight. The partiers were showing no signs of slowing or heading home, so breaks were rationed. It took Blue a little longer to weave her way through the tables to reach him. Baird had been distracted all day, working out problems in his head while his hands were on autopilot pouring drinks.

"I gotta answer this." Baird held up his cell phone that had since stopped ringing. "Could you take over with the shots for a while? I could use a break. I'm starving."

Blue nodded. "Five minutes," she warned, knowing she could neglect her tables only so long before they got riled up and it started affecting her tips.

Though there were three lines of drinks already poured, she knew they would be gone in a moment. Baird usually did two dozen at a time, but Blue wanted to do more. She lined up six rows of twelve miniature glasses and began dragging the flowing green liquid across the tops in a clean, even sweep.

Ten minutes later, Baird returned to the bar, saying nothing as he traded places with his sister. It was hard to believe that if all went according to the very new plan, she would be leaving the diner she'd just started working at in less than a week. He could tell that Blue wanted to ask him what Joe had said, but knew it was not the time to talk. "Hey, I thought you had tables to wait on. And that line at the door won't seat itself."

"Yeah, yeah. You know me. Slacker extraordinaire."

Baird did not jump back into bartending immediately. Instead he moved slow, not bothering himself with the bottles on the ledge in front of him. His gaze was fixed on the hostess stand where Steve was actually doing his job for once. Blue followed his line of vision and saw Liam, Alec and Sam.

The three Vemreaux scanned the diner until Liam found Baird and Sam located Blue. Alec had his eye on Blue as he surreptitiously kept his sensors up for any danger that could be more of a threat than the young girl standing by the bar, holding an empty tray at her side.

The moment Sam's gaze fell on Blue, he could not help the delight that appeared in his eyes, nor the slight hopeful wave that his hand made in the air to greet her.

This so confused Alec that he dropped his defensive focus for a moment to stare at the man next to him. "What are you doing?"

The three watched as Blue lifted her hand to curl and uncurl her fingers in a veiled acknowledgement of Sam's greeting, and then dropped her tray by accident.

Sam grinned at Blue in a way that summoned the now familiar blush to invade her. "I'm just saying hello. You know, waving. Is that a problem?" His accent stood out in the American bar, and a few nearby Femreaux gave him the glad eye.

"Stop being a freak," Liam whispered.

"Oh, I'm a freak because I'm waving to her? Could this be misconstrued as 'take your clothes off, love'?" He shook his head as a Femreaux who'd overheard his last statement responded with a flirtatious smile. "Not you."

"I think the direct translation is 'I'm already wrapped around your finger, so here, take my whole hand and lead me wherever you want.'" Liam held his hand out slavishly before Sam batted it away.

"WAITRESS!" CALLED A VOICE FROM ONE OF HER TABLES. BLUE DUCKED her head and went back to work.

A song was blaring from the jukebox that Blue had never heard before. She tried to listen to the slurred and often unintelligible words of the high-voiced male singer as she averted her eyes. She trusted Steve to seat the Vemreaux she could feel watching her from across the bar.

The last hour of the night passed with little of the levity diminishing in the Vemreaux who insisted on keeping each table full. Baird had sent Stephanie home at twelve-twenty, judging that Grettel could handle closing up the kitchen herself. "Hey, don't seat anyone else," Baird instructed his sister when she came up to the bar to get more shots.

"Sure thing, boss."

Steve came up to the bar and stood beside Blue. He took no notice of her and nearly knocked her out of the way in his beeline for Baird. "It's twelve-thirty. I'm tired, and I've got a sore back," he stated with just enough whine to make the complaint believable. "I've pulled this shift too many days in a row, so I'm going home now. Blue can handle the rest of the tables." Without waiting for a response, Steve took off his apron and tossed it to Baird, who looked like he wanted to give Steve something more to cry over than a troublesome lumbar. The Vemreaux left the bar; it was the fastest he'd moved all night long.

When the round clock behind the bar finally clicked to twelve forty-five, Baird sighed. "Alright, guys. Bar's closed for the night."

"Come on, Baird. Just one more for the road," Martin slurred.

"Really, man. Usually you give me a ten-minute warning or something, so I know to order another. You can't send me away like that," Lawrence complained.

"You should really branch out next time, Lawrence. You know I can make other drinks, right?" Baird made another round of shots and lined them up on a tray behind him for the booth he knew would not leave at one. The barflies grumbled, but stood and made their exit together.

Blue and Elle began collecting bills and clearing tables, subtly conveying that it was high time for everyone to leave. Some

Vemreaux begrudged giving up their well-earned seats after a long day of work, while others took the hint and headed to their vehicles soon after paying down their tab. Finally, it was just the lone booth and the staff that occupied the diner.

"Hey, midget. You up for one last order?" Baird called into the kitchen. "It'd be great if you could make a platter of pancakes for these guys. I can tear down the patio."

"Of course, Baird," Grettel consented.

Blue saw Elle's stiff and deliberate demeanor and recommended she sit down. "No, no," Elle insisted, shaking her head. Blue could tell by her hooded eyes that she was pushing through a headache from the lack of sleep and loud music that had thankfully stopped. Blue pulled out a chair and pointed to it, imitating Baird's firm way of commanding.

Elle chortled. "Just for a minute, okay? I want to get out of here at a reasonable hour tonight so I can actually rest."

Blue reached for the large square bucket she was using to bus the tables, but found Sam holding it instead, smiling around his freshly lit cigarette. With a look of disgust, he picked a dirty plate up off the nearest table and rested it in the gray plastic bin.

"What are you doing?" Blue tried to keep the smile out of her voice. She watched him pick up the next plate with just the tips of two fingers to avoid the smear of curried blood ketchup that dripped over the side.

"I'm trying not to lose my lunch," Sam admitted. "Oy! Liam! Grab Elle's bin and make yourself useful." He motioned with his shoulder to Elle's bucket that rested on the ground at her feet.

At the suggestion of a Vemreaux lowering himself to do her job while she was still able-bodied, Elle shot up out of her seat with new life.

Liam stood uncertainly and moseyed over to Elle. "So, what do I do?" the prince asked, lifting the gray bin up off the floor.

Elle tried to take it from him, but he raised it over his head and out of her reach. "Not so fast, blondie. Sit down and tell me what I'm supposed to do."

"Um, does Baird know about this?" Elle made another swipe at the tray in the air with her left arm and immediately regretted it. "Ah!" The stitches pulled at her skin. She winced at the sting. She held her side to soothe it. "On second thought, I think I will sit down a little bit longer." Elle stared at Liam, taking in the same blue she saw every day in Baird and his sister. "Oh! Your eyes! They're the same as Baird's. Weird. Never seen 'em on anyone but them." She sat down in the chair, unable to tear her eyes from his alien ones.

Liam lowered the bin to his waist. "Yeah, but mine go with a much better face, so you know, I'm still more handsome than he is." The prince tossed her a dazzling smile and a wink, and then looked at the table in confusion. "What do I do?" he repeated.

Elle stared up at him like he was a puzzling insect that just told her a very complicated riddle. "Uh, you just take the dirty dishes and put them in the bucket. Nothing to it."

Liam scooped up two plates at a time and dumped them with a clatter into the bin. "Like that?" he asked for confirmation, pleased when Elle nodded. He repeated the action with seven shot glasses. "Hey! Look at me, Sam! I'm bussing tables!" His theatrical, joyful voice boomed across the diner with too much volume.

"Where's the paparazzi when you need them?" Sam was beginning to regret offering his help as he approached a particularly disgusting plate. "This is sick." He played up his reaction to draw a second smile from his favorite waitress' lips.

"I'll be outside making myself useful," Alec informed his friends. "Baird looks like he could use some help with the patio. You got Liam, Sam?"

"Every mouthwatering eyeful of him."

Liam flexed animatedly for his friend, drawing out a tired whoop from Elle.

Blue giggled, and Sam endeared himself to the sound. With every dish that he blanched at, Blue's smile unveiled itself a little more. By the time they finished the third table, she gave birth to a full-blown, teeth-bearing grin and a quiet laugh. The boys would finish clearing off a table and she would wipe it down and put the chairs atop it.

Grettel opened her mouth when Sam handed her the tub of dirty dishes to wash, but no sound came out. "Thank you," she whispered before ducking back into the kitchen.

Sam threw Blue a quizzical look. Blue shook her head sadly in response. Blue was beginning to hide her face less and less, now that the diner was closed to outsiders and it was just them. The more she glanced over at Sam, the more relaxed his shoulders became. When Sam finally slumped into the booth with Liam, he patted the seat next to him.

"Come on, little Wayward. Take a load off."

As Blue judged the decision to sit next to him, her eyes darting from him to the patio where Baird was, it caused the confident smile to wash from his face. Sam realized that he had not made as much progress as he would have liked. As soon as that thought crossed his mind, he began silently shouting at himself, berating his vulnerability.

Instead of wallowing or dissecting his longings to have an A-blood sit next to him with all of her sulfuric stench, he began listing conquests in reverse chronological order. Each Femreaux had to have possessed a name, surely. He tried to recall the third one from the week previous. He was pretty sure she had dark hair. He was positive she had long legs.

Blue shook her head at Sam's offer, whispering, "I can't. I don't want to set off Baird again."

As Blue excused herself and walked away from the booth into the kitchen, Sam realized a sobering thought: he did not want to think of any Femreaux. They all seemed plain compared to Blue.

Liam glanced down at his best friend and shook his head as he, for once, managed to keep his voice low. "Man, now you're working at a diner for her? Did you really think that would impress her?" The platter of pancakes sitting in front of him was too tempting to resist, so he piled three onto one of the plates and shoved a forkful into his mouth.

Sam decided to stop playing dumb since Elle was the only other person in the dining area, and her head was resting on the table out of whispering range. He took a drag on his cigarette, wide eyes staring at nothing. "Like you said last night, her brother hates me and she does whatever he says. Even if I did want to be, you know, with her at all, it couldn't happen."

Liam's mouth fell open that Sam conceded his denial so easily. "Would you hear yourself being all sensitive? Who are you? What happened to my boy who'd screw first and ask questions later?"

Sam shrugged. He had been wondering the exact same thing. He righted himself when Baird and Alec came back in. They both were inflexible with the colder air and moved stiffly.

Sam cast a warning at his friend. "Not another word, Liam."

Liam looked up at the ceiling, pretending to weigh the options of poking more fun or giving in and being a good guy. "Okay, okay," he consented, lacing his hands together behind his head. "Do you think you could do me a solid and cut down on the Romeo eyes? It'd make jerking you around a little less... Well, just quit it. Either I throw jabs at you or Baird actually throws punches, so you know, tone it down. Let her come to you." He shook his head at his friend in mock disappointment. "You know how to bait the Femreaux. Why're you acting like a virgin?"

Sam kicked Liam under the table hard to shut him up when Alec slid into the booth next to the prince. "Pancakes!" Alec exclaimed as he reached over Liam to grab a plate. "Finally! This is all I wanted."

"So how'd you like working in a diner?" Liam queried between mouthfuls. The excitement at having cleaned off tables danced in his face like a kid promised a new toy.

Alec, not being one for self-revelatory conversation, replied in monotone. "I think I made the right career choice, despite the monkey I'm supposed to be guarding." He inspected the syrup before drizzling it onto his steaming stack. "And Sam, that was maybe your worst attempt at flirting. Ever. What's your deal with her?"

The dig at being referred to as a primate didn't even touch Liam. His pride at working a few minutes as a common man displayed proudly upon his puffed up chest. "Wait till ole' Emperor Freddy hears about this. Prince Liam: Man of the People."

Alec cocked his head toward the prince as Baird emerged from the kitchen with girls behind him. "We still have to figure out how much you're actually going to tell your dad. I hired Brody, you know, and I've been with your family since before Frederick was even born. We're not exactly supposed to keep secrets regarding your safety from him."

Liam rolled his eyes. "I wasn't going to get hurt putting dishes into a bucket. Francis' pants, I'm not that fragile." He pounded his fist to his chest once like a caveman.

"Not bussing tables, which I'm sure will get adequate media coverage back home. I mean the fact that you're buying the Light. We'll be traveling with an assassin capable of killing the thing Vemreaux haven't been able to catch or even photograph." Alec tried to convey the seriousness of the situation to the goofy man next to him.

"Technically," Sam intervened, "she's probably not killed anyone yet, so she's not an assassin. She hasn't actually done anything that's too big of a red flag."

"Sam, she threw you up against the wall and attacked Liam's guards. That's cause for trial back home, at least," Alec reminded him.

Sam grumbled, "Well, we're not at home, Alec. I don't think telling Frederick about her will do anything to calm her brother down. I love Uncle Freddy, but he's the emperor. He's got an obligation to the public that we don't. It's too risky telling him about her. Or anyone, for that matter."

Alec shrugged, conceding for the moment.

The three watched as Baird instructed Grettel and Elle to hurry home and lock the door behind them so they could settle in for the night while he stayed and sorted things out with Blue. They were all a little surprised at the gentle kiss he placed on Elle's pouting lips and the affectionate ruffle of Grettel's hair that he indulged in as he said goodnight to the girls. They were treated entirely different than Blue was.

The moment of tenderness faded as Baird turned to the booth

and tightened his shoulders. He snapped his fingers at his sister, who followed obediently a few paces behind him, clutching onto a plate that housed a nibbled sandwich.

Liam ground his heel into Sam's foot. "Keep your eyes to yourself."

Sam punched Liam under the table just above the knee in response. "Keep your mouth shut."

"I'm sorry, was that you trying to get to third base with me?" Liam joked. His smile turned into a grimace at Sam's glower.

After setting a tray of shots down on the table in front of the three Vemreaux, Baird slid into the booth next to Sam so that Blue could not, though she made no move to. She sat next to her brother and kept her head down, eyes on her sandwich.

Baird was not one for wasting time when he could be home, so he cut right to the chase as Liam unabashedly downed the first shot. "Keep it to two shots, Liam. You're unchanged, and that's absinthe." He cleared his throat. "Joe called me a little while ago and told me he talked to you, Liam. I told him I could find a decent replacement for Blue if he could call The Way and speed things along. It took months longer than it should have for them to sign her over, and we just don't have that kind of time now. He's gonna call the headmaster tomorrow to see if it can all be expedited."

"Who'd you choose?" Blue asked quietly. Alec was surprised she spoke at all.

Looking a little guilty at being confronted with this, Baird glanced at the shaded window behind Liam to avoid his sister's question. "It doesn't matter. You'll be gone by the time he's here anyway. He'll do fine."

The other three were mildly curious at this unimportant piece of information, but Blue suppressed her prying questions and trusted that Baird knew what he was doing. She had grown to understand that there was little use in pushing Baird to do what he did not want to. She was not the only sibling born with a strong will.

Liam spoke up. "I've been keeping current with Joe about paperwork and everything, so that won't slow anything up."

"Perfect," Baird said with a nod.

"So if all goes according to plan, we'll have ownership of Blue by Wednesday." Liam reiterated bits of the plan they all knew. "And we'll be gone the next day."

Alec cut in with the questions he needed to ask to do his job as he reached for the green liquid in front of him. "Is there anything we need to know?"

Sam's scowl betrayed him. "She's sitting right there, guys. She can answer for herself, you know."

Baird ignored Sam and spoke for his sister. "She hasn't done most things that Vemreaux have. She's only been in the world a month, so don't assume she knows things that everyone else does. She picks it up quick enough, but you know, don't take anything for granted. And like I said last night, don't leave her alone, either."

At this, Blue cut her eyes over to him, but said nothing to what she considered an insult.

Baird elaborated, "Once she gets over there, if things get clearer to her how she should kill your predator, someone should be there so she can do whatever it is that needs to be done. If she needs a specific weapon, you get it for her. If she needs a ride, you take her. Stuff like that."

The clarification gave Blue back a little of her dignity.

"It wouldn't do well for us to go through all this trouble just to have her get arrested or lost over there because of something stupid that could've been prevented."

Liam scratched the five o'clock shadow on his face with his fingertips. "She'll be my personal servant." Remembering that she was at the table, he addressed Blue directly, though she was partially obscured behind her brother. "Is that okay with you? It'll make sure you're with me most of the time. I've never had one before, but my sister has one. It wouldn't be too weird. Might be strange that she's a girl, but they'll just have to get over it." Liam stretched his large arms behind him and draped them on the back of the booth. "What else do we need to know? Does she like, shed her skin or Hulk out if we leave her out in the sun for too long?"

Baird didn't understand the "Hulk out" part, but he got the rest just fine. He sighed and looked down at the table, trying to find the right words. "Actually…"

"Baird, don't," Blue warned. "I've got it under control."

Baird stared at his sister and shook his head. "You know that's not true."

"It didn't happen last night, or when I took them down," she motioned to Alec and Sam. "Not worth mentioning. Please," she pleaded, turning the full force of her otherworldly eyes on him.

"I don't believe you," he ruled. "And I won't be there to hide the bodies in Europe. They need to know what they're getting themselves into. They have Liam to protect." Baird turned his attention to the wary men. "There is something you should know. Blue…she can't always control her temper…her abilities. You have to understand, everything's an effort. She's far stronger than anyone you've ever met, so she has to really try hard with even normal things to stay under the radar. Sometimes it's too much for her to hide."

When Baird paused, Alec eyed him. "Like when she attacked Sam in the hallway?"

Baird chuckled. "Nah. He's still breathing, isn't he? When Blue's cornered, sometimes she blacks out and goes on sort of a…a killing spree."

Whatever they'd been expecting Baird to say, it wasn't that. They all turned as one and stared at her, mouths agape.

"Sometimes!" Blue emphasized defensively as she took a bite of her sandwich. "And it hasn't happened in a while."

"That's what I said," Baird argued. "And it happened a month ago. And it almost happened last night when Sam and I got into it."

Alec paled. "That's what that thing with the towel over her head was?"

Blue cringed. "But before that, not for, like, a long time. And I didn't go totally dark last night or a month ago with those two Vems with that stupid green car, Baird. You had to kill those guys for me. I didn't lose control completely."

Sam started his sentence twice before sound came out. "A green Humvee with fire decals?"

Baird turned to Sam. "How'd you know?"

"I saw the car! I could tell it was a murder cover-up. That...that was you, Blue?"

Blue's face darkened. "No. That was Baird. And they were robbing us, by the way. I don't just go around slaughtering innocent people at random. And I didn't black out, so I couldn't kill them. Just gave one of them brain damage." She frowned at her brother for bringing up the sore subject. "I told you I hadn't blacked out in a while, Baird. I controlled it that time, so it doesn't count. Leave me alone about it."

"A few months back when I was visiting Griffin, he told me that you almost blacked out and killed some guys that were messing with him."

"Almost doesn't count. If you *almost* spill a glass of water, it's not actually spilled, is it?" She huffed, her face turning red. "Plus, I didn't kill anyone that time. Just broke a few arms. It was pitch black! They didn't even see me there. Griffin took credit, and he got the respect he needed to keep other people from picking on him. You're welcome!" She crossed her arms over her chest as she tried to ignore the dumbfounded stares of the three men she wished were not privy to this conversation.

"Griffin was scared of you."

Blue gasped, forsaking her sandwich. "He didn't say that! I would never hurt him."

The men watching the two vacillated between horror over the situation and amusement at her feisty personality finally being drawn out. "Well, this is a problem," Alec muttered.

Baird eyed his sister. "Griffin *did* say that. You don't know what you're doing when you black out."

She glared at him, all pretense of submissive behavior gone. "I never attacked Elle, Grettel or Griffin!"

"You punched me in the face once! That time you killed the dozen or so guys Trisan sent after me?"

"Who said that was by accident?" Blue challenged. "You'd been asking for that black eye for days! Kinda like right now."

Sam sniggered as he sucked on his cigarette, unable to keep the attraction off his face as he watched the kitten turn into a tiger.

Alec held up his hands to force a truce. "Alright, you two. Enough. So how do we deal with this? What's the trigger?" He watched as her forced timidity melted away.

Blue held her chin up, daring them to question her. "I don't like being threatened. Do you? I told you in the hallway, I don't like it when people put their hands on me. Just like anyone else, I'd imagine."

Liam cocked his head to the side. "Yeah, but everyone else doesn't go off killing left and right when they're in trouble."

Baird spoke for his sister. "In The Way, that's how girls end up raped or dead. In the real world, that's how you end up abducted for a prostitution ring."

Alec lost his appetite for pancakes and put down his fork as he continued the conversation. "Well, it won't be like that where we're going. No one's going to hurt her or sell her off for sex. If she's going to be with Liam, she'll be very well guarded. But there might be times she's cornered or scared, and she'll have to be able to handle it."

Blue flopped her arms on the table and laid her forehead down to hide her face. "I can handle it!" she growled.

"Clearly," Baird snorted. "Tell me the situation, and I'll work on it with her before she goes."

"Liam's photographed all the time. Sometimes the paparazzi get a little overzealous and corner him. If she's with him..."

"I'll just slip out of sight. I'm fantastic at being invisible," Blue argued, head still buried in her arms.

Alec addressed Baird. "Look, I'll do whatever I can to make this happen. Vemreaux can't keep dying over there. The emperor's worried. The king's getting desperate. I'd love to get her over there and let her end it. But if she's a danger to Liam or any of the royal family, I just can't risk it."

Blue banged her forehead against the table in frustration, causing the silverware to clatter and Liam to jump.

Baird nodded. "I understand. She'll be ready. I'll see to it."

Blue slammed her head on the hard surface again, drawing a noise of protest from Sam.

"I'll need proof, Baird. Solid as your word is," Alec instructed.

"I know. I'll take care of it."

Blue lifted her head to look at her brother. "You really think I'd hurt Liam?"

Baird's mask of composure settled back into place after being ruffled at their argument. "No, but Alec doesn't know you like I do." He turned to Liam. "Will she wear a uniform?" he asked, changing the subject.

Liam shook his head. "No, she's a civilian. You know I'm not buying her to own her, right?" It was obvious that Baird needed the clarification when the Wayward's eyebrows rose. "The emperor doesn't own slaves. It's normal here to do that, but it's not a good example for our family to own people. I'm buying her from Joe, so I'll be her owner, like, that day, but she'll technically be a freed A-blood after I file the paperwork and make the payment to liberate her." He raised his hand when Baird began to protest at the wasted money. "My dad wouldn't have it any other way. Since you want her under the radar, I'll buy her from Joe to cover his loss so he can purchase a new Wayward. Once she's mine, I'll free her and she'll magically choose to come work for me. Her wage will be the same as a Vemreaux and she'll have the same rights. She can vote, walk around wherever she wants without a problem and be, you know, free."

The sandwich in Blue's hand dropped to her plate, immediately forgotten. Her mouth hung open in surprise as she stared up at Liam. Her chest moved up and down, but her eyes did not fog up on principle.

Though she was clearly affected by the words, Baird spoke up. "That's unnecessary. She might only live with you for a week or two. You can't waste your money like that. It wouldn't be right."

The usually happy-go-lucky Vemreaux's face darkened as he

leaned forward. Baird began to wonder if Liam's bodyguard was only there as a formality. "What's not right is that I'm in the position to own human beings. It could have just as easily been reversed, you know. The only real difference between us is blood type. I just got lucky. Does that mean your sister should be a slave her whole life because she was born with the short end of the stick? My family doesn't own slaves. It's insulting to think that we would. Now don't fight me on this, Baird. You may run this place, but you're trusting me with your sister. You should want this for her." His tone conveyed the disappointment of an older brother to a younger, foolish sibling. "Wouldn't you be happier knowing she's out there, free?" Liam noticed the look that Sam gave him and turned to his friend. "What?"

"You sound just like your dad. Never a bad thing, that," Sam commented as he smoked.

It was odd to witness Baird at a loss. He was always so sure of himself and his duties. For the briefest of moments, Blue saw a flash of Griffin's insecurity in him. Embarrassment mixed with defiance and settled into his chest to tighten the muscles there, but he said nothing controversial. "Okay. If she's freed, doesn't she have to find lodging?" His brain worked quickly to factor the new information into the existing plan.

"She's a personal servant, so she'll live in the mansion with me. I have a guest bedroom next to mine. My sister's servant lives in the room adjoining with hers five days a week. Blue would just stay all seven with me."

"What's the rent?" Baird asked, trying to find the catch.

Liam's nose crinkled. "There's no rent. She wouldn't have any bills to pay except for what she charges outside of her expense account."

At this, Baird could no longer attempt a poker face. "Expense account? For what?"

Liam didn't see what all the fuss was about as he picked up another shot and downed it in one satisfied gulp. "You know, for eating out when we're on the go. She's supposed to travel with me places if I say I need her, so she'll also have to eat out with us. If she wants personal things like clothes, hair stuff..." he trailed off as his hand lifted to make circles in the air. "I don't know what chicks buy. She'll get a green card that's linked to an account. My dad'll put money in it every month for her to use for that kind of stuff. You know, like an allowance. Her paycheck's a separate thing. I'll set up a bank account for her over there. Don't worry."

Baird tried to be delicate, so that the words did not burst out unpolished. "And all she'll be doing is household stuff for you? Nothing else? Nothing I'd have to kill you for?"

Liam nodded, taking the insult with grace. Deciding to play it off as a big joke, he winked at Blue. "Well, if I want a sandwich and a smile at two in the morning, then..."

Sam's hand flew up and smacked the back of the prince's head. "Then you'll get it yourself."

Blue's wide eyes met Liam's with a combination of shock and confusion. Her mouth opened like she wanted to say something, but words would not reach her throat.

Liam seemed to understand everything she wanted to say, and he acknowledged her inexpressible gratitude with a polite bow of his head and a gracious smile.

For once, Baird was speechless. He looked down at his sister with wonder that was tinged with the hardness of jealousy.

Blue felt an odd gloss come over her eyes. She stood up and left the table for the kitchen without a word. Baird made no effort to follow.

"Is she okay?" Liam asked for Sam's sake. His friend looked like he wanted to go after her.

Baird shrugged, thinking the answer to that question inconsequential.

"What's the matter with you?" Sam growled at Liam. "She's afraid of being raped or sold as a prostitute. You think your dodgy sex jokes are funny to her? Or her brother, for that matter? Sandwich and a smile," Sam grumbled.

"Sorry. Forgot about that."

Baird shot Sam a confused look of appreciation.

Liam switched tacks. "Uh, I don't know if this is relevant," Liam spoke into the hushed moment, "but I did ask Joe for both of you, Baird." He watched Baird's face jerk up and the air leave his lungs. "He wouldn't part with you. Called you irreplaceable." To cover over the wound, Liam spread some more sugar on it. "Said he wouldn't give you up, even for double what he paid for you. Which, if you think about it, is a pretty high compliment." Liam cleared his throat. "I put in a call this morning to Wayward Services. They're going to be looking into your housing arrangement to see if it's up to code, which it's not. Joe'll have to put you three in a better house if he wants the government out of his hair, which it sounds like he does. I gave him the heads up."

Baird looked uncomfortable at receiving the help that was already in motion. "Um, you didn't have to do that. We're fine the way we are."

Liam waved his large hand, signifying that it was done. "How are you going to make a move on that blonde of yours with no proper bed? Consider me your guardian angel."

"More like a fairy without the wings," Sam murmured under his breath. "Is there anything else we should know?"

Baird paused, humbled at being looked after so kindly. Then, regaining his manhood, Baird postured. "There's something *you* should know. I see the way you look at my sister. I also saw you in here with a few nice pieces on your arm yesterday. I'd go for the Fems. Blue isn't one of you, so leave her alone. She's never had a boyfriend or even kissed a guy before. She's *pure*. You get what I'm saying?"

Before Sam could answer, which it looked like he was gearing up to do, Blue returned from the kitchen holding a plate with a sandwich on it. Without a word, she set it on the table in front of Liam.

The prince looked at her down-turned eyes in confusion. "Aw, thanks. What's this for, kitten?"

Blue sat back down next to Baird and ducked behind his sturdy frame. "You said you wanted a sandwich," she spoke quietly. "It's almost two in the morning."

Curiosity twisted into a sickened expression, and Liam looked at the plate as if it contained a human head. "Aw, *bambina*. I was only kidding." As soon as the word slipped from his mouth, Liam covered his offending lips as Alec and Sam both slapped him in the back of the head.

"This is not your house, Liam," Alec reminded him sternly. "You can't call her that in public."

Though he looked like he agreed, Liam threw out the token argument. "You call this public?"

"I call this not your house." Alec shook his head as if it pained him to watch over such an imbecile. "Or your father's country."

Blue looked up at Baird for him to explain what had just happened, but he shrugged, indicating his own ignorance.

Liam held up his hands apologetically. "Thank you for the sandwich, Blue." He made sure to say her name and not anything resembling another forbidden language. "I was kidding, though. I won't make you get up and wait on me in the middle of the night. It was a bad joke. That's something you'll have to get used to. I only mean about half the stuff what comes out of my mouth." He reclaimed his swagger. "The other half is pure gold, though. You're lucky to be traveling with such a smart guy like me."

Before he could make another faux-pas, Liam reached for the sandwich because it was there and begging to be eaten. It was peanut butter and jelly, which he hadn't had in years. When Liam opened his mouth, his words were jumbled from the bits of sticky sandwich impeding his speech. "Anything else before we call it a night? Will she be all ready to leave by Thursday?" He unglued his tongue from the roof of his mouth with very little grace.

Alec averted his eyes at the sight of the food rolling around in the prince's mouth. He struggled to keep himself from blanching as he recounted the number of decorum lessons the man had been given, all with limited results.

Baird nodded. "Almost. She's got one more job to do before she'll be ready to kill the predator. I trained her myself, and she's practically perfect." The praise made Blue happy, but she did not show it.

"If you can spare one of your guys for a couple hours, you can head home now."

"Sure," Liam nudged Alec, who did not look thrilled at the prospect of babysitting. "What for?"

Baird debated whether or not to tell them in front of Blue. He did not want her to have too much time to think about it. He wanted her to just go and execute without having hours or days to plan it out. He sighed at the late hour. "She's supposed to be able to kill this predator and put an end to tyranny," he paraphrased the familiar prophecy that at times seemed to simultaneously run and ruin his life. "The thing is, she's never been able to kill someone without blacking out. I don't want her to get out there face to face with it and freeze up. And you wanted proof that she can handle stressful situations without losing her mind, Alec."

Liam paused his attack on the sandwich. "You want her to kill one of my guys?" He raised an eyebrow. "Well, then I change my mind. You can have Brody instead. He's back at the hotel nursing a hangover, so he'll be an easy target."

"I've already got a criminal in mind that's gotten out of prison twice now for running a Wayward prostitution ring. I just want one of yours to go with her and make sure she does it. It'll put any of your fears to rest that she isn't the Light, or that she won't be able to handle herself without blacking out."

"Well, shoot. I want to see that!" Liam exclaimed.

Alec and Sam both shook their heads like they were tied to the same string. "Not a chance," Alec protested. "If you get caught at a murder scene, it'll get back to your father and become a public thing along the way. We'll take you back to the hotel first and then I'll go with her."

Blue wanted to say something, but she knew that Baird's mind was already made up. Baird had taught her just about every take-down tactic there was, but snuffing the life out of someone and seeing their last breath escape their lips awakened both her conscience and something cold that she tried to suppress before it claimed her soul. She'd never been able to kill someone in her right mind. Part of her had to go blank to carry out the gruesome task.

Baird stood up, so Blue mimicked him. Alec watched as they moved together, her following him like she had no choice to her movements. He hoped that she would be as easy to control in Europe. He did not relish the thought of being laid out on the ground every time he made her do something she did not want to do.

Baird stood directly in front of his sister so the two saw only each other. His eyes bored into hers as he leveled his finger to her face. He spoke quietly just as Liam let loose a dramatic yawn to cover any chance of eavesdropping. Blue did not put up any semblance of a fight, but nodded once when he'd finished his instructions. Baird held up his finger to the others, indicating for them to wait there while he retreated into the kitchen for a moment.

"Does this seem wrong to anyone else?" Sam asked, putting out his cigarette on Liam's empty plate.

Alec shrugged. "I see his point. Man! He'd make a fantastic guard."

The kitchen door swung open, and Baird strolled out at a moderate pace holding a plastic grocery bag. "Alright." He spoke again only to his sister, but did not bother lowering his voice this time. "Remember, don't bother doing the civil thing and making him face his killer before he snuffs it. If he sees you, it'll count against you and I'll send you out again after someone else tomorrow. The predator doesn't deserve to see who's going to kill it, and neither does this guy. Stealth, Blue."

It was clear that the men wanted to speak up, but Baird held his hand out to silence them. "If any of those guys helps you? Same thing. I'll send you out again tomorrow, too. Now, he touched Grettel's face, so I want whichever hand he used." Baird's gaze grew intense as he gave the orders to his sister, shoving the plastic bag at her. "He was looking at her, too. I want both of his eyes intact and out of his head." Baird could tell that his sister was doing her best not to look shocked. "Bring them both home to me, Blue. I don't want to see any blood on your shoes either, so you'll have to wear your old ones from The Way, in case you screw that up. I see blood on your shoes, you'll have to go out after someone who doesn't deserve it like this guy does. If an innocent person has to die tomorrow, it'll be your fault. Do you understand me?" When he spoke, it was more like a punctuation at the end of his command than an opportunity for her to ask any clarifying questions.

"Why do you need his eyes?" Blue questioned quietly.

"Alec does." Baird jutted his chin toward the booth. "We need proof that you can kill without losing your mind. That means when you do take him down, you have to keep him in one piece before you remove my parts and bring them back to me. The guys can help you deal with what's left of the body, but if they're not good at that sort of thing, have them call me, and I'll take care of it."

Baird noticed the dread beginning to creep into her cerulean eyes, so he held his finger up two centimeters from her nose to distract her from it. "Hey, this is nothing. You're doing us a service. After you leave, I'll still be here watching over the girls. Grettel's too naïve and scared of her own voice to scream for me if he gets too close to her again. If you didn't find him the other day, he could've taken her. Do you want that? Do you want him to sneak off with our Grettel after you're gone? You can't just leave without making sure it's safe for her, Blue. She's your responsibility just as much as mine. She can't lift her hand to push him away from her. You can. So do it. Push him so he never comes back for her or anyone else."

Blue nodded once, and Baird was convinced that she was ready for the task. "Oh," he remembered. "Your weapon." He pulled something shiny out of his pocket. It was an ordinary butter knife, like the one she'd thrown into the dartboard the night before. "You seem to like showing off with them."

Blue took the excuse for a weapon from him and pocketed it along with the balled-up grocery bag. Removing her short black apron, she pulled out a thick wad of bills and handed it over without batting an eyelash.

Alec was amazed at Baird's authority. Sam was sickened at the subservient sister who was parading around, trying to hide all traces of the girl who'd shoved him up against the wall and threatened to break Brody's arm.

Baird added one last low threat. "If you don't do this without blacking out, I won't let Liam buy you or free you. I won't send you out to the island if I think you'll be slaughtered because you can't control the final punch. Liam's a good guy who's risking a lot for you, so I won't let you live with him if I'm not certain you won't go dark. There'll be no more trials for the pimp, Blue. No prisons he can get paroled from in a year. Just justice. Clean and quick."

Blue nodded, though her eyes were on Baird's shoes, studying them as if they held the secrets of the universe. "He works the corner of Liberty and 5th this time of night. Wait till he sells off his last girl, so there are no witnesses. He usually has about an hour or so by himself." He dismissed her as he walked away toward the front door. "Guys?" He indicated the exit. "I'll see you later. Stop by tomorrow night if you have more questions or want more drinks. Except you, Liam. I told you two drinks a night. You're cut off." His tone left no room for arguments. "Otherwise we'll see you around on Peace Day."

The three just stared at him, thunderstruck. Even Liam lost his ever-present laughter.

Baird pursed his lips and pushed the door open, reminding them of the late hour. "Goodnight, guys. I'm locking the doors now."

Alec snapped back to himself first and nudged Liam forward. He waited for Blue to follow the men, her head down, as usual. It was more than just the need to hide her eyes that drove her gaze to the floor. Alec thought to himself that her shoulders now seemed weighted, like they carried too many burdens to stand erect.

Alec put his hand on her shoulder to lead her out of the door, but she stiffened, telling him that it was the wrong thing to do. The guard caught Baird's eye and nodded once to communicate that he'd be there the entire time to make sure she did everything he told her to.

Liam noticed Baird taking off toward the woods. "We can give you a ride home, Baird." Before Baird could protest, Liam turned his back so he would not be able to see the token hesitation the man put up at accepting any help.

When they reached the car, Baird slid in the back seat beside his sister, obscuring her from Alec's view, who sat on his right. Blue's fists were balled up and tightened around her stomach. "You know," Baird said quietly as the car started up, "if the predator sees that kind of fear in you, you don't stand a chance."

Blue relaxed her fists, but then moved them to clutch at the interior of the car that was available to her. "It's not that." She corrected herself, "Well, it's not just that. I don't like riding in cars, Baird. But at least in yours you can feel it moving. This one barely jerks at all. I can't tell where it's taking me, and I don't like that." She swallowed once. "If I just knew how to take it apart and put it back together by myself, I think I'd feel better about it."

"They have books like that at the library, but we can't use the library, Blue. Citizens only. You'll just have to get over it." Baird shrugged, his arm brushing uncomfortably against Alec's.

Sam's eyes frequently darted up at the rearview mirror to look at the siblings, but at this, he stared only at Blue in between focusing on the road. He could not help the anger that flared up in him when she responded with an obedient "okay."

"You got something to say, Vemreaux?" Baird leaned forward to stick his head closer to Sam's threateningly.

"Sam," Alec cautioned as he grabbed Baird's shirt collar and pulled him back.

"I just think it's great you've trained her so well."

"Sam." Alec threw him a dark look to indicate that he should stop.

"What? You can't take five minutes to explain how a car works so she's not so scared? Excellent job, chief. I mean, now we have our very own pretty little homicidal puppet to..." But Sam never got to finish his sarcastic sentence or the bitter monologue he was building up to in his head.

Baird lunged forward toward the driver's seat, but Alec was faster. "Not tonight, you two," Alec warned. He wrapped both arms around Baird and clamped them to his body, limiting the threat.

Blue let her vice grip on the seat go and punched Baird in the throat, which stopped him from further attacking Sam. He shot her a look of betrayal as he choked. "What? You hit the driver, Liam could get hurt. You wanted Liam to be safe, but you throw a fit this easily? How'm I supposed to learn control if you don't have any?"

Alec nodded, shooting Blue a look of gratitude. "You're the boss in the diner, but you answer to me around the prince. That means no attacking the driver, no matter how asinine he is."

Liam shook his head at his friend, but no one said anything else.

Blue had her work cut out for her, trying to be invisible in such a cramped space. She did her best to push down her anxiety about the car and her impending mission, and focused on forcing the seat she occupied to swallow her as best it could.

It was not a moment too soon that the vehicle pulled up to the unlit hut, and Alec ushered Baird out of the car. He ducked down and spoke over Alec to his sister, who was still trying to disappear. "Be back before your shift, Blue. You'll need to change out of your clothes and wear Elle's for her scent. Yours are starting to lose Grettel's smell. Give your uniform here." He extended his hand. "You can't be getting blood on that or your shoes. I'll bring out your old ones."

She obeyed and took off her shoes and the powder blue collared shirt, exposing her bare arms in the form-fitting tank top. Sam picked a tree in front of him to stare at without bothering to blink.

Baird departed into the hut, reemerging with her worn Wayward white sneakers. "Fellas," Baird tipped his head and turned toward his home.

3 2

DEADLY DEEDS DONE IN
THE DARK

The atmosphere changed as the four drove away from the hut. The pressure lifted enough to make breathing easier. Liam reclined the passenger seat and closed his eyes. "You can relax, kitten. Your guard dog's gone now. What a night." Then he turned his head to his left, his tone sharpening. "Did you have to start with him?"

"He's the one who started it, ordering her around. Would you let someone talk to Suzette like that?" Sam countered, not in the mood to be blamed for the mess that was Baird's.

Liam chuckled as his eyes drifted shut again. "Shoot, I'd *pay* to see someone talk to my sister like that. She'd tear them a new one in a hot second. Suzette's not afraid to go off when she needs to."

"Or when she doesn't," Sam amended.

"True enough." Liam nestled into his seat to get a little more comfortable. "You've got to admit, though, she does what he says. When's the last time Suzette did anything anyone asked her?"

Sam's teeth ground together as he tried to focus on the road, his speed picking up with his temper. "You're doing it, too! Stop talking about her like she's not right behind us." He glanced in the rearview mirror at Blue, only to find her braced against the door with her head down. "Hey, are you okay back there?"

Blue nodded, but Sam was not convinced. He opened his mouth again, but Liam reached out and nicked his friend's shoulder with his knuckles. "Leave her alone, Sam. She'll be fine. Right, kitten?"

Blue did not respond, but no one expected her to.

Alec spoke up. "What was that about Grettel's smell? Why do you have to wear your friend's clothes?"

Without looking up, Blue spoke just loud enough for her voice to drift into the front seat so she did not have to repeat herself. "I don't smell like an *A*-blood to the changed Vemreaux. Baird thinks it's part of being the Light or something. So I wear their dirty clothes to blend in." Blue's hands were plastered to the car and gripped onto the leather as she revealed the well-kept secret. "It wears off by the morning, though."

If the boys weren't awake before that, they sure were then. Liam's serious expression matched Alec's. "Then why does Baird smell? Not as strong as a normal Wayward, granted, but he's still got the scent," Alec wondered. "You have the same eyes, same genes, but you don't smell the same? How's that work?"

Blue shrugged, though she did not release her grip on the car. "He's probably my half brother. We're not sure."

"How can you not know something like that?" Liam questioned, unaware of his rudeness.

"How do you expect me to? It's not like we get to know our parents or see them after our first year. Building One of The Way is separate from Building Four, which is where the adults live. We aren't given names unless two siblings ask specifically and file a petition to know if they're related. Lucky we look so similar, really. Baird found me and knew we belonged to each other before they even told us we were brother and sister. Our eyes are the same just by chance, I guess. Our younger brother Griffin has the same eyes, too, and he smells just like Baird does. It's rare for siblings in The Way to be true siblings, though. Most of us are halves."

"So you don't know who gave birth to you?" Sam asked unhappily.

"No, but no one knows that kind of stuff in The Way. That's a Vemreaux thing. Baird, Griff and I all have the same eyes, same hair and the same ears, but there's no way to tell who our parents were. They'll have moved on to Building Four or Five, or they're terminated once they hit life expectancy."

No one spoke for a moment. Then Sam rolled down the window to bring in a bit of fresh night air. "That's a sad story, little Wayward."

"Is it?" Blue contemplated this new thought. "I'm sorry."

The four drove the rest of the way in a thick silence filled with pondering, breaking the peace only when they dropped off Liam. Sam parked the car, taking the keys out of the ignition. "I'll take Liam to his room and wake up Brody, but I'm going with you tonight."

Alec shook his head. "Sam, I don't know about that."

"Good thing you're not the future emperor." He turned to Liam, who was reaching for the door handle. "Liam, do you want me to stay with you tonight, love? I'll sleep right next to you and sing Perry Como to you all night long. Come on, you can be the little spoon to my big, fat..."

Liam shuddered. "Brody can take the guest bed tonight. I don't want that wanker anywhere near me while I'm sleeping," he informed Alec. "And I'm not the future emperor. That's Killian's job, thank goodness."

"There's a comforting thought for the nation," Sam sneered with a glower.

"Fine." Alec sighed as he got out of the car. "But you're not a guard anymore, Sam. You can't be responsible for him. I'll take him up to his room and kick out whatever Fem Brody's got tonight. I'll be right back." Alec got out of the car and started walking toward the hotel. "Come on, Prince."

The title felt like a jab, and Liam gave Alec a half-hearted shove. Liam turned around and ducked to look at Blue in the back seat. "I only need guards because I'm so dashing. People see my face, and all the Femreaux maul me. The blokes don't like me. Think I'm too good looking." His white teeth set off his teasing smile nicely, but Blue still would not look up. She nodded, which deflated his mood. "See you 'round, kitten."

As soon as the two men were away from the vehicle, Sam tried to think of something clever to say, but came up empty. He pulled out his cigarettes and lit one up. "Are you alright? You don't have to do this, you know."

Just when he was about to give up on conversation, Blue answered in a whisper. "You heard Baird. If I don't kill him, I'll have to kill someone innocent tomorrow."

"He can't make you do anything you don't want to do," Sam countered as he turned in his seat to face her. He was glad that, at the very least, she had not said "okay" again.

Her brain spat out a mixed regurgitation of Baird's words. "He touched Grettel when she wasn't his property. If I don't kill him, he'll do it again after I'm gone. I can't..." she considered her words carefully. "I can't let that happen. I won't leave if they aren't safe."

Sam wished she would look up at him. He was beginning to be annoyed by the thick waves of auburn that insisted upon obscuring his view of her face. "What I mean is that Alec and I can do it. You don't have to do this."

At this, Blue raised her chin and allowed her eyes to meet his. The steadiness she'd achieved left her, her breath dragging in and out unevenly. They were both stunned at the intensity of their unspoken connection, and Blue had to remind herself that she needed to come up with a response to his offer. "But I *do* have to. Baird's right. If I can't kill someone who's a threat to Grettel without going dark, how can I kill for complete strangers I'll never meet? Besides, he'll know if I'm lying. I gave up lying to him years ago. No point, really."

Sam allowed silence to fall between them. He realized that he couldn't correct the first thing that came out of her mouth. If he grew too argumentative, perhaps she would stop speaking to him altogether. For whatever reason, he could not have that. Instead, he drank in her face, which was finally revealed to him.

Beautiful, he realized. It was subtle, hiding beneath a thick iron wall that had "stay away" inscribed on it. Most Femreaux he knew screamed for attention. Their gobs of permanent and temporary makeup painted on their often lifted or reconstructed faces held nothing to Blue's natural features and simple beauty. Thinking back to her brother's threat earlier in the booth, Sam wondered how it was possible no other man or boy had noticed the rare find. Then again, perhaps they had, and were just too afraid of her brother.

Their connection did not waver even as Sam spoke. "Why don't you come sit up here? If you want to learn about cars, I can show you."

Her lips pursed and drew to the side of her mouth as she considered this, weighing the uncertainty against her blatant curiosity. In the end, her curiosity won. She unbuckled her seatbelt and let herself out of the car, tingling with excitement.

As she walked around to the passenger door, Sam turned back around happily. He managed to have a little conversation with her without scaring her or saying something inappropriate or stupid. He had to fight against every natural tendency as he reminded himself how to speak to a woman he was not trying to bed right away.

Blue dipped down and sat next to him, their close proximity making both of them a little nervous.

"So this is the dashboard," Sam pointed out, tapping on the surface in front of him. "Do you know what a kilometer is?"

This drew out a simpering look from Blue that seemed to say to him, *"Please, I'm not an idiot."*

Sam laughed aloud at her adorable face and had to temporarily glue his hand to the dash so that it did not jump off and stroke her cheek. "Good. This is the odometer. It tells you how fast you're going. There are speed limit signs on the side of the road. You can't go above those limits." He backtracked. "Well, you can. I mean, they're more like suggestions to drivers like me. But if the cops see you speeding, they can pull you over." Blue's eyes widened at the idea of the police pulling them over. Sam tried his best to cover over his indiscretion. "Hey, don't worry. I'm a good driver." He waited until the panic died off her features. "Does the smoke bother you?" He blew a mouthful out of the open window. Sam grimaced. He'd never cared to ask permission or preference concerning his favorite escape.

"Can you smoke and keep telling me about the car?" She saw a true grin erupt on his face as he nodded, and she smiled in return. "Continue."

Continue he did until there was nothing more in the interior for him to explain. He kept waiting for the glazed look of too much information at once to settle in, but it never came. He was explaining how the gear shift and the clutch worked when Alec came up and let himself into the back after depositing a shovel and garbage bag into the trunk.

Sam waxed poetic about manual transmissions and how there used to be cars made that were automatics and required no shifting from gear to gear. However, with the terrain in many areas still torn up from World War Three, it was not realistic to continue making cars without the extra push to them.

"Did I go too fast?" Sam questioned as he turned the key in the ignition.

"No." At her next words, she retreated behind her hair again and looked forward at the dashboard. "You were p-perfect. Thank you."

He grinned at her slight stutter. Suddenly, an idea occurred to him. "Do you want to try shifting?" This earned another direct hit from her blue eyes. It never ceased to quicken his breath. "I mean, I'll help you."

"Really?" she asked with a rare flash of girlish intrigue. Her silly grin leapt off her face and pulled his back to the surface.

Alec remained quiet and patient in the back seat, glad that, at the very least, Sam had started the car.

"Sure." Sam reached over the console that separated them and lifted her hand, enjoying the thrill of such simple contact. Hand holding had never been something he invested in. In fact, for the most part, he batted away any attempts from a Femreaux to claim him in such a possessive, nonsexual way.

Things with Blue were different. Her skin was slightly chilled from the early hour and her knuckles were brittle from hard labor, but her palm felt soft, like how he imagined her lips would. He made the most of the brief touch and stroked the inside of her hand before placing it on the gear shift. Reminding her again where each gear was, he earned a second *"Please, I'm not an idiot. I heard you the first time, and it's written right on the panel"* look that made him chuckle.

"When I tell you, push the button in on the side and move the gear up to the one I tell you to. It'll always go in order. I can't jump around from first to say, fourth. Just so you know."

His foot pushed down on the clutch and he realized that this was the most power he'd ever given away, and she hadn't even asked him to. "Are you ready?"

After she buckled her seatbelt, Blue nodded. Her focus was completely on the gear shifter. Her heart jumped into her throat when Sam's hand rested on hers to guide it. She could see faint traces of scars he'd not had removed before bathing in the Fountain of Youth, and wondered how he acquired so many.

"Okay, first." The stick was slower to move than she anticipated, but after she felt the resistance, she adjusted her thrust accordingly. Sam did not move it for her, but still kept his hand on hers. It felt odd to have that kind of support. Usually on her new ventures, Baird sent her off with sometimes cryptic instructions and forced her to sink or swim. Not a fan of sinking, she learned to pay close attention to everything so she would not fail. Having Sam's hand on hers as a backup just in case she needed it allowed her to relax, despite this very new lesson being taught her on the open road.

Blue's fingers remained on the stick the entire car ride, moving it where Sam beckoned, and only when he told her to. When he was sure she had the hang of it, and they reached a steady speed that allotted for little shifting, his hand drifted up from the back of hers, feeling the skin there as if he'd never felt the slope of a woman's wrist before. In a soothing motion, his fingers began to slowly brush up and down the back of her hand and arm.

Though she wanted to give the stick her full attention, her eyes drifted shut on more than one occasion as his gentle touch lulled her imagination to places it certainly had never gone before.

Heated tingles shot up her arm and ricocheted through her body at each pass of his fingers, immediately followed by warmth that was completely other. She had to remind herself to give him directions to the cross streets where the pimp worked, nearly failing to inform him of their last turn as she shuddered when his hands trailed to the sensitive underside of her wrist.

Her words jumbled and came out all wrong, but somehow he understood that she wanted him to turn the corner and park on the next street down to avoid their car being anywhere near the scene of the crime. By the time he instructed her to shift the car into park, her resolve was a complete pile of mush. "How did you do that?" Blue stared at her wrist. Her skin was practically humming from his touch.

"Do what?"

"That's the first time I haven't felt like throwing up in a car."

Sam sized up her smile with a crooked one of his own. "Guess I'm just good for you."

"Are you ready?" Alec asked her as he flung open the car door, reminding them both of his presence and reality.

Blue swallowed and nodded as she pulled her hand reluctantly from Sam's. His face fell at the loss of contact. "I can't think when you do that," she informed him. Her words made his expression lift into a cocky smirk.

She glanced down the alley through the thin layer of fog that gathered in the early hour, and for a second, hoped that the man wouldn't be there. She frowned when her keen eyes found him leaning against the brick wall of the university. "Oh, no."

"What?" Alec's vision followed to where she was looking.

"It's the university. I just...I wish Baird would've told me. I had a friend who works there. Doesn't feel right."

"Best do it quick, then," Alec advised, motioning that they should cross the streets further down to maintain the element of surprise.

"Is it cheating if I kill him first and then take his eyes and hand?"

Blue tried to scrub the sweetness out of her wrist that Sam had rubbed into it over the course of the drive.

"I'd prefer you took Baird's trophies after the fact. I'd also prefer you not make any large blood splatters on the concrete. It's easier to wash away on the grass."

She arched an eyebrow. "How do you know that?"

Alec eyed her as he sized up her loyalty. "I wasn't always a bodyguard, Blue."

Blue nodded as she pictured how much blood would come when she removed his hand.

Sam shook his head in disgust. "You don't have to do this," he offered. "I've got my knife and Alec's always got his on him, too."

"Yes, she does. Baird was right. If she can't keep her head while killing, she can't be trusted on the battlefield, and probably not with Liam, either."

"Shut it, Alec. She's a girl. At least give her the option."

"You heard my brother. I'm not a girl. I'm the stupid Light. I don't have any options, Sam. This is who I am. It's already decided for me." Even the coo his heart felt at her saying his name did not settle him. He had an argument waiting, but she beat him by turning away. "You two stay here. I'll be back." After a few steps toward the empty moonlit street, she could hear two sets of shoes behind her. Without looking at them, she called over her shoulder with just enough volume to carry to them and trail no farther. "I can sneak up on him, but I don't know how good you two are at it. Just give me a little space so nothing gets messed up."

"We'll be fine, Blue."

"My assignment. My call. Fancy shoes like you're wearing make too much noise. Now stay back and let me do this." When they did not back off, she whirled around to face them, all pretense of timidity gone. "Look, I've mostly got the blackouts under control, but if something were to go wrong, I don't want to hurt you. Baird was right; I need to pass this test."

Both men were offended at the insinuation that they could ever mess up on something so basic, but they obeyed. They remained several meters behind her with the shovel Alec had stolen from the hotel.

Despite her resistance to the task, Blue was relieved to find the dirty man in front of the college, propped up against the brick of the building away from any windows. She didn't know where else he would have been otherwise, and Baird would have counted that as failing. The very idea of failure made her heart beat erratically. She could feel her brother with every cautious step that she took. She could practically hear him whispering for her to sneak, but it was of little necessity.

"I'm trying," the man complained into his phone. "Nah, all six girls are entertaining right now. Should be back by the hour mark."

Blue decided to wait for his call to end. Her window was small, but it would be made even tinier if the caller was cut off prematurely.

If there was a protocol for humanely killing someone, Blue did not know it. Her fingers twitched several times as she worked up the nerve to reach out and end his life. Each time she felt ready for the kill, the threat of the black coming back nearly choked her.

Finally, Blue closed her eyes and thought of Grettel. Sweet, innocent Grettel with this man's hand on her scared, tear-stained face. In a matter of days, Blue would be on another continent, leaving Grettel exposed to his evil desires.

Her hands steadied. She did not need to lose herself to end him; she would be there for every second of it to ensure that Grettel would be safe. Her blue eyes held their vision. She fended off the darkness that begged her to sink into it. There was enough black to the situation already.

"Fine. Leeza can replace her... No. I'm working on it. The girls want their cut up front this time, though. It's time for some fresh talent... Yeah, fine." He hung up the phone and pulled out a flask from his old leather jacket.

There would be no hesitation to speak of, no prolonged moment of indecision to report back to her brother. Silent as the night itself, Blue ran through the grass, out of the shadows, leaped onto his back, and did not falter as she twisted his neck with more force than necessary for the job. She heard and felt his neck snap beneath her capable fingers as the momentum forced them to the ground. The nameless man's only course of action was to open his eyes and mouth as his final breath exhaled onto her shoulder in a sigh that sounded mistakenly like contentment. His last moment came and went with all the gusto of a spinning toy top before it gave up its fight to stand erect. Like snow falling. Like every other death she'd caused, only this time, she was wholly there for it.

His chin jutted out in an unnatural angle, making his surprised and soulless eyes lock with hers, whether by coincidence or by choice, she was not sure.

The last glimpse of his life hit hard in Blue's gut and sunk like a rock through the ocean of her self-loathing. She could scarcely believe the hands that she saw were actually attached to her body. Unfathomable though it was, she was the bringer of doom, despite the rationale Baird would no doubt feed her wounded soul later.

In that moment, there was no Light, and no dark. Just death.

WITNESS TO A MOMENT OF WEAKNESS

"*I*f you use that butter knife, you'll probably end up accidentally piercing the eyeball and squishing it. I'm sure Baird wants his prize in one recognizable piece." Alec instructed her which nerves she was cutting through with his knife. In the cover of darkness, she allowed a grimace when she felt the eyeball pop out of the socket with a sickening slosh as it rolled into her grocery bag.

Sam drew no masculine merriment from this, and his weighty expression was not veiled. He left his cigarettes in the car, so as not to attract attention to the wooded area behind the university they'd dragged the body to. He desperately wished for a smoke to relieve the tension.

"What?" Alec turned to his friend. "You've seen and done worse. You're acting like this is all new to you."

"I've done my duty by the free world, but I've never had the displeasure of plucking out a person's eyeball," he pointed out.

"Well, you've killed a fair few protecting the throne," Alec pointed out. "Baird's right. You can't think of her like a normal girl, Sam."

Blood began to boil beneath Sam's controlled outward appearance. He noticed Blue's stiff shoulders and guessed that she hated these comments every bit as much as he did. "How about she pulls out your eyes next?" he suggested gravely. "Then maybe I can use them to show you that, in fact, she *is* a girl. And this is wrong."

"Wrong?" Alec guffawed. "When did that become a judgment instead of a challenge to you?"

Blue made quick work of the second eye, and eventually Sam could no longer deny the boyish fascination that made him watch her swift and clean movements.

Alec then explained to her in the pleasant tone of mere instruction the usefulness of a makeshift tourniquet when doing dark deeds as they were. He shook his head when she handed his sharp knife back to him. "No, you'll need that to saw through the bone in his hand."

"Maybe *you* do," she muttered. Alec and Sam watched with morbid interest as she picked up the victim's wrist and crushed the hard bones beneath the butts of her palms with what looked like a calm, meditative pose. "Now I'll take the knife."

"Did you just... Did you just crush the bones in his wrist?" Alec asked, astonished.

"Of course. How else am I supposed to do it? Easier this way." Blue held up the deflated and floppy arm and jiggled it for his benefit. Her eyes were focused and her motions precise as she sawed through the contorted skin. She refused to lose herself now that the end was so near. The veins and stubborn sinew were reluctant to give up Baird's trophy, but conceded defeat when she yanked the hand free of its death grip, making sure that the blood splattered away from the men.

"Tourniquet's got to be tighter than that next time," Alec instructed, shaking his head. "Do you need some help, kid? I don't think Baird would mind if we dug the grave. Give you a break."

"I don't need anything," Blue spat out a little too forcefully. "And I'm not your kid or anybody else's." Wiping the sweat from her forehead, she unceremoniously tossed the appendage into the grocery bag. "Didn't get to be a kid. Too busy training for this kinda thing."

Sam made good use of the shovel as he began to dig what would be an unmarked grave by morning. He was glad that he had opted for black pants and a button down shirt instead of the suit he'd worn when greeting the Emperor of the Americas.

Blue held out her hand to take over for him since this was her task, but he refused on principle. He would not be the only one who did nothing other than drive the getaway vehicle. This was her moment, and he wanted to be a part of however she decided to feel about it after it was over.

To ensure that it was deep enough, Sam dug uninterrupted for thirty minutes. When it was three meters deep, he motioned for Alec to roll the garbage bag-wrapped body down into it. Blue was faster, though, and she pushed the body in with eyes that were devoid of the spark he'd been drawn to. In that moment, Sam began to hate Baird.

Blue held out her hand for the shovel after Alec dumped in most of the man's personal affects, but Sam refused. "I should do it," she insisted.

"I'm not arguing with you over this," he said as if they bantered like this all the time. "You did the kill, we'll do the cleanup. Cleaning up won't teach you a thing you'll need to know when you're up against the predator. They'll want his ugly head on a pole and a big parade when he dies." He grunted when he hefted in a particularly stubborn clod of dirt and rock. "With twinkly lights and the token baton twirler. Everyone'll love it. They'll eat cotton candy and throw confetti in the air in your honor."

"Do you want me to take the shovel from you, or are you gonna give it to me?" she asked threateningly. "I have to finish the job. I… this is my friend's school. People actually learn things here and study and get degrees. It's not right that I ruined his university like this." She sighed. So desperately had she wanted to attend there and learn everything they had to teach her, but now her mere presence besmirched its higher purpose. She felt the need to rid her inbred savagery from the institution to somehow make recompense. "Even if it's not important to you, it is to me. I made the mess. I should clean it up. Baird would say the same thing."

This was clearly the wrong thing to say, but Sam barely got out, "I don't give a..." before she jerked the shovel from his tired hands with more force than he anticipated. Her small frame always threw him when she did things with more strength than her slight physique seemed to allot for.

Alec bit back a snide comment at Sam being robbed so easily.

"Alright, you pushy woman. Just save the grass patches for last. Those should be put back in place by hand, not with the shovel so it doesn't look so obvious that there's a dead body under it."

She worked quickly, her muscles not tiring as a normal Wayward's or even a strong Vemreaux's would. After she handed the shovel back to Sam so that she could kneel down and replace the sod, she eyed the rest of the dirt that did not fit due to the displaced volume of the man's body beneath her. "Spread it out over the bloody patches so the dirt's not all in one place," Alec instructed calmly, as if he was telling her how to turn on a washing machine. After he observed her handiwork, he gave his approval. "It'll do."

The mild acceptance instead of praise caused her shoulders to sink. She looked over the grass and dirt under her hands to see where she'd gone wrong. Smacking down a stubborn edge of unearthed grass, she found yet another small pool of blood that was too visible. She picked up a chunk of dirt and packed it over the offending area so that it was obscured from sight.

"It looks good," Sam assured her, offering his hand to help her up off the ground. She surprised him by taking his hand and using it to pull herself up next to him. Without thinking or recalling his personality, he wrapped his arms around her and pulled her to his chest.

Before she made contact, her forearm flew up to shield her breast while her other arm guarded her stomach from his body.

It was the strangest embrace he'd ever had, including when Liam would try his hand at different wrestling holds by sneaking up on him from behind. Sam hoped that she could allow a modicum of softness to surface, but the hug only caused her to stiffen against him, like she did not understand the concept of an embrace from a man.

Alec did not need to be asked to leave. He granted the two a moment of privacy as he picked up the discarded shovel and Baird's plastic bag. He ironed out a few more dirt patches and wiped off his knife on the grass before leaving them in the darkness.

Blue's rigid body frustrated Sam, but he feared that he would make her even more uncomfortable if he said anything overtly selfish. "Hey." He willed his voice to be gentle. "You can relax. It's over now." He rubbed long, deliberate circles into her back.

So quiet that he almost did not hear it, Blue whispered. "It's not over. It'll never be over! This is just the start of what I'll have to do."

Sam considered this a moment as he traced a line down her side, stretching from her shoulder to her hip. "How about for tonight we just pretend that it's over. You can be someone else if you want. Some gorgeous Femreaux whose biggest problem is how to fit ninety-seven dresses in a closet that only holds eighty-six."

Blue suffered her cheek to lean against his shoulder, and felt his chest swell at the contact. Despite her devastation, she managed a short chuckle. "Wow. That is a problem."

Sam smiled. "Then I'd come along with some brilliant solution."

"Like what?" she prodded, her defensive fists loosening their death grip on her body.

"I don't know. You could shove the dresses that don't fit into my closet or something," he suggested, mentally moving Blue into his house.

"That is brilliant," she conceded, her tone going flat. "Sam?" she choked out in a whisper. "It's not working!" The weight of her foul deed nearly pulled her into the freshly dug grave along with her victim. The blackout was safely at bay, but she sensed the guilt from this never would be. Dread coursed through her as she lifted one hand to the Vemreaux's chest and clutched onto the front of Sam's expensive shirt, using it to keep her body upright. Her face pressed between his shoulder and collarbone to muffle the single shudder that rocked through her and threatened to shake her apart. "This wasn't my choice!" she pleaded with nobody for absolution. "Why does it have to be me?" Her knees shook under the weight of the bleak world and nearly gave way beneath her.

Sam scrambled to keep his grip around her finally pliable body as she deflated in his arms. With all of his might, he struggled to hold the girl together as she came unglued. "I'm here," he promised.

"I just killed that guy, and I don't even know his name!" she confessed, the ugliness of her violence rang out in every word as torture. "I'm a murderer, Sam. You're holding a murderer! I've lost count of how many people I've killed. I'm a d-dangerous p-person!" She released his shirt to rake her nails down her arm, letting out a little of the tension she could not contain.

"You were following orders, Blue. I've killed people I didn't know, too."

"But he wasn't even armed! I killed someone who couldn't fight back. What kind of a person does that make me? Killing the predator's one thing, but this guy's just a regular person." She buried her face further into his chest, willing the tears to stay tucked away inside of her as she scraped at her own flesh. "I'm a monster."

Sam said nothing to this, for there were no words that would make her feelings or deeds disappear. Instead, he settled for holding her while she shook unnaturally in his arms. He reached out and grabbed her hand to stop its punishment of her arm. "Stop that. Don't hurt yourself."

When her tremors quieted, he brushed his fingers through her auburn hair, releasing her pheromones from the tangles. "Hey, this emptiness and regret that you're feeling is what makes you a person instead of a killer. If you weren't upset about all this, *that* would make you a monster." He could tell that she was thinking up an argument, so he distracted her by trilling his hand down her side once more.

"Why aren't you afraid of me?" Blue fought as best she could against the shiver that replaced her shaking. "I can see it in the guys every now and then. They get scared sometimes when they learn more about what I can do. Why're you being nice?"

"Shh," he whispered into her hair. "Just let me hold you until you're not so scared of yourself."

"That might take a while," she warned.

"Good." His arms around her loosened from their vice when he judged that she could stand without assistance. The loving embrace became soft with its gentility, coaxing both of them into an understood hiatus from the severe stress of the night.

After several minutes of breathing in and out together, Blue closed her eyes and nuzzled her cheek into his warmth. His hand covered her jaw and stroked the filthy flesh lovingly, bringing her further into the tender moment. "So tell me more about this Femreaux with the millions of dresses."

Sam smiled as he lifted his other hand to cover the one she still had bunched into his shirt. He pried her blood and dirt-stained fingers loose and entwined them through his. He heard her breath catch as he pressed her knuckle to his lips and gave it a small kiss. "I've heard," he began, moving on to the next knuckle as he spoke, "that the guy she's with is really good looking."

"Is that s-so?" she replied when she found her voice again. "I d-didn't know you noticed other men like that."

"Ha." Sam paused before kissing her third knuckle. "Man, I like you," he admitted. "This you. Not the one who's always hiding." His other hand found her waist and squeezed mischievously, bringing out a squirm from Blue.

"W-we should probably get going. Scene of the crime and all."

"Just let me finish kissing your fingers, you silly woman."

Miracle of all miracles, she let him.

THE HOTEL

Though there were no tears, Blue felt that she had purged entirely too much emotion. Enough weakness had been shown for one day, and hopefully, a lifetime. She finally pulled away from Sam.

Reluctantly he let her body part from his, though he would not relinquish his grasp on her hand. He did not want her to hide herself again. They walked hand in hand across the street over to the car where Alec was patiently waiting in the back seat.

"Can I drive you home so you can wash up?" Sam offered as he opened her car door for her.

Blue was confused at this repeat of chivalry, which was a new thing for her. She wondered erroneously as she stood outside the car if he thought she was too shaken to open the door for herself.

"No," she shook her head. "I don't want to wake them up. I have to be back in a couple hours. I'll just jog home to kill time." She grimaced at her poor choice of words.

Alec spoke up from the back seat. "You look like you just killed someone and buried the body, Blue. If you don't want to go home, you can come back to the hotel and clean yourself up there. It's no good for you to be running out in the open with blood on your face."

Her eyes widened while Sam smirked, ushering her into the passenger's seat. Though both of them were filthy, Sam reached out after he resumed his place at the wheel. He took hold of Blue's hand, kissing it again before placing it on the gear shift. "You ready for it?" he asked, his eyebrow cocked in her direction.

"I'm ready."

Alec called Baird from the back seat to assure him of her whereabouts, the courtesy of one guard to another. Alec felt the kindred spirit to Baird's watchful presence. "Park around back," Alec instructed. "Don't use the valet."

"You don't want the hotel staff seeing me without my hair done?" Sam joked. "I know, Alec. I'm not stupid."

Alec did not comment, but glanced at their clasped hands and sorely disagreed.

Blue kept her chin down, and for the first time Sam was glad that she kept her lovely features from view, given that they were covered in dirt and blood. When they reached the elevator, Blue entered hesitantly, having never been inside of one before. When Alec pushed the button to the penthouse suite, the elevator began to move. Blue's hands flung out to the nearest wall. She grabbed onto the flat silver railing that clung to the sides of the box.

Alec shot her a look like she was a camel instead of a girl, but Sam spoke first. "Hey, what's wrong?" Sam's hand lingered in the empty space between them.

She looked up at him as if he was crazy. "We're moving!"

"Yeah." He pointed to the button marked PH that was lit up. "We have to go up to get to the room." It began to dawn on him how different their worlds were. "You've never been on a lift before?"

When she shook her head and eased her knuckles off of the railing, he explained the mechanics of how elevators worked, remembering her earlier request to understand how a car functioned in order to feel safe in it. Admittedly, he did not know much about the inner workings of the elevator, but he did his best with Alec filling in the gaps he left. By the time they reached the suite, Blue did not feel quite as ruffled about the moving box as she initially did.

"Are you taking her home?" Alec asked Sam.

"Yeah, no problem." Sam slid his plastic key card into the door and held it open for Blue.

Alec arched an eyebrow at him as if to say, "I bet."

Though Sam had invited many a Femreaux in that very hotel room, it was the first time he felt nervous.

Blue gasped at the opulence. "Wow! This...this is amazing! You live here? I've never seen anything like it!" Alec left them for one of the bathrooms, but Blue was too overwhelmed by the decadence to think about washing up. She could not stop her astonishment. "Seriously? You have a kitchen in here? Do you even cook? Two couches? Plants? What is that, a bar?" She moved into the suite without asking permission. "Look at that table! You could fit, like, twelve people there! Whoa, that is the biggest TV I've ever seen. It's bigger than I am!"

Sam kept his comments confined to quiet laughter until she got it all out of her system. It was the most he had ever heard her speak, and the longest she kept her face unhidden.

"Sam, I can't believe this is all for you guys. I mean, what do you need all this space for?"

"Well, Liam snores, for one. And two, he's who rooms like this were built for. Royalty gets the best as a show of respect between countries. If we're going to be away from home, why not be comfortable?" He watched her observe the suite from top to bottom. "You want to shower? Give you a chance to see the wicked huge bathroom we've got."

"Sure. After Alec's done." She could hear the water running.

"Nah, my room's got its own bathroom. Come on." Without hesitation this time, he reached out and held her hand, leading her through his room to the bathroom as she looked around in wonder. "There's shampoo, soap and towels and stuff in there. Do you need anything else?" Looking down at her dirt-smudged tank top and shorts, he did the chivalrous thing and offered her fresh clothes in the form of his most fitted t-shirt from the dresser. "You can wear this if you want. It's clean. No signs a gorgeous guy like myself ever wore it." He grinned, trying to force the confidence that usually came natural to him.

Blue took the shirt from him and tried not to sully it too much by running her filthy hands over the smooth material unnecessarily. It was a light gray color and the fabric was unlike anything she'd ever felt. It was soft and stretchy while still being thicker than an average t-shirt. Not bothering to hide the indiscretion, she lifted the garment to her nose and inhaled. "Mmm. It smells like you."

"And what do I smell like?" Sam reached out to slip a lock of hair behind her ear.

"Sweet smoke and Vemreaux deodorant."

Sam frowned. "I really smell that bad?"

Blue's nose wrinkled, wondering what she said wrong. "You smell like you."

Sam regained his cockiness. "Well, you should feel privileged. I don't give out my clothes to just anybody." On occasion, if he was excessively spent from the night to care much, a Femreaux would come out of the bathroom in nothing but one of his shirts, smiling in a way that was supposed to be coy. Not one for sharing, he would insist she change back into her own clothes immediately. Now here he was, voluntarily giving up a shirt so Blue could be more comfortable.

"Thank you," Blue replied without looking up at him. The fact that they were alone in his room did not escape her notice. She did not want to push herself too far over the edge by looking up at the face she was growing increasingly fond of.

"Hey," Sam tucked his finger under her chin and lifted it so that he could get a better look at her face. "You okay? You went all quiet on me."

"Yes. I mean, n-no." Blue began breathing unsteadily at his close proximity. "I think I'm nervous, is all."

"Do I make you nervous?" he asked, a slight tease to his voice.

Blue gulped and glanced around the room, then threw him a withering look. "You know you do. You. The room. The blood. You. We're so different."

Sam did not hide his cocky smile, which pronounced her blush that much more. "Well, I can't do anything about me. I'm your ride home. The room's not so bad, though. The guys are right next door, just a phone call or a shout away. No need to be nervous about that. And we can take care of the blood." His eyebrow wrinkled. "I meant *you* can take care of the blood. In the shower. I'll wait out here."

"Okay." Blue nodded, pulling away from him. She turned and walked into the bathroom, cringing as she tripped on the way. She cursed the klutz he turned her into as she assessed the tools she needed to bathe herself. "Where's your bucket?" she inquired, noticing its absence in the tub. "I bet you could fit Grettel and Elle's bed in here with room to spare. This bathroom is huge!"

"Bucket?" Sam tried to imagine where a bucket would be needed in the fully functional bathroom. "I don't have one. There's one for ice out here. Did you want some ice?"

"No, I mean to catch the water in so I can, you know, wash myself." When this did nothing to bring revelation to him, Blue explained in more detail their bucket at the hut and her bucket in The Way.

Sam's confused expression grew grim as it transformed into pained disgust. He walked past her into the bathroom and turned on the shower, testing the water as it fell from the silver head. "We don't use a bucket, Blue. Water comes out up here and you stand under it to wash yourself. The water won't shut off on a timer. You just use it till you're finished."

Her eyes showed him her confusion as she watched all the droplets fall needlessly from above. "But isn't that wasteful? I mean, look at all that water, Sam. It's just going down the drain!" Her voice was strained as the beads of moisture added up.

"Trust me, it's fine. I can't believe they make you all take military showers." He shook his head as he moved past her out of the bathroom. "Man, this is a day of firsts for you. First time using a gear shift, first ride in a lift, first real shower. Any other firsts you want to try while we're here?" The moment the inappropriate words slipped out, his cocky smirk mutated to chagrin. "That was stupid. I shouldn't have said that." He ran his hand over his tired face in an attempt to start over. "How about after this, we slow it all down. We can do something G-rated, like hold hands and trade stories that have nothing to do with anything serious," he suggested as he yawned, covering his mouth. "Talk more about that Femreaux with ninety-seven dresses."

Blue nodded, not completely sure what all of his odd references were. Her main focus was still on all the water that was being wasted. It was not the only thing Baird would disapprove of.

SAM SHUT THE DOOR TO GIVE HER PRIVACY AND LEANED AGAINST IT with his head in his hands. The verbal vomit that flowed in the unassuming girl's presence was disgraceful. He was the loquacious one of the four. There was not a pick-up line he did not know, or a woman he had ever misspoken so many times around.

Over and over he berated himself for turning soft so fast. Never had he let a girl borrow an article of clothing from him. Even Julia or Suzette weren't granted that privilege, sisters as they were to him. When he'd been semi-serious with Celilia, there had been precious few tender moments or letting her into more than just his bedroom. The kicker was that Blue had not even asked for it; he just volunteered himself time after time with no hope of ever bedding her.

He pushed himself off of the door and walked over to the mirror hanging above the dresser to examine who he hoped he still was in the glass. Though his face was smudged with dirt, it was still him. His study revealed the cocky sarcasm that usually pulled his features down was not as prominent. He opened the dresser drawer and pulled out fresh clothes for him to change into after his shower. He sniffed them, unhappily noting that they did have a faint odor of the changed Vemreaux cigarettes, though he had not smoked in at least an hour.

Sam's phone rang, drawing his attention from the mirror. "Go back to sleep, Liam."

The prince's voice sounded tired on the other line. "Are you alone with Blue in there?"

"She's rinsing off right now. We couldn't send her home with blood and dirt all over her."

The prince's words were squeezed out in between yawns and stretches. "Do you...need a...chaperone? Or can you...manage to avoid making her brother crazy...this once?"

"Shut up, Liam. I'm out here while she's in the shower, aren't I?" Sam pointed out to defend his innocence. "Besides, I don't care what Baird thinks of me."

The prince sounded more awake now. "Well, you should. If he reneges on this whole thing, we can't get her over to the island. So keep your hands to yourself for once in your life."

Sam glanced at the bathroom door to ensure it was safely shut. "Would you all stop worrying? I'm just letting her clean up like Alec wanted. Then I'll take her home if she needs a ride. Give me a little credit. I do have *some* self-control."

"I'm just saying. Be careful."

"Quit 'just saying' and go back to sleep," Sam grumbled before hanging up on his friend.

IN THE PRIVACY OF THE BATHROOM, THE WATER FROM THE SHOWER FELL so fast that Blue had to remind herself that it was apparently okay it was mostly going to waste. She surely did not need that much to get herself clean, but as there was no bucket, she decided to be as quick as she could.

The shampoo was real. It wasn't Brand A, either. The label bragged of an herbal goodness, and when she squeezed some into her hand, the pungent scent matched the description on the bottle with an artificially sweet stench that masked itself as natural. Though the pampering felt amazing after the horrible thing she'd just done outside the college, she was still very aware of the water that was being thrown down the drain with every moment that she dallied.

When she finished scrubbing the blood and dirt from every part of her body, she quickly turned off the water and stepped out, trying to locate a used towel so she wouldn't dirty a fresh one. It seemed, however, that Sam did not have any wet or crumpled ones. They all were rolled tightly and resting neatly on a shelf. Reluctant to use all the nice things in his bathroom before he'd even had the chance to shower, she pulled one down and unrolled it. Though it was prickly as it swept over her skin, it was the first truly dry and clean towel she'd had since she'd left The Way. Making good use of the luxury, she wrapped it around her hair to sop up as much liquid as possible while she dressed.

It did not feel great to pull on the same dirty shorts and underwear, but when Sam's shirt slid over her head and down her torso, she felt like a new woman. She inhaled with her nose bunched in the supple material. Her eyes rolled involuntarily as she smelled his scent beneath the smoke that was laced through the soft strands.

Deciding that this indulgence was too much, she unwrapped her hair from its towel, lifted Sam's comb up off of the counter and dragged it through her snarls. When she replaced it, she realized that everything on the counter was on a right angle to the gargantuan mirror she was desperately trying to avoid looking up at. She wondered if he preferred it this way or if a maid had come and put them straight for him. She made sure that everything was perpendicular and perfectly clean when she left.

Blue emerged from the bathroom quicker than Sam expected. Sam was used to Femreaux washing up for half an hour once they discovered the built-in hair dryer in the wall. He did not trust his tongue to say anything as he traded places with Blue so that he could scrub up from the night's deed as well. She looked too good with wet hair. She looked too natural and comfortable in his clothes. Her lower lip was too inviting for his to maintain a respectable distance if they were alone in the same room for too long.

Yet, here was Blue, wearing the shirt he'd handed over, and she was modest enough to wear her dirty shorts underneath. He wondered if walking around in just a t-shirt would even occur to such a pure soul. Her sincere shyness was the bait to the fishes that swam low in his belly at the sight of her fully clothed form in his hotel room.

Ten minutes later, when Sam rejoined her in the room in fresh clothes and a clean body, he found her standing in the exact spot he'd left her. "Did you move at all while I was in there?"

"No. Of course not. This isn't my room, Sam. I'm not gonna invade your personal space."

"I invited you in, you know. You don't have to be perfect around me."

Blue shrugged, but offered no other response as he flopped on the enormous bed.

"You still got a couple hours before the sun comes up. Make yourself at home." He patted the mattress, relieved when she complied and sat daintily on the edge of the bed. "You hungry?"

Blue shook her head. "You're tired," she commented, observing his yawn. "Why don't you go to sleep? I can just run home."

He frowned. "You want to leave?"

She cracked a smile. "No, but I'm sure you want me to. I'm not the one who needs rest."

"I'm fine." He sat up to prove to them both that he was up for anything. "Besides, I don't want you running home. Who knows what kind of hooligans are out at this hour, just waiting for a helpless girl like you to run by."

"At least you've still got your sense of humor when you're exhausted."

"Naked without it." He sighed as he glanced at the clock. "How about a little TV? I didn't see one at your house. And if I just so happen to close my eyes for a few minutes, so be it. I won't fall asleep. My eyes are just a little tired."

Blue laughed at his yawn. "Yeah, okay."

Sam lay down and grabbed the remote on the nightstand, turning on the news for her. Even as his head rested on his pillow, and his body groaned for slumber, Sam was nervous. He only ever allowed himself to fall asleep next to Celilia once, and he scared her so bad that she never slept in his bed again. Of all the things he wanted to do with Blue, scaring her off was not one of them. "Hey." Sam lifted his hand to touch her back. "Lay down for a minute."

Blue swallowed. "Like, n-next to you? In the bed?"

"I won't try anything. Honest. I just like you near me. Got my taste of it tonight, and I'm not ready to give it up."

Sam relaxed muscles he did not realize were tensed with anticipation when she finally consented and laid down atop his outstretched arm, her head on the pillow next to him. He drew her to him slowly, so she would have plenty of time to pull away if she wanted.

Blue wanted so many things in that moment, but settled for cuddling into his side and tucking her head into the crook of his neck. She had never been in a bed with a man before, and was hyper aware of every body part that might be too intrusive. The only person she ever shared a mattress with was Elle, who would sneak onto her cot in The Way on the nights Blue volunteered to take a beating for her friend. Even though Blue was the one who had been bloodied, Elle would softly weep for Blue's marks. In the cover of darkness, Blue would permit her friend to hold and comfort her. Baird would not have approved of the obvious coddling, but some nights, Elle's sisterly love was the only thing that kept Blue from losing herself completely.

Being next to Sam was exciting...and dangerous. Blue fought the urge to look over her shoulder to make sure Baird was not somehow towering over them, waiting for his moment to make Sam disappear. After much debate, Blue placed her hand on Sam's chest.

"Mm...perfect." Sam breathed into her hair. "Nope. Still not close enough." His hand reached over, guiding her knee to rest over his thigh, tangling their legs together. Then he lifted her palm and pressed it to his lips, giving her a kiss she could hold onto. When his lips dragged to the sensitive spot on the inside of her wrist, he smirked at her gasp. "Don't let me fall asleep, alright? You wished me 'sweet dreams' last time, but it didn't work."

Blue's entire arm tingled as she rested it on his chest. "Sweet dreams, Sam," she whispered into his neck.

"Don't let me fall asleep, Blue. I mean it." Her presence relaxed and excited him simultaneously. The early hour coerced his eyes to close and his breath to steady as he gave in to the tranquility she provided.

And for once, Sam slept without his demons. They were chased away by the Light.

For three hours, Blue scarcely moved, distracted only by the quiet babble coming from the TV. Every detail of Sam was catalogued and relished so that the memory would never have a chance at leaving her. His chest moved up and down calmly. In slumber, his sarcasm, borderline OCD and anger were gone. His face was serene, unassuming and utterly stunning in rest.

When the clock would allow her to prolong the inevitable no longer, she breathed his name into the crook of his neck. "Sam. I think it's time to wake up."

He frowned, but did not open his eyes.

"Sam. I've got to get home for my shift."

"*Tranquillo, dolce ragazza,*" he mumbled, still mostly asleep. "Not yet." His arm tightened around her as he rolled on top of her petite body, pressing his full weight into her.

"Huh?" She laughed as she rolled Sam onto his back again, amazed how open she had become around him, and how well their bodies fit together. "Yes, yet. I'll just run, though. You need your rest."

Sam grumbled unintelligibly, but the moment her hand left his chest, he felt the absence, and knew he would go wherever it went. "No. I'll drive you. Just give me a minute." He turned onto his side, wrapping her waist in his arms as she sat up, so she would not get far. "Not yet."

Blue laughed. "You're not going to make this easy, are you? Just go back to sleep, Sam. It's fine. I promise. I'm a lot faster than you know."

"Sun's up," he pointed out as his eyes opened reluctantly. "People aren't supposed to see you run as fast as you can."

"Fair point. I'll wake up Alec, then. Seriously. You look exhausted."

"You look like you need to be exhausted." He frowned, not sure if there was innuendo in his statement. "I'll take you."

Blue broke from his tired grip and stood to find her socks and shoes.

"Alright, I'm awake," he declared, sitting upright.

His rumpled t-shirt and haphazard hair made her laugh again, and the sound softened his morning mood. "Something funny, little Wayward?" He picked up his pillow and tossed it at her.

"Not sure you want to give me a weapon when you're this out of it," she teased, flipping the pillow casually. Blue covered her smiling mouth when he scowled at her. "You. You're funny. You sleep so peacefully, but you wake up so angry."

"Yeah, well..." He tried to think up something clever, but came up empty. He stopped his sarcasm and looked up at her in shock. "I slept peacefully?"

Catching the astonishment in his voice, Blue observed his surprise. "Barely moved. You smile in your sleep, too. What were you dreaming about?"

"I don't remember," he admitted, scratching his head as he processed. "Really?"

"Why is that so strange?"

"I...usually I..." Sam looked up at Blue in confusion, the angel of deliverance he expected to scare off by morning. "That's...unexpected. Didn't I say not to let me fall asleep?" he asked both of them rudely. Then he stood without further explanation and went into the bathroom while Blue put her shoes on in shame. Even when he came back out, he did not speak, but remained deep in thought. It wasn't until he had his jacket, wallet, keys and some of his bearings that he opened his mouth at all. "You ready to go home yet?" His tone was clipped, all traces of levity gone.

Blue nodded.

"You can talk, you know," he snapped maliciously. His tone slashed at the glow she'd acquired from lying in his arms. His mood shifted for a reason she could not pinpoint, but she'd been around Baird enough to know that the problem was usually her, and that she should quietly wait out the storm before standing up in the middle of it. She took her penance with grace, and tilted her chin to the floor in an effort to be invisible. She followed behind him out the door, glancing up only enough to see his shoes to know where she should go.

This irritated Sam. "You don't have to walk behind me, you know. It's creeping me out that I can't even hear you walking. Here." He slowed down so that he was next to her. "Just be next to me. Make me feel like a beautiful woman like yourself would want to walk down a hall with me." He tried to regroup with humor, but waking up with a woman in his bed was a new experience. Not having had a night terror was downright unsettling.

When her pace began to fall even slower, he sighed in irritation. "It makes me nervous to have anyone, except maybe Alec, behind me. He actually makes a little noise, so I don't feel like I'm being stalked."

"I'm sorry." She looked disgusted with herself, the splendor of their intimate evening shattering around her. She felt like a fool. "I... you're m-mad at me."

Sam internally berated his temper and sighed. "No, *I'm* sorry. I'm not mad. I'm just not...I'm not mad."

As they strolled together down the hallway, Blue began to drift behind him once more. Sam told himself that he simply *had* to link his fingers through hers, so that she'd keep pace with him. He ignored the silent cheers inside when his lonely hand got its wish. The brightness was short-lived, however, when he realized she would not look up at him anymore.

DIFFERENT WORLDS

"Yeah, yeah. I'm smoking," Sam grumbled obstinately as he pulled out a cigarette. "I smoke in the morning and pretty much all day long, and I'm fine with it."

Blue had not said a word, but crawled further and further into her shell as he lashed out.

"My clothes smell like smoke, too, apparently, and I bloody love it."

The plastic bag had been stowed under the front passenger's seat for safe keeping, but Blue still checked that it was there when she ghosted past the door that Sam opened for her. She kept her face from him and tried as hard as she could not to anger him further.

"Why don't you ever look at people?" His tone had too much edge to it. Sam stood, leaning on the open passenger's side door.

Blue did not answer, nor did she move to show him her face. She shrunk down into her seat, head bowed and shoulders hunched to ward off his aggression. Her voice was so small; he had to close his mouth to hear it. "I'm sorry."

Sam paused, and then shook his head as his hands cast out in frustration. "Why are you apologizing?"

"Because you gave me a direct order, and I disobeyed. You told me not to let you fall asleep, and I did it anyway. I got confused. The Vemreaux Supervisors never put us in charge of that kind of thing back in The Way. Forgot that you're Vemreaux, and you never disobey a Vemreaux Supervisor. So, I'm sorry."

Sam paled. Once words finally came to him, his tone was gentler. "Blue, I'm not your supervisor. You don't have to obey me."

"Yes, I do. You're throwing a fit right now because I didn't."

"Throwing a fit, eh? Well, I guess that's true. But you don't have to obey me. We're equals, here. I was just being a jerk for no good reason. You should cuss me out, and then call me a dick for being mean to you."

"Okay."

"Okay? We're back to that? That's all you have to say? Why don't you ever fight back? Where's the girl what threw me against the wall a couple days ago?"

She shrugged. "Fine. You're a dick, then."

"Good. Now tell me you think smoking is bad, and I should stop."

"But I don't know anything about smoking. Never saw it until I got out of The Way."

"Well, it's a bad habit, and you should throw a fit about it."

"I'm not going to throw a fit." Blue sighed. "You losing your temper's just hurtful and petty. When I lose mine, it's dangerous. When you hurt people, they just want to die. When I do it, they could actually die." She shook her head, still not looking anywhere near him. "If you don't want to smoke, then don't. I'm not here to boss you around or make you mad at me. I'm not your supervisor. I'm just trying to get home, which I already told you, I don't need you for."

The morning air worked its magic of finally smacking sense into him. He closed his eyes. "Ah, Blue. I'm sorry."

"Okay."

He cringed, but fought to control his temper. "I am. It's not you. You didn't do anything wrong."

"Okay."

Seeing her hide herself from him and knowing that this time, he deserved it brought about the rare emotion of humility in him.

Instead of shutting her door, he knelt down on the pavement and placed his hand on hers. "Blue, I'm sorry. I'm a jerk, and I'm sorry. I'm not a morning person, and well, I don't usually let girls stay the night in my bed. Kinda threw me."

She held her face far from him to keep her hurt feelings private. "I didn't ask to stay the night, Sam. I told you I could run home. If you didn't want me to be there, you should've let me go. I don't understand your Vemreaux politics, so you shouldn't mess with my head like that. Just say what you mean. I didn't...I didn't ask you for anything."

"I know that. I'm not upset that you stayed. I'm really glad you did. I..." He ran his hands through his dark chocolate-colored hair in frustration and humiliation. "And now I've been a jerk to you, so I have to tell you why." He made a frustrated noise, and then exhaled, steadying himself. "You said I slept peacefully. I don't do that. I have night terrors and I wake the guys up screaming every night. That's why I get my own room. Peaceful sleep? I can't remember the last time that happened."

"I don't know what night terrors are, Sam. I don't know why smoking's bad. I don't understand elevators, and until last night, I *never* laid down in a bed with a guy. Never. So stop being mean to me. This is new to me, too."

"Blue, I'm so sorry. Please look at me."

"No. Not until you're worth looking at."

"Ouch. I deserved that."

"More than that. You're just lucky I have more control than you do."

"I guess you're right." Sam shook his head, unsure how to clean up the mess he made. "Have you ever had a nightmare?"

She shrugged. "I don't remember. Haven't slept since I was a kid."

"Well, mine are like bad dreams that you can't get out of. Like, I can feel everything happening to me in mine. I can taste it. Smell it. Like when you first bathe in the Fountain of Youth and everything's heightened, or like you're on acid." He shook his head. "I'm not explaining this very well."

Blue moved her head to look down at her lap instead of far away from him. "So you have bad dreams usually? And you scream, so you don't let people see you sleep. Is that it?"

"Yeah. Kinda embarrassing."

"Why is that embarrassing?"

"Do you want people to watch you cry for help or suffer through things that... Would you want anyone to see you like that?"

"I guess not. But why are you upset now? You didn't do any of that last night. I was there the whole time."

"That's just it. I scared off the only girl I let sleep next to me a couple years ago. She did it once, then never again. I was expecting you to be gone, too. I was *not* expecting to sleep like a normal person and wake up still holding you."

"Did you want me to be gone?"

"No. But if you were going to leave, I'd rather you do it now rather than later, when I get even more attached. Give you a really good reason, like me being partially insane when I'm passed out."

"Is that supposed to be rational? Because I don't get it."

"Do you get that I'm sorry, and I acted like an idiot?"

"The idiot part, sure." Blue sighed at the complications in their non-relationship. She was beginning to understand why Baird avoided being in one. "Look, if you want to smoke, do it. If you don't, then stop. If you don't want me to be next to you, then just say so. I was so...so happy last night, even after everything I did. Then you just took it away because...what? Because nothing bad happened? I don't understand Vemreaux."

Sam cocked his head to the side and sized her up. "I guess we're pretty different."

Blue hissed humorlessly. "You have no idea."

He looked her over, then stood, shutting her door and moving around to the driver's side. He sat down next to her, started the car, and reached for her hand. He took her flinch in stride, knowing he deserved it. He placed her hand on the gear shift and spoke to her with determination to make things right. "Okay. What's it like in The Way?" When she looked up at him and quirked her eyebrow, Sam relaxed a little and offered a small smile. "What? I don't know any more about Waywards than you do about Vemreaux. I'm not allowed to try to figure you out? You do it to me all the time."

"I do *not* understand you," she admitted.

"That's my whole point," he agreed, his accent thickening. "If this is going to work, we should probably try to understand a little more about each other, yeah?"

"Um, okay."

"First gear," he instructed, and she obeyed. She did it so fluidly now that it was almost like he was doing it himself. There was no jarring or trying to fiddle with the proper gear to get it where it should be. She was a quick learner. Still, he deemed it necessary that his hand should rest on hers. "Second. Now tell me all about The Way."

"Um, well, it's a lot of the same. We all wear the same clothes, do the same rotation of chores for the most part. We each had a cot on bunks for sleeping. I belonged to The Way West, which mostly did paper pressing, fertilizer, housing bricks, and of course, S-bricks. Baird let me be out in the yard and do fertilizer for a couple years, did a little time in housing bricks, but then he had me go to the Paper Unit with the rest of the girls."

Sam was beginning to despise the sound of the older brother's name. "Which one did you like best?"

"Oh, fertilizer. No contest," she admitted. It felt strange to be asked her opinion, but as soon as he did, she found she had one that no one knew about. "Paper's pretty boring." She lowered her voice, even though no one was in danger of eavesdropping. "Have to pretend to not be able to lift really light weights all morning long. Not so fun. With fertilizer, you at least get to shovel the scratch and use the fun tools. It's a good workout if no one's watching."

"Sounds like you had to hide yourself a lot there." He cleared his throat. "Third."

"I have to do that everywhere." Blue shrugged. "Imagine being Grettel who can barely lift one of the weights. Baird was right to put me on paper. Grettel woulda had to eat a lot of scratch if I wasn't her partner."

"Eat scratch?" Sam wrinkled his nose. "Is that Wayward slang for something?"

"No. If we drop the weights and they break, we have to clean them up. If there's any shards left, we have to eat them. The weights are made out of the parts of scratch that are leftover after making the S-bricks. Like how the housing bricks are made. Same thing, different shape is all."

Sam turned his head so that she would not see him gagging. "I knew you worked in manure, but I thought The Way was mostly a school."

"What's manure?"

"Fourth gear. Manure's another word for scratch, Blue. It isn't used all that often anymore, though. Doesn't have the same ring as 'made from scratch'."

"Oh, well there's some school that's required, but after that's finished, you could sign up for more classes or you could learn a trade. But scratch duties always come first."

"What kind of trade do the Waywards aspire to?" Sam made every effort to be conversational, though he could not stop his stomach from lurching as he pictured the girl with cow pies smeared on her lovely face. Cow pie burger. Cow pie...pie? He shuddered.

"You know, normal stuff. We sewed clothes, assembled furniture, made socks and soaps and stuff like that. We cleaned a lot. You have to. With that much scratch around, you can't allow even a little dirt. Flies flock to any trace of it. I took all the school they offered for my age group, even though Baird said it was probably a waste of time."

Sam hissed. "So you don't always do everything your brother says?"

Suddenly her hand felt wrong under his, so she removed it, sliding it out from under him so that his rested on the shifter all by its lonesome. "No, I don't. But I do what he says when he's right. I may not always want to hear the truth, but he tells it to me. He's got a good view of the big picture, and I sometimes don't." She fiddled with the seatbelt across her chest, but then remembered that she was making her nervousness obvious, so she folded her fingers in her lap instead. "It's good that he's the way he is. If he wasn't, then I wouldn't be going to the island, and all those Vemreaux would keep disappearing. I'd be selfish and do what I wanted instead, which wouldn't be right." She sighed. "Baird's not the easiest to get along with, but he does what needs to be done, even when it's hard."

Sam had to go against everything in his nature to speak softly and hold his tongue from spouting off the first sarcastic retort that popped into his brain. "What do *you* want?"

Her response was quick, robotic and rehearsed. "I want to end the tyranny."

Sam's frustration was harder to harness than he would have thought. He blamed it on the early hour and loss of contact. "That's rubbish, and you know it. If you weren't the Light, what would you want?"

Blue blinked, showing him that the question made no sense to her. She mulled it over in her head as if for the first time, kicking around different possibilities that all seemed as unlikely as the next. "I want to be here," she finally replied just when he thought she wasn't going to answer him.

"Here in the Americas or here in the car?" he asked with too much hope.

"Both." Her thumbs twiddled in her lap as she spoke nervously.

"It's a good car," he commented, evading the almost compliment he'd tricked her into giving him. "What else do you want?"

"I want my brother to be happy. Every now and then I see him smile, and it's nice. I make him so miserable." She shook her head at her shortcomings. "I wish he could be happy when I'm around instead of always worrying that I won't be ready when it's time for me to go." She looked forlornly out the window at the trees rushing by. "He used to joke around with our little brother, Griffin, and it always made me a little jealous. I mean, I can be fun, too, if he'd let me. We'll have, like, a minute of fun, and then he'll come down hard. He's like you. Being too nice makes him mean. Thinks I won't be able to leave him, but I will. I want him to enjoy himself someday. He can't do that with me in his life."

"I am *nothing* like Baird. And I told you, I just got thrown for a minute this morning, is all. I'm back, though. For better or worse." He sighed. "You were talking about Baird."

"Elle makes him happy when they're not fighting. Well, sort of happy. Whatever Baird's version of that is, I guess. I want him to be nicer around her. She deserves at least that. He's the only thing she wants, other than to keep us all safe."

Blue thought further when Sam made no attempt to interject. "I want Grettel to stop being so afraid of everyone. I want her to be able to look a Vemreaux in the face and smile like Elle can. She's seen me black out a few times in The Way, and it scared her. She denies it, but sometimes I can tell that I still scare her." She stopped speaking then, for the next words that wanted to come out of her carried a hitch in her voice with them, which she would not tolerate.

"Blue, what do you want for *you*? Not your friends or your brother. For you," Sam clarified.

"All the rest of that *is* what I want for me, Sam. If they're happy, I'm happy. When I leave, they can all try to have a normal life without worrying about me being found out. Elle won't have to put up the show so no one notices me. Grettel won't have to be so afraid that she'll slip up and say something about me to the wrong person." She concentrated on her short fingernails as she veered closer to honesty than she usually cared to venture. "Baird'll be relieved when I'm gone." Though she'd thought the words before, saying them out loud in the privacy of the car was a declaration she had been trying hard to deny the truth of. Immediately she was engulfed by sadness that punched her in the gut and pushed her spirit down past the floor with the passing of the words through her lips. "Do you think we could talk about something else? If this is what it feels like to talk about myself, I don't like it."

Sam mulled over her words, though she still had not answered the question to his liking. "Baird mentioned earlier that you hadn't had a boyfriend in The Way. Is that true?"

An unexpected short laugh lightened her demeanor. "Yeah, that's true. I doubt anyone even knew I was there half the time. Most of my life's been spent trying to be invisible, not that anyone would've looked anyway. I had one guy friend who was only around because he was Griffin's best friend, and you know, *had* to be around me. Marxus, too, I guess. But he only checked in on me occasionally because Baird asked him to after he got bought. The only other man I really talked to was one of the professors who was nice to everyone. Liam's Uncle Jack. Baird made sure that I hid my face as much as I could because of my eyes."

"What do you mean 'no one would've looked anyway'?" Sam shook his head at her berating tone.

She kept her face fixed away from him and went back to staring out the window. "I don't look like Elle. I'm not deluded or anything. I know what I look like, Sam."

Frustration flared up in the man, forcing only words of ire into his brain. Sam took a deep breath. He reached back over the console and picked up her hand, not to place it on the gear shift, but to run his fingers along her palm once again so he could see her spine straighten.

Sam turned to her and took in the beauty she could not see. "I seriously doubt that, Blue."

3 6

PEACE DAY

Age of Peace Law 3, Subset 2a
No musical instruments may be played in public.

Age of Peace Law 3, Subset 2c
Privately owned establishments may play prerecorded music, but televised
events must play only the preferred, government-approved prerecorded
music.

The next few days were the last Blue would spend with her makeshift family in the confines of the hut and the diner, yet they seemed to blur by. It was Tuesday, and her last day of work in the diner. She would leave on Thursday.

The paperwork that had taken months when Baird tried to buy her from The Way took no time at all for Prince Liam and all of his connections. Another waiter was already picked out and would be working at the diner by the end of the month to replace Blue. Baird still would not say who, but by his evasion, Blue had a guess which Wayward it would be.

"Is it Androo?" she asked as she helped her brother put new bottles of absinthe behind the bar. "Please don't say it's Marxus."

"How will it matter to you at all? You'll be gone."

"It would be a mistake only you would make to buy Androo. Don't think I've forgotten the three fights you got into in The Way with him. I don't care if he's the next biggest Wayward. It's a bad move." She wiped off her table. "And Marxus? Well, he needs to be in The Way. The whole structure you two set up would fall apart without one of you there. He's the one they're all afraid of. He's the one keeping the peace in there. Keeps them in check. Who knows who'll rise to power if you take him out of there. Could undo everything you two worked for."

"Who I pick is none of your business." He still would not confirm her theory.

"Baird?" Her lowered voice caused his head to raise. "When I was out on your assignment, after I was done, the guys wanted to rest, so I watched some television while they slept." She conveniently left out the part where she laid in Sam's arms. Her eyes darted around the diner to reconfirm that they were alone. "Back in The Way they let us watch the Peace Day celebration on TV every year, and the king would make some big speech at the end, right? You know how we always kinda suspected something was off about King Sinclair?"

Baird nodded, moving closer to her so the conversation could remain quiet. "I saw a short report with him talking about the island. Baird, I figured out one of his tells."

Baird stopped working and sat down at the table she was cleaning, and then motioned for her to do the same. "Tell me everything."

"He does this thing when he's talking about someone or something that he's trying to distance himself from. He pauses right before saying their name. He did it three times in the news announcement. I'm sure of it."

"Who's he trying to pretend he doesn't know?"

"Not just doesn't know, but like, he wants to make sure he's separate from that person. It was Emperor Boniface, then the king's own son, Everest Sinclair, and the A-blood island. He either is close to them and doesn't want the world to know about it, or he wants it clear he isn't in the loop with whatever's going on with them, which means he knows more than he's letting on."

Baird mulled over this new information. "Good to know. Huh. I'd be careful around Liam's dad, then. Either he's doing something he shouldn't that the king knows about, but it hasn't been made public yet, or the king wants us to believe there's a united world power, but there really isn't."

"That's where I landed with that, too."

"Watch yourself when you go out there. He can't know about you if he's involved in something shady, or if the king's gunning for him."

"You realize I could get in a lot of trouble for saying all this, right?"

"Yeah. So don't mention it to the guys."

"Okay."

"Just keep it to yourself and maintain your distance. The emperor comes into a room, you leave it."

"Okay."

"Under the radar, Blue."

"Okay."

PEACE DAY ARRIVED THE FOLLOWING MORNING, BUT THE FOUR WERE more relieved and excited that the diner would be closed for the entirety of the day. So rare was it to work a five-day week that they did not know what to do with themselves.

Grettel scrubbed the hut from floor to ceiling while Elle thoroughly washed every bit of fabric they owned, which wasn't much. Baird worked on a leak he hadn't had the time to fix in the bathroom, borrowing tools from the diner. Blue kept herself busy assisting Baird by bending things into place for him to fix that were almost beyond use at their current angle. She also lifted the major appliances so Grettel could clean under them.

By noon, Elle hit her limit. "I can hear the music from in here, Baird. There's nothing more for us to do inside. Could we *please* go to Capital City?"

"Oh, fine." Baird consented with a sigh, as if the notion of enjoying their day off was wasteful.

They ventured out to Capital City on foot toward the already crowded streets. No cars drove on Main Street, for there were simply too many people. A long route that went through several large towns was blocked off so that everyone who wanted to could join the largest celebration in the Americas. The entire parade would travel on for most of the day, ending very far south by nightfall. The most energy was at Capital City, where the parade began.

All the Vemreaux were decked out in their partying best. The brightly colored clothes were almost blinding to look at in such a wide smattering. People were hugging, dancing, kissing and shouting joyfully, as if they were at the first Peace Day that ever was. If there had been inhibitions before, there were next to none now.

Blue compared this heightened celebration to the old TV set and half-day off from scratch duties that the Waywards received. She thought of Griffin and George reveling in their few extra hours of freedom. Guilt flooded through her when she realized that her baby brother's greatest perception of glee was Peace Day in The Way. When compared with the unburdened and under-clad shoulders of the Vemreaux surrounding her, she wondered how those who knew of both worlds could stomach such a great divide.

Grettel let out an eager squeal. "It's the jugglers!"

"You wanna go see them up close?" Baird offered. "I could run up ahead with you so you can get a better look."

The little hesitation that came to her face was only from the idea of being mixed in so thoroughly with the Vemreaux. "Um, okay."

"Don't be scared, short stack. I'm stronger than all those

Vemreaux put together," Baird bragged, hoping to make the girl smile.

His phone rang, and Baird's face fell when he saw the number. "Yeah?" he barked with no attempt at respect or politeness. It was Sam informing him of their whereabouts. Baird told him where they were before ending the call and glowering at Blue as if it was all her fault he had to deal with the man he was beginning to despise the sight, and now the sound of.

He was about to open his mouth and crush Grettel's elation with more talk of duty, but Elle placed her hand on his shoulder and spun him around. "We'll be right here," she assured him. "Now get going before you say something you'll regret."

Baird looked very much as if he'd like to argue, but thought better of it when he noticed that Grettel had stopped bouncing with delight. It was their one day to let loose together and enjoy each other. He decided that if he couldn't be civil, he would step back and allow them their fun, at the very least. "Come on, shorty." Baird watched as her disappearing smile bloomed on her youthful lips once more. Grettel was so filled with excitement that she jumped a little before running away with Baird at her side.

Though Blue knew it would be her only Peace Day celebration out in the real world, she was content to watch it from afar. Elle wrapped her arm around her friend's waist.

"You're my best friend, you know." Elle cut right through all the small talk and took advantage of their precious little time alone.

"You're a better friend than I deserve," Blue echoed, being careful not to touch her hand to the sore spot on Elle's hip. Instead, her wrist rested on Elle's back in a half hug. "After I'm gone, I want you to relax. You don't have to train anymore, you know. You can just be a waitress who's in love with the bartender."

Elle smiled sadly. "He won't be the same after you're gone." She looked off in the distance where Baird and Grettel disappeared into the crowd.

"Good. Maybe he'll be happier and nicer. You know, easier for you two to live with." The words stung Blue, but she did not hold them back.

"Yeah, right. You have no idea what it was like with you in The Way and us out here." Elle recalled the memories with a sour expression. "It'll be just like that. All he did was worry about you and make plans for you. He's not himself without you to work with."

"You mean work *on*. There's a difference."

Elle ignored this. "You two speak the same weird language that none of us really gets."

"Elle," Blue began, "do you remember that time Grent and those guys cornered us in the furnace room?"

She felt Elle stiffen as she nodded in response.

"Did you...were you afraid that I would hurt you?"

Elle shook her head absolutely. "Not for a second. I was afraid that you would be found out and they'd take you away from us. I know you'd never turn on me, even if you aren't sure." She eyed her friend. "Don't let Baird get in your head like that. You know who you are." She squeezed Blue's hip affectionately to pull them both out of the sadness that loomed. "So you'll have some time in Europe before you fly over to the island?" Mischief danced in her tone.

"I suppose. Don't know how much, though." The massive throngs of partiers accumulated yet more bodies as the girls talked and observed from the outside. Thousands of Vemreaux cheered and danced in the streets, giving them plenty to watch. Elle lost count of the visible underwear she so loved to add up.

"Please tell me that you'll master the art of flirting with Sam before you go. It pains me to see him watch you with those puppy eyes and you shying away like you're Grettel or something."

Blue shook her head. Ever since their night out when she wore Sam's t-shirt home, she had grown unbearably shy around him. She did not think she was as bad as Grettel, but she was not as stoic as Baird felt she should be. "Sam is...confusing. And you know I don't know how to flirt. Besides, Baird would kill me."

"Haven't you been watching me? It's like, my one teachable skill," Elle joked, evoking a laugh from Blue. "Seriously, though. The boy's smitten. You don't smell Wayward. He doesn't seem to mind that you are. Once you get away from Baird, don't be afraid to go with it."

"Go with what?" Blue's eyes followed a group of Femreaux wearing nothing on top except for fluorescent-colored bras covered in sequins.

"Go with *him*. Wherever he wants to take you, Blue. I say this with love, honey. You've got to take your eyes off the prize every once in a while. This obsessing about the predator that you and Baird do is too much. It's unhealthy. When are you gonna live? You saw how much Baird needed our kiss," she said smugly.

"There's no way I could ever do...that. And besides," Blue spluttered, "I don't think Sam would ever want..."

Elle cut her off. "All I'm saying is that you should try to be open to it." She sighed dreamily at the many strapping Vemreaux who wore their retired military uniforms for the celebration. "I just love a Vemreaux in uniform. Baird would look so great in one."

As if on cue, the black eyes that made Blue's heart jump into her stomach found her amidst the sea of faces. Blue pinched the skin on Elle's back roughly enough to divert the conversation when she saw Sam strolling toward them. The first time she'd seen him, he'd been in expensive-looking clothes, but it was nothing to the perfectly pressed military uniform he wore as he parted through the massive crowds of Vemreaux to reach them.

Blue's breath caught in her throat at the sight of the navy blue fitted suit with a white stripe down the sides and medals decorating the breast. Sam's shoes shined and his usually haphazard hair was calmed down by the hat he wore on his head. When he met her eyes, his shone with the relief of finding his destination.

"Do you feel that?" Elle whispered in her ear. "That's attraction, Blue. You may not know it yet, but you do want him to kiss you. And if you'd let him, he'd do it in a heartbeat, judging by that silly grin he gets whenever he sees you."

"Shut up!" Blue scolded her when he reached proper hearing range.

Sam removed his hat to tip his head politely to them. "Ladies."

He greeted both women respectfully, but with a smirk that revealed he knew exactly how good looking he was in his uniform. "Where's Baird and Grettel?" What he really meant was, "how long do I have before Baird comes back?"

Elle knew what he was trying to say. "They went up to see the parade for a bit. You look very nice in your uniform, Sam. Did you really earn all those medals?"

Sam nodded with a modest smile. He had been unusually well-mannered around Blue ever since he lost his temper after his one good night of sleep. "Yes, ma'am. I was honorably discharged just before the army was disbanded, so I'm afraid this little collection's all I'm going to get. Are you two enjoying the festival?"

Once again, Elle answered for Blue, sending the silent alert that she really was turning into Grettel in his presence. "Why yes, we are. Has the Light been announced yet? We can't understand the loud-speaker from back here."

"It's some Wayward named Willa Anders?" He spoke the name like it was a question.

Elle's pretty face darkened. "That's the jerk that got me. I hope the predator takes her down hard."

Blue shot her a look. "You know you don't mean that."

Sam smiled that Blue finally spoke. She had been uncommonly quiet in his presence since that night she showered in his room. He did not like the change. She hid herself even more after her brother forcibly returned the shirt Sam had let Blue wear home.

"I suppose not. But I do hope that at the very least the predator takes a chunk out of her hip while she's unarmed. Cowardly bitch." Elle tossed her blonde hair back over her shoulder as she repeated the insult she'd heard a barfly utter one night. "So where're the others?"

"Brody and Alec are guarding Prince Liam." He spoke the title as if it were a joke. "The emperor sent him over to represent Europe, you know. So he's got to stand up there and look official. He hates that kind of stuff, but plays the part well enough. You'd never know that he wears boxers with cartoon characters under his uniform."

Streamers blasted out of a popgun that a clown on stilts was holding. Blue had never seen a real clown in person before. The thick makeup hid the facial features well. Blue thought it the perfect way to hide in plain sight.

A loudspeaker was blaring big band music that whipped everyone into a frenzy. The law permitted instrumental music of all kinds, and happy songs from the 1950s, so long as they were not played live. Strangers danced with each other in the streets without bothering to exchange names or intelligible words. The music was their language, and they all spoke it fluently as their movements flowed into one another. It was as if the country had been storing up all of its energy for one day a year to let it all explode with glitter, lights, drinking and twirling.

Elle watched everyone gyrating with a wistfulness that suggested a wish to join the world in celebrating. "Do you dance?" Elle asked Sam, shouting above the occasional recorded trumpet blasts.

Sam nodded as his foot continued to tap without him telling it to. "Every now and then."

"Can you believe that our Blue has never been dancing before?" She slung her arm over Blue's shoulders to keep the girl from ducking and running out of embarrassment.

"I think we can remedy that." Sam picked up on Elle's prodding, grateful for the push and how easily Elle seemed to accept him. She was a welcome change from Baird's firm disapproval.

"Real subtle," Blue grumbled as she glared at Elle.

Sam's fingers started at Blue's triceps and trailed down the length of her arm until they latched onto her hand, beckoning her to come of her own accord instead of being taken against her will.

The nervousness that always peaked when he touched her flooded up and threatened to choke her. "Just, I really don't... Sam, I can't do what they're doing!" She gestured to a nearby Femreaux who was being flipped up in the air, mini skirt flapping and tiny panties displayed proudly. She shuddered to think of the loss of control that move would cost her, and knew that no matter how much she wanted to follow him, she could not permit that.

"Wherever he wants to take you," Elle reminded her.

"Don't worry." Sam leaned to speak in her ear so he could be heard above the recorded trombones. His breath tickled her ear, and without meaning to, Blue trembled as she involuntarily pressed closer to his body. "We'll go slow."

It was just the thing she needed to hear for her feet to unglue themselves from their spot next to Elle.

"I'll be right back for you, blondie," Sam promised, knowing that Baird would never offer to dance with her. Out of his gratitude for her acceptance of him, he felt the need to be charitable. He watched Elle beam at the hope of joining in the celebration and wave the two away, gently swaying to the music as he trotted away from her, hand in hand with his girl.

It was with great control and focus that he drew Blue to him after they moved into the crowd of dancing Vemreaux, placing his hands on her hips so that she knew which way to move them. He was really a great dancer, capable of much more than swaying back and forth, but it seemed to be all that she could handle. Her eyes darted around defensively while she tried to hide her face from the thousands of people surrounding them. "Hey," he said, trying to draw her attention. "Don't you know by now that I won't let anything bad happen to you?"

"What if I die of embarrassment because I'm such a bad dancer? Or what if the embarrassment takes you down, too, from being seen with me like this? I'm already doing it wrong. I can feel it. Ugh!" Blue cringed as she tried to understand how she was supposed to move. "I suck at life!"

Sam laughed at her theatrics. "You suck at life, yeah? That, well, that's just terrible. Good thing there's more to life than dancing. And a very good thing you have an excellent teacher." Sam pulled her hips to his so his body could move hers where it saw fit. One arm wrapped around her waist, and the other held her hand out to the side as they began turning to the music. "What's the worst that could happen?"

"I could draw attention to myself. I'm a Wayward dancing with a Vemreaux, Sam."

"I believe dancing is allowed."

"Okay, I could trip and pull you down with me. What if I'm so bad at this that I accidentally break your leg or something? It could happen, you know. What if I..."

"Shh," Sam interrupted her growing concern. "Seems like you've thought a lot about this. Is that what you spend your time doing? Thinking about dancing with me?"

"I, um, I didn't mean..." she stammered as she swayed where Sam directed her.

Sam laughed. "Relax, little Wayward. Why do you think I came over to see you?" He gave her an appreciative look. "You were built for dancing."

"I know you're just being nice, you know," she sassed.

"I wonder what sort of compliments you'd actually accept. Beautiful? Graceful? Funny? Alluring?"

"Alluring? Really? That's where you're taking this?" She rolled her eyes. "Real believable, Sam."

"Well, the other things'd just make you blush, so I'll stick with those for now." He lifted her hand and kissed the barcode on the inside of her wrist, enjoying the look of all further arguments dying on her parted lips. He grinned at her fluttering eyelashes, laughing when she came to and yanked her arm from his mouth.

"Sam! Not where people can see!"

He quirked his eyebrow at her. "So, you're saying you want to get me alone first? Clever girl."

"That is *not* what I meant, and you know it."

"See, now you're sending all these mixed signals. First you want me in dark, secluded corners. Now you want me in public. Which is it?" He smirked, enjoying the ease of teasing her. "Unless what you're trying to tell me is that you just want me all the time. Can't say I blame you. I'm very good looking."

Blue narrowed her eyes at him. "You're trying to make me blush."

"Oh, Blue. If that's all I wanted to do, I'd just tell you how pretty you are."

"Sam," she protested.

"I know, I know. I'm too charming for my own good. I'll do my best to be less attractive. Don't want you sneaking me off into your dark American corners and having your way with me."

Blue guffawed, hoping he did not notice the pink coloring her cheeks.

About halfway through the song, Blue's shoulders began to loosen up when she saw that this was the extent of the dancing she'd be expected to do in public. She listened more closely to the beat so Sam did not have to do all the work. Before the song morphed seamlessly into the next, she was smiling, even allowing him to twirl her slowly under his arm once, leaving the safety of his embrace only seconds before returning like a magnet to the comfort of his chest. All thoughts of The Way, her doomed future and the life of duty temporarily left her. The elation of becoming suddenly unburdened was so rare and precious. She could scarcely recall ever feeling so alive. She laughed at her own daring, her eyes meeting his as they shone with wonder and happiness at being so very free in that moment.

Of course the thought of planting a celebratory kiss on Blue's pink lips occurred to him, as it had several times a day since he met her. He had to remind himself of his promise to go slow with her, and just how much he did not want to scare her off.

He hoped she would not notice when the song changed into the next, but she did. Blue stopped dancing immediately so that Elle could have her turn. They walked back hand in hand like it was the most natural thing in the world. Their bodies compensated for the other's easily, dodging the crowd without either one falling behind, due to the other's consideration.

Though he was disappointed to exchange partners, he gave Elle her fair turn. The blonde was infinitely freer, practically begging to be spun and dipped as he danced with the quick learner. He felt bad that her heart was so set on Baird, who was not the type to learn to dance to woo a woman. Though, Sam reasoned, in some ways he was that man, too. He knew how to dance because it was a part of his culture, but there were a great many things he had never considered doing to please a woman until that week.

Elle was a natural dancer with a dazzling smile that demanded attention, but Blue's introverted and guarded awkward movements were much more rewarding when he finally made her come undone and enjoy her first dance. Elle's song ended, and though she was ready for another dance, he felt he had wasted too much unsupervised time away from Blue.

On their way back to her, Elle unexpectedly grabbed Sam's collar and jerked his body down to her level. Her usually joyful eyes were suddenly dead serious as she stared him down. "You listen to me, Sam Boniface. That girl's my best friend. I don't care what any old prophecy says. Don't you let her get killed by that predator." She threatened him with every bit of seriousness she possessed. Sadness mingled with her command. "And when you both survive, don't you dare bring her back here. You take her away from all this and you marry her. You buy her jewelry and give her status so she can vote and walk around like a real citizen. Love her till she dies of old age, not life expectancy. I love her more than anything, but she deserves to be happy for once. If you can make her happy, then don't waste it. She's my special thing, and the world's treated her like garbage. I'll only give her to you if you promise me that you'll treat her like she's your special thing, too. Do you understand me?"

He had to admit, the girl had moxie. Were it a few weeks ago and Elle a Femreaux, he'd have already slept with her and forgotten her name by now. As it was, he nodded once to indicate that she had been heard. "Yes, ma'am."

The sadness and urgency fled from her face, chased away by a girlishly confident smile. "You're a peach and a half, you know that? Don't worry about Baird; he hates everyone."

Spinning away and letting her grip on his collar go, she led their way through the dancers and partiers to find Blue accompanied by Baird and Grettel.

Sam tried to hide his disappointment while Baird pushed back his anger at Sam making off with Elle. The blonde sashayed right up to Baird and planted a light kiss on his scowl to see if there would be any change to it. Though the shift was small, it was gratifying to her to know that she possessed some small amount of control over the immovable man.

Sam did not bother with an obligatory greeting to the brother, but instead smiled politely at Grettel. "Do you want to dance, too?"

Grettel shied away from the kindness, shaking her head as she moved behind Baird and Blue. She mumbled a "no thanks", but it was lost to the music that still trumpeted on. Grettel had never danced with a man either, but she did not dare leave Baird or Blue's side with so many Vemreaux about.

Sam took his hat off and ran his fingers through his smashed down hair, not liking it so trampled to the crown of his head. "Liam wanted me to tell you that we still have to stop by The Way West before we leave for home. We'll call you on our way over to the diner. Can Blue be ready in the afternoon?"

Baird nodded, but Blue surprised him by speaking up. "Can I come with you? My brother's there, and I'd like to say goodbye and explain things to him before I leave."

Before Sam could agree, Baird interrupted. "No, I'll take you there before work in the morning. He's my brother, too. I'll wait around until you guys get there. You can have her then."

Blue did not appreciate being treated like a toy to be passed back and forth, but true to form, she did not say anything.

Sam consented to Baird's plan and bid them farewell, nodding to the girls as he left. Baird mumbled under his breath, "I can't stand that pushy Vemreaux. It's like he's just asking someone to punch the cocky smirk off his face."

"Would you stop being such a downer?" Elle snatched up Blue's hand and Grettel's, pulling them forward to join the colorful crowd. "If this is Blue's only Peace Day, it'll be done right."

PARTING WORDS AND ARGUMENTS

Griffin's chin mimicked Baird's, which stayed level to the table with a stern determination. The visitation room that the three occupied was fortunately bereft of professors or any other listening ears and prying eyes. Such was not necessarily the right of family members coming to visit their relatives in The Way. It was thanks to Jack, who escorted them to the visitation room and allowed them their privacy while he waited outside. There were chairs, but only the boys sat in them. Blue stood off to the side, ashamed to look at her younger brother.

Though Griffin did not understand everything that had taken place in the short time since he'd said goodbye to his sister, he did grasp the finality of this parting. The prophecy always loomed in the back of his mind. Even when his sister would talk about his future in The Way or out in the world, it was with the understanding that she would not be there for it. Though it was a reoccurring theme, it never ceased to upset him when he would allow himself the privacy for such unwelcome emotions. Now, as he sat across from his intimidating older brother whom he felt very little affection for, it took all of his concentration to keep his chin from breaking its hold and setting off into a quiver. "So that's it?" he questioned, trying to be brave.

"It's our only shot, Griff." Baird rested his hand on the table between them and traced an invisible line into it. "I can't see another way to get her over there without breaking a whole lotta laws."

"So I don't get to be on the outside with my own sister, ever? By the time I get out... *if* I get out, she'll already be dead?" the boy asked, forcing his agony into misplaced bravado.

"That's right," Baird replied with no hint of emotion. He was well practiced in suppressing the misery that often grabbed him in the middle of the night. "So now's the time to say your goodbyes." He stood, knowing that his mere presence was a hindrance to the proper farewell that his siblings deserved. "Is Jack around? I wanted to say hi."

Blue shot her older brother a suspicious look that told him she knew just how odd that sounded coming from him. "Yeah, he should be just outside the room still."

"I'll be back in a few minutes." Baird tried to sound gracious, but was really offering Blue a warning to make it brief.

When Baird left the room and shut the door behind him, he was met by the black eyes of the professor who'd taken a special interest in the siblings from the beginning. He watched Jack look politely up from the book he was reading. With too much venom, Baird spoke. "Hi, Dad."

Jack's eyes grew wide. He dropped his book on the floor, sending the light sound echoing down the deserted corridor. "Baird! I-I... Who? Who told you?" he finally asked when his voice came back to him, not able to think of a better response. So many times he'd dreamed about his son knowing who he was, but even in his wildest imagination, Baird never smiled. True to form, Baird scowled at the man.

"Why didn't you tell us?"

Jack's head whipped down the hall to check again that it was empty. "Your mother wasn't... How did you figure it out?"

"I met your nephew, Liam Boniface. He's got my eyes. Original Vemreaux eyes are pretty rare. Makes sense one of our parents was Vemreaux. And, apparently, Blue looks like his dead sister." The silence that fell almost strangled the stunned Vemreaux. "I was under the impression that Vemreaux couldn't marry Waywards who weren't free."

"They can't." Jack's voice came out in a pained whisper, his Western accent falling by the wayside in his distress. "I loved your mother, Baird. I named you and Idahlia. Your mother named Griffin."

"Don't call her Idahlia. She hates the name you gave her."

Jack swallowed. "Your mother died just after giving birth to Griffin." Jack knew that his son could see the hollow darkness that haunted his eyes, and that it was enough to convince Baird that he hadn't been raping a Wayward. "We were in love, or I thought she was in love with me, anyway. But buying her wasn't an option." He swallowed again and nearly choked on his saliva as the words that had been trapped inside of him for decades finally spilled out. "All three of you are mine, Baird. Mine and your mother's." Jack began to sweat. The European cadence he'd worked so hard to iron out thickened. "That's why I delayed Blue's purchase. Even without you knowing, it killed me to have you out in the world where I couldn't see you."

When Baird glowered at him instead of bursting out in anger, Jack fumbled through more explanations. "I always wanted you three to know, but if anyone else found out, it would be bad. You know the laws against relations between Vemreaux and A-bloods living in The Way. I thought it would be better if I could at least keep an eye on you kids. I kept my mouth shut so I could be near you." He nearly cried when Baird's grim expression did not lighten in the least. "I'm so sorry, Baird." Jack hung his head in shame, knowing that there was no forgiveness for keeping his identity from them.

"Save it," Baird spat, working to keep his anger in check. "I'm just telling you because my master sold Blue." The words hit Jack like a well-aimed punch in the face that knocked him speechless. "She's leaving today. Now's your last chance to say goodbye when you walk us out."

A low cry escaped Jack's mouth. His black eyes showed Baird more hurt than he was willing to behold. Blue was his only daughter, and though she did not know this, Jack always reserved a special spot in his heart for her.

Baird cleared his throat. "I don't want you telling her who you are. She's leaving, and it won't do her any good now. She's got a lot on her mind, and I won't have you messing with her head to clear your conscience. Do you understand me? Being your daughter didn't do her any good while she lived here, and it won't help her out in the real world either, so save it." He glared at Jack with a veil of disinterest, allowing a small amount of his hatred to peek through. "You may be her father, but I'm the one who raised her. I make those kinds of decisions for her, not you."

Jack looked like he could barely recall his own name, but eventually he nodded. An entire minute of silence covered both of their mouths until Jack found his voice again. "Who bought her?"

"Your nephew did."

"Liam? She's going to live in Frederick's house?"

"Liam's taking her over to Europe to be his personal servant. He... he even said that he's going to free her and employ her like a real person – not a slave. It's the best she'll get, so say goodbye and let her go."

Jack nodded, unable to hold back his tears. "My brother's a good man. She'll be safe there."

Baird took a step forward to enforce his law. "You will not call to check on her. You will not tell your family who she is to you. You will not tell her who you are. She has a job to do, so leave her to it." There was no mercy or pity that could be found in his fist as it clenched at his side. "You have no idea who you abandoned. It's too late for you to claim her now. Or any of us, for that matter."

Jack let out a short sob of agony. Baird had the decency to look away.

A loud crash came from the visitation room. "Clean yourself up. I'll bring her out in a few minutes."

Leaving Jack to his mournful weeping, Baird slipped into the visitation room to check on things. Griffin had thrown a chair and was yelling at Blue, who just stood there and took it, shaking before him while nodding. It was not the farewell the girls had shared with Blue that morning in the hut. There were so many tears between Elle and Grettel that Baird had to excuse himself to escape the flood.

"I hate you!" Griffin roared childishly. "You're both supposed to be my family, and now you're going off to die! Stay here! No one's making you go, Blue. The predator's killing off Vemreaux, not Waywards. You're fighting for their team! You're gonna die for the people who locked you up in here, but you won't stay and live for me?" He threw another chair, not even calming down at Baird's presence. "What do I have to do? Train with you? Keep your stupid secret? Be your brother? Why are the Vemreaux more important to you than I am?" Griffin pounded his fist to his chest. "*I've* got Baird's shovel now! *I'm* the big name on the yard! When are you finally going to listen to me?"

Baird righted one of the overturned chairs, taking the rage in stride so that Blue could follow his example of controlling one's temper. Though Baird did his best to appear unaffected, Blue was slowly losing her battle. He hated it when she shook. When Griffin spouted off a particularly intolerable accusation, Baird decided that he'd had enough space to let loose. He wouldn't have his brother be the first one to make Blue cry.

"Enough!" Baird cut him off.

"Don't you tell me what to do!" Griffin postured, daring his large brother to treat him like a man. "You're just as bad as she is! I wish I never knew either of you were my family! I'm nothing like you!"

So quick that Griffin didn't have a chance to react, Baird crossed the room and pushed his brother up against the wall. The force was smooth and did not hurt the teen, but it scared him into a stunned silence as Baird spoke barely above a whisper, just centimeters from his face. "I said that's enough. Like it or not, our sister's leaving and you're never gonna see her again. How many beatings did she take for you? How many times did she take the blame because she loves you? She deserves better from her family. She may not live long enough to be haunted by this little outburst, but you will. When we're old men together and all you have is me, you'll remember the last things you said to our sister." He looked deep into his baby brother's cerulean eyes and saw the same pain, anger, defiance and rage that haunted his own. "I'll give you one more chance to say something you won't regret for the rest of your life."

Mortified tears pricked Griffin's eyes as his conduct changed. It was not often that Blue's scars on her back from the lashings she'd taken for him surfaced in conversation. Self-loathing overtook his demeanor, and he let go of the fight in his fists. Griffin slumped against the wall before his brother.

When he decided Griffin was sane enough to speak to Blue, Baird released him.

"I'm sorry," Griffin mumbled as he looked down at his white shoes, watching as one of his angry tears melted down his cheek and fell between his feet. "I killed someone, Blue!" Griffin croaked out in a whisper. "Joodas. I didn't mean to. It was a yard fight, and a bunch of guys jumped Marxus." He hated that Baird was watching him cry, but he could not hold it back any longer. "That's how I got Baird's shovel."

"Oh, Griffin!" Blue buried her face in her hands. "No, Griffin! No! You don't want to be like Baird! You don't want to be like me!"

Baird nodded solemnly at his brother, letting Griffin know with a look that he had passed from boyhood into the realms of being a man. It was not a joyous thing.

"I didn't mean to," Griffin whispered. "I didn't know it would feel like this." He shook his head. "You kept me calm, Blue. I need you here. Sometimes I feel it growing in me." He tapped his heart. "Something dark. Please! Don't leave!"

Blue closed her eyes, shutting out the image of her beloved baby brother mutating into Baird. "Oh, Griffin."

Baird looked like he might be sick. He rubbed his hand over his face so his sister would not see the horror running through his mind. He had done everything he could to make sure Griffin did not turn into a monster.

Griffin swiped at his running nose. "Blue, I don't want you to go. I...I don't think the Vemreaux deserve to be saved."

Blue nodded again and continued her shaking. She did not focus on hearing him; she only wanted to fill her vision with the sight of his tenacious innocence. Orange jumpsuit. Auburn hair. Glowing blue eyes. Peak in his left ear. A face capable of every emotion imaginable. She loved every bit of him, tantrums and all.

Baird placed his solid hand on his younger brother's shoulder and nudged him forward. "Give your sister a hug before she leaves, Griffin."

Griffin jerked away from his brother, not wanting to be told what to do. Still he obeyed, moving forward and awkwardly wrapping his arms around his sister, whom he'd long since surpassed in height, but felt he could never truly outgrow.

Blue let out a short, high-pitched whine that served to replace the sob that threatened to pull her apart. Her arms banded around her stomach as Griffin held her.

"I love you, Blue," Griffin whispered through his tears. He hated that he was crying and she was not. It was hard enough to maintain one's masculinity with an older brother who saw everything as a combat lesson and a sister who was destined to destroy an unstoppable foe.

Unable to relinquish her grip on herself, Blue pressed her cheek to Griffin's chest to get closer to him. "When you get outta here someday, be good to Baird. He doesn't know any better, Griffin. Promise me you'll be good to him. Look after him." Her brother held her firmly as a tremor tried to tear her in two. "He needs you!" She inhaled his scratch-laced scent and stored it in her memory, not wanting to exhale him out of her senses.

Baird shot her a dark look, which she ignored.

Griffin wiped his tears on her uniform. "If I don't, will you stay?" He felt his sister chuckle in his arms and shake her head. "Please stay," he begged. When his sister quaked more violently, he squeezed her tighter until her feet were ready to support her again. "Had to try," he muttered. Depression overwhelmed Griffin as he gave one final hug to the body that was destined to be broken.

Not one to prolong the inevitable, Baird opened the door the moment Griffin pulled away and motioned for Jack to come in. "You can take us out now, sir."

Jack looked completely different to Blue. She remembered him quiet and reserved, but as he walked into the small room, he looked just as shaken as she. "Jack? Are you okay?" she asked, trying to pull herself together.

The man merely nodded. He was a terribly unconvincing actor.

Baird exited the room to indicate that even though they needed an escort to be in The Way, he would not follow the man. He would leave on his own accord as the leader, not the follower.

Jack's voice was gravelly, and Blue judged correctly that he'd been crying. "Griffin, you can go back to the mess hall." Jack pulled a signed slip from his pocket and gave it to the boy in case he was stopped along the way.

Griffin nodded, but was reluctant to leave, as was Blue.

Baird stalked back into the room, unhappy with the addition to the party, and placed his hand on Blue's shoulder. She was starting to shake again, and he would not have her making a scene that might evoke compassion in her father. He glared at Jack to give them some space.

Leaning down to speak so that only she could hear him, he whispered coldly, "You walk out of this room and you don't look back. There's no point in moving forward if you're gonna spend your time looking back at your life." Baird noticed her hesitation. He lifted his hand and pointed to the hallway, his words dripping with the spit of anger. "Don't expect any help from me. I won't be there to push you after today. If you can't do this, then don't bother getting on that plane. Let that Willa kid die while you rot at the diner for the rest of your life."

One heavy foot after the other, Blue found that she barely had the strength to walk out of the room, turning her back on her younger brother and all that she wanted to be there to witness in his life. Each step that she took fell with a sickening weight like bricks on the floor, echoing her pain along with it. Her brain began to frost over and glaze her eyes with ice that could not observe the world as she passed it. The greened walls and chipped ceiling unraveled in her periphery, but she took no notice. By the time she reached the end of the hallway, the pain was covered over with a buzzing sound that cancelled out all she could not bear to feel. Baird, for once, walked behind her and next to Jack, ensuring that she did not sneak one last look at her baby brother before they turned the corner.

It took Blue, Baird and Jack twenty minutes of passing through hallway after mundane hallway to finally reach the entrance. Not that he was surprised, but Baird was relieved that Blue did not turn around once, trusting that he was behind her all the way and that there was no going back.

Liam leaned against the wall at the reception desk at the south entrance of the massive series of buildings. Alec was standing at attention, clashing with Liam's foot pressed to the wall behind him. Brody's nose was still a little swollen, and his eyes had black wells beneath them, but he stood before Liam as a front of protection anyway.

Sam slouched next to Liam. Though he was not a guard anymore, the training was in his bones. His eyes drifted to each doorway every few seconds, his lazy demeanor a cover for his years of experience.

Sam's molded face broke down and relaxed when he saw Blue round the last corner, her auburn hair obscuring what was becoming his favorite sight. As she neared, he realized something was wrong with the perfect work of art. She did not return his smile or even look up to acknowledge his stealthy flirting. So covetous was he of the small moments that he noticed when each miniscule inflection of affection was stolen from him.

"We'll wait in the parking lot," Baird informed the men. "Take your time."

"Uncle Jack! How are ya?" Liam boomed, his indoor voice having never been properly installed.

Jack put on a smile that convinced no one as he watched his only daughter walk away.

THE HARSH END OF THE BEGINNING

The siblings waited in the parking lot for half an hour in silence, Baird giving Blue the space she needed as he sorted through all the possible ways he'd worked out in his mind to say goodbye.

When he sensed that enough time had passed and it was safe to talk, he stood next to her and leaned back on his 4x4 so he did not have to look her in the face. "You got everything in your sack?"

Blue nodded, but offered nothing more to ease along their last moment.

"Good. I, uh, I got you something." He reached into his pocket and pulled out a butter knife from the restaurant that he paid for with his tips. "I know they'll probably get you all sorts of fancy weapons over there, but I don't want you forgetting who gave you your first one." He did not look to see the little smile that played on her lips, but he knew it was there. There was not much that he couldn't predict about his sister. "Just remember everything I taught you, and you'll be fine."

Immediately he regretted his choice of words. He knew that she would most likely not be fine. This was the last time he'd spend with her, and he was saying all the wrong things. If Elle had been there, she would have kept him in check. He was horrible with moments like these. He cleared his throat and looked away. "So, I know you know, but I love you."

At this, Blue's head shot up. "What? How would I know that? You've never told me before." She seemed to come back to herself a little.

His lips pursed as he fought back the guilt that tried to tie his tongue even more. "Yes, I have. Don't you remember?" He was a little insulted that she had no recollection of something he recalled so vividly. "We were kids in the old building. Building Two. I was teaching you how to run with your eyes closed and you tripped and fell. You skinned your knee." He smiled as he pictured it. "Man, you were small. Tough kid, too. Didn't cry at all. I tried to pick you up, but you wouldn't let me. You said you weren't a baby and you could do it yourself. You said that you were just as big as me, which, you know, has never been true." He breathed to steady his voice. "You said you wanted to be just like me, and I told you that I loved you." He shook his head. "I can't believe you don't remember."

"How old were you?" she asked, dumbfounded that he remembered something obviously very important to him and she had not.

"I don't know, like seven? A month or so before I turned eight. It was just before I left for Building Three," he guessed.

"Baird, I was five when you were seven!"

"Almost six! Five's plenty old enough to recall important stuff," he defended himself.

"How could I remember something that long ago?" She laughed, the mild sound relaxing both of them. When she sobered, she kicked his foot with hers. "I love you, too," she admitted.

"Good thing I wasn't waiting on that one," he joked, tapping her foot in return.

"I wasn't gonna be the first girl to cave."

"Oh, so now I'm a girl?" Baird smiled, enjoying the turn of levity.

"Yup. A big, giant girl." Her face changed after a moment. "So when's the last time you told Griffin that you loved him?"

"He knows."

Her response came swift, with no room for counterpoints. "No, he doesn't." She watched Baird shut his mouth, for he had no retort to that. "You have to tell him. He's not me. He actually needs love from you. Promise me that after I'm gone, you'll take care of each other."

"You know I will," he assured her.

"Not just physically. I mean, he needs you to love him. So be nicer. Tell him every time you see him. Tell Elle, too, and don't be stingy with Grettel. I may die first, but you'll spend your whole long life dead if you don't start admitting to us that you love us. It won't make you weak, Baird. We deserve to hear it from you every day." She paused, steeling herself to say her next piece. "After everything we've been through, I deserved to hear it more than once."

Baird ran his tongue in between his teeth as the guilt crashed over him. "Twice," he corrected her, though he did not understand why he was arguing.

In their quiet, unsupervised moment, Blue broke down and began to quake, hating herself through every tremble. "I deserved it every day you told me not to look up at people when they spoke to me or how to get the drop on someone from behind. I deserved to hear it when I was sent to bed bloody for taking Griffin's beatings. I deserved to hear it when I had a stomach full of scratch shavings after Grettel or Elle would drop a paper weight. I deserved to hear it when no one would come near me because you'd covered my face in scratch." Her voice rose, now with anger tainting the sadness. "I did everything you told me to, Baird, and I deserved more from you!" The bitter words came out of her after having spent years in rehearsal. "Griffin deserves more, too." She shook her head. "You give up all your time, your money and your energy to watch over us and train me, but you withhold the one thing that's so easy to give. I don't get you sometimes."

"Stop it," he scolded her, warning her that he got the point and she was traipsing into dangerous territory. His stone wall was ready to be thrown up at a moment's notice, and then used as a weapon against whoever angered him.

"It's my last wish," she whispered, laying it on thick. "Promise me that you'll tell Griffin every time you see him that you love him. Tell me that you'll be nicer and you'll love Elle well and Grettel, too."

The tables turned, and Baird found that he did not like being on the submissive end. Swallowing, he took the advice he'd given to his brother. "Okay. If it's that important to you, then fine."

"Tell me," Blue insisted obstinately, and in that moment he could truly tell that he was the one who had raised her.

"I'll tell Griffin every time I see him that I love him. I'll be better to Elle and Grettel, too. I'll be nicer to all three of 'em." The words were hard to say and tasted bitter in his mouth, but he knew once he repeated them that he would have to find a way to make them true. "I don't love Elle like you want me to, Blue. Can't force that."

"Yes, I can."

Baird snorted, and then quieted. He stood next to his sister, working up the courage to speak openly the things he hated thinking about. "I do love you, Blue. You're the only one who really gets it all." Baird swallowed, gearing up for the big guns. "You're my best friend. Do you think I liked making you do those things? I couldn't tell you how proud I was of you, because I didn't want it to turn you soft. But I am. I'm so proud of you."

At this, Blue's control faltered. She started shaking even more. For some reason, this hit harder than his admission that he loved his family. Quickly she suppressed the moment, storing it away in her memory so that she could pull it back out unharmed when she next needed to hear it. She tapped her foot to his again. "It doesn't count if I'm your only friend."

To indicate that he'd gotten her point, he grabbed his chest like she'd sent a dagger through his heart. "You got me."

A few minutes of shared silence calmed them both down. "Hey, do you think long after it's all over they'll like, write songs and tell stories about us and everything we went through like they do with Francis Vemreaux?"

"Maybe." Baird shrugged, considering this for the first time. "In the stories, though, make sure I get the girl in the end."

"I'd like to be a little taller and, you know, prettier in the poem versions," Blue joked, her insecurity poking through.

The front door to The Way opened, and the four Vemreaux they'd been waiting on emerged. Alec spotted Baird and nodded as they made their way across the parking lot to the two. Shaking his head, Baird corrected her. "Pretty doesn't matter…"

"…when you're slitting throats." She joined in, spouting off one of his many lessons. "I know, I know."

"Oh, I almost forgot." Baird reached into his back pocket and pulled out a thick wad of bills. Blue's eyes widened bigger than he'd ever seen when he picked up her hand and shoved it in her palm, closing her fingers around it. "Just in case."

"No, Baird. That's not my money." She tried to press it back into him. "It's for Griffin, not me. What would I need with money?"

Baird shook his head and moved her outstretched hand back to her body. "They're just your tips from Tuesday night. Everything else'll go towards buying Griffin. Don't worry. This is just in case. You might need food or a ride somewhere, and I don't want you not to have the money." He rolled his eyes and sighed. "I won't let you not take it, Blue, so you might as well just accept it and be done."

After much internal debate, Blue realized that she had very little choice in the matter, since her brother's mind was made up. Grudgingly, she took the bills, folded them in half the way she'd seen Baird do it every night when they closed up, and shoved them in the back pocket of her jeans. "Thanks," she muttered, though her tone suggested something other than gratitude.

"You ready, kitten?" Liam was oblivious to the tender mood between the siblings.

Baird saw the man in a new light now that he knew they were cousins. Reckless with a smile and incapable of being serious, Baird thought Blue would probably laugh a lot in what he hoped would not be her last days. The whisper of a promise that she was guaranteed a grin in the near future gave him just enough fuel to leave her with the foreigners and trust her to fate's wretched choice for her life.

Blue did not respond to Liam, for nodding would only have been a lie. Baird and Liam exchanged a bit more information and paperwork concerning her purchase and impending freedom, which Liam assured him would happen the following day when they could file the papers in Europe.

When all was said and done, it was Baird who had trouble leaving. Despite their audience, he pulled his sister into the first hug he had given her since he had been bought by Master Joe and left The Way.

Before he could pull her to him, her arms flew up, one forearm blocking her stomach and the other crossing her breasts. He had seen her do this before when someone would get too close and try to hold her against her will. It was her way of bracing herself for an attack of emotions and love that she did not think she could handle. He could feel her fists balling up against him as she shook in his arms. In his periphery, he saw her face turning red as she held her breath to stave off the onslaught of agony that ripped them both apart.

He decided to be brave and throw caution to the wind by placing a kiss atop her head. "Hey," Baird whispered as he grabbed her to him so tight that he could feel her heartbeat through her back. He flexed his muscles so that she didn't even have the room to tremble. Baird squeezed her so fiercely that a short sob escaped from her before her mouth clamped shut. "Hey, I love you."

Baird wished that she had not braced herself for the hug. He wanted her to return the gesture and hold him together, as well. He took it as a just repayment for all the times he told her how important it was not to get emotional. Of all the things he taught her, hugging was never one of his instructions for survival, though he needed it now more than anything.

"Goodbye, Blue." Baird squeezed his sister one last time with the brunt of his strength before releasing Blue and turning his back on her as she stumbled forward miserably, collapsing to her knees.

"No, Baird! Don't leave me!" Blue shouted after him. "No! I want to stay with you!" She allowed the child she always tried to quiet inside of her to finally speak. "Don't let me do this, Baird! Please! Don't let me die!"

True to form, Baird did not look back as he climbed into the car and drove away without a second glance at his only sister.

Blue willed Baird to come back, to say something that would rescue her from her anguish, but he remained gone from her vision and her life. She sagged hopelessly on the pavement, and did not even notice when Sam lifted her and carried her to their car.

HELD TOGETHER

Sandwiched in between Sam and Liam in the backseat, Blue had little room to air her grief as Brody drove them all to the private airport after they left The Way. Sam's arm stayed around her, permanently affixed there through her anguish, and she realized that she did not stiffen at his touch anymore. She was so wrecked from leaving her family that she could scarcely breathe without feeling the crushing weight of despondence. His breath tickled her hair, but she did not thrill at the sensation. His thumb rubbed soothing circles into her shoulder, but even that was not strong enough to pull her out of her pit of despair.

Sam's warm body drew her to his side, and although she had precious few other places to go, she allowed him to lean her head on his sturdy shoulder until the shaking subsided. Even Brody had the decency to allow her a moment of silence before making a crack about the Americans and their terrible driving habits.

"Okay, old man," Liam teased from the back seat, shifting uncomfortably from one too many bodies stuffed back there. He was tall, but did his best to accommodate the girl.

"Old man? Hey, just be glad it's not Sam driving. We'd get hit for sure with his lead foot." The attempt to bring Sam into the conversation fell to the wayside, for the Vemreaux was intent on stroking the woman's sullen face with his free hand, and could pay attention to little else. This irritated Brody, but he didn't push it with Alec sitting next to him in close punching range.

"You ever been on a plane before, kitten?" Liam asked, trying his luck at pulling the more diplomatic of the two out of their shared funk. He reached over and rubbed her back gently with his palm.

"No," she answered, too depressed to resist the contact.

Liam grinned. "You'll love it. Your first flight's on a New World One airplane? Man, who else can say that? The seats are way bigger than a regular airplane."

"Since when have you ever been on a *regular airplane*?" Brody challenged, glancing in the rearview mirror at his friend.

Liam decided not to dignify that with a response, even though Brody had a fair point. "The ride's real smooth. Better than driving with this pothole magnet behind the wheel."

He indicated Brody with a silly look that Blue missed entirely, due to her head still enjoying its new home on Sam's firm shoulder.

Though her mind told her body to tremble, it would not obey anymore with Sam's command of comfort on her cheek. Eventually the tremors stopped, and a buzzing filled her ears so that she could not understand any of the banter that was picking up around her. She thought of Baird's last bone-crushing hug, Griffin's angry tears and Grettel's endless sobs, but it was Elle's words that surfaced above the agony of deep depression.

With perfect clarity, she recalled the goodbye in the hut that morning as she left the girls. With Grettel barely able to make out an intelligible word, Elle was the one who found her voice amidst the tears. She had pointed directly into Blue's face like she was Baird giving an order. "Don't you lose that fight, Idahlia Jane."

Blue cringed at the use of her real name.

Elle yanked her into a hug and whispered in her ear. "I love you, Dolly, and you're not going out there on your own. You've got a whole team of guys who believe in you, so don't be scared. Kill that predator and never look back. Let them take you anywhere. And let that Sam take you *everywhere*."

Even though Blue was pressed right against Sam, it was still not close enough. Huge, gaping holes in her psyche stung where they were exposed. "Tighter, Sam! I'm still falling apart. You're not close enough," Blue whispered into his neck, ignoring his goosebumps that responded readily to her soft breath on his sensitive spot. When he gave her a reassuring squeeze, she shook her head. "So tight, you think you're gonna hurt me. I mean it, Sam. I can't feel it! I can't feel you." She swallowed hard. "I can't feel anything."

His serious black eyes met her unfocused blues, and nodded. Despite the movement of the vehicle, he lifted her off the seat next to him and slid her onto his lap. Strong arms banded around her torso and squeezed, slowly increasing his strength until he was certain he was hurting her. "You feel that? Is that better?" Sam asked through gritted teeth.

With the increased force compressing her joints, Blue's muscles began to relax, releasing a bit of the tension and misery that pulled at her. She let a portion of it go when Sam's grip was more firm than the grief that clawed at her. Blue shivered as the body heat collected from shaking for so long left her. "Cold," she whispered, staring vacantly in Liam's direction.

Brody turned on the heat to full blast, though the car was already warm. He met Sam's eye and nodded in solidarity. They looked after Julia, why not her doppelganger?

Liam met Blue's soulless eyes with compassion. Her cheek was pressed to Sam's shoulder, defeated by the day. The prince took off his jacket and draped it over her body, moving closer to the two. "It'll be okay, kitten. We'll kill that predator, and then send you right back home. Just think of it as a little holiday." His thumb met her face and traced the arc of her cheek tenderly.

Alec shifted his body and shook his head at Liam, indicating that lying to her would not help the situation. Then he spoke, directing his quiet words to the window. "Hold her tighter, Sam." Alec cleared his throat. "Hardest part's over, Blue. That pain you're feeling? It'll dull. It always does." His tone was hollow with suppressed sorrow, and Blue could tell, beneath her own unhappiness, that Alec was the only one in the vehicle who could somehow relate.

That would have to be enough. The four of them would have to be enough. Someone to understand her plight. Someone to make her smile through the fight. Someone to bicker with and distract her. Someone to hold her together and love her. They would be her weapons. They would make her strong. Together, they would fight to free the Vemreaux from whatever tyranny dared rise up to meet them.

Love the book?
Leave a review!

THE TRUTH

ENJOY A FREE PREVIEW OF BOOK TWO IN THE VOLUMES OF THE VEMREAUX

It had been four days since Prince Liam indulged the world in a smile. The garish grin that was once a permanent fixture on his face seemed to have found a new home entirely. Where that new abode was, no one could say. Much of Europe was not given to merriment as of late.

The washing machine offered the only noise in that section of the gargantuan house. To call it a house was not accurate, but saying "mansion" sounded so odd to Blue that she could not wrap her mind around it. The laundry took a little time. In The Way they sorted laundry, but it was barely a chore. All the orange jumpsuits went in one pile, white underthings in another.

After a brief rundown of how to sort their garments by the succinct and tight-lipped elderly housekeeper, Blue adjusted to the new method. Apparently, clothes had to be separated by color and delicacy of the fabric here. Blue was a quick learner, having to be told things once, if catching on by observing was not an option. Josephine, however, was not one whose constitution tolerated errors.

Since they had landed in Europe four days ago, Blue began making a tally of her mistakes so that, during dull moments, she could recite them to herself as a sort of verbal beating. She kept her mouth shut as she stumbled through the long list of domestic tasks, speaking only when nodding would not suffice.

Josephine ran the domestic aspect of the household like a captain might command his ship of top-notch sailors. That is, if a sea captain had brown hair with streaks of gray pulled up into a bun so tight, it provided a temporary facelift.

On her second day, Blue managed to mop the floor with the wrong kind of solution, and then had to clean the sticky surface all over again. The mansion was so expansive that Blue had to tap into her heightened abilities so that she did not get lost in the maze. It would have been a great help if someone could have shown her around, or at the very least, drawn her up a map. Everyone was so preoccupied with more important things than getting her acclimated that she was, for the most part, left alone to figure things out. Blue counted this a blessing, for many of her blunders went unseen this way.

The room she had been given was enormous. It was larger than the hut by far, and her bunker in The Way that housed twelve girls. The bed was beyond the capabilities of a Wayward's imagination. It was bedecked with tall iron posts and crimson curtains hanging down from them so that she could shut herself inside for optimum darkness. The comforter was light beige with gold and ruby swirls sewn into it. It was so gorgeous that she categorically refused to touch it, for fear of sullying the beauty. The small red accents were subtle, but when paired with the deep rouge of the hanging bed curtains, it made the whole sumptuous nest look warm and romantic. Blue thought it looked as though the bed was lit by constant candlelight, even in midday.

A tall and intimidating dark wood wardrobe stood proudly at the northern wall of the room, begging for her to put it to use. Blue did not touch this, though, either. It was too perfect, and she could not bring herself to put her burlap sack with the two changes of clothes she'd brought with her from the hut inside of it. Her sack looked pathetic and out of place. It was not much of a leap to think of herself in that way – the one thing in the immaculate mansion that did not belong.

Josephine wrote the duties for the day on the dry erase board in the main kitchen in the morning. Blue spent the rest of the day trying to decipher her tightly scripted handwriting and figure out what each assignment meant. Frustration often threatened Blue's meek demeanor when she was given a job that was foreign to her. She wished she could ask questions, but it had been beaten into her that speaking out of turn was not an acceptable practice for Waywards when interacting with Vemreaux. Blue was keen not to earn a beating in her new home.

The scent from Elle and Grettel had faded. Blue no longer smelled Wayward, so Josephine made the assumption that the new servant was Vemreaux. Perhaps it would make no difference if she knew that Blue had been raised in The Way and had no knowledge of things like polishing wood or sorting laundry. Perhaps Josephine would not frown at Blue's clothing if she knew they were all the girl had. Those revelations would fall under the category of exposing herself to people, which was not something Blue would do without the proper aggressive prodding.

Sam, Liam, Brody and Alec left the first night they'd returned to the mansion, and had not been back since. No explanation was given, and Blue did not think it her place to ask Josephine where her new owner had gone. She wished Sam at least had told her where he was taking off to.

Not my place, Blue scolded herself as she folded laundry. *Just because he was nice to you doesn't mean he owes you any kind of explanation. He's Vemreaux. You're Wayward. You're not equals, no matter how many times he looks at you like that.*

The mansion was uncommonly noiseless at night. The quiet was overwhelming at times when the autumn sun would attempt to deceive her into thinking that the day held promise of change or movement other than what came from the few servants. A weight settled over everyone, and Blue wondered when she would be allowed to disturb it.

The trip to Europe was not for recreation, nor was her sole purpose to be a household servant. She was supposed to be taking the steps to get to the island that housed the O-bloods. There had been three more Vemreaux disappearances since they had left the Americas, which was the reason for the deafening silence and Liam's hiatus. Prince Liam had purchased her and brought her to live with him as a servant so that she could get to the island and kill whatever was butchering all the Vemreaux. It had all seemed so important a few days ago. Blue was confused as to the sudden drop in urgency.

Though she did not want to admit it, the most unsettling shift was found in Sam. The attractive Vemreaux spent almost the entire airplane and armored car drive over to the mansion attached to her in some tangible way. When the fear began to rise in her as the small aircraft lifted off of the runway, he had held her hand, speaking calming words that, to the others, may not have sounded like the perfect thing to say, but to her, made all the difference.

Not knowing much about the mechanics of an airplane, Sam had explained everything that was happening as best he could, down to running through Newton's third law just so she understood as well as he did. He even asked the co-pilot to come back when he was not busy so he could fill in the gaps that were left. While some might find that kind of one-way conversation boring, it was just the medicine Blue needed to feel safe so high up in the air. She still wished she could take apart the plane herself and put it back together so she could understand all there was to it, but this was better than nothing.

Sam's hand never fell away from hers, even as his mind drifted into unconsciousness. Blue had been left to her wonderings. She made sure to close her eyes whenever the flight attendant walked through the cabin so that it appeared she was capable of sleep, but her mind never stopped processing all the new information.

After landing at the airport in Europe, the only time Sam's hand left hers was when he let her slide into the backseat of the chauffeured vehicle. The moment he ducked in and sat next to her, his fingers once again stroked hers, as if he needed the contact to properly breathe.

The car ride had been long, but Blue did not mind. Conversation picked up in the back of the vehicle that sat all five of them somewhat comfortably. There was one bench that faced forward and one that angled toward the back. They all had enough elbow room so they were not on top of each other, though this notion did not persuade Sam to move so much as a few centimeters from Blue's side. One hand held hers, while the other draped around her back to affix her to his side, where he would occasionally brush his fingertips along the curve of her hip. Each time he did it, Blue had to work to hide her blush and the shiver that exploded up her spine. Occasionally, Liam would glance up from his stack of paperwork to examine their connection with an approving twinkle in his eye.

Brody's irritation in the car at their closeness had spewed out of his mouth in the form of sarcasm and outright criticism. Blue had responded by removing her hand from Sam's.

Brody argued with Alec, giving Sam the chance to address Blue's closed-off demeanor he had worked so hard to open up. "What's wrong?"

Blue shrugged. "It makes Brody mad when we hold hands, I think. He's right. I'm Wayward. You're Vemreaux. I don't know why I keep forgetting I shouldn't be holding your hand like that." Instead of looking up at him, she had stared down at his lap so he could not see her eyes.

"I like when you hold my hand. I want you near me." Sam had turned to his friend with a warning in his tone. "Seriously, Brode. Leave her alone. She's not used to your mouth, and I'm barely tolerating it right now."

Brody let out a gust of air, regarding Blue with an expression of utter mockery. It seemed most of the things he did and said were done to taunt, and Blue was the new object of scorn.

Sam's phone sounded, and when he had pulled it out, Blue

glanced over at the screen. "Who's 237? Is that a person's name?" She only ventured to speak to change the subject from Brody's sarcasm.

Brody and Alec had sniggered while Sam blanched, ignoring the call. "Not a name. It's no one."

Brody's mirth came out in a chuckle, while Alec had subdued his reaction to a smirk.

"What?" Blue questioned, jutting her chin out to demand being taken seriously by those she had not meant to include in the private conversation. "What's 237?"

"Nothing. It's just a number, Blue."

"Now, now." Brody pretended to scold Sam as a teacher might. "That's not all it is. Go ahead, Sam."

"Do you want me to thrash you right here?" Sam had leaned forward, looking darkly into Brody's still laughing eyes. "Quit messing with her."

Blue frowned next to him. "I don't understand. Why are you mad?"

Alec folded his arms over his chest and sized up Sam, daring him to own up to his actions. "That's a pretty high number, Pan. You hit the grand two hundred mark just before we left for the Americas."

Brody tapped his finger to his chin. "Is it 237 bills you make a week?"

Sam's eye roll had made Blue smile. "No. Maybe it's 237 punches in the face I owe you. You're working your way up to 238, so knock it off."

Liam looked up from his paperwork, as if only just realizing there were people next to him. He glanced from face to face for someone to give him a clue as to what he had missed.

Alec chimed in, though his tone had been less antagonistic than Brody's. "237 times you've done something selfless?"

"237 fishes?" Liam suggested. The bewildered looks he garnered told him he was off-topic. "What are we talking about?"

"What? No, Liam. Leave it alone, guys. She's new to the real world."

"Then shouldn't you be educating her on it? I mean, she asked you a direct question. Most she's spoken in a few hours," Alec commented. "If you don't tell her, I'm happy to. Actually, let Brody educate her. He looks like he's been dying for the chance."

Brody's laugh cut short, and he and Sam had turned to glower at Alec. Brody had grown red in the cheeks. Once again, Blue was in the dark.

Sam exhaled, tucking away the scowl he'd cast at Brody and Alec. "It's nothing, Blue. I keep a tally on my phone. Sometimes I put a girl's phone number in here. That's all. It's just a person's phone number."

"Okay," Blue responded, keeping her eyes on her hands. She could sense the tension in Sam's body, and though she still did not feel like her question had been answered, she had not dared to question him again.

Wayward or Vemreaux, boys were still boys. Sam was no exception. When Blue had been sitting next to Sam in the car, she wished she could disappear. Especially when Liam finally answered her question.

"You're up to 237 Fems already, Sam? That's higher than I thought."

Sam had let out an exasperated groan. "Seriously, Liam! I'm trying, here."

Blue blinked up at Liam, trying to make sense of the conversation. "Sam has 237 Femreaux friends? Why is that a bad thing? That sounds good." She had turned to Sam, cocking her head to the side. "Why are you embarrassed by that? I only have two girl friends. You're very popular." Blue held in her sadness at being so limited by her brother about whom she could befriend.

Before Sam could conjure up an adequate excuse, Liam cut in. "237 is the number of Fems Sam's had sex with, kitten."

Blue had cringed at her stupidity. Of course that's what they were talking about.

Sam had been just as mortified, and they both stared out the window of the car to mask their chagrin. Never had it been clearer how different their worlds were.

"Thanks, Liam," Sam grumbled venomously.

Brody laughed, his blond hair shaking as he held his stomach. "Poor Pan! Found himself a cherry, and he hasn't got a prayer."

"I told you to leave her alone, Brody!"

Alec saw the potential for escalation and intervened. "Knock it off, guys. We've still got a while till we get home. Let's try to make it back without bloodshed, for once."

"Was it supposed to be a secret? I mean, it's right there on your phone, Sam. Since when did you stop bragging about that?" Liam looked over at Blue, light dawning in his eyes. "Oh. Sorry. I was just trying to answer her question. You can ask me anything, kitten. Even if Sam's too embarrassed to tell you the truth, I will."

"Alright," Blue had said, challenging his offer. Brody's teasing and Liam's reveal loosened her tongue. "Why do you call me kitten?"

"Because you're small and cute, but you're feisty, too. Like a wee kitten."

"Bloody tiger when she's mad," Alec amended.

Liam rifled through his papers. "If you don't like kitten, I could always call you by your real name. Idahlia Jane Anders?" He grinned like a naughty boy who wanted to be in trouble.

Blue's muscles tightened, and her mouth projected the scowl that hearing her name always evoked. "My name's Blue," she had corrected him, though she knew he would call her whatever he pleased. Prince Liam was used to getting away with anything he wanted, due to his status, good looks and adorable smile.

"Why don't you like your name?" Liam asked her kindly. "Very proper."

Blue had known that Sam was watching her. Her answer came out fast. She'd been storing up her disgruntled feelings about the subject for years. "Because it's not mine. Names are randomly assigned in The Way. Someone just picked the next name on the sheet, and that's that. Jane isn't even a name."

"Jane is so a name," Liam countered.

"No, it's not," she had argued – a thing she never would have done with a Vemreaux a week ago. "Every girl who's nineteen this year has the middle name Jane. It tells the professors what age I am. Grettel and Elle have the same middle name. It's Louise, because they were born a year ahead of me. So I go by a name that's mine, not theirs."

This new bit of information had puzzled the men. Though Europe housed The Way East, they had rarely been inside the facility, and did not know much about its operations. So it was with most Vemreaux. Sam touched the side of his shoe to hers. "So, when is your birthday?" Sam attempted to steer the conversation in a more positive direction.

Blue's face had scrunched up as if he'd asked her what it was like to live inside of the sun. "How would I know that?"

Sam was stunned. "It should be on your birth certificate. Liam? Is it in there?" He'd lifted his chin to indicate the pile of papers in his friend's hands.

Liam shook his head. "Don't need it. Waywards don't come with a whole lot of documentation." The prince looked over at her sadly. "You seriously don't have a birthday, kitten?"

Blue shrugged. She could not have cared less about the oversight. "We all turn the next age on January first. Does that count?"

With a compassionate melancholy smile, Liam turned back to his papers. "Yeah. That counts."

The remainder of the ride to the mansion had been much the same. Blue looked out the window to soak in the scenery before the speed of the vehicle became too much for her. Brody picked a couple more fights with Sam's shortened fuse. Alec ignored them both, while Liam studied document after document, adding his signature here and there. When the car pulled down the long drive that led to the largest home Blue had ever seen, a crowd of seventy-eight people was waiting. The car slowed as a few approached too near the tires to be safe. Fists knocked against the windows and doors to get at the vehicle's occupants.

"Sam?" she called out, her voice strained. She backed up into him, away from the demanding fists. "They know it's me!" she fretted. The people shouted, some excited, and others concerned. "Make them stop!" she begged as the familiar black she dreaded began to seep into her vision. She'd assured Baird the blackouts that ignited her killing sprees were under control. And yet, before she'd even stepped foot in her new home, one was already threatening to take her under, stimulating her body to kill without discretion.

Sam's arm slid around her again, shielding her as much as he could from the insistent faces and fists. "I can't, baby. We're almost to the gate, though. Give it a few more seconds, and they'll be gone."

It was overwhelming. As Blue ducked her head down to focus on fighting the darkness, Sam redirected her cheek to rest on his chest. "They can't see you. Don't worry about that. They just want Liam."

"Liam's in danger?" she clarified, stiffening in his arms.

"Nah. They want to know about Liam's trip, is all. Ask him questions. Get him to smile for their cameras. They don't even know you're in here. Promise."

"Buzzards are out early today," Liam had commented, though he barely glanced up at the ruckus.

Alec frowned. "There are more than usual. We're due to meet with Harold in twenty minutes. Think something's up?" he asked Brody, who also judged the count of reporters on the lawn to be about thirty too many.

Knowing that Blue would not ask what was going on, Sam had explained the situation to her to ease the fear she would never admit to. "Those are reporters from just about every major paper and magazine. They hang out on the lawn to catch a glimpse of the royal family so they have something to write about. Liam's a big deal here." The car crawled past the gate, shutting out the chaos. Sam relaxed as Blue breathed a sigh of relief in his arms. They drove further on the massive property and pulled into the dim light of the lengthy garage.

Liam shuffled his papers into one neat stack so they would slide into the briefcase a little easier. "They get like that because I'm Europe's most eligible bachelor. The Femreaux can't get enough of his gorgeous face. Can't say I blame them." He beamed at earning a meek smile from the girl. "I mean, if you had to go a week without this mug, wouldn't you be a bit batty?" He was satisfied when the corner of Blue's mouth lifted. Liam had cracked jokes all the way from the car into the house, enticing levity from her soldier-like stance.

"Josephine, you minx! I'm back!" Liam had announced upon Blue's first step into the new home. Josephine was a Femreaux who was one of the rare *B*-bloods that had chosen not to bathe in the Fountain of Youth. Blue had not seen many aging people, but she guessed the woman to be in her mid-sixties. If Josephine had been Wayward, she would have been terminated already. "Did you miss me?" Liam asked, though when he took a good look at her upset face, he'd stopped in his tracks. "What's wrong?"

Josephine shook her head once and took Liam's briefcase from him. "Harold's waiting for you in the study. Don't dawdle, boys." She was a woman of few words, but they were all the right ones. Liam did not even get a snack from the kitchen, which he had mentioned a desire for several times in the last half hour of the drive.

"Sam? Take Blue up to my guest bedroom. She can wait there and get settled in while we meet with Harold." Liam handed his suit jacket to Josephine. "This is Blue. She'll be working in the house now. Picked her up in the Americas."

Josephine had given her a scrutinizing look that made Blue's head dip down, but said nothing. Sam placed his hand on Blue's back and took her out of the room and down several hallways without a word. The flight of stairs he led her up were the very first ones she'd ever been on, but she did not stop to enjoy the experience, nor to look down at how high up she was. The urgency in his step told her not to dally or ask questions. Down more hallways and up yet another flight of stairs led them to a door that he popped open without hesitation. Flicking on the lights revealed the biggest and most beautiful bedroom Blue had ever seen. "This is you, *dolcezza*." He'd paused to tuck a lock of auburn hair behind her peaked ear. "Stay here until one of us comes and gets you, yeah?"

Blue nodded, but was reticent to go in right away. Though her shoes were not very dirty, they did not feel welcomed by the cream-colored plush carpet. Sam was long gone by the time she decided to remove her sneakers and enter the perfect room.

She waited in the bedroom, familiarizing herself with everything around her, except for two doors on opposite walls that she would not even touch, for fear of going where she was not supposed to. Though Sam told her that one of them would come and get her, the day turned into evening without a single knock at her door. At one point, Blue recognized Liam's feet shuffling into the room next to hers, but he did not come for her. A muffled crash came from the other side of the insulated wall, but that was all she could make out. Shortly thereafter, Liam had left, taking with him Brody, Alec and Sam. She'd pressed her ear to the door, but she did not dare disobey her first order given in her new position.

Blue did not know what she should do, so she waited. She sat in front of the door with her legs crossed on the dream-worthy carpet as she reread her Geometry book. When her need won out over duty, Blue turned the knob on the door opposite Liam's wall to find, with great relief, a lavish bathroom. She flicked on the lights, and immediately turned them off with a muffled gasp.

Mirrors.

Sink-to-ceiling mirrors covering an entire wall stared at her, daring her to face herself. Even with the lights off, she could still tell where her reflection was. She used the bathroom as quick as she could and darted back out, heart racing at the garish sight.

Her stomach growled sometime around two in the morning that first night in the mansion, but she'd ignored it. She had gone hungry before. She reasoned the guys were testing her, probably vetting her to see if she was tough enough to get through a night without food. She scoffed at the insinuation that she was anything less than prepared for whatever they threw at her.

The next morning, she was still alone. Blue wondered what had happened to the guys.

She remained curious for four days. In the afternoon of the

second day, Josephine came up to her room and scolded her for hiding when there was work to be done. She assumed Blue had slept the night and most of the next day away. Josephine informed the girl that that sort of behavior was not tolerated.

Blue stared at her feet and nodded, apologizing when the rant was over. She followed the housekeeper down the two flights of stairs and through the many winding halls to the kitchen, listening as Josephine explained the dry erase board that contained all of the daily chores.

Josephine was not overly friendly like Liam, and Blue judged that she was not a person to be asked obvious questions. So when Blue did not understand a job, she did it to the best of her ability without begging for clarification. Josephine critiqued her several times that first work day, telling Blue that she was too slow cleaning the windows, or that she did not need to be so thorough with polishing the floors on the first level.

The only time Blue did not hear Josephine's critical correction was her second day in the mansion around dinner time when her stomach rumbled, which she thought for sure would earn her a severe talking to. She did not know how to stop the noise, though. It was not as if she did it on purpose. Josephine surprised her by speaking about something not related to chores. "Have you eaten tonight, young lady?"

"No, ma'am."

"I can set something out for you, if you'd like."

"Just rations would be fine, ma'am," Blue requested meekly. They contained all the necessary nutrients a Wayward needed for a day's work, and she'd been two days without them.

"Goodness! You're Wayward?" Josephine examined the girl curiously. "Your demeanor, certainly, but your eyes are Original Vemreaux. I can't tell if you smell, of course." Josephine indicated her light gray eyes that told Blue the old woman had forgone a dip in the Fountain of Youth.

The seasoned woman frowned at her, as if Blue purposefully chose to starve herself. Josephine rummaged in the cupboard and set out Grade *A* rations, telling Blue to eat before she started in on cleaning each of the thirteen bathrooms. Blue did not dare inform Josephine that she was allergic to Grade *A*, and only consumed Grade *V*.

Though she knew what would happen if she ate the rations, Blue popped open the lid on the tin, unwrapped the standard plastic fork that came with it and dutifully placed bite after bite in her mouth, chewing slowly, though her stomach was screaming for a faster pace.

She had not finished the scrubbing the bathtub before the wave of nausea came over her. Bending over the toilet, Blue's stomach emptied itself of the rations she had known would not stay down. Though they were considered the best variety, it did not matter. They always made her sick. She was grateful that her own bathroom came stocked with toothpaste. The mouthwash took some getting used to, but she began to rely on it as a necessary asset.

By the end of the fourth day, Blue had thrown up three times, each after Josephine would set out the Grade *A* rations for her, usually as her breakfast. After that, her stomach was so tender that it did not warm to the other food provided for her throughout the day.

Music was piped in via speakers that were built into the walls of the main rooms. It was soft in volume, but almost overwhelming at times with its beauty. Blue knew next to nothing about music, but she knew for certain that the gentle songs stroked her loneliness into submission and distracted her from the grief that leaving her family behind threatened to choke her with.

Meals were a dreary affair. Josephine would set the table in the fancy dining room, but no one ever came for dinner. Two plates were set out, one for Blue and one for another young woman, who looked at Blue as if she were a bothersome insect.

Bonnie's nose in the air as she spoke of her closeness with Princess Suzette grew tiresome after five minutes. Blue knew that Bonnie used the princess' name to assert her clout over the Wayward. Blue did not want clout or even introductions. She wanted to be left alone in her misery and chores. Bonnie purposefully sat farther from Blue than her stool suggested, angling her body away and dramatically holding her breath between bites, so that she would not have to inhale the sulfuric stench of the Wayward servant. Of course, Blue was born without the signature scent, but as soon as Josephine introduced Blue as "the Wayward servant Liam hired to help with the housework", there was nothing for it. Bonnie kept a healthy distance from Blue at all times, as if she were afraid her poverty and inferior blood type might be infectious.

Bonnie had announced to Blue several times that she was Princess Suzette's personal servant in a way that made Blue think that must mean Bonnie's station was above her own. Blue did not bother to mention that she was Liam's personal servant. Bonnie needed the validation. Bonnie cried loudly during dinner on the third night about the state of Princess Suzette and how she felt lost without her mistress. Blue thought the display was a little showy, though her opinions remained secret. She pushed her food around on her plate, trying not to vomit while attempting to remain invisible, so as not to further anger Bonnie with her presence.

Instead of calisthenics, which she barely had the energy for after such malnutrition, Blue kept her nights occupied with chores. When she'd finished her list for the day, she got a head start on the ones for the next morning. When those were completed, she discreetly crossed off items from Josephine's list. Josephine said nothing of this, but her criticisms came less often, so Blue guessed that she was pleased.

Though it was only a few days ago, she could still feel Sam's reassuring grip on her hip like it was yesterday. In the quiet of the laundry room, Blue folded a pair of pants and tried to shake the euphoria from her mind. *It was nothing. Sam wasn't being romantic. He's Vemreaux. You're Wayward. He's out who knows where with any number of much more beautiful Femreaux. Fems who actually know what they're doing and don't get confused so easily. Stop being stupid. He doesn't want you. Look at you! You're a servant. His best friend owns you! He doesn't think of you like that. It's just the way Vemreaux are. Flirt with anything on two legs. He left with no explanation, and he's probably not coming back.*

Blue permitted the whirring of the dryer to calm her nauseous stomach. She was glad for the distraction that kept her from wondering if she'd been abandoned by the men in the foreign country.

Read *The Truth* tonight.

ABOUT THE AUTHOR

USA Today bestselling author Mary E. Twomey lives in Michigan with her three adorable children. She enjoys reading, writing, vegetarian cooking, and telling her children fantastic stories about wombats.

While she loves writing fantasy, dystopian, and paranormal tales for her readers, Mary also writes romance under the name Tuesday Embers, and cozy mysteries under the name Molly Maple.

Visit her online at www.maryetwomey.com, and sign up for her newsletter, so you never miss a new release.